THE
WORLD
WE
MAKE

I *can* walk all night so sometimes I do, for days at a time. I need the sidewalks rising to meet my feet the way bodega cats lift their asses when you knuckle near their tails. I need to slip over the barrier at the edge of the subway platform, past the patches of fermenting piss, to breathe the mingled aromas of rat poison and ozone. I need to crouch down by the East River to poke the slime growing on the rocks, wondering what kinds of chemicals are trying to soak through my skin. People who travel, they talk about how clean other cities are. Not much gum on the sidewalk in Toronto; wild. In Bern, crews empty street garbage cans ten times a day. Nice, I guess? But to be New York, I gotta stay dirty. Even if I shower every day and do laundry every week—with a washer and dryer in the house! living in the lap of luxury—I still gotta know the trash. I gotta *be one with* the trash, owoowoo, ommmm.

THE WORLD WE MAKE

THE GREAT CITIES: BOOK TWO

N. K. JEMISIN

orbit

orbitbooks.net

ORBIT

First published in Great Britain in 2022 by Orbit
This paperback edition published by Orbit in 2023

1 3 5 7 9 10 8 6 4 2

A CIP catalogue record for this book
is available from the British Library.

ISBN 978-0-356-51272-3

Printed and bound in Great Britain by
Clays Ltd, Elcograf, S.p.A.

Papers used by Orbit are from well-managed forests
and other responsible sources.

Orbit
An imprint of
Little, Brown Book Group
Carmelite House
50 Victoria Embankment
London EC4Y 0DZ

An Hachette UK Company
www.hachette.co.uk

www.orbitbooks.net

UPSTATE

WESTCHESTER

YONKERS

hop? hop?

THE
BRONX

BRONX
ZOO

BRONX
ART
CENTER
(underwater)

THROGS
NECK

COLLEGE POINT

FORDHAM

HIGHBRIDGE

INWOOD
HILL
PARK

RIKERS

LGA

WELCOME TO
NEW YORK

JACKSON
HEIGHTS

FLUSHING

JAMAICA

QUEENS

THE
NYCbe

HARLEM

ASTORIA

L.I.C.

MANHATTAN

FDR DRIVE

Roosevelt

Hell's Kitchen

Times Square

Little
Brittain

WILLIAMSBURG
BRIDGE

MANHATTAN
BRIDGE

BKLYN
BRIDGE

CITY
HALL

NEW JERSEY

HOBOKEN

Hudson

JERSEY CITY

CHECKER CAB DREAM WEDDINGS

VINTAGE NEW YORK CITY
CHECKER CABS

📞 (215) 555-0199

Prosperity & Progress

BETTER NEW YORK FOUNDATION

A SUBSIDIARY OF T.M.W., INC.

SYDNEY • NAIROBI • BEIJING • ISTANBUL

NEW YORK • CHICAGO • MIAMI • HAVANA • RIO DE JANEIRO

LIBERTY ISLAND
RED HOOK
BED STUY
JFK
Bed Stuy do or die
Crown Heights stand up
Flatbush represent!
S.I. FERRY
ST. GEORGE
BAY RIDGE
FLATBUSH
BROOKLYN
BENSONHURST
YUCK!
COLLEGE OF S.I.
VERRAZZANO BRIDGE
HEARTLAND VILLAGE
STATEN ISLAND
CONEY ISLAND
the Rockaways
S.I. MALL
FRESH KILLS
LONG ISLAND
HERE THERE BE DRAGONS
SHARROT'S SHORELINE
SÃO PAULO
LAGOS
PARIS
CAIRO
HONG KONG
LONDON
~~NEW ORLEANS~~
~~PORT AU PRINCE~~

PROLOGUE

Call me Neek.

No, I'm not hunting no fucking whale. Giant squid, maybe. Got some homoerotic shit going on, too, yo. Maybe I should write a book. Instead of *Moby-Dick* I'll call it *Suck My Interdimensional Dick*—a thriller, or maybe a horror, with some comedy and romance and tragedy. Little for everybody. It's gonna be a hit 'cause I got publishing and Madison Avenue all up in me, plus like a million hustlers and grifters and corner boys who all can sell you your own kidneys before lunch. *All of whom.* Guess I should talk proper when I'm slinging shit about literature.

Pssh, fuck it. Point.

Neek. New York City. NYC, only pronounce the *Y* like "ee," not "why." I know why. It's not the name my mama gave me, but she claim I'm not her son anymore anyway, so fuck it. Been time for changes.

New York always changes. We who become cities are evolving, dynamic entities, constantly adjusting to the needs of our citizens, endlessly pushed and pulled by state politics and international economies. Lately we gotta deal with multiversal politics, too, but whatever. We can take it. We're New York.

Been three months since the city came to life. Three months

since the Williamsburg Bridge got smashed by a giant tentacle from beyond; three months since millions of citizens got partially infected by a multibodied, mind-influencing alien consciousness and walked around looking like gotdamn Sasquatches 'til we fixed it; three months since a whole-ass extradimensional city started trying for squatters' air rights over Staten Island. Most New Yorkers can't see or hear all this shit. Lucky. But ever since New York became the newest and loudest member of an international resistance against the encroachment of hostile quantum possibility collapse, we been dealing with more than the usual day-to-day fuckshit.

Por exemplo:

Periodically R'lyeh sends forth a hollow, tooth-aching, atonal song that echoes across the whole city. The song's a problem; listen to it for more than a few minutes and you start thinking Mexicans and birth control are what's really wrong with the world, and maybe a nice mass shooting would solve both problems. But then, like, mad numbers of New Yorkers feel the sudden urge to turn up their bike-handle speakers so the whole neighborhood can hear them blasting Lady Gaga, or they throw a house party that bumps 'til dawn despite a million complaints to 311, or they start walking around their apartment in heels knowing it's gonna piss off their downstairs neighbor, or they start loudly complaining about all the other motherfuckers being loud. All of this drowns out the song. So, thanks to so much of New York being *so* damn New York, we okay.

Also been three months since six of us became something more than human, closer to eldritch abominations ourselves—or gods, or living symbols, or hairs on a dog's back that occasionally steer its teeth. I carry within myself the hopes and hatreds of almost nine million people. I'm also just me. Still human in all the ways that matter: I bleed, I sneeze, I scratch my ass when mosquitoes bite—and they still bite, little evil-ass zebra-striped motherfuckers as resistant to pest control as the rats and pigeons. I still sleep, though only when I want to now. Went a whole week without once, just to see, and it was fine. But I spent too many years not getting enough sleep when I was on the street, so these days I like doing it whenever I can.

Weirdest change is I don't need to eat. When I skip that for a week, I don't get shaky and cold the way I used to, but sometimes I get, like, phantom food in my mouth? Cheesecake dense as concrete, burnt too-salty pretzels, a Coke and a slice. Sometimes it's roasted chestnuts, even with no street vendor around. Sometimes what I pick up is stuff I never had before, but I know what it is because I am New York. Lobster Newburg and red clam chowder and a lot of other weird shit got invented here.

But mostly? I eat, even if I don't need to, because I still get hungry. New York is always hungry.

New living arrangements these days. Manny got us a five-bedroom in Harlem, in an old building that's been gut renovated to make it fancy. Place is nice: three bathrooms, a kitchen that's *not* galley, a loft that the floor plan calls a "study," a huge common space that's big enough for a sectional and a dining table, wraparound balcony, pretty tin ceiling. Roof-deck. Penthouse, even. I like it: fancy as fuck, a little old New York and also some new. Manny don't like it because he's the part of New York that wanted a new start from his old life. He wanted ordinary. Shouldn'ta become Manhattan, then.

And since it turns out Manny's rich as fuck—he paid the whole year's rent up front—the landlord lets him move in whoever he wants. Breaking the old lease left Manny's roommate Bel out in the cold, so Manny made an offer: take a payout for Manny's half and stay at their old Inwood place, or claim an open bedroom in the new apartment for the old rent. Bel picked the latter 'cause usually a place like this would be three times as much. Me and Veneza—Jersey City—got two of the rooms. She's paying her old rent; I get it free. Fifth room is still open because Manny's hoping one of the other New Yorks will take it. It don't really matter if we live together. Easier for Veneza since New Jersey Transit is a pain in the ass, but it ain't nothing for everybody to get together when we need to do city stuff. City magic's faster than the subway, and all of us are getting good at using it. We didn't need this apartment.

I get why Manny did it, though: for me. City picked a little homeless batty boy who didn't finish high school to be its rep. Manny's cool with the rest but didn't like the homeless part, so now I got a permanent address and a roof over my head for whenever I want it. I don't always. Sometimes I just be . . . over it. Artist, got other shit on my mind. I *can* walk all night so sometimes I do, for days at a time. I need the sidewalks rising to meet my feet the way bodega cats lift their asses when you knuckle near their tails. I need to slip over the barrier at the edge of the subway platform, past the patches of fermenting piss, to breathe the mingled aromas of rat poison and ozone. I need to crouch down by the East River to poke the slime growing on the rocks, wondering what kinds of chemicals are trying to soak through my skin. People who travel, they talk about how clean other cities are. Not much gum on the sidewalk in Toronto; wild. In Bern, crews empty street garbage cans ten times a day. Nice, I guess? But to be New York, I gotta stay dirty. Even if I shower every day and do laundry every week—with a washer and dryer in the house! living in the lap of luxury—I still gotta know the trash. I gotta *be one with* the trash, owoowoo, ommmm.

Veneza asked if it bothers me to have somebody paying my way, and maybe? A little? The fuck else am I supposed to do, though? This ain't the kind of city where you can start from nothing anymore and have a real chance, and I started with less than nothing. American Dream *been* a sucker bet. I do my part around the apartment. Can't cook for shit but I clean when they let me, oh and also? I keep the whole fucking city from dropping off the face of existence. So there's that.

Anyway. Not the first time I had a sugar daddy. Just the first time I wasn't actually fucking him for my keep.

(Ay yo, I *offered*. I ain't a savage. He said no.)

So now it's late-ish, close to midnight. I stand on the balcony staring out at Harlem and the Heights and the Upper West Side, not thinking about anything. It's autumn now, getting chilly at night, so after a while I head in 'cause I'm cold. If Veneza's awake, she's not making noise in her room. If Bel's up, his TV is still on, because I see light flickering under his doorsill. My room's on the other side of the house, near Manny's, 'cause that's the room I picked. (In case.) When I pass the bathroom, the door is ajar and I see Manny leaning on the counter, staring at himself in the mirror. I don't really mean to creep, but he's pretty as hell and right now he's wearing satin pajama pants with no shirt, so yeah, I take it in. He's all kinds of cut. (Muscle, I mean. He won't let me see the other part that might be cut.) The muscle don't usually show with the preppy way he dresses. Likes to play harmless. The truth shows now, though: there's a long scar on his lower back that was obviously stitched at some point, and another scar on the shoulder blade, old and keloided, wider at the bottom than at the top. I seen scars like that on dudes who look ten times harder: knife marks. Guns attract too much attention for some kinds of business, see. I'm guessing the long scar is from surgery, because it crosses a smaller, fainter scar. If he got stabbed or shot right around there, he probably lost a kidney. That's my Manhattan: neat and proper on the surface, walking near-death experience underneath.

He's either lost in thought or checking out an ingrown hair real hard. At first I figure he doesn't know I'm there, but then his eyes shift to me in the reflection. That part kind of shuts down the horny, because for once he isn't trying to pretend he's not . . . whatever he was, before the city claimed him. (My bet's hitman. Veneza's got ten on corporate espionage. Bronca's stuck on CIA, but she came up in the Sixties and thinks everybody's CIA.) I get why Manny feels like he needs to play nice, but when a Black man puts on a friendly mask like that, it means he thinks less of you. Means you're too chickenshit to handle the real him. I like that for me, he shows all his beauty and all his beast, all the time.

"We're getting complacent," he says. I like that he doesn't waste my time with small talk, either.

I push the door open more and lean against the sill. "Maybe we just taking a break after all that crazy shit last summer."

"The Enemy still floats over Staten Island. Think she's taking a break?"

"Nah. But Squigglebitch ain't human, so—" Whoops. I cut myself off with a little wince.

He smiles thinly and says the obvious. "Human beings get time off, yes. *We* are the city that never sleeps."

"A'ight, fine, I get it, Scarface." I sigh and fold my arms. "Well, you probably got bazooka money. So let's roll up on Staten Island and start shooting up in the air."

He smiles. It's got a tired edge 'cause I know I'm being a pain in the ass. Then he turns to face me, leaning back against the sink edge. Aww, bye booty, but hello to the front, mmm. He catches me looking and *blushes*, which is hilarious. Fine as he is, I know full well Manny been drowning in pussy, bussy, and all the ussy in between, his whole grown life—but with me, sometimes it's like I'm talking to a virgin. Even now he ducks his eyes, bites his lip, spends a second trying to figure out if he should flirt back and what he'll do if I take him up on it . . . and then he takes a deep breath and decides to act like everything's normal between us. It's not as insulting as if he pretended to be nice. That's mistrust and disrespect; this is something else. Fear, maybe. Wish I could figure out what the hell it is about me that scares a dude like him.

"No bazookas," he drawls, "and I can't think of a construct that could possibly have enough power to even reach R—that city, let alone hurt it." By unspoken agreement, we mostly avoid saying the name of our enemy. It hurts to say, and none of us likes stinking up the conversational air. I don't like saying "NYPD," either.

Manny continues: "But there are things we *can* do. Strategies we should consider—like asking around to find out if other cities have useful intel. Maybe figuring out which alternate dimension she came from, and dealing with her at the source."

There's a big ol' chunk of knowledge that pops into the heads of baby cities when they get reborn—a lexicon, compiled by the other living cities to give the babies at least a fighting chance. I don't know how the other cities compiled it or how they make sure new cities get it at birth. It's missing a lot of important shit, too, which is why they also send the next-youngest city to help out and explain. And the process still got some bugs, because when the others woke up after I went down, only Bronca got the lexicon, out of the boroughs. Bottom line—I got the lexicon and Manny don't, so I explain: "We already know more than the other cities. None of them ever had to deal with her after birth, and all they ever seen was fucked-up tentacles and shit. She wasn't even *she*, for them."

"But now they know there's more to her. They know she has a name, and that she works through manipulating institutions and systems as much as individuals. If I were a living city who suddenly realized the Enemy was in *real estate*, I would look back on every bit of city planning over the last fifty years with a different eye. Education budgets, policing, zoning, liquor licenses, public transportation, even popular culture—and the signs would be there. She's been playing the long game, stifling progress and weakening cities to make them easier to destroy, and once you know what to look for, the cancer is everywhere."

Yeah, but. I sigh. "My daddy died of cancer."

Manny blinks, sobers, and doesn't say anything. I never talked about shit like this with him before. Don't know why I'm saying it now. "He knew something was wrong, but he also knew he had other shit to worry about, like trying to keep a roof over our head. So he ignored it when stuff hurt, or when he pissed blood. Health insurance was shitty so he didn't go to the doctor, who was just going to tell him something he didn't want to hear and push him to start treatments he couldn't afford. He figured he could leave us a bunch of medical bills, or he could leave us life insurance." I shrug. It hadn't even been that much money. Our family still fell apart after he died. But that was the choice he made.

Manny chews on this. "You think the other cities would rather deny the obvious than acknowledge how bad the problem really is."

"Some of 'em, yeah. Denial's easy, fixing shit is hard. And what's the alternative, putting the city through chemo?" I shrug. "Ain't everybody up for—"

Before I can finish this thought, something hits me. That's what it feels like—not a punch but a goddamn truck, smacking me out of nowhere and hitting so hard that for an instant I go blind. It's not physical, though I grunt and fall to my knees as if it is. It's sensory, and extra-sensory. It's here and elsewhere. It's *screaming.*

den of iniquity

full of ANTIFA fucking terrorists

everybody's leaving, New York is over, turn it into a for-profit prison and wall up anybody left behind

LIBTARDS LIBTARTS LIBARTS START SREADING THE NEWS FUCK NEW YORK

And more. So much more. I already have eight million voices in my head but this is way, way more than that—so many it almost drowns out the voices that are supposed to be there. But then, some of the eight million start shouting back.

9/11 didn't happen anywhere near you, STFU

NY and Cali put money into the country and you racist flyover corn-eaters just suck it out! Suck on this!

SHUT YO BITCH ASS UP

So much. Too much. It hurts, both my physical head and my mind, and it's not supposed to be like this. A living city blends the will of its citizens with the impressions of outsiders, as filtered through legends and media. We are amalgamated gods sprung whole from the fusion of belief with reality, but usually, the beliefs are pretty steady. People still think New York is a great place to live despite 9/11, nightmare housing prices, and the media making us out to be a combination Mad Max sim and Taco Bell. Meanwhile there have always been people who hate New York without ever setting foot in it—because they hear too much about it and get tired of the hype, because they "lost" a cousin who moved here from TinyRepublicanVille and turned socialist, because they secretly wish they could live here, too, but are too scared to try, whatever. But 'til now all this was constant. Background radiation. What's hitting me now is a sudden ramp-up of outsider hate like nothing I've ever felt before. All these voices from Iowa and Alabama and England and Nigeria echo not our legend but its opposite—all the shit that people think about New York which not only isn't true, but contradicts what is. Those concepts jam into my mind like shrapnel: crackheads vomiting on every corner, children being kept in Omelasian basements by cannibal pedophiles, sneering intellectuals in kippahs and wild-eyed billionaires in turbans scheming to take over the world, seedy public bathrooms that will turn you trans even though we barely have public bathrooms in the first place.

The reality of New York is being assailed by a thousand other

New Yorks that don't exist . . . but a bunch of people suddenly *want* them to. And, oh God, I can feel their belief actually dragging at me, trying to pull me away from who I actually am.

Hands take my shoulders. Manny, but Veneza too, and those are Bel's "if you can read this I'll take a footrub, thanks" socks. Shit, I'm on the floor. When did that happen? Somebody pulls me up.

"The fuck," I mumble.

"I caught some of that," Manny says. He looks freaked out in a very calm, serious way. "I don't know what it was, though."

"Me neither, homme."

"Maybe you have epilepsy?" Bel asks. He knows the scoop about us on account of having almost got ate by tentacles in a park once. Still, he thinks like a normal human being, so he looks first for normal human reasons for things. "Wait, can living embodiments of cities have epilepsy?"

"Sure," I say, though I don't know how I know this. I push myself upright, shaky enough about it that Manny puts a hand on my back for support. I hate that I need it. "Epilepsy ain't what this was, tho. Felt like . . . I don't know." A blurring of existence. An unmaking.

Veneza looks toward the window—specifically, toward the south-facing window on that side of the apartment. Great view of Manhattan below 125th. It's also where, amid the wispy night clouds, I can just see the ghostly, jagged spires of an alien metropolis hovering like a guillotine over what used to be my fifth borough.

"Nah," I say to Veneza. "It ain't her either. Not this time, anyway."

She looks skeptical. "You sure? I don't put anything past

Squigglebitch. Even if it didn't feel like it was coming from her, it's probably something she did."

Manny's and Veneza's phones suddenly bling with several texts all at once—Brooklyn and Padmini hitting up the group chat, probably, to ask what's going on. Then Veneza's phone rings outright: Bronca, who's old and hates texting. Veneza sighs and steps back to answer the call. My head has started to clear. "Something's changed," I say. "Somebody, somewhere, is talking shit about us. *Declaring war* on us. And whoever it is, they got enough people listening and agreeing that I actually felt that shit."

Bel mutters something to himself along the lines of "Yeah, fuck this nonsense, never want to become a city, migraines are bad enough." Manny nods at me, his expression grim and strained. They all felt it, I realize, but the boroughs are each one-fifth of New York. I'm the only one who got the full whammy. Veneza's trying to get Bronca off the phone. "I don't *know*, Old B, and he doesn't either. Look, I thought old people didn't sleep that much anyway—Oooh, nice, you kiss people with that mouth? Yeah, g'night."

That's pretty much it after that. Manny helps me up and to my bedroom. Bel herds Veneza and Manny out to give me space, and I guess Manny handles the group chat. I don't look because I got one of those shitty prepay data plans, so I keep the phone off when I don't need it. Not sure I want to waste money on seeing what's got New York trending on social media, or whatever.

In the morning, we understand.

Bel's got a crush on NY1's Pat Kiernan, so he watches news every morning on the big TV in the common area. I half listen while I brush my teeth and pretend to shave, even though I only got like twelve chin hairs. Over the sound of Veneza blearily cleaning the coffee pot, Pat says there was a big to-do online the previous night, when a bunch of Republicans started "spontaneously" tweeting about New York City needing to be punished for stuff like trying to defund the NYPD and make sure poor children don't starve. I guess they hit viral mass or got bots, so for a while #NewYorkIHopeYouDie was trending number one on Twitter. Pat screencaps some of the tweets: surprise, most of the "facts" getting tossed around are made up and most of the charts are wrong. The most popular retweets feature either footage of individual people doing dumb shit, which they claim is proof that the whole city is full of dumb shits, or clips from different cities altogether. I just roll my eyes and sit down at the kitchen island to eat my cereal, but Veneza gets a weird look on her face and pulls out her laptop. It's wild to watch her hands actually blur as she types and clicks. Then she curses. "*Thought* so."

The Froot Loops are hittin' today. "What," I ask with my mouth full.

"That hashtag smelled like a marketing campaign, especially seeing how it hit right before the news. Lo and behold."

She turns her laptop around, playing a clip from the PIX11 website—the previous night's news broadcast. Bel's rummaging in the fridge, but he stops at the noise and meanders over, munching on a carrot. Manny, still buttoning his shirt, comes out of his bedroom to see, too. We're all riveted, suddenly, by a sallow-complexioned fiftysomething Italian guy with a bad frontal hairpiece.

"New York needs not only new leadership, but a new soul," the guy says. He's in a room full of people, standing at a podium and grinning while camera flashes go off all around him. "This isn't what New York—America!—is supposed to be like. My ancestors came here legally. They didn't expect handouts. They didn't whine about discrimination when the police gave them a hard time; they *joined* the police and abided by the law. The men were men and the women were women and we didn't have any of that, uh, confusion." He laughs. Bel mutters something. "We gotta fix all that. This is *our* city, not theirs."

Cheers resound in the room. The guy grins, feeding on their excitement, excited himself. He turns to a drape-covered easel that stands nearby, and with a flourish uncovers it to reveal a campaign sign: PANFILO FOR MAYOR in lurid red and black, superimposed over a blue outline of New York's cityscape, love the color symbolism. The guy—Panfilo, apparently—then turns to look dead into the camera, grinning and raising his arms. "We're gonna Make New York Great Again!" More cheering all around him.

The clip stops. Veneza closes her laptop. Manny looks at me, and I remember our conversation from the night before. The doctor just called, it's cancer, and it's about two seconds away from metastasizing. So how *does* a city of eight million people put itself through chemo? Guess we 'bout to find out.

CHAPTER ONE

Living Just Enough in the City

It's job offer day at Evilcorp.

Padmini knows she probably shouldn't think of it as Evilcorp. Yes, it *is* evil—a multinational financial services company that makes billions per year in exchange for the small price of the environment and economic stability and anything resembling human decency—but it is also her employer. She knew what she was getting into when she accepted the offer of an internship with them, and for the most part this devil's bargain has worked in her favor. She's gained a ton of experience and gotten paid for the privilege, while many of her grad school peers are struggling along on SNAP benefits, forced to do all their professors' dirty work if they want to graduate. The money's been good enough that she helped Aishwarya buy clothes for the baby, and sent something back home to her family in Chennai for the first time ever. She can remember her mother, a quiet but determined woman, working all day in a government position and then doing call center shifts at night from home, surviving for years on only four or five hours of sleep just to make sure Padmini's education fund kept growing. Now Padmini is contributing to the education fund for her younger brother. This is late-stage capitalism; evil is everywhere. But if she can help her family, then at least she's getting a little good out of it.

(Such an odd term, "devil's bargain." Hinduism is full of "demons," but half of them are just gods having a bad day. As far as Padmini can tell, the same applies to Christian demons, who are supposed to be fallen angels. But Hindu demons don't run around trying to trick people into shady spiritual contracts; they mostly just start fights and kill people while obsessing over their own personal affairs. Christian demons really need to get a life.)

Padmini and her boss are meeting in the prettiest conference room on the fifty-sixth floor. It's got a big mahogany meeting table, elegant exotic plants that someone gets paid well to keep alive, and actual wood-paneled walls instead of the ubiquitous glass that's supposed to suggest transparency. That small measure of privacy is why it's being used for this meeting, since HR matters have to be kept confidential. Padmini picks a seat facing the window, which takes up one whole side of the room, gifting them both with a bright midmorning view of lower Manhattan, the East River, and, ah yes of course, Queens. Nice to have her emotional support borough here with her.

Remember to call him Joe, Padmini reminds herself for the umpteenth time. Her supervisor is Joe Whitehead. All the other interns call him Joe. Padmini's tried on his given name a few times, but using it still feels disrespectful and overly familiar, so she always reverts to "Mr. Whitehead" when she's not thinking about it. Thing is, she's *not* the same as those other interns, and no amount of fake-casual familiarity is going to make her ever forget that. Most of the others are Ivy Leaguers while she's from NYU, which is just an Ivy League–priced wannabe. A lot of them are getting MBAs, PhDs, even JDs—terminal degrees—while she's in a STEM master's program, hired only because nobody else can handle the data crunching. She gets along with all of them, of course, because she knows how important workplace relationships are. She laughs at their unfunny jokes; she answers their questions about how to make good chai even though she hates the stuff. Meanwhile she works longer hours than everyone on the team, Joe included.

But whatever. Here she is at last, at the finish line.

"Padmini, how's it going?" Joe asks, as he strolls in and sits down, laying out several documents in front of himself. She sees that the top one carries the letterhead of HR, which is a satisfying-enough sight that it almost distracts her from the mangling of her name. *Padmini* is not that hard to say, but he frequently transposes the consonants: pah-dee-mee instead of pad-mee-nee. She grits her teeth into a bright smile.

"I'm doing great, Joe!" Excellent, got that "Joe" in. It works like magic; he relaxes visibly, which is good because he's always a little stiff around her. "Just enjoying this beautiful view."

"Oh, is it?" He glances at the window and then back at his paperwork, which he's shuffling around. "Always preferred the harbor view, on the south side of the building. Statue of Liberty and all. I figured you'd like that yourself."

There was a time when statements like this went over her head.

These days she pings on them immediately—but a meeting with your boss, who's about to offer you a permanent position, is not the time to point out that not all immigrants like the Statue of Liberty. Especially immigrants for whom the whole *Send me your tired, your poor* schtick has turned out to be more like *Send me your smartest and hardest working so we can suck the life out of them then ship the exhausted dregs right back*. So Padmini shrugs and plays it off. "Well, but facing that way you have to look at Staten Island, Joe."

It's not a fair joke. First because the southern view also features Jersey City. Second because Staten Island is going through some stuff right now, and people in the city are likely less sympathetic toward it as a result. Sure enough, Joe laughs, too loudly. He's always so loud. "Perish the thought! You're so funny, Padmini." Then he sighs, pressing his lips together in awkward discomfort. "That's what's going to make this so difficult."

It's such a swift change in the meeting's mood that it takes Padmini a moment to catch up. "What do you mean?"

He hesitates, then puts on a neutral face that immediately makes her tense. She tries to think of all the possible scenarios that she's prepared for. He'll say, *The salary is below market, unfortunately*, and she'll have to find a politic way to say that she'll accept anything, even minimum wage, as long as the company sponsors her H-1B visa application. Or he'll say that she didn't get the title she requested—something without *Administrator*, and hopefully with *Researcher* in it—and she'll counter with, "Well, maybe we can consider that at my first performance review." She's rehearsed this with a career counselor, and practiced interviewing with her uncle. She's ready.

He says, "I'm afraid our department wasn't able to come up with a line item that would fund a postgraduation position for you, Padmini."

There's a beat of silence between them.

Then she blurts, "What the actual fuck did you just say?"

He's already halfway to saying something else; the f-bomb stops him in his tracks, and he blinks, then lets out an uncomfortable chuckle. "I'm sure this comes as a shock, so I'll let that slide. But I just wanted to say that I'm sorry—"

She interrupts him. She knows better, but she can't think. "Why?"

"Well, the management team met, and there was concern about your organizational fit—"

It hits like a punch to the belly. "My *fit*?"

"Yes." Joe looks defensive, probably because her tone communicates clearly that she thinks this is the shittiest excuse that ever got shat. Her facial expression's probably helping to convey her open disgust, too; she's always been the face journey type. "As you know, fit is extremely important to teamwork, and since we do solicit feedback from other interns about anyone we're considering for a permanent position, there were . . . concerns, as I said. Some of the others seemed to feel that you were, well, condescending at times." When Padmini continues to just stare at him, he resumes, with visible unease. "Others felt that you were unwilling to listen to feedback."

She narrows her eyes. "Is this about Wash still insisting that my projection was wrong?"

"This isn't about anything specific—but yes, that was one of the incidents that got discussed. And your reaction to Wash was professional, certainly, but..." He spreads his hands, as if she's supposed to know what that means.

The horrible thing is that she does know what it means. Wash—family name Washbourne—is one of the PhD interns, with several years of experience as a tech company CFO and an unhealthy tendency to assume that his quantitative skills are much better than they are. During an analytics review a few months back, Padmini took care to speak to him deferentially even though they're both interns with the same rank, but she also did not back down when he got defensive over an error that she pointed out. When he insisted he was right, she asked for time in another team meeting and then used that time to walk everyone through the details of her point, including white papers on the common error Wash was making. Joe agreed, the team agreed, and Wash even apologized and laughed it off afterward. Now, though... Padmini narrows her eyes. "Wait, did Wash file some kind of complaint? Because there was nothing about my *fit* in my performance review, and... and even if there was, that..." She shakes her head, her mouth faltering because she's completely unable to believe what she's hearing. It's the stupidest reason she can think of not to hire someone, especially given that they *need* her. "What was I supposed to do, let him put that error into the final report?"

"Of course not. And no, he didn't file a complaint; if he had, I would've told you. Padmini." Joe sighs and leans forward. "You're getting very emotional about this. Honestly, I didn't think you had a temper at all."

"You're telling me I'm going to have to leave the country I've spent almost half my life in because I'm not polite enough to let incompetence slide, and you think I shouldn't be *emotional?*"

Joe sets his jaw. "And that's part of the problem, too. You're only here for the visa." When she audibly gasps, Joe presses the case. "You don't care about our organizational mission. You don't have any curiosity about other departments or teams; no one outside of Data Analytics knows you—"

Oh, hell no. Padmini pushes herself up to stand, palms planted on the edge of the mahogany conference table. If the thing didn't weigh a ton, she'd flip it. "I don't know anyone in other departments because I put in sixty-hour weeks on a regular basis," she snaps. "I'm not supposed to work any more than twenty-four hours per week, remember? Because I'm also a full-time student. I didn't report the excess to my internship supervisor. I could lose my student visa for that—but I did it, because I thought that was the way to prove I was worthy of long-term investment. I spend half of my time correcting other people's work as well as doing my own, *to make sure the team looks good.* I go home exhausted every day and still do my coursework at night, I barely see my family even though we live in the same *house*"— She's shaking with rage, but has enough presence of mind to rein it in when she hears her voice echo off the walls—"but I don't complain. Not when Ed makes his little comments about how different my lunch smells from his Trader Joe's vindaloo, or . . . or when Judy keeps stroking my bloody hair like I'm a *doll*, and when Rajesh won't even look me in the eye because he can tell I'm Dalit! And you think I don't care about *the mission?*" He opens his mouth and she runs over him, too furious to care anymore about treading carefully. "This organization's mission is to make money, which I support by making 43 percent less than Wash, who can't be bothered to check his fucking math!"

"Padmini—"

But she's done, done, done, and her heart is in her throat and her eyes are blurry with anger-tears as she shakes her head and starts snatching up her things. Joe gives up and watches in awkward silence while she *emotionally* walks out of the conference room. And as she storms past Wash's cubicle, of course she sees that he's facing its opening, watching for her. *Grinning*, at the look on her face. Then Padmini hates herself for not being able to hold in the tears anymore, though she at least keeps it to a silent trickle as she passes Wash and heads to her own cubicle.

She's already on her way out when security arrives to escort her. That's standard practice in tech and finance companies, and she expected the escort given that it's her last day. It still feels accusatory to have two hulking men walk along with her as she carries a box containing the sum total of her professional belongings: a tiny aloe plant, some reference books she'd kept in her office, and the WELCOME TO NEW YORK! snow globe that someone gave her at the last office Christmas party. She's concluding an internship that would be counted successful by most measures, but it still feels like she's leaving in disgrace. Probably because she might as well be.

Then she's outside and they shut the doors behind her and she stops on the sidewalk for a moment to try to regain her emotional feet. That's impossible because those feet are numb, like her heart and her mind. Some part of her clinically, cynically notes that she's going to need to apologize to Joe pretty quickly so that she can maybe scrape a good referral and internship review out of it, at least. But *How could you?* is what she really wants to say to Joe, and she's pretty sure she's right to feel that way. It *is* a betrayal. She was the best employee on that damn team. A postgraduate offer would have meant she could relax a little, for the first time since she came to the US. Make a mistake every now and again. Take a whole weekend off, even.

But now when she graduates, she'll have to find different employment before her student visa expires. That won't be too difficult given her skill set, but what she needs is an employer who's willing to sponsor her for the next step in the process: the H-1B specialty worker visa. It can easily cost ten thousand dollars for a company to hire lawyers and file all the different fees required, and whether the attempt is successful is a crapshoot because the government only gives out so many per year. Given the added cost and risk, few companies are willing to take a chance on an entry-level employee who hasn't already interned with them. Padmini can continue to work in the country for a couple of years and at least earn some money, but after that she'll have to go home to Chennai, a city she hasn't seen in more than ten years. Her chances of being able to legally return to the US for work or citizenship after that will drop from slim to infinitesimal.

She makes it to the subway, at least, before she breaks down sobbing.

There's nothing particularly esoteric to New York in how people react to a woman crying on public transportation, though the range of those reactions does vary depending on what borough one is in. Nobody says anything while she's in Manhattan. It's still early afternoon; not many people on the train this time of day, except tourists who just gawk at her. As the train approaches the bridge, however, the Manhattan passengers leave and Queens-bound passengers replace them. Somewhere around Queens Plaza an old white-maybe-Jewish woman leans over and says, "You okay, honey?" In the same moment another older woman, this one Desi with a soft Mumbai accent to her Hindi, says, "Younger sister, why are you crying?" while a Latino guy somewhere near Padmini's own age goes, "Hey, you need tissues? I got tissues," and pats his pockets.

It's like a group hug of concern, her borough folding gentle arms around her and slapping away all that Wall Street coldness, and for a moment Padmini cries harder. Can't help it. "I'm okay," she blurts, taking a tissue from the packet that the young man waves at her. "I'm sorry. It's just... hard, sometimes. This damn city."

There are nods around her. "Fuck this city," says the old lady. "That's how you gotta be to live here, sweetie. Fuck it right in the ass." There are more nods at this bit of nonsense, and a few enthusiastic "Yeahs" of agreement from people who are watching. It's enough to pull a laugh from Padmini, which helps a lot even though absolutely none of her problems have been solved. Well—maybe one problem. In a moment when the world has made her feel valueless and alone, this little bit of human connection is exactly what she needs.

And then suddenly, out of nowhere, she gets booted into a different reality.

It's a familiar reality, at least. The subway lights shift from their infamous green-toned white to something more red-yellow, almost twilit. The people that were around her, the anxious young Latino and the foulmouthed Jewish lady and all the rest, are gone, though Padmini sees a packet of tissues on the bench across from her, where the Latino guy left them. Padmini herself isn't present anymore, either, not in any visible form—but she's used to the peculiar re-centering of her awareness that occurs whenever she shifts into this place. It's a metaphysical paradigm shift, a background process switchover from the perspective of a small flesh-and-blood human being into something vaster, stranger, many-minded. One of the reasons she and the others became cities is precisely because they are capable of making this leap of identity; they are not driven mad by the sudden ability to see and think as gods.

But never mind all that. Why has the city suddenly brought her here?

Padmini visualizes herself going to the windows for a look outside the train, and fortunately her disembodied consciousness cooperates. Beyond the windows she sees not the graffiti-limned buildings of Queens, but something at once familiar and unnerving: the metaversal tree. It exists at a scale great enough to encompass all worlds, both nowhere and everywhere at once, where one can witness the dynamism of the entire multiverse in an exponential cauliflower-cluster fractal spread of possibility. *Spreading from where?* she wonders for the first time, craning her figurative neck in an attempt to see beyond the nearest churning cluster. In the very far distance—farther than human eyes should be able to see, handy not being quite human anymore—she can make out a massive, impossibly long trunk below the tree. The trunk is universes that came into being countless aeons before Padmini's own, and whose growth was obviously less varied and chaotic than what dominates the tree's canopy. Figures; there probably wasn't a lot of thought impacting the multiverse back when life was nothing but amoebas.

But Padmini can't see to the trunk's roots—if a mass of endlessly spawning universes can have roots. That's because what she can see of the trunk eventually vanishes into a blaze of light so bright and white that it's impossible to see beyond. *We aren't supposed to go there*, she feels with sudden instinctive certainty. But that makes sense, doesn't it? A leaf dies when it drops from a tree's canopy onto the same soil that nourishes its roots. Not the leaf's fault, or the soil's; the leaf is just specialized for a different role in the tree's life cycle, and what it requires to survive are things that simply aren't present down on the ground. Also, this light is *too* bright. There's sunlight, and then there's whatever this is: a supernova of radiance, overwhelming by degrees. Even without eyes, Padmini has to stop looking in that direction, because it hurts.

What are you trying to show me? Padmini asks her borough.

The borough responds in the language she knows better than any of the other three she can speak—not words at all, but numbers and symbols and equations, writing themselves in panicky black strokes into the air around her. It's all quantum state stuff, she recognizes at once, and in particular it's

$$-\frac{\hbar^2}{2m}\frac{d^2\Psi(x)}{dx^2} + \frac{1}{2}m\omega^2 x^2\Psi(x) = E\Psi(x)$$

which is one of the Schrödinger equations. The one for the collapse of a wave function? As she watches, variables fill themselves into the equation and begin cycling with increasing speed. Counting *down*, as the train's wheels scream and the subway car rocks faster and faster. She only got to take elective physics courses in undergrad, and she doesn't remember all of it, but she thinks this might have something to do with eigenstates? The measure of how much quantum energy is in a system, basically. But what does it mean here? Damn it, she should've at least done the physics minor back in undergrad, but she was worried about her GPA, and . . .

. . . And for some reason, as she floats bodiless amid the branching, churning expanse of ten billion universes, she feels like she's being watched. But when she "looks around," there's no one there. What the . . . ?

perception dampeners inadequate, awareness imminent, abort abort abort

Then reality snaps, and Padmini is a human-shaped person on the R train again, clutching a small packet of borrowed tissues in one hand and leaning on the Mumbaikar lady, who's crossed seats to put an arm around her shoulders. What the fuck.

Okay. "Thank you," Padmini mumbles, trying to smile and trying not to look too disoriented as she pulls herself together. "Thank you, I'm sorry, you're so kind, I love you all, I'll be all right."

But that is a lie. She has no idea what the hell she just saw/felt/heard/became in that other place, but she knows when something's wrong.

The train's at Jackson Heights, though, so she gets off and just stands there for a moment as the premonition of wrongness escalates.

Something in the station? The platform here is aboveground like most Queens trains. The air smells off in a way that's not exactly bad, nothing stinks (for once), but nevertheless is different enough to make her wonder. Things sound weird, too—flatter, softer, a little tinny. The cardboard box has softened from the humidity and is starting to sag in Padmini's hands, and her fingertips feel numb. Is that because she's been holding the box too long, or...

...or is it because Queens is no longer alive?

Holy shit. It's only been three months since Padmini became New York, but in that time she's gotten used to perceiving the city through senses that ordinary, unidimensional human beings lack. Suddenly those are gone. But how is it possible for Queens to not be alive? *She's* still alive. There hasn't been any kind of mass catastrophe that's left a crater between Brooklyn and Long Island— but suddenly, for the first time since the city awakened, Queens is just a place. Not dead, but nothing special. And Padmini is also... nothing special.

In a daze she wanders out of the station, letting habit guide her feet toward home. Same route every day. Strange to see it in daylight, given that she rarely got to go home before dark while she was working. So much stranger to feel her steps just land on concrete, without sending little reverberations into it and receiving emotions and energy in return. She breathes and the city does not breathe with her. Before becoming Queens she used to get winded going up even one set of subway steps; the internship plus maintaining a 3.9 GPA haven't left her a lot of time to exercise. Stations like Times Square, where the interchange to reach the 7 train is such a marathon that the MTA actually emblazoned its longest stretch with a poem about how it felt to be *So tired*, always left her sweaty and out of breath before. For three months, however, she's been breezing through it without her heart rate even going up and she *didn't notice*, until now. How—

"Fucking chinko bitch," mutters a voice behind her.

Padmini flinches and immediately regrets it. She's had to deal with street harassment in both Chennai and New York pretty much since puberty, so she knows not to show any sign of discomfort or fear. Guy might not even be referring to her; she's not Chinese, or whatever a "chinko" is supposed to be. Maybe he's saying *chico*? Mistaking her for Latina, or trying to insinuate she's a man? Doesn't matter. The guy notices the flinch.

"Yeah, you," he says, louder. She hears him get up from where he'd been sitting, hears feet start to follow. Other people on the street, those walking in the opposite direction, start frowning at something behind her. Padmini speeds up her pace a little even though this is a reaction as well, but the guy speeds up to match. "I'm talking to *you*, chink. Li'l brown turd. *Illegal*. Comin' over here and spreading viruses everywhere and stealing our jobs."

That, on a day when Padmini has just lost her chance at a job because a less-competent white man disliked her, hits like a slap. She's already turning, already furious, already shaping her mouth to blurt "Fuck off" before her more sensible self can rein it in.

The guy following her is a dude she's seen before around the subway station, Black and maybe fortysomething, dressed in pajama pants and a Mets hoodie and flip-flops. She doesn't think he's actually homeless; he's always clean and well rested, locs groomed, and she's seen him going into a big apartment building down the block from Kebab King. He's a fixture in the area, though usually he just sits against a wall and mumbles to himself while occasionally asking for spare change. She thinks she's given him a few bucks over the years. But he's on his feet today, and more focused than she's ever seen him, though he stops and looks confused when she rounds on him.

"*Fuck off,*" she says again, "and kiss my fat brown ass. Nobody's taking a job from you! Or if they are, maybe it's because you spend all your time shitting on other people? Fix yourself, you stupid son of a bitch, and leave me the fuck alone!"

Someone nearby laughs. Someone else claps. The dude looks genuinely hurt, however, and that breaks the back of Padmini's rage. Poor fool is probably schizophrenic or something. Doesn't mean his insults are harmless or that he can't help himself—he clearly chooses to feed his delusions a diet of stereotypes and Fox News—but beyond just getting him to shut the fuck up, she's taking out her day on him. When he falls silent, she turns away and resumes walking, with a little snarl of frustration. Fuck all this shit. Fuck this city, whatever's happening to it. She just wants to go home.

But just as Padmini steps out of the shadow of the elevated tracks, there is a crack like thunder from the sky.

She turns in surprise to see something long and sinuous curling down out of the half-overcast clouds. At first it looks like a loose power line, somehow snapped free from a building connection or pole... but there's no building or pole that tall in the immediate area. And then she realizes the long thing is moving on its own, wending toward her against the wind. And, oh shit. The cable is *white*.

Then an even greater chill freezes her: Queens is no longer alive. Which means that Padmini is just an ordinary woman without any sort of extradimensional powers—

—so there is absolutely nothing she can do as the long white cord, which *is* a power line of sorts but definitely not installed by ConEd, slips almost playfully around the elevated tracks and loops around a lightpole... then curls around the legs of the man who insulted her. He's still staring at her, not at it; can he not feel it? Then as the cord reaches the back of his head, it suddenly becomes not the cut end of a thick wire but something like a flower, flaring out a radius of plasticine petals. At the core of the cable is not braided wire, but something thinner and more familiar. A white tendril. It wriggles wildly at first, but after an instant of this it stops moving and orients, with uncanny intent, on the nape of the man's neck.

Padmini lifts a hand and opens her mouth—

—and then she just stands there, helpless and horrified, as the ugly cord-flower strikes with snakelike speed. The man jerks a little, his eyes widening as it sinks into the back of his head... and then he goes still. Not dead or unconscious. He blinks once, twice, frowning to himself and tilting his head as if he hears someone else speaking. She can see the "petals" of the thing, wrapped around the back of the man's neck and the edge of his jaw; they shift a little before settling, like fingers getting a good grip on something.

And then, slowly, the man's face begins to distort.

No one else seems to see. It's Jackson Heights; there are at least a hundred people in viewing range, walking down the street or perusing the fruit vendor's stall or eyeballing their phones. None of them react as, slowly at first, the man's left eye moves down, and his right eye gets bigger. The color begins to wash out of his skin, not in patches like vitiligo but everywhere, not the fade-to-blond of Black albinism but a starker, inhuman white. His cheekbones broaden, sharpening into impossibly fine edges under his skin. He's getting bigger as well: two feet taller than her now, rapidly gaining bulk. Padmini blinks and he has four arms. She takes an inadvertent step back and now he's got six legs. Blink blink blink because she can't believe her eyes and it's eight legs, *twelve*. He's getting lopsided, with more legs on his left side than his right. He opens a mouth that is froglike, stretched across his face and lined with too many small square teeth, and *no one sees this*. Some do flinch, at least, when he suddenly yells in an echoing foghorn voice, "FOREIGNER. FUCKING FOREIGNER." They can hear him, or an echo of him, or maybe they just hear the malice that ripples under the words. But they do not *see* as he spreads too many sharp-clawed hands and takes a rolling, centipedal step forward. "FUCKING FOREIGN CHINKO BITCH."

"Yes, no, *hell* no," Padmini blurts as she turns to run. It's not her nature. Queens never gives up—but someone has pulled the Queens out from under her, so atavistic self-preservation takes over. She gets maybe three steps before there is the thud-feel of something huge and heavy jolting to a halt right behind her, as if the man has leapt the distance in pursuit. Something hits the back of her head. It's not a painful blow, probably because she's running away already, but the sheer force of the hit is enough to throw her forward by a good ten feet. Padmini lands on her box with a grunt; the box crumbles instantly beneath her. One book and the ceramic pot that contains her little aloe jab her in the ribs and tits respectively. She manages to catch herself partially on one hand and a knee, which hurts abominably, but the pain is nothing to the sound of rumbling lopsided feet coming closer, and the dread that accompanies this sound.

"Hey!" someone shouts nearby.

Startled, Padmini looks up. Centipede Man has stopped with three of his feet in the air. He's staring at a tiny brown woman in a hijab who has interposed herself between them. She's older, maybe in her sixties, and is that an actual copy of the *Daily News* rolled up in one hand? Padmini hasn't seen anybody read a physical newspaper in years. The headline that she can make out reads TAKE THE F U TRAIN, PANFILO, with the *F* and *U* in brightly colored circles like subway line markers. Oh, that's right; some new guy just declared himself for the New York City mayoral race, didn't he? Padmini remembers overhearing people in the break room at work talking about this dude being a real piece of work, and... She's getting distracted. The old lady is still talking.

"What's wrong with you?" the lady says. Her hand clenches around the paper and—Padmini gasps—she *swats* the monster with it. It's not a particularly good swat. It's been a while since Padmini held a newspaper herself, but she remembers that you have to roll it up tight if you want to achieve maximum swattage. Pages scatter, however, because the old lady really put her back into it. "How dare you? What's *wrong* with you?"

"FOREIGN FUCK—" the monster starts to say.

"*You* the fuck," says another dredlocked Black guy, about the same age as the old hijabi but bigger and wearing a UPS uniform. "You hit some little girl half your size? Fucking bomboclaat, man. Leave people be! Go wash your ashy feet!"

Abruptly there are other cries around them, taking up the man's name-calling and echoing the woman's *What's wrong with you?* Other voices, other wills, other angry energy, the reverberation of which is enough to tint the air—

Wait. Tint the air?

Padmini pushes herself upright just as the nearby reverberations of energy seem to gather strength and send forth additional waves. By the time she staggers to her feet, she can see these waves reflecting off every surface around them, building in strength as each ripple fuels others. Off the sidewalk. Off the wall of a nearby bakery. Off the Centipede Man, who flinches at their touch and stares at Padmini with wide, vertically aligned eyes that once again look hurt and confused. Continuing, building, the energy cycling from point to point faster, each wave palpably strengthening the others, until—

Like jump-starting an engine, Padmini thinks in wonder, even though she's never done that in her life and has no clue how to do it. But the metaphor works, because an instant later Padmini feels the sidewalks start to purr and sees the sky suddenly brighten and she inhales as the power of the city flows back into her limbs and mind and soul. *She is New York again.* She is the borough of the city's besieged working class, huddled masses done with everybody's shit, and they've got her back. *Queens* has her back.

Padmini smiles, barely feeling the scrapes and bruises this time as she turns to face her foe. Centipede Man takes a step back as she steps forward—but twenty legs apparently don't back up easily, so he stumbles. Doesn't matter. She's got his number now. She's got all the numbers, always.

The snow globe from her smashed box has rolled to a stop at her feet, because that's how city magic works. She raises a hand and it leaps into her palm, "snow" swirling wildly within, but not so much that she can't still see the WELCOME TO NEW YORK! within. A tiny King Kong holds this slogan on a sign, while the Statue of Liberty claps her hands and cheers King Kong on from nearby. When Padmini smiles at how nonsensical the whole thing is, the snow swirls even harder, and she feels the plastic sphere grow icy cold against her palm. Welcome to New York, huh?

"Glad to be back," Padmini says. Then she turns the snow globe and smashes it against the man's distorted face.

It shatters instantly, splashing him with ice-cold water that sizzles on his skin with an awful searing-meat sound. There is an outcry from nearby; the man's mouth doesn't move, but nevertheless Padmini hears the high-pitched, agonized *skree* of nothing human. An almost electrical snap follows this cry as the power line from Dimension X detaches from the man's head. In the next instant the man is himself again, blinking water and fake snow out of perfectly human eyes set in a perfectly human face, above just two arms and two legs.

"Don't fucking touch me, bitch," he murmurs at Padmini, wiping water from his eyes in disgust. He sounds confused again, as if he's suddenly not sure why he's got snow globe all over his face.

A moment later, however, the guy goes flying. A big balding white-maybe-Italian dude has come out of the bakery and hit Padmini's harasser with a sweet shoulder tackle. "Well, don't fucking hit people in the head, then!" he shouts. The small crowd that has gathered applauds and cheers him on. The man formerly known as Centipede groans and flails weakly on the ground, while Bakery Guy lifts his hands and turns, grinning, to accept the crowd's adulation.

Bomboclaat Guy shakes his head and turns to Padmini. "You all right?"

"Yeah," she says. "You?"

"Mi deh yah. Nobody smack *my* face wit a snow globe, see?" He grins, and Padmini can't help laughing back. The laugh's a bit hysterical, but badly needed.

"Don't let them hurt that guy," she says, even though there's no reason to expect Bomboclaat to do anything more than he's already done. "He's an asshole, but you know what the cops are like." Nobody deserves to die just for being an asshole.

"Queen," Bomboclaat says, in amusement. "Too nice. Fine, tho, I gotchu."

Nobody hurts ex–Centipede Man. A random other guy helps Padmini pick up the scattered contents of her box. She looks around for the old Muslim lady and spots her on the other side of the crowd, tucking the now-ruined paper into a bag of groceries as she walks away. Padmini calls another thanks after her, but she doesn't think the woman hears.

There are police sirens in the distance. Probably unrelated to this little fracas; it's only been maybe five minutes since the guy hit her, and NYPD never shows up fast in this zip code. Still means it's time to move on. She needs to tell the others about this. The tendril from the sky, the fluctuation of the city's power, the quantum weirdness; nothing like this was supposed to be possible anymore. Team meeting time.

But before all that, Padmini's going home. She needs her family. Her scrapes and bruises have already healed, but she decides she also needs a long soaking bath with scented Epsom salts, and a pillow to cry into, and maybe some of those little brigadeiro things she's been loving ever since they met São Paulo. There's a Brazilian bakery on the way home.

Thus does the Queen of Queens reclaim her throne—only to belatedly realize somebody stole her aloe plant. Fucking city. She loves it so much.

CHAPTER TWO

It's a Hell of a Town

Manny sits in his office, trying to decide whether to quit his graduate program.

He's doing well, in spite of his recent transcendence beyond purely corporeal, unidimensional existence. Finished both his late-summer courses with As. Now that it's the fall term, he's just finished teaching a half-semester intro course for undergraduates, and his course evaluations are stellar. On Rate My Professors he's got a 5 out of 5 rating, with tags including "caring" and "tough grader" but also "really interesting lectures that suggest he spends a lot of time thinking about ethics and ontology." At least three comments have been flagged inappropriate because they speculate hopefully about his sexual proclivities and penis size, but it could be a lot worse.

He came to New York for this. It must have been important to the person he was before. But now that he *is* New York, or at least a significant part of it, getting a PhD in political theory suddenly feels like a colossal waste of his time.

He doesn't need to work as a teaching assistant, either. The bank account attached to his name—or rather, the name that used to be his—contains roughly three hundred thousand dollars. That's apparently just his pocket money. It receives regular infusions from several sources, including a consulting company, a venture capital firm, a hedge fund, one trust solely in his old name, and another attached to some corporation whose principal shareholders include several other people who share his family name. He also gets money from his partial shadow ownership of a national sports team—not any of New York's. He's had to do some digging to figure out all of it, because each of these sources is shielded from easy discovery through a complex layer of incorporations, offshore accounts, and accounting complexities that seem designed to do nothing but provide layers of obfuscation for anyone who wants to know where Manny's really getting his money. As he did the digging, he was surprised to realize he knew exactly how to dig and what sort of layering—or laundering—to look for. If he didn't set all this up himself, he knows exactly how it was done.

There are a couple of conclusions that Manny has drawn as a result of discovering that he's apparently, clandestinely, worth a few million dollars. The first is that he needs to stop digging. He doesn't want to know what his pre–New York self was into, and there's a chance the other people involved will notice his snooping and consider it an invitation to make contact. His second conclusion is that he definitely doesn't need a PhD . . . but he does need New York.

He needs to spend his nights standing on rooftops, staring at the cityscape around him and breathing its air. He needs to lie awake in the mornings, listening to the stop-start of hydraulic bus brakes and ambulance sirens. It isn't just an aesthetic or spiritual craving, either. On some not-quite-natural level Manny has begun to understand that when the borough of Manhattan is in tune with him and vice versa, everything flows better. Fewer car accidents, and those less deadly and more quickly cleared. Less illegal garbage dumping, fewer rats. New York as a whole is struggling right now. In the wake of Bridgefall, as the Williamsburg Bridge disaster has come to be known, the city's economy has taken a hit. Traffic jams, as the whole city now has to cope with four main bridges instead of five, have been epic despite Manny's best efforts. Worse, the Williamsburg, a rusty old workhorse of a bridge with none of the architectural cachet of the Brooklyn or the Manhattan Bridges, was the one most residents of Brooklyn and Queens— the city's most heavily populated boroughs—used for daily commuting. As a result, many small businesses on both sides of the bridge have shut down, with a corresponding catastrophic loss of jobs and shuffling-around of the population. Many of the city's denizens have jumped boroughs; Manny can feel a steady drain into Brooklyn, with a thinner trickle into Queens and the Bronx. Not much inflow to make up for the deficit, but that's because Manhattan has lost so many neighborhoods to gentrification over the past decade; there are whole swaths of the island that contain more never-occupied investment units and illegal Airbnbs than rentable apartments. Newcomers to the city mostly go to the boroughs, given this. A few New Yorkers have left the city altogether for quieter locales, frightened by Bridgefall's stark demonstration of the city's vulnerability. This fear has been fanned by right-wing conspiracy theories about what caused Bridgefall, ranging from ISIS to space aliens hepped up on Critical Race Theory and invited to conquer Earth by George Soros. Despite this, the city's overall population has increased.

Churn happens in any major metropolis. It's just a normal part of city life. Still, the end result is that New York is restless, and its unsettled movements ripple across the multiverse in odd ways. It's a strange feeling—somewhere between the creepy suspicion that one is being watched, and the sensation of falling.

Manny wants to do something about that precarious, looming-disaster feeling. It's not what city avatars should do, he suspects. There's something ethically wobbly about an avatar taking action that will change the city—a metaphysical conflict of interest, bringing quantum theory to a policy fight. But why shouldn't a city try to take care of itself? Manny eats right, gets recommended vaccinations, attends regular checkups for preventative care—or he did before he became semi-immortal, anyway. Isn't active involvement in his city's "health" the same thing?

Manny sighs and pushes up from his desk. He needs to get going if he's going to make it to Brooklyn's place in time for the meeting.

It's only been three months since those hectic days in June when Manny and the others ran all over the city trying to thwart the terrifying minions of the Woman in White, but he will not be caught helpless again. There are few words for the peculiar abilities that come of being a city—and really, so much of it is less skill than instinct, resonance, comfort, self-acceptance. It's nature, though reflective of an ecological complexity that defies current human understanding. It's acculturation to a posthuman identity shared by only a few dozen individuals all over the world.

"It's just . . . being Manhattan," he murmurs to himself, and smiles as his city thrums in agreement.

He's standing at the Columbia gate nearest the 116th Street subway station, but that's only so he can get his bearings. The others say it's harder to do this at rush hour than any other time of day, and it is—but there are a few tricks Manny's found that make it easier. He moves to stand on a nearby subway grate, through which he can hear a 1 train idling on the platform below. He spreads his hands to feel the gentle waft of warm, funky-smelling subway air along his skin. (No one pays attention when he does this, because few people bother paying attention to odd behavior in New York, and he wouldn't care if they did, because few New Yorkers care what other people think.) Shutting his eyes for a moment, he takes a deep breath and relaxes enough to let his mind unlock itself from the constraints of human flesh. There. Ready.

When the subway ding-dongs to warn that the doors will close, Manny opens his eyes. In one moment he's on the corner in front of the Columbia gates, baring his teeth in a smile that is half-snarl, the summation of thousands of annoyed, impatient subway riders who just got off work and are ready to be home already. Then Manny is gone, vanishing to human eyes as he is carried along by the train's momentum. He uses more than just the train, however. That's the trick. The 1 is a local, after all, stopping every few blocks and making the overall journey gratingly sluggish.

Better to gather close not the train itself, but the concept of *hurry-ing home*. This lets Manny balance the subway's intermittent speed against the more relentless progress of a nearby delivery guy hustling on an e-bike, and a teenager riding a Lime moped without a helmet—though both mean he occasionally experiences the agony of getting doored. No reward without risk. But now he's passing Lincoln Center, spreading his arms and inhaling as elation makes him want to sing. He twitches through Times Square, resisting the urge to gawk like a tourist, groaning in native-New-Yorker frustration when the tourists get in his way—but in an eyeblink he's at Fourteenth Street, hurrying along a sidewalk and wondering if he should stop and pick up something for dinner from the farmers market, and wondering if the doctor called in his prescription, and oh is it going to rain? Hard to wrench out of that because Fourteenth is such a commuter nexus, but he manages by latching on to an especially aggressive NYU student on an electric unicycle. Suddenly he's at Battery Park, being carried along by a power-walking young man who's finally starting to understand that a high salary isn't worth much if the hundred-hour weeks kill him before he gets to spend it.

Overshot again, but not by much this time. Manny backtracks by following a roller derby team out practicing together, then lets his mind skim along with the NYC Ferry toward Red Hook in Brooklyn. Easy transfer there to a dollar van that's cruising for a pickup. Finally Manny stumbles back into corporeal existence at the corner of Bedford and Fulton, laughing as he catches himself against a lightpost. Someone actually does see this, because people in their neighborhoods tend to be more observant than commuters going to and from work, but he doesn't look dangerous so still, no one cares. An older woman curses at Manny for stumbling against her in his disorientation, and for a moment his awareness snaps sideways, thoughts developing a non-English lilt—*Stupid graceless ass, probably high, God willing these children will learn respect someday, my feet hurt so much*—and then he is firmly himself again, just a graceless ass in khakis stammering out an apology in Arabic while the woman sighs and pivots around him. Okay, best to walk from here.

Jojo, Brooklyn's teenage daughter, opens the front door of the brownstone almost as soon as he rings the doorbell. "Hi, Manny," she says, a bit breathlessly. "Mama said you were coming. How have you been? Do you like New York? Hey, do you do school-to-college teaching?"

"I, uh," Manny says, thrown by the rush of questions.

"Girl, if you don't calm the hell down," Brooklyn says, appearing behind her. Jojo sighs and rolls her eyes (where her mother can't see), but she finally slips around Manny—taking care to pivot and wave goodbye to both of them—before heading down the street. "Be back by the time the streetlights come on," Brooklyn calls after her, and Jojo waves back in impatient acknowledgment.

Brooklyn gazes after her with fond exasperation. "I think someone's got a li'l crush."

"Oh," Manny says, blushing a little as he finally catches on. "Uh...sorry?" He's never been sure what Brooklyn thinks of him.

Brooklyn snorts at his discomfiture. "When I was her age I had a thing for men with Jheri curls, so at least she has better taste. Come on in."

Inside, Manny's relieved to realize he's not the last to arrive; Padmini is nowhere to be seen. Brooklyn's fetching drinks for everyone, and Veneza and Bronca are in the kitchen arguing about... collard greens? Okay. Neek stands at the apartment's front windows, tinted pink and amber by cast-off sunset through the stained-glass uppers, though he turns and jerks his chin at Manny in greeting. Manny nods back, a little awkwardly, because everything between them is awkward. The urge to go to him is strong.

Slowly, whispers Manny's borough, from the eternal place where its voice lurks in his soul. Manhattan is a city of passion and bold declarations—and cold, calculated strategy. *Be cool. This is a hunt; rush it and you'll spook him. Give him what he needs to feel safe and let his guard down.*

Manny-that-is-not-a-city sighs. Yeah. Okay. He can be cool.

Veneza emerges from the kitchen clutching a tied-up sheaf of dark green leaves, which she then stuffs into a backpack propped against a nearby ottoman. "Oh. 'Sup, Mannahatta."

He eyes the greens. "You stopped at the farmers market in the middle of an extradimensional crisis?"

"Dude, we're always in some kind of crisis. Meanwhile, these were on sale! Though Old B says they still cost too much. I've been trying to do better about eating my vegetables." She frowns and plops down on the ottoman. "Even though I don't really have to eat anymore. Man, I wish the city would make it so I don't have to pay rent—I mean thanks for the cheapo penthouse spot, but generally speaking."

"There probably *is* a way to avoid paying rent, you know,"

Manny says, taking his own seat on the couch. (Neek is just behind him. He is always aware of where Neek is.)

"Ooh! See, that's why I like you, Manny. Tell me—"

"That," Bronca says, emerging from the kitchen with a wry look on her face, "is why you shouldn't listen to Mannahatta, Young B. *He* can probably get away with it. Jersey City ain't got nothin' on Manhattan for scams."

"Speak for yourself. I'm fulla scams." Veneza pushes up her sleeves and wiggles her arms. "Look, scams up to my elbows. I'mma get some scam nail art. I..."

She trails off as Manny hears Brooklyn let someone else in. As Padmini comes into the living room, the aura of hovering misery about her is immediately palpable from the young woman's blotchy face and red eyes. She's in schlubby casual, sweatpants and an oversized hoodie, and smells of something herbal, like a bath bomb or potpourri. And for some reason she's got one of those little cheap souvenir snow globes in one hand, which she turns in her fingers now and again, as if it's a fidget toy. It's still got a lurid red price tag stuck to its base.

"Hi," she says to all of them. She sits down, heavily, on the couch.

"You okay?" Veneza asks, frowning. They know about the attack, but it's clear now that Padmini underplayed its impact on her. "You...don't look okay."

"I'm fine, now that all's said and done, but it keeps hitting me..." Her expression tightens, so much that Manny debates preemptively fetching a box of tissues. Then Padmini squares her shoulders. "Well. I left this out of the chat because it was more personal than city business, but now that I think about it, it's city business, too. Before my borough temporarily died and I got attacked by an Asian-hating centipede monster, I...I found out I'm not getting a job offer from my internship. Instead, after I graduate, I'll have to go back to my country."

And then, while they all stare in appalled silence, she chuckles. It sounds as tired as she looks. "But that's kind of minor compared to the city destabilizing, so don't mind me."

"Okay, wait," Brooklyn blurts. "That's not how this city shit is supposed to work, is it? Hong said it was a matter of luck. Things just happen for us, because the city makes them happen. Right? So you *should've* gotten that job."

Everybody starts up at once. "A lawsuit," Manny starts to suggest, but he is immediately talked over by Brooklyn's persistent, "If you had good evaluations, then—" and Veneza's "Could the city have turned your boss into a bitch?" and Padmini's own frustrated, "No, no, he was a bitch long before that," until finally Bronca purses her lips and pierces the chatter with a loud whistle.

"The city's power doesn't always work the way we think it will," Bronca says when everyone focuses on her. She's leaning back against Brooklyn's breakfast bar, arms folded as she frowns in concentration. "I mean, if it was that neat, it wouldn't need us, would it? We have to guide it. It has to understand what we want and need."

"Whoa," Veneza says, frowning as she ponders the matter. "But *want* and *need* aren't always the same things. If you're saying the city can't tell the difference, then...like...c'mon, Queen P, you never liked that internship. Maybe—" Abruptly Veneza looks horrified and cuts herself off, as she reaches the logical conclusion of what she's saying.

Too late, though. Padmini stiffens. "You're saying this happened because of me, then? That my asshole boss was right and I didn't get the offer because I wasn't *happy* to be worked half to death with no overtime? If only I had been *excited* about working for a megacorporation that destroys nations for profit! Then my family wouldn't have mortgaged their whole future for nothing!"

"It was the wrong job for you," Manny says. When Padmini rounds on him, furious, he belatedly realizes he's compounding Veneza's error. It's the wrong thing to say in this moment, while Padmini's wound is still raw. But now that he's said it, he might as well finish. "We keep forgetting that the nature of our boroughs complicates things. *Manhattan* is the land of social climbers who'll shank their mothers for a big-enough payday. Queens, not so much." Manny doesn't have a good read on what Queens *is* yet, but he gets what it's not.

"Queens is families," Neek says. It's soft. He hasn't turned to face them, speaking to the window, but all of them fall silent and turn to him. "Little-big dreams. An apartment with rent stabilization, parking for a car the neighbors will admire. Queens is people climbing out of hell and dragging everyone they care about along with them, just to make it to purgatory."

Padmini makes a disgusted noise. "I could help my family a lot better with a Wall Street job than I can working at a call center in Chennai!"

"You barely saw your family anymore," Brooklyn says gently. "I remember you saying that. You're a full-time student, and that was a full-time job even though it wasn't supposed to be, and you've got city stuff to deal with on top of everything else. *Three* high-pressure jobs. Sure, hustling is the Queens way, the *New York* way, but how long could you have kept it up? What good are you to your family if you break?"

That seems to strike home. Padmini opens her mouth to retort, but nothing comes out; after a moment she looks away. Veneza sits beside her. Padmini glances at her, sighs in rueful acknowledgment of this silent apology, then subsides.

Bronca takes a deep breath as a segue. "So we got *another* crisis. Why can't this goddamn city ever just have one at a time? Don't answer that, it was rhetorical."

"The city *un-citying* is a really good one, though," Brooklyn says. She's in the kitchen, resting her forearms on the other side of the same breakfast bar as Bronca. "If we're rating crises, I'd give that one 5 out of 5 stars. Also yet another old bigoted white man running for mayor, but we get those all the time so it just gets 2 stars. What else? I feel like I'm missing something."

Neek answers: "Squigglebitch sending down fiber-optic cables from the sky."

"Right, of course, how could I forget." Brooklyn eyes Padmini. "That dude hurt you, honey?"

Padmini touches the back of her head. "No. There isn't a bruise or anything anymore, and no whiplash that I can tell. It was just scary." She bites her lip. "I bought a new snow globe at one of those ninety-nine cent stores. Just in case, you know?"

The truly scary thing is that none of the rest of them had even been aware of the problem happening, Manny thinks. Normally they can sense one another's presence and well-being, but for a harrowing few minutes Padmini—and Queens—had simply been an odd numb spot in the back of Manny's mind. A name he kept forgetting, an area of the city he suddenly found it difficult to think about. But that had been just his own, borough-specific perception. At the time of Padmini's trouble, Neek had been home alone while one-fifth of the city flickered like a cheap lightbulb. Manny frowns, surreptitiously checking for any sign of another collapse, but if it happened, Neek's not letting it show.

Oblivious to Manny's scrutiny—maybe—Neek says, "That dude you ran into sounds like the fucked-up thing I had to fight back when the city first woke up. Looked like a couple of cops at first. Then they changed into...something else."

He doesn't elaborate, but he doesn't need to. They've all seen the kinds of horrors the Woman in White can summon. Padmini grimaces. "Yes. 'Something else' is a good description of it. But this isn't supposed to happen anymore, is it? I thought we were *done* with her."

"Not as long as she's still parked over Staten," Bronca says. "Guess that's no surprise. People—and Squigglebitches, I guess— who think they got the right to just *take* something don't stop 'til they get it."

"Well, why us, for fuck's sake?" Veneza demands. "Why are we the only city that can't completely get rid of her?"

"Bad luck on our part and advance planning on hers," Brooklyn says, shaking her head. "But I agree. I'm tired of being on the back foot with this shit. Isn't there some way we can take the fight to her?"

"How?" Veneza gets up and starts pacing. "Can we even go to Staten Island, now? I haven't tried since that one time. And nobody got the avatar's number before she teleported us away. Shit, even if we had, Squigglebitch done probably *ate* that dumb-ass by now."

"She's alive," Neek says. When they all stare at him again, he shrugs, leaning back against the windowsill. "She's still part of me. It's like . . . like my leg's gone to sleep, but it ain't cut off. Anyway, I confirmed already that we can at least go there, though it goes to shit past that point. The ferry and ferry stations are still me."

Cold washes through Manny. There's only one way Neek could know this. "You went there?"

Neek's expression is frank and unashamed. "Yeah. Wanted to see how far I could get. Answer is, to the St. George ferry station—but not beyond. Even one step past the station grounds is *her*. Thought I might be able to do the railway there because it's MTA, but no."

"Whoa, are you nuts?" Veneza says, half a breath before Manny can. "Neek, dude, why didn't you bring one of us with you? What if you'd been attacked?"

"I wasn't." Neek shrugs again—but Manny can see his annoyance. He's a chill guy, the living embodiment of New York; not much fazes him, angers him, or impresses him. He's getting close to anger now, though. "And what you gon' do? I don't need a sitter. I fought her by myself, remember, before any of you even knew she existed."

Veneza puts her hands on her hips. "Yeah, and that's how you ended up in a magic coma. Sorry, *enchanted slumber*."

Bronca rubs her face with her hands. "Young B, shut the fuck up, please." When Veneza throws up her hands in a mute *Yeah but did you hear that shit* protest, Bronca glares her down. "I don't want to be here all night, and it's obvious at this point that we need each other." She turns an equally formidable glare on Neek. She's a grandma now, and must have been a terrifying mother back in the day; this glare is fierce enough that Neek sets his jaw and looks away. "All of us. Whether some want to admit that or not."

Neek rolls his eyes. "Look, I could tell the ferry was safe. I know what's mine." After a moment he sighs and adds, resentfully, "Ours."

"We're getting sidetracked," Padmini says, rubbing her face.

Veneza sighs while Manny exhales and tries to think. Bronca shakes her head, visibly troubled. "There's nothing like this 'un-citying' in the lexicon," she murmurs. "The history in it, everything living cities know about becoming living cities, goes back tens of thousands of years. Still nothing in it about cities spontaneously becoming not-living in spots. I guess we're trailblazers. Again."

"Panfilo," Neek says. "That's what set this off."

That makes everyone flinch as they realize he's right. Brooklyn murmurs a soft, horrified "Oh, fuck." But—

"Bullshit," says Bronca, although Manny suspects this is more her habitual harshness than any real anger. "Look, New York has had shit mayors for most of my life. If that was all it took, Giuliani alone should've sunk the damn city into the sea."

Brooklyn snorts in amusement at this. The two of them are getting along better these days, probably because Brooklyn and the Bronx are the two most similar boroughs in the city, though

Manny knows better than to doom himself by saying so out loud. "True that," Brooklyn says. "But it does feel like there's something special about *this* prospective shit mayor. Something that makes him more than just another corrupt politician."

"*Is* he corrupt?" asks Veneza. She reaches for her laptop as she says it, probably to look up Panfilo's record. "I mean, I figure most politicians are, but I like to leave a little wiggle room for reasonable doubt."

"Oh, Senator Friendly is 100 percent corrupt." Brooklyn rubs at her temple. "So corrupt that I'm amazed he's running. I remember him doing the whole 'socially liberal / fiscally conservative' song and dance back when he first started out—as if you can be socially liberal when you're against funding social justice—but like every other Republican since then he's figured out there's more profit in being owned by this or that billionaire ideologue than in democracy."

"'Senator Friendly'?" Bronca asks.

"Yeah, like those old community-relations reels they used to make us watch in school, with Officer Friendly? Supposedly Panfilo really wanted to be a cop at some point but got kicked out of the academy. The joke is that he gets his cop fix now by shoveling copaganda." Brooklyn's frown deepens. "The thing I don't get is, I heard he has his eye on the presidency. He's already a senator. Winning the mayoral race won't raise his profile any further, and could even weaken him. Ex-mayors of New York don't do well in national contests."

Manny shakes his head. "I don't believe this is all a coincidence. Panfilo, what happened to Queens, Padmini being in danger of deportation, the Woman in White still being parked over Staten...Somehow all those things must be connected." But he can't fathom how.

Brooklyn straightens up to begin pacing in the kitchen, a calmer echo of Veneza's frustrated pacing in the living room. "Okay," she says, folding her arms and thinking out loud. "Panfilo is a threat because of his 'us versus them' framing, which suggests that only certain kinds of people really belong in New York. Stock Republican Play Number Five these days, but it's also good strategy. New York is pretty progressive, but that energy gets spread across a lot of small constituencies, like the local-control-of-schools advocates, the police defunders and abolitionists, the marginalized communities, and all the unions that aren't cops. If Panfilo can get the bigots in line, it'll create a voting bloc that can wedge through all of that, and maybe even attract a few subgroups that currently vote Democratic—the dirtbag leftists, for example. Those fuckers'll vote for the KKK if it promises them basic income." She purses her lips in thought. "But a coalition like that will fall apart as soon as he's elected. This isn't the Eighties or Nineties anymore; the city's not struggling, and we've got more of a police violence epidemic these days than a drug-fueled one. The only way..." Abruptly Brooklyn stops pacing, her eyes widening. "Ohhhh."

"What?" asks Bronca.

"It *won't* work, short-term," Brooklyn says. Her voice has grown softer, almost talking to herself as she narrows her eyes. "Not on its own. Back during the Giuliani era, he polished up some hack academic theory about broken windows and used it to set the police like dogs on Black and Brown neighborhoods." She turns to them. "But it was really about real estate. Crime was bad all over the city back then, but Giuliani made it seem like *those neighborhoods* were the only problem. Between the predatory policing and the economy, and Giuliani undermining rent stabilization, people of color were getting evicted and foreclosed-on all over those 'hoods. Now, nearly all of them have become predominantly white, and homes that used to be affordable are now worth millions. Panfilo must be planning to try something similar. Target an ethnic group to please his base, then take their stuff to make the landlords and businesspeople happy. The latter will keep him in power for a while."

Bronca's nodding along grimly. Padmini frowns in confusion. "Wait, but . . . cities change like that all the time! It isn't always some conspiracy. Do living cities usually yeet whole sections as soon as there have been a few demographic shifts?"

"The change we're talking about wasn't just demographic," Bronca says. "It was *spiritual*. Once, New York City was known for its art. Fashion, fine art, the performing arts, music; we were the center of the world for all of that, creating new genres and even new ways of thinking on the regular. Notice how many of us come from that background?" She eyes Neek and Veneza. "But not all of us, because New York's not such a good city for art anymore. That wasn't an organic, grassroots change; it was imposed from the top down, over decades, and it *worked*. Now we're best known for overpriced real estate and money laundering. In barely forty years we've completely transformed. So maybe, if the change happens too fast and we don't change enough to keep up . . ."

She lets this fall into silence, which no one interrupts. They all have to chew on the implications of that for a moment. And there's the elephant in the room: if Panfilo is being used by a certain someone to suit her inhuman agenda, then any changes he might impose as mayor will surely make her stronger. Maybe even strong enough to overcome the city's magical protections. And then what?

"Yeah, fuck this," Veneza finally says, scowling. "We need to call the other cities. Maybe they know something we don't. Paulo mentioned something called a Summit, let's give them a call."

"Agreed," Manny says.

Neek makes a soft derisive sound. "Paulo also said the Summit didn't want to help three months ago—even when half the city was eaten up by Squigglebitch. We still got a whole-ass city floating over Staten, and this Summit ain't sent so much as a 'u ok' text."

Padmini sits with her elbows on her knees, staring at her own limp hands. "We have to try," she says softly. "We need *help*."

Everyone looks at Neek. Neek groans and rolls his eyes. He never seems to like it when they treat him as their leader. "Oh-*kay*. I'll hit up Paulo . . ."

He trails off on an up-note, frowning a little as his gaze grows distant. Then Manny hears it, too. New York is never quiet, but in the near distance there is a sudden chorus of car horns. That's nothing; since moving to the city Manny's heard entire four-movement symphonies whenever someone blocks an intersection. But they're all listening now, attention caught, because if Neek's noticed it, then it's important. Manny begins to hear voices, a lot of them, rising louder than the horns. Angry shouting. Scornful laughter, alarmed questioning. A single piercing shout: *"Get the fuck out of here!"*

Brooklyn goes to the window that Neek's not at, pulling aside the designer drapes to look outside. "That sounds nearby," Padmini says.

"Can't tell," Brooklyn says. Then Manny gets the backwash of a flicker from her other self, that massive and graceful collection of old buildings and endless audacity that is Brooklyn-the-borough. Brooklyn-the-woman scowls. "Something's wrong."

Abruptly she turns away from the window and heads for the front door of the apartment, grabbing her keys along the way. While all of them stare at each other, thrown by the sudden change, she stops and glares. "Well?"

Manny pushes to his feet at once, and the others do, too, following Brooklyn once more into the breach.

CHAPTER THREE

You Might Be Fooled If You Come from Out of Town

Brooklyn thinks of herself as an amateur historian. The amateur part is because she never studied history in any formal way. The historian part is because Clyde Thomason didn't raise no fool, and she figured out a long time ago that the history being taught to her in school was patchy, propagandistic, and flat-out wrong in a lot of ways. Like Tulsa's Greenwood Massacre in 1921; it's in pop culture now, but when Brooklyn was coming up it was little more than a whispered legend, acknowledged only by Black newspapers and proto-hoteps preaching Afrocentrism on the corner. Sometimes Brooklyn wonders what it was like for her ancestors who survived these thoroughly American pogroms, building lives and futures for themselves again and again only to have it all shot and lynched away. Did they hear the mobs coming? Were there warnings ahead of time—whispers over the wire, soldier instincts astir, sympathetic officials pulling aside favored servants or even clandestine lovers and telling them to brace for attack?

What *could* they do, those proud but powerless people, in a country where no law protected them and even basic human decency turned its back? Where could they go, with no ancestral homes to return to and no one to rely on but themselves?

Maybe it felt a little like this.

Brooklyn stands on Nostrand Avenue where it crosses Fulton, staring at a honking caravan of cars and trucks that has taken over the street. Most are pickup trucks, with a few SUVs and vans scattered amongst; all are bedecked with lurid, professionally made signs and flags. The flags are a grab bag of ugly: Thin Blue Line and several variants thereof, DON'T TREAD ON ME, Confederate crisscrosses, LIBERTY OR DEATH, and Nazi swastikas of course. A handful of American flags, probably tossed in as an afterthought, never mind any inherent conflict with some of the other flags. The printed signage is more uniform: FRIENDLIES FOR SENATOR FRIENDLY, MAKE NEW YORK GREAT AGAIN, OUR CITY NOT YOURS. No handwritten signs. None display the official campaign logo that Brooklyn's seen on the Panfilo campaign's ads, but that's probably just because Panfilo only unveiled the logo that morning. Brooklyn knows exactly how much signs like that cost, and also that they cannot be printed on a dime; you need days' or weeks' lead time for big orders. This is no spontaneous, grassroots show of political support.

And she's pretty sure there's a reason they've come to this street, in this neighborhood. Nostrand Avenue is one of the main thoroughfares of the borough; it runs from Williamsburg all the way to Brighton Beach, and is probably better known for its potholes and bad traffic than anything else. For the length of its run through Bed Stuy, Crown Heights, and Flatbush, however, the avenue is a showcase of Black-owned business, from fast-food joints like Golden Krust to locticians and braiding salons to top-notch African restaurants. There are plenty of other ethnicities' businesses present, including Korean-owned produce stands, a Jewish deli or two, and the odd Italian-run fish market, but if you want to shop from the full breadth of the Black diaspora in New York, Nostrand is one of the best places to do it. And if you're a bunch of racists who are feeling themselves, this is the place to start shit.

Around this sore thumb of a caravan, the sidewalks are packed with shoppers and merchants and commuters, nearly all Black, none of them with any chill. Plenty are just going about their business, but quite a few of the folks on the sidewalk are watching, taking video on their phones, and shouting back at the caravanners. The caravan's drivers have deliberately spread out so as to block the intersection, so a good bit of the honking is coming from other cars trying to get around them. On one corner, a cellphone vendor has put out a six-foot-tall speaker that's bumping Biggie. It's mostly drowning out the honking and whatever country-music nonsense one of the trucks is trying to blast, but the result is auditory chaos.

It's all a little corny. And yet Brooklyn cannot bring herself to find it funny. Open racists usually don't come to Black areas, preferring to target isolated individuals, or other ethnicities that they think won't fight back. That sort are cowards at heart, and they know coming to Bed Stuy is a great way to get knocked the fuck out. That they feel so emboldened by Panfilo's campaign after barely one day is a bad sign. Worse, Brooklyn's been doing the avatar thing long enough to understand that if her intuition is this off-the-charts, it means that something about this pathetic display has attracted the city's attention. It's Brooklyn's job to figure out what.

Then a caravanner rolls down his passenger-side window to yell back at a young woman who's stepped into the street to deliver her insults up close and personal. She apparently strikes a nerve, because the guy gets even redder-faced and reaches behind him, pulling out *a gun*. It's only a paintball gun, at least; that pellet hopper on top is distinctive. The young woman recognizes it, too. It's not clear whether the guy is just brandishing it to scare her or if he means to use it, but while he's fumbling with it, she laughs in his face and swings her purse to knock the gun out of his hands. He curses and actually tries to scramble through the window after her, but the window isn't open all the way; he gets briefly stuck. She rolls her eyes and walks off. By the time the guy manages to get out of the car to retrieve his gun—delayed further because a child has run forward to grab it with a finders-keepers gleam in his eye; the guy snatches it back, but it takes some yanking—she's gone.

Half the block starts pointing and laughing. In a fury, the guy curses at them . . . then raises his gun and sprays everyone on the sidewalk.

It's a switch-flip, comedy turning instantly to chaos. The sidewalkers start screaming as windows break and people fling themselves behind cars for cover—and in that frozen instant of horror, Brooklyn sees blood. Way too much of it, on people's clothing and on the ground. Paintball pellets hurt like hell, but they're just liquid in little soft plastic capsules; they can put your eye out, but usually clothing is enough to protect against broken skin. The wounds that Brooklyn glimpses as people fall to the ground or run aren't bright with red paint, but something much darker and more vital.

She ducks behind somebody's classic Oldsmobile before she can think otherwise; too many drive-bys back in the day, old instincts kicking in hard. Bronca's down, too, flat on the sidewalk with hands over her head; her gaze meets Brooklyn's and it is wild, furious, full of *did-you-see-that-shit* incredulity. Padmini, Neek, Manny, and Veneza belatedly drop behind the same car as Brooklyn. "What the fuck?" Veneza yells over the gunshots and screaming. "What the actual fuck?"

"Frozen," Manny says. In less terrifying moments, Brooklyn has wondered if he's aware that he's got resting serial-killer face. In this moment, however, he's looking at a nearby business whose corrugated-steel rolldown door has a noticeable dent in which a paintball—still mostly solid—is embedded. "The paintballs must be frozen."

"Who the hell would shoot frozen paintballs?" But Brooklyn already knows the answer: someone who actually wants to kill people, but with plausible deniability.

The guy is still unloading on Nostrand, laughing and yelling insults while his targets run, and Brooklyn can see other people in the caravan pulling out weapons of their own—more paintball guns, pepper spray canisters, water guns sloshing with something too dark-colored to be water. One asshole even has a crossbow. Projectiles start flying, including some thrown back by people on the street; the first paintball-shooting guy staggers back as someone's ice-filled soda smashes into his face. But it's a pretty one-sided battle.

Then Brooklyn inhales as she spies an NYPD vehicle idling behind the caravan, about a block away. Two cops, a Black man and a white one, sit inside...just watching. One of them's speaking into some kind of mic, maybe issuing a warning over the car's PA, but if he's saying anything, it's drowned out by all the screaming and shooting. The other is *grinning* like he's heard the best joke ever, while unarmed citizens of the city he's paid to protect get shot right in front of him. Maybe he thinks they're just paintballs so no big deal, but it's not the first time Brooklyn's seen cops ignore a violent incident if the wrong kind of person was on the receiving end.

So that's when Brooklyn gets mad.

She pushes to her feet. She's a city; no little projectile's going to hurt her. Her hands form claws at her side and her head tilts from old habit. She's got her sneer on: upper lip curled, cold smile on her lips, her own resting serial-killer face fully engaged. "Mic check, mic check," she snarls. "One-two, one-two. *Drop.*"

A curtain of absolute silence slams down out of nowhere. There's no physical force to it, but the instant cessation of street noise and even her own harsh breathing is so shocking, so impossible, that everyone present stops whatever they're doing, stumbling or looking around with wide eyes. It's localized, because the rest of the borough doesn't deserve to have its day disrupted by these fools, and because Brooklyn has envisioned a circular radius around the intersection, roughly encompassing a block in every direction.

The cop car is just outside Brooklyn's zone of control—and to her bitter amusement, *now* the cops look alarmed. The one on the PA lifts his handset again. "Order to disperse," he says, his voice crackling but jarringly clear amid the silence. "This is the NYPD.

If you're visible on the street right now, you are engaged in an illegal protest. We are ordering you to—"

Motherfuckers. But Brooklyn's got their number and Nostrand's got her beat.

She twitches a finger, and the speaker in front of the cell phone shop starts up again, instrumental only and tweaked for extended play by some long-ago DJ. It's just the bass bridge from Biggie's "Can't You See": *beat-riff and*. This time, however, the sound is infinite, all-encompassing, short of auditory damage but a psychic hammerblow. And this time Neek stands up with her, and the others do, too. What she's already started begins to echo, amplify, sharpen in focus. With Neek and the other boroughs' power added to her own, the caravanners have already lost this battle. Time to let them know it.

Beat-riff and

At the edges of her vision, Brooklyn is aware of other people on the street standing up as well, others who are 100 percent New York no matter where they came from and no matter that they are not avatars. They're the ones who belong here, not these wannabe-lynch-mob motherfuckers with Jersey or Pennsylvania plates, and by their collective outrage is Brooklyn empowered.

Beat-riff and

"*You* disperse," she murmurs, and the cop car, with the cops inside, vanishes.

Beat beat beat beat-riff and

"Disperse, motherfuckers," yells a man across the street, and the caravanners' weapons vanish from their hands. One of the few women in the caravan starts shrieking as if someone has mugged her, but no one can hear the shrieks. Brooklyn hasn't enabled sound for them yet. Right now, only New Yorkers get to speak.

Beat-riff and

From a sturdy Haitian grandmother who has her hand tight on the shoulder of a little boy: "Dispèse! Don't even belong here! Pa janm!" As she does this, the caravan's flags and Panfilo banners vanish. The guy who shot the first paintball stops wiping Sprite out of his eyes and stares at his suddenly denuded truck.

Beat-riff and

"Vete pa la pinga!" That's from a middle-aged balding Cubano who's shouting through the window of his black limo and shaking a fist for emphasis—and then the trucks themselves are gone. The people inside are suddenly sitting on air, whereupon they promptly fall, hard, onto the asphalt. There are startled shouts, cries of pain, probably a cracked tailbone or two. Brooklyn finds it hard to care.

Beat-riff and beat-riff and beat-riff and beat-riff and beat-riff and beat slow-riff, go the speakers, before finally letting the bridge go. But the city's work is done. Brooklyn releases the circle of silence and breathes out slowly as the ordinary sounds of her borough resume. Cars start honking again, but that's just the usual Nostrand traffic. A bunch of dumb-ass tourists are sitting in the middle of the street, after all.

Neek laughs. Brooklyn isn't smiling, however, as she steps off the curb and walks toward the now-pedestrian Friendlies, until she stands over the man who started the shooting. In the distance, there is a chord of ambulance sirens drawing closer; on the sidewalk behind her, Brooklyn can still hear the caravanners' targets weeping or groaning as they nurse their injuries. Their pain is an offense that grates under Brooklyn's skin, tickling the roots of her teeth. The borough's hunger for justice thrums in her blood, but she restrains the urge to unleash vengeance on these interlopers any more than she has. It isn't necessary and they aren't worth it.

"You might want to leave now," she says. The first shooter cringes from her. Another man who was in the car with him grabs for his shoulders as if to pull him back. They both look utterly terrified of a middle-aged Black woman in a pantsuit. "Some of these folks you hurt are gonna want payback. I'd advise you to stick together 'til you get out of the neighborhood. If you stay in a group, they probably won't jump you. Probably." She starts to turn away, then pauses as a new thought occurs to her. "If you'd rather try to get a police escort or something, then the nearest precinct's up Tompkins, about six blocks thataway." She jerks her head in that direction.

"Oh, God," the first shooter blurts. He's hyperventilating. "Oh my God, what did you do? Where's my, my truck? How, how . . ." He shakes his head and keeps shaking it.

Brooklyn snorts. "I made Brooklyn great again. Now get the fuck out of my borough."

She heads back toward the others—but as she steps back onto the sidewalk, she is jolted by a familiar call, shrill enough to break through the street sounds. "Mama! Mama!"

Brooklyn has pivoted in that direction before the call's echo fades, and she sprints faster than anyone in heels should be able to safely manage. Behind her, she can hear the others exclaim in surprise and move to follow. They all round the corner and stop at the sight of a handful of frightened teenage girls crouching around another of their number, who is down and clutching her bloodied arm. It's Jojo.

Newcomers to New York are always surprised by how frequently one crosses paths with acquaintances in the city. Happens all the time, really. Brooklyn goes to Macy's and runs into a fellow council member, or she heads up to Harlem for an event and sees her next-door neighbor, or she gets on the subway and there's her old eighth grade English teacher, whom she hasn't seen in thirty years. New York is huge, but considering the sheer number of interpersonal connections one makes in the ordinary course of life, it's actually kind of amazing that Brooklyn doesn't randomly run into people she knows all the time. No big deal to find Jojo and her friends on one of the most heavily traveled streets of their neighborhood.

Also no big deal to encounter one of the best-known reporters in the city, Mariam Dabby from NY1, when Brooklyn steps outside the hospital for some fresh air. She's not going to find it here; Dabby has clearly been working on her cigarette for a while, and the whole area is thick with smoke. Brooklyn just sighs and tries not to feel how tired she is as she toes off her heels. The avatars of living cities aren't supposed to need rest, but tired isn't always a physical thing.

Mariam snorts smoke, then strolls over. "Small world, Council Member," she says. "You got a hypochondriac mother-in-law, too?"

Brooklyn laughs, once, in spite of herself. "If only." Her late husband's mother went out only a little before him. Wonderful woman. Brooklyn could've used her help all these years. "That mess on Nostrand earlier got my little girl." She pats her upper arm, because she's too tired to explain that Jojo's arm was broken badly enough that they're waiting to see if she'll need surgery. Brooklyn's father is with Jojo, and will call her as soon as the specialist shows up.

Mariam's eyebrows shoot up. "I heard about that incident. Weird rumors, though. People are saying the caravan's vehicles vanished, NYPD's missing a car although the officers turned up back in their precinct confused . . . There are videos, but people have claimed they're doctored. They *look* doctored."

Living cities aren't supposed to reveal the workings of their will. Usually when people witness the what-the-fuckery that is city magic, they just . . . forget. Brooklyn supposes the city doesn't have to bother with all that anymore, here in the era of deepfakes. "I don't know about the videos or any of that other stuff, but the attack was real," she says. "The paintball plastic they fished out of Jojo's arm sure as hell was."

She sees a whole process of contemplation work its way around in Mariam's expression, as the woman decides whether what Brooklyn's saying is interesting enough to merit working off the clock. Then she sighs in a self-exasperated way, shakes her head, and reaches into her purse. "Care to go on record?"

No. But it's not just about Brooklyn and her outrage. Dozens of people got hurt by that damn caravan. Jojo's injury isn't even the worst; one woman lost an eye. She nods. Mariam pulls out her iPhone, slaps on a windscreen mic attachment, and holds it up to Brooklyn's face.

"You gonna ask some questions?"

Mariam shrugs. "Too tired to think of any. Just talk. You know we'll pull out the good bits."

Fine, then. So Brooklyn talks. She has to keep pausing in her summation of events because she's furious, and the city is even angrier, still seething that outsiders have attacked its people while its supposed defenders, the NYPD, did nothing. Some of the fury comes out anyway, because Brooklyn's still human at her core, and her child has been hurt. But she's also lived her entire political career knowing that Black women don't have the same leeway for righteous anger that everyone else gets.

Well. Politics is a step show. You have to get your audience engaged before you throw down the big crowd-pleasers.

"These people," Brooklyn concludes, "they come here for a weekend maybe. Usually never leave Midtown, watch movies about us made in LA by producers who grew up in Kansas. They think they know us. They tell each other that New York is the boogeyman of cities, full of scary—" She catches herself and takes a deep breath. Puts on a yeah-I-almost-slipped smile, which makes Mariam chuckle. "Scary Black people and eeee-legal criminals and trans women who'll beat them up in a bathroom. And then they have the nerve to come here waving banners that say *Our city not yours*. People like this only want to *use* New York. They steal our tragedies to hype themselves up. They claim ownership of a New York that never existed outside their imaginations. And they actually think they can tell *us* who we are!"

Her voice echoes in the car park area. Shit. But Mariam hasn't stopped her, and words have always flowed through her like the

Hudson when she gets heated enough. Strange to realize they can flow even without the momentum of a backbeat—but then, Brooklyn hasn't been MC Free for twenty years. Figures this part of her would have adapted over time. And New York's politicians have always known the power of a good catchphrase.

"*We are New York*," she snarls. Mariam's eyebrows rise, and Brooklyn's smile widens, turning fierce. "And we are the ones who get to decide what that means. You don't get to step on New Yorkers on your way to greater power, *Senator Friendly*. You don't get to invade, because we fight back. And we *will* hand you your ass." She's shouting again—tightly, controlled, but her voice rings. There is a ringing in her ears, too, and in her mind, and deep in her conjoined, million-voiced soul. She is Brooklyn, and in this moment she speaks true.

"Quite a declaration of war, Council Member," Mariam says, sounding genuinely impressed. Then she narrows her eyes. "Or a declaration of...something else?"

Brooklyn knows what she means at once, because suddenly Mariam leans forward with a hungry light in her eyes. *This* is a story. And, well...It's a thing she's never wanted, because she's been famous before and she knows exactly how much it sucks—constant criticism, never knowing friend from exploiter, the loss of privacy and safety. Her family deserves better.

Then again...her family also deserves a city worth living in.

So Brooklyn closes her eyes for a moment, then speaks the city's will. "That's right," she says. "I'm declaring my candidacy for Mayor of New York City. So let's go."

INTERRUPTION

Tokyo

When the woman currently known as Tokyo walks into her office, she is extremely displeased to see a stranger there waiting.

The stranger is another city. Obviously not Japanese—though he looks half, maybe, with the other half being something other than the usual European. In any case, because there is something indelibly American about the way he stands, and because he has been vulgar enough to intrude upon her like this, she's fairly certain she knows who this city is.

The door has shut behind her. Tokyo has the room regularly scanned for RF signals. Outside of this space and moment, she is the stylish and youthful-looking CEO of an entertainment company that develops J-pop bands for corporate investment. Right now, however, she is the two-hundred-and-fifty-year-old avatar of a four-hundred-year-old city, and she ran out of patience for rude behavior back in the 1800s.

"New York," she says in English, folding her arms.

He bows with passable respect, but it's as stiff and awkward as any Westerner's attempt. "There are no excuses for my intrusion upon you," he says, in formal and fluid Japanese, a preamble to whatever else he means to say.

"Then why have you done so?" She sticks to English. Easier to be rude in ways that English-speakers will understand.

He pauses for a moment, registering the rudeness, and then to her relief he discards formality. Doesn't fit him anyway. "Manhattan," he corrects, finally conceding to English. "New York is someone else. And I wouldn't have intruded, if not for the fact that we're all facing a deadly crisis."

"*You* are, as I understand it." Tokyo brushes past him and goes to sit behind her desk, folding her legs and leaning back in her chair. "And while I sympathize, I don't share your problems. I cannot help you. Leave."

Manhattan takes a deep breath and sits down as well, without her permission and with unsubtle stubbornness. "I understand that only the elder cities can call a meeting of the Summit."

"I'm not an elder city. You should probably try this with them." And when he does and they immediately kick him out of their city limits, Tokyo is going to eat a whole pizza in celebration.

He crosses his legs. "I also understand that if the elder cities won't call the Summit, the younger cities can override them with enough votes."

Tokyo sighs. "You are so American. This isn't some gerrymandered pretend democracy like what you're used to. If enough of us want to meet, the meeting will simply *happen* as reality responds to our collective will. No vote needed. And no, I will not support a meeting, if that's what you've come here to beg for. Again: I am aware that your city is in danger, but this sounds like a 'you' problem."

Manhattan looks surprised to hear how the Summit works. Tokyo can remember being that new to her role as a city, though now it seems almost incomprehensible. She supposes he has done this, coming here and not taking no for an answer, because he's the sort of man who prefers action, even futile action, to complacency. For living cities, however, existence itself is an active choice to ensure their city's health and peace. When living cities take too much action, and get hurt, innocent citizens die. This is also why those with any sense don't *invade* other cities, barge into other people's offices, then refuse to leave. A fight between them would kill thousands.

Manhattan leans forward, propping his elbows on his knees and steepling his fingers. "Were you aware that the head of the Kansei Group is on the payroll of the Enemy?"

Tokyo freezes. The Kansei Group is her company's biggest rival. She's in the middle of amending all their contracts right now because Kansei found a loophole that allowed them to legally poach her biggest up-and-coming idol. And yes, she's heard rumors that the Enemy has developed new tactics, but…this? It sounds absurd. The monster that dogged her youth? It was an amorphous horror of a thing, covered in the hands and leering faces of enemy soldiers. Old meets New goes the Tokyo tourism slogan, and thus did she strike down the rude newness of the Enemy with her family's ancient naginata, passed down from mother to daughter since the Heian period. She has changed greatly in the centuries since, and she supposes extradimensional monsters can change, too. But…they buy pop-culture influence now?

While Tokyo ponders this, Manhattan stands up and sets a

paper file on the desk in front of her. Clipped to the file is a familiar face, photographed in a candid moment—the chairman of the Kansei Group, smiling at a tall white woman in a pale suit, with white-blond hair. Then Tokyo frowns. "You need better digital artists," she says, tapping the woman's blurry, unrecognizable face.

"That's the unaltered photo my private investigator took," Manhattan says. "Every attempt to photograph her ends up like this—or the camera malfunctions. But even if the photo was perfect, you wouldn't believe me, would you?"

At last he learns. "How much would you listen to someone who barges into your private office and makes unreasonable demands?"

"The demand that we simply meet to discuss the threat? A threat which looms over all of us, not just New York." He nods toward the file. "This is everything we know about the TMW Corporation— the Enemy's parent group. They have subsidiaries in forty-two cities, living and not-yet-living. Back home they go by the Better New York Foundation; here in Tokyo they're known as Municipal Improvement Holdings. I don't believe they're actually after you, though they're definitely trying to influence housing policy in several Japanese cities. Kansei's chairman has a brother in the Diet; that's probably why they're interested in him. I also notice a lot of TMW activity in Kyoto. Look for yourself, then draw your own conclusions."

With that, Manhattan bows again, and vanishes. Infant. She's always careful never to go macrostepping anywhere that others might see; at technology's current pace of improvement, they cannot always assume city-made "luck" will continue to conceal their purpose and abilities. He's not cautious enough.

Which is why Tokyo picks up the file Manhattan has left, gazes at it for about ten seconds, and then tosses the whole thing in the trash.

She's not a fool. If there's even a possibility that he's right about Kansei, then she needs to look into the matter. Her own people can do that. But there are reasons why it's improper for newborn cities to make demands like this, and she's not about to ignore propriety for the sake of some arrogant, entitled American haafu.

Kyoto, though.

It was the oldest of the Japanese living cities, once, though its avatar died in the devastating Ōnin War of the 1400s. The city has struggled ever since, buffeted by politics and Westernization, but there are signs that it might have finally settled into itself enough to be reborn soon. If the Enemy is somehow interfering with that process . . .

Tokyo pulls out her phone, thumbs through its contacts, and stops on the one labeled "Fai." It's five in the morning in Egypt, but that's fine. If Tokyo has to suffer this sort of affront, everyone around her is going to feel it, too.

The line clicks as someone picks up. A sleep-bleary male voice sighs in English, "You had better be dying."

She shakes her head. "How lazy you are. I haven't slept in ten years."

"*Some* of us aren't infamously workaholic cities. Some of us spent centuries as farmers, and thus we enjoy sleeping *past* dawn now and again. What do you want?"

She sits back in her executive chair. "Tell me everything you know of what's been happening in New York. Also, I'd like to file a complaint."

CHAPTER FOUR

These Vagabond Blues

By the time Aishwarya bangs on Padmini's bedroom door, it's 10 a.m. She pulls the covers down to see her room awash with midmorning sunlight—shockingly bright, given that she's spent the past year getting up before dawn. How long has it been since she saw her own room by daylight?

It doesn't help that she hasn't slept much or well. After the awfulness of finding poor Jojo injured and groaning on Nostrand, Padmini and the others accompanied Brooklyn and her family to the hospital. Since Jojo hadn't been bleeding profusely or judged otherwise in danger, that meant a wait of several hours in the emergency room before she could be assessed for possible surgery. Jojo was fine, however—well, she had a fractured humerus and needed to stay overnight, but it could've been a lot worse. After they got that news, Brooklyn pushed Padmini to go home, given Padmini's own bad day. Padmini resisted until Manny—who has no business being both deeply kind and a manipulative bastard—urged her to step outside for some fresh air, then stood with sad puppy eyes until she accepted the Uber he'd preemptively summoned for her. Once home and in bed, she lay awake for most of the night, only falling off around dawn.

She's still in her jammies when Aishwarya knocks a second time. When Padmini opens the door, Aishwarya shoves a baby into Padmini's face. The baby is Vadhana, Padmini's eighteen-month-old cousin, who grins with Aishwarya's smile and shyly says hi. Automatically Padmini takes the child into her arms and is painfully reminded of how much time she wasted working herself to death at Evilcorp. Vadhana has grown noticeably bigger since the last time Padmini held her.

"There," Aishwarya says, nodding decisively. "That's better. Stop moping and come out to eat. Don't think I didn't hear you up all night."

The last thing Padmini wants is breakfast. "I don't need to eat anymore, Aunty—"

"Bullshit," Aishwarya says, putting her hands on her hips. "You're always full of bullshit these days. Come out before I drag you out." When Padmini reluctantly steps out of her room, Aishwarya moves behind her and starts clapping to hurry her along. "Now, now, now, bullshit kunju, the food is getting cold."

"There is so much wrong with you," Padmini says, deliberately not speeding up, although she does at least start walking. But she cannot help smiling.

In the months since Padmini became Queens, she has often contemplated whether there are human embodiments for other existential concepts. If all it takes is enough human minds sharing space and thought, then why aren't there human embodiments of countries, races, subcultures? Many religions incorporate the concept of an avatar, but shouldn't even the ones that don't still spawn a few? Why don't sports teams have avatars? Why *isn't* Gritty immortal and magical by now? Because if the same thing can happen for any concept, then Aishwarya is surely the human embodiment of a tropical cyclone. Padmini feels increasingly certain of this.

Already at the kitchen table is Barsaat, Aishwarya's husband, squinting at his phone. He glances up and beams. "It's been so long," he says. "I'm glad we got to see you again before your funeral."

Since Vadhana's birth, Barsaat has gleefully embraced the concept of dad jokes, though naturally his contain a generous helping of Tamil gallows humor. Padmini just sighs and sits, adjusting Vadhana into her lap. There's a plate in front of her laden with her favorite: pani pol stuffed with sweet coconut, with a bit of fish curry on the side. An extremely pleasant surprise given that Aishwarya hates making pani pol; rolling the little pancakes can be a pain.

"No, it isn't your birthday," Barsaat says, amused by the look on her face. "Aish is trying to spoil you while pretending that she isn't. Quick, act like you don't care."

"Hush," Aishwarya says, rolling her eyes and sitting down as well. "You'll ruin my reputation as a wicked, meddling aunty."

It's almost pathetic. How are stuffed pancakes supposed to make her feel better about the end of her future? And yet Padmini finds herself touched. Some people have no business being both manipulative and deeply kind. When Vadi asks for one of the pancakes, Padmini hands it to her; this helps her fight off tears.

"*Much* better," Aishwarya says with satisfaction, as Padmini finally eats. "I don't care if you've transcended human bodily needs or not. Everyone needs a good meal to get their head on straight. Especially in your case, since you have like a million heads inside you now."

"Two million people in Queens," Barsaat says, pushing up his glasses and returning his attention to his phone.

"Well, she'll need seconds, then."

It's all so normal. Aishwarya and Barsaat are making Padmini feel better and she doesn't *want* to feel better, damn it. She wants to wallow in her feelings. "You're making jokes?" she says, even though she knows it sounds petulant. "I lost my job, the city's in danger *again*, and I have to hear your terrible jokes before we all die?"

"Yes," Aish says, sipping tea. "Why not? Would you rather die miserable, on an empty stomach?"

"You said we were all going to die back during the summer, too," adds Barsaat. He holds out a pancake on his fork for Vadi, and she grins and leans over to bite off a piece. "Yet here we still are. Were we supposed to mope about our imminent death all that time? I don't think I have that much moping in me."

"*Uncle.*" Padmini puts her fork down to sigh at him.

"Seriously," Aishwarya says. "Last time, you made us drive all the way to bloody Philadelphia to stay with Barsaat's cousin Edgar, and you *know* I hate that man. Always staring at my tits. So since you say the city is in danger again, I want you to know that we will *not* go to Philly. If that bothers you, then you'd better simply fix the problem. All right?"

"I did punch him that one time," Barsaat says, looking hurt.

"Yes, and it was a lovely punch, my love, you just didn't use enough shoulder." She pats his hand. "Now he only does it when he thinks I don't notice, but he's stupid and has slow reflexes so I always do. Next time let me handle the punching, all right? I've been taking cardio kickboxing at the gym."

Padmini rubs a hand over her face. "I don't know what to *do*," she says. "Do you hear me? I'm going to have to go back to Chennai, and everyone will know I'm a fu—" She catches herself, just. Vadi loves to repeat curse words. "—a failure, and I'll have to just *endure* that until the Woman in White turns us all into calamari, or—"

Aishwarya sighs. "You *will* think of something," she says, serious at last. "You're always so dramatic, but things work out for you, don't they? As long as you don't give up and just let everything go wrong." She shakes her head. "You need to believe in yourself more, kunju. Why can't you be more like that nice lady from Brooklyn? She's an avatar *and* a city councilwoman. So accomplished."

Padmini stares at her, incredulous, until Vadi carefully puts a piece of mangled pancake into Padmini's open mouth. "Eat," she says. She is so Aishwarya's child.

"—Thank you, Vadi." She has to chew before she can speak again, but that gives her a moment to compose her thoughts. "Aunty, how will *believing in myself* keep me from getting kicked out of the bloody country? My options are going to work for one of those awful tech sweatshops over in Jersey, where they'll probably take my passport and treat me like a damned slave for years, or, or . . ." She shakes her head. She hasn't been able to think of anything else.

"That isn't your only option," Aishwarya says. "There are other good jobs—hard to find, but they exist. Also, you should sue your old company."

"But if I—" Padmini starts, hard enough that Vadi looks quizzically at her. "*Sue* them? For what?"

"Wage theft." Aishwarya starts ticking things off on her fingers. "Illegal employment practices. They weren't paying you overtime and they made you do too many hours. You did say you thought they didn't like you because you were Indian, so discrimination, too."

"It was more that I was an immigrant, I think, but probably a little of both, and being a woman besides," Padmini says, frowning. "Is that discrimination?"

"Yes. Well, I don't know, but it's worth looking into. I used to date a lawyer—"

Barsaat narrows his eyes. "A *tax* lawyer. Also, ugly."

"Yes, my handsome and manly beloved." He settles, mollified, and she returns her attention to Padmini. "But he might know a good employment lawyer. I'll ask. In the meantime, you could also get married." Then Aishwarya blinks at their expressions, because both Barsaat and Padmini are now gaping at her in horror. Vadi glances at them and does it, too. "What?"

Padmini manages to recover enough to speak, but it's a hard thing. "I am poor," she says, with as much heat as she can express without upsetting Vadi. "Dark. Fat. Descended from a 'lineage' of garbagemen and underpaid civil servants. I put my biodata on some site and what, people just laugh? I don't even—" She catches herself, feeling her face heat. There are things she's known about herself for years, but never discussed with her family. They just don't talk about certain things. But Aishwarya rolls her eyes.

"Yes, yes, you don't like men," Aishwarya says, waving a hand impatiently. "We noticed that years ago. Marry a woman, then, it's legal now. Also, you aren't fat for goodness' sake, you're only a size fourteen, try having a baby at forty-five and *then* see what you look like—"

Padmini's so floored that she forgets to not talk about certain things. "I don't like women that way, either! I don't like *sex!*"

"Ha!" Barsaat slaps the table hard enough that Vadi gasps and starts crying. He winces while Padmini quickly jiggles the child to soothe her and Aishwarya turns a glare on him. But he adds, "We had a bet on. Aish thought you might be hiding a girlfriend on the side, but when would you have time? And there aren't any sex toys in your room, even with all your stress—"

"Oh my God, you *looked through my room?*" Padmini gasps.

"I did," Aishwarya says, though she has the grace to look chagrined.

"Are you *serious?* How could you!"

Barsaat winces, probably because he's now going to be in trouble with Aishwarya. "It was just a quick peek. You know what she's like." Which has probably just gotten him in deeper hot water.

Aishwarya swats his hand, then sighs at Padmini. "All right, I'm sorry, but I was just worried for you, kunju. Look, my point is, take up with however many, I don't know, Netflix-and-actually-watch-Netflix partners you like. But make sure you marry one of them, please, if they're a citizen. And at least consider having a child, because you're so good with babies, and a lot of insurances cover intrauterine insemination—"

"Enough, enough, my God, please, enough." Padmini tries to focus through the cringe. "Have you also forgotten that I'm a *city*? Semi-immortal, possessed of uncanny extradimensional abilities, attacked every other minute by strange creatures? Even if I had someone I liked enough to live with, and you *have* to live with them if you're getting married for citizenship, I couldn't in good conscience subject them to—"

And then it hits her.

Aishwarya exchanges a look with Barsaat, and both start grinning. "You've thought of something," Barsaat says. "So quickly, too. That means the problem is solved."

"I—" But Barsaat is putting away his phone, and Aishwarya is pouring herself more tea. Matter settled, apparently. Vadi asks to get down so she can roam the living room, and Padmini finishes breakfast quickly after that. The part of her that is a city might not need it, but the part of her that belongs to this ridiculous family knows better than to waste good food.

After that, she dresses and spends a while playing with Vadi while Aishwarya, who works from home, does some sort of meeting on Zoom. Barsaat then takes the child and heads off to his own job, which has day care for Vadi on site. Not for the first time does Padmini envy her aunt's and uncle's work hours and benefits. Barsaat is a natural-born citizen and Aishwarya has her Green Card; they get choices. Will she ever have such freedom, herself?

Maybe. Maybe they're right, and she just has to keep trying.

Because it's not a class day, Padmini heads back into her room to try and do some course reading. She's about to be reduced to an absentee avatar of New York, but that's no excuse for letting her grades slip. (Though first she moves her lone sex toy to a new hiding spot. Just in case.)

She's barely done more than pop her earbuds in, however, when the door buzzer for their apartment sounds. She ignores it and keeps working, because Aishwarya has always told her to treat study time as work time, not to be interrupted except in emergencies. She hears Aishwarya come out of her room, grumbling a little as she keys the intercom. The first reply to her query is an unintelligible garble of words, so Aish repeats her "Who is it?" More gibberish. In her room, Padmini frowns at this. Their intercom is cheap nonsense installed by their asshole landlord, but normally the thing has good audio. When Aishwarya, now sounding highly annoyed, asks "Who?" for the third time, the male voice on the other end still says nothing clearly. It's almost like the guy is intentionally trying to make himself incomprehensible.

If Padmini had been the one to answer the door, she would have just buzzed the person into the building by now. The shortest distance between two points is a straight line, and the easiest way to quickly get back to her own business is to assume goodwill and bad enunciation. Aishwarya, however, believes firmly in the philosophy of "Well, if they can't be bothered then I won't be, either," so she walks away from the intercom without bothering to let them in. The buzzer sounds a few more times, enough to start grating on Padmini's nerves. She's about to get up and let them in herself, when it finally stops. If they're a delivery person, they'll either drop the package behind the planter that stands near the building door or buzz someone else who will hopefully let them in. Relieved, she gets back to work.

She's reading a paragraph for the third time when a fist bangs on the apartment's front door, heavy and violent enough to make her jump. That . . . does not sound like a frustrated delivery person.

She cracks open the door of her room, from where she can watch while Aishwarya—fists tight and shoulders belligerently squared under her sari blouse—stomps over to the door. "*What,* for fuck's sake? Who is it?"

"This is the NYPD," says a male voice on the other side of the door. Same voice from the intercom, but clear-spoken this time. "We need to speak with you regarding an incident."

Padmini gasps. Aishwarya looks incredulous as well as furious—but then she blinks and glances at Padmini, and her expression grows more opaque. "Fine," she says to the door, less angry than wary. "Speak."

"Could you open the door, please?" The politeness rings so false. Polite people don't bang on doors like that.

Aishwarya folds her arms. She's standing away from the door and to one side of it, Padmini notes, but that's still too close for Padmini's tastes. Aishwarya is fearless, however. "You don't need me to open the door. Say what you need to say."

"Ma'am, you're making this unnecessarily difficult. We don't want to broadcast your family's business to the whole building, do we? Just open the door."

"Do you have a warrant?"

"Yes, ma'am, we do."

"What kind of warrant and for what purpose? Is this an arrest warrant, or Form I-205?"

There's a pause from the other side of the door. Aishwarya laughs into this conspicuous silence. "Yes, I thought so. You're ICE, aren't you? I heard what sort of games you people like to play. Everyone in this home is in status, so what do you want?"

The pause continues. Padmini's mouth has gone dry and her thoughts are a bluescreen of panic. Fending off overzealous immigration officers isn't something city magic can do, can it? Do ICE agents carry guns? What possible construct could she imagine to protect them if these cops start shooting at them?

Nothing. There's nothing she can do. Queens is the borough whose heart is immigrants. With that identity comes the ugly knowledge that sometimes those immigrants get attacked in their homes and dragged off by secret police who put them into camps and take all their belongings on a whim, or because some politician thinks he can score points by seeming tough on "illegals," or—

Politician. Padmini whirls into her room to grab her phone with shaking hands. To the group chat, she texts: *Is Panfilo against immigration?*

As she does this, the voice on the other side of the door finally speaks. "We're acting with the authority of the NYPD, ma'am. But you don't have to open the door, fine. We're looking for a Padmini Prakash, who's registered to this address. May we at least speak to her?"

Padmini opens her mouth, then freezes when Aishwarya throws her an immediate quelling glare. She *is* scared, Padmini can see now, but it sounds like belligerence when she scowls and says to the door, "What do you want with her? She's in status, too, like I said."

"No, ma'am. We have a report that she's out of status, having worked illegally while on an F-1 visa."

Padmini blurts, "What?" before Aishwarya can glare her silent. It's soft, however, because Padmini is honestly confused. F-1 visas allow legal work. She did work *more* than she was supposed to, but those hours weren't shown on her pay stubs because HR at Evilcorp—being evil—used some trick to hide the overtime. She also never told her advisor that she was doing more than the maximum hours. How...?

"False," Aishwarya says. "Who made this report? Someone who doesn't know anything about international students, I assume."

"The report was anonymous. But if you really want to know, it was someone from the company that formerly employed her."

Padmini's mouth falls open. "Those *sons of bitches.*"

Aishwarya face-palms and mouths silently at Padmini, *Will you shut up?* Back to the door. "The school can verify her status. That's nothing her coworkers should have anything to do with. You could check her status yourself with five minutes on SEVIS! This constitutes harassment, and—"

The voice behind the door sighs. "Do you really think we care about you playing half-assed lawyer, ma'am?"

That startles Aishwarya into silence. Then Padmini's phone vibrates with a new message; Padmini jumps violently. Three texts have come in at once. From Veneza: *Yeah, of course, he's a*

Republican. Following closely on this comes Brooklyn: *Yes. He used to pretend he was only against illegal immigration but lately he's praised ICE harassing legal immigrants too, especially ones from nonwhite countries.*

Then there's Manny, right to the heart of the matter. *What's wrong?*

The voice on the other side of the door speaks again. It sounds exasperated—but also smug. Aishwarya's silence seems to please him. "Consider this a warning. We're watching you, Ms. Prakash. We're watching your whole family. Don't forget that we can make things hard for even citizens, if we want." She can hear the man smile. How can a smile make a sound at all, let alone a sound so chilling? "You have a nice day, now."

And to Padmini's enduring relief, the heavy boots move away from the door. At least three sets of boots; God, how many of them came to participate in this tacit threat by Evilcorp? Because that's what this is. If she does take Aishwarya's suggestion to sue, all Evilcorp has to do is tell the truth and she'll be kicked out of the country before she can blink. They might have to pay a fine or something, but they'll consider it a bargain compared to giving Padmini the back pay she's due. Or maybe it's not a threat, and she's overthinking this? Maybe it's just pettiness—Wash or someone from her old team adding insult to injury. People like that are never content just to win. They also want Padmini put in her place.

She comes out of the room and goes over to stand beside Aishwarya, both of them silent as they listen to the men finally exit the building. Then they are silent for a few moments longer, just because. Aishwarya is shaking a little, Padmini discovers when she puts a hand on her aunt's shoulder, which makes a perfect match for the hollow fear roiling in Padmini's own belly. There's been no attack, no freaky white tendrils coming through the door, no monsters in the swimming pool. She doesn't know if this has been some sort of flanking maneuver on the part of the Woman in White, and it doesn't matter, because no corporation needs help from eldritch abominations to do awful things. Neither does ICE.

And yet.

Three hours later, with a suitcase in tow and a tightly packed duffel bag on the other shoulder, Padmini knocks on the door of a penthouse apartment in Harlem.

When Neek opens the door, he just stands there for a moment, expressionless. Then he reaches out to take the duffel and assist her with the suitcase. "C'mon."

Her throat is tight. She hasn't called ahead. Didn't have a chance with Aishwarya and Barsaat and half her relatives back in Chennai talking and texting at her, trying to change her mind while she packed. "I need to—"

"Yeah. We got you."

It's too quick. "I didn't—"

He lets out a little breath of not-quite-laughter. "I said we got you." So that's that, then.

Bel's there with Manny, both waiting and worried. Veneza's at work, but in the group chat she's been threatening to show up at the nearest ICE detention facility with a lawyer she knows, so Padmini hopes she'll be okay about suddenly gaining another roommate. It's more than a relief, these people's welcome; it is both bulwark and reassurance. Even if it does feel like a retreat to leave Queens before her family can be harmed by her presence.

"S'bullshit, innit," Bel says, as Neek moves past him to put Padmini's bags in her new bedroom. "Like that 'hostile environment' business they keep pulling in the UK. You're doing everything you should and they're still giving you hell? Bullshit."

Padmini can only smile in weak response. It is, but just because something is bullshit doesn't mean it can't hurt her and everyone she loves. "Are you sure you're all right with me staying here?" she asks him. "I don't want to put *you* at risk. You're on an F-1, too, aren't you?"

"J-1. Research scholar. But close enough by ICE standards—and yeah, even so, I'm all right with it." Bel sets his jaw. "They're not going to bother me much because I'm not from one of the 'bad countries,' even with my funny foreigner name. Worth the risk to help you, if sharing the shower a bit more counts as helping. Welcome to Casa New York with Bonus London Decor."

It does help to hear the words. Then Padmini turns to face Manny, taking a deep breath. "So, um. While we're on the subject of huge favors, I need you to do me one more. For New York. Let's get married."

CHAPTER FIVE

Tentacles Rule Everything Around Me

Everything is great again for Aislyn.

No more strangers accosting her on her doorstep. No more half-psychic summonses from a city she does not want to be part of; no more hallucinations about a young man sleeping on trash. Staten Island stands alone, a proud and independent city in her own right at last, even if the state of New York isn't quite ready to acknowledge a strictly metaphysical secession. Aislyn's people might still have to ferry off to the strange and hostile foreign land of New York City in order to make a living, but that doesn't matter. Lots of cities are exurbs of other cities for reasons of finance or infrastructure. True Staten Islanders always come home in the end.

She's not lonely anymore, either. She has friends now! A couple of acquaintances she met back in college—people she didn't talk to much, but from study groups or her work-study job—have reached out to suggest coffee dates. The other ladies who work at the library with her have also started inviting Aislyn to the movies or baseball games. And if the coffee conversation is nothing but stilted pleasantries, or if there is something fixed and blank about the library ladies' expressions—something entirely too familiar in their smiles and awkward "human languages are hard" slips of the tongue—well, that's fine, too. Though the Woman in White is easily capable of being in many places at once, Aislyn feels honored to be the dedicated recipient of so much of her attention. Between the library ladies, and the crossing guards who know her name and say hello, and the store clerks who laugh and wave her money away, Aislyn feels like a real VIP. She feels *special*. It's nice.

And now she's at the ballpark with several *thousand* of her new friends, eagerly awaiting the start of a rally by Senator Ruben Panfilo, also known as the next mayor of New York City. When Aislyn showed up at the rally with her ticket, she and her friends and parents all got quickly ushered over to a fancy-looking private entrance and up to an even fancier luxury skybox. From here, the whole field is visible, with the part of it that contains the stage perfectly framed. There's a small bar serving the suites, where all the drinks are comped and the bartender is a very pretty and exotic-looking young man like someone out of Aislyn's favorite romance novels. The hors d'oeuvres and plush seating aren't bad, either. Her family is absolutely delighted. Her father beams proudly at Aislyn in a way that he's never done in the thirty years preceding. Then again, the Woman in White has made him great again, too, and these days he is every inch the father Aislyn's always wished for. Aislyn's mother sits quietly beside him, smiling and happy. She doesn't talk anymore to Aislyn when they're in private, except to say pithy, empty things. That…bothers Aislyn, in spite of everything. But Kendra hasn't drunk herself into a stupor in weeks, so there's that, too.

There's always a price to be paid for imagination, the Woman has told Aislyn, which seems an odd thing for anyone to say. But maybe the Woman just means that poor Kendra Houlihan, who gave up a life of artistic self-direction in order to please her insecure husband, is not served well by yearning for what might have been. That yearning has been killing her, slowly, over the years. Isn't she better off simply leaning in to being Matthew Houlihan's shadow and helpmeet? That was the choice she made, after all, and now she can enjoy it free of regrets. Why should Aislyn feel guilty about that?

Aislyn rubs at the back of her neck and sighs. She should just find a seat and enjoy the rally.

Down on the field, giant screens arranged around the stage start to light up. So does the big screen that takes up one whole wall of the luxury suite. Very exciting! She sits down with a beer in hand to watch as the senator himself comes into view. (Her father usually says women shouldn't drink beer, but he's also less opinionated these days. That doesn't bother her so much.)

Ruben Panfilo isn't much to look at. He's short, unimposing, and it looks like he's gotten his money's worth on frontal hair implants. There was a time when Aislyn's father would have laughed at the idea of voting for such a man. Panfilo is too obviously built for glad-handing and desk work, with no visible markers of "toughness." *Just another greasy dago foot soldier*, Aislyn can almost hear her father saying. (Matthew Houlihan thinks all

Italians are in the Mafia.) *The kind of guy who might talk shit but be the first one screaming and running if there's a real fight. Fucking chickenshit.*

Now, however, Aislyn sees her father start clapping and cheering, as does most of the crowd in the stadium when Panfilo steps up to the mic. Even the little white tendril on Matthew Houlihan's neck, just to the left of his third or fourth cervical vertebra, is jerking and whipping around as if cheering, too. Aislyn feels a tremendous surge of relief at the sight of Panfilo, who has promised to make New York once again a place where people like Aislyn don't have to be afraid. That's what her parents told her the city used to be like back in their day, when everyone knew their place and people were safe and happy, and it sounds like a version of New York that Aislyn might have liked.

"Friends," Panfilo says, holding up hands after a few moments, because the crowd seems determined to cheer for the next hour or so. "Friends! Come on, now, you're gonna make everybody believe that old saw about Staten Islanders talking too much." Good-natured laughter greets this, and Aislyn beams. He gets her! He gets her island. Finally. The cheering subsides, allowing Panfilo to begin his speech.

It's a little rambly because he's talking without a teleprompter or any sort of prepared remarks. This makes him feel more real and believable, but it also means he occasionally says things that don't quite make sense. Still, the crowd loves it, and Aislyn loves it. He wants to give more money to the NYPD and stop making them waste time on diversity training! He's going to fire the city council! Fire everyone running the MTA so that the trains will finally run on time! Stop funding CUNY, since all it does is crank out "wokeism" and socialists anyway—Aislyn doesn't really understand this part, because the College of Staten Island is part of the CUNY system and Aislyn doesn't think she ran into any woke socialists while she was a student there—but the crowd seems to love this statement, so it must be a good thing. It's an *amazing* thing. She had no idea the mayor of New York had so much power.

But the best moment is when Panfilo pauses for dramatic effect, then leans into the mic and says, "And we'll be pushing for Staten Island to split off from the City of New York, too. Right? Right?" Cheers start to rise, and he grins. "They don't want us anyway. So why don't we just take our balls and go home?"

The crowd goes wild. People are stomping their feet, blasting off air horns. Aislyn sees one guy who's standing on his chair start jumping up and down, miss his seat, and take out half his row when he falls. His neighbors just help everybody up, stanch the blood, and resume cheering.

It's glorious, and Aislyn floats on that glory, buoyed by her fellow islanders' joy. There's a niggle of a quibble in the back of Aislyn's mind; how's Staten Island going to pay for everything if it doesn't have the city's money to help out? But these are minor worries. Political expediency has to fudge the truth sometimes, she knows. Politicians always lie, so why not elect one whose lies will get you what you want?

That's apparently it for the talking portion of the rally. Panfilo walks off the stage to cheers as the Beastie Boys' "An Open Letter to NYC" starts playing over the speakers, which makes Aislyn wince. She does actually love that song, but it feels inappropriate—a song about the whole city's unified spirit, right after Panfilo has called for Staten Island to secede. People are grooving to it anyway, so Aislyn dismisses her thematic doubts and gets up to pee while her parents and library friends are gleefully chanting the song's chorus over sloshing drink cups.

The skybox bathroom is unbelievably posh, with an elderly white woman in uniform as an attendant, even. Aislyn feels a little self-conscious about doing her business when this poor woman is forced to listen to people's farts and tinkles all day, but so be it. Afterward, she washes her hands and is startled when the woman steps forward to hand her a thick cloth napkin, as if Aislyn can't pick one up for herself. The look of suspicion and unease must be really visible on her face, because the attendant smiles in a grandmotherly way. "You can take it yourself if you'd rather," she says, holding forward the basket of napkins. Aislyn does so. But this makes her feel foolish and ignorant, because if fancy people normally just accept what's handed to them, then Aislyn has just revealed herself to be low-class. She presses her lips together and ignores the conspicuously placed tip jar on her way out of the bathroom, even though normally she prefers to tip service workers. The woman shouldn't have made her feel so low, damn it. Who expects tips for handing out napkins, anyway?

On her way back to their luxury box, Aislyn passes another suite full of people. They include Senator Panfilo, who's laughing with a small knot of hangers-on at the center of the room. It's also where the event DJ is spinning, his gear spread across a set of tables in the back. He's a gray-haired skinny white man wearing a backward baseball cap, holding headphones to his ear with one hand and bobbing his head as he works. He's doubled the Beastie Boys song into extended play, probably because Aislyn can hear half the stadium singing along. On impulse, Aislyn turns into the room to approach him. He looks up when she comes over, and Aislyn blinks; there's a translucent white tendril growing from his left cheek, right above the scruffy jawline beard. She hardly notices the tendrils anymore—guidelines, the Woman calls them—though this one's a bit hard to ignore given its placement.

The DJ grins, gaze roving up and down her body in an unpleasant way. "Hey there, honey," he says. "Got a request?"

"Yeah," Aislyn says. His wandering eyes have stopped on her tits. An instant later his guideline curls back and tickles just under his eye, however, and he focuses on her face again. *Good guideline*, she thinks. Then she says, "Why don't you play some music that's, I don't know, more in line with what Senator Panfilo talked about? Like . . . independence and standing up for yourself and . . ." She shrugs awkwardly.

"Oh, yeah, I got you, honey, we got lots of that lined up. Some Springsteen, little Linkin Park, 'Fortunate Son,' oldie goldies and newie twoies! Whole stadium's got a party comin'."

"Yeah, but . . ." Aislyn can't think of how to articulate her frustration. "What about, like, Wu-Tang Clan or, or RZA? They're actually from Staten Island. And, like, Joan Baez, and—"

"Baez, maybe," the DJ says, a little dismissively. "I think I got that Dixie song she did somewhere? When things slow down a little I'll spin that one. No Wu-Tang or RZA, tho. I don't play that jungle music shit."

It's a slap in the face, even though the guy at least used the "at-home" version of the word Aislyn suspects he really wanted to use. What frustrates her is that race shouldn't matter—not here, not now, not when something as simple as a music choice can help Panfilo. She gets that not everyone likes Black people, but everybody likes *Wu-Tang*. Don't they?

She's too flustered to talk anymore, so she smiles awkwardly and bobs her head and turns away. This positions her to see that Panfilo is now talking with the Woman in White, who for the time being has taken the shape of a tall middle-aged ice-blond woman in a tailored business suit. She looks almost normal for once, or normal for the important and well-connected prospective donor that she's pretending to be . . . except that her head is tilted completely to one side, at nearly a ninety-degree angle, as she stares at him. Oops. Panfilo's handling it better than Aislyn would have, continuing to smile and talk, but maybe that's why he's a politician and she's just a part-time librarian.

Then the Woman's gaze alights on Aislyn. She beams, straightens her head, thank God, and beckons Aislyn over. "This is my dear friend," she says when Aislyn steps into their circle, taking Aislyn's hand and squeezing it with honest enthusiasm. Aislyn immediately feels better. "Why, Aislyn here is the very embodiment of your constituents! Aislyn, dear, please meet my latest weapon against the mess that is New York."

Panfilo laughs at this moniker. "I like that! Might steal it for a slogan." He focuses on Aislyn and she can see a slight puzzlement in his expression as he does so, as if he's trying to fathom how a mousy young woman in a Target dress could possibly be friends with the glamorous, wealthy woman he's currently schmoozing. Still, to his credit, he offers his hand to shake. "Lovely to meet you, miss. I was just telling Ms. White here that this is my first time on Staten Island since I was a teenager."

Usually Aislyn is overcome with shyness in situations like this, but it's always easier to talk when the Woman in White is near. And she can talk about her island forever. "That's better than most people, Senator. A lot of New Yorkers never come here at all."

"Well, we're gonna change that." He grins at the Woman and either doesn't notice or chooses not to remark upon the unblinking, predatory stare she's got fixed on him. (Aislyn nudges her with an elbow. The Woman blinks, then smiles gratefully and resumes focusing on Panfilo, this time remembering to blink and occasionally change facial expressions.)

Panfilo turns and gestures out at the stadium, in the direction of Manhattan. "People think New York is just Manhattan— skyscrapers and Broadway and Park Avenue. Maybe they go see a ball game in Queens, or hit up the Bronx Zoo or the Brooklyn Botanic Garden . . . but they don't come to the *Staten Island* Botanic Garden. They ride the ferry here so they can see the Statue of Liberty for cheap, but then they turn right around and leave again. We're gonna change all that."

"How?" Aislyn asks, out of genuine interest. Because she might love her island, and she knows they've got zoos and ballparks and all sorts of nice attractions, but she also knows that the borough's leaders have struggled to overcome tourists' misconceptions of Staten Island for years via endless promotional campaigns, to little effect. And then there's another incontrovertible element to consider, which is that some part of Aislyn—the part of her that embodies the will of her fellow Staten Islanders—is *glad* when those tourists don't visit. Staten Island doesn't like being gawked at. So she adds, "And...*why* would we change that?"

It's like Panfilo doesn't hear the latter question. "Well, there's a long-term plan and a short-term one. Long term, we need more real people in this city, people who aren't freeloaders or gang-bangers or, uh, sexually confused." He grins. "And they need to see that Staten Island is where all the *normal* people of New York live—hardworking all-American people, who understand family values. If we play it right, get some movie shoots in to showcase how beautiful this borough is, maybe open up to new development, Staten Island can grow. Imagine if this borough had as many people as Brooklyn! We could get anything we wanted out of the city, then."

Aislyn frowns, then quickly tries to smooth over that frown with a pleasant look—but she's never been good at lying or lying-adjacent behavior, so she does a bad job of it. Too much development, too many new people, would inevitably mean the loss of the Staten Island Aislyn has always loved. No more farms. Less parkland. No more stately Victorian houses with twenty rooms for the same price as a two-bedroom condo in Midtown Manhattan. Everything might end up as dense as the North Shore of the island, which is so packed with multifamily high-rises and traffic that Aislyn kind of hates going there. Feels too much like the rest of New York. And would regular people still be able to buy beachfront property after an influx like that? She doesn't know economics, but it's not hard to guess that if a lot more people are buying houses, then no, Staten Island would not remain as afford-able as it is.

While Aislyn stews on this, the Woman in White beams. "I'm delighted that you want to Make New York Great Again," she says to Panfilo. Somehow the capital letters in the slogan are audible, when she says them. "That's the whole idea, isn't it? Bring this troublesome city into alignment with more sensible parts of reality, stop all that pesky, viral replication of new universes. The more we unify the city, stop catering to"—she goes blank for a second, then brightens—"*special interests*, yes, the faster we'll travel through the aethers of the multiverse."

Panfilo looks confused for a moment, but he recovers quickly. "Special interests, exactly. Right now New York City schools are a complete mess because we've got people from the projects, peo-ple who never even finished high school themselves or went to college, influencing policy! We need sensible businessmen—and women like yourself, of course—to take charge and make sure our kids are prepared for the workplace. Instead of pouring tax-payer money into hopeless schools where the kids are too crimi-nal and lazy to learn, just let those schools die! Parents can send their kids to better schools, with no CRT or indoctrination into problem lifestyles. Parent-centered education, am I right?"

"Right!" The Woman in White looks at Aislyn, and Aislyn manages a weak smile in response to her excitement. "Why, if I want to teach my hypothetical and impossible child-city how to *darkle* and *tinct*, no matter how dangerous such practices might be, then I darn well ought to be able to do that, don't you think?"

Panfilo looks glassy-eyed, but he keeps the conversation going.

Aislyn is impressed. "You definitely should! It bothers me that this country has changed so much over the years. We used to be number one for education in the world! Then liberals got into the schools and used taxpayer money to teach all sorts of godless, perverted, useless things. Sex ed for elementary schoolers! Diversity. *Art therapy.*" He laughs at the very idea. "It just has to stop."

The Woman in White leans over to touch his arm. Aislyn's seen other women do this during interactions, a little bit of flirting to make sure a man is paying attention, but there's something off about how the Woman does it this time. She rubs Panfilo's upper arm and gives it a little squeeze—not like she's trying to figure out the size of his biceps, but in a more measuring way. Figuring out whether he's got enough meat on him, maybe, or needs more fattening up. "I like how you think, Senator," she purrs. "Well, I have a great deal of, uh, money, and you have a clear vision for this city. Let's remake reality together."

She sticks out a hand, and he brightens and reaches for it. Aislyn knows what's coming. It's different now, seeing it from the other side. There was a time when she found the guidelines alien and disturbing, but no longer. Clarity is nice. Knowing herself to be on the side of righteousness is, too.

And yet.

The Woman and Senator Panfilo shake hands, then let go. Aislyn frowns as Panfilo excuses himself and moves away to join another cluster of people. Aislyn cranes her neck to see better, but...no fronds uncurling from his arm. He's not rubbing the palm of his hand where the Woman touched him, either.

"Oh, aren't you a dear," the Woman says, smiling as she notices

Aislyn's confusion. "No need for additional guidance with that one. He's going to go exactly where I want without any help from me. Now stop fretting, and go mingle. Everyone is here for you, after all, aren't they? A whole stadium of people wanting Staten Island free and strong." She squeezes Aislyn's arm, and this time it feels genuine, reassuring. Aislyn manages a smile, and the Woman offers her a huge grin in response. Then she, too, turns away to resume schmoozing.

Everyone is here for Staten Island. And yet, as the DJ starts playing more thumping, feel-good music made by someone from New York but not from Staten, and the bartender hands out free Manhattans but has no idea how to make a good Staten Island Ferry . . . Aislyn finds herself just standing there for a long moment, feeling lost. No one talks to her. The Woman in White always makes time for Aislyn, but as Aislyn watches her loop an arm around one of Panfilo's bodyguards, murmur in his ear, and then move away as a frond curls down from the man's earlobe, she isn't sure she wants to interrupt. The Woman is a busy entity. She has dimensions to flatten and Staten Island to . . . make great, again.

A New York where everyone gets along and everywhere is safe. Where people know their place and don't fight for more, don't even *imagine* more. Is that even possible? What would it take to stop every conflict, smooth over every prickly personality, make every minority group see past the little injustices and just be happy with whatever it's got?

She could ask the Woman—whose true name is R'lyeh, the city from beyond reality, where the buildings are all curved and the streets are all straight and there is never conflict or ugliness or fear. She should visit R'lyeh, to see what it's like. It's odd that the Woman has never invited her there, isn't it? Maybe that's just because she knows Aislyn is agoraphobic. But friends *invite*, don't they?

(*Maybe the Woman is not really your friend*, whispers her borough.)

Something burns, suddenly, on her shoulder. Aislyn winces and claps a hand to it. Did she get stung by a bee? She fingers the site, then goes back to the ladies' room. The attendant that she didn't tip gives her a flat look, which Aislyn ignores as she leans close to a mirror and yanks her blouse aside to peer at the skin. Nothing. *Completely* nothing: the guideline is no longer there. Something has burned it away.

After a long, taut moment, in which Aislyn stares at herself and does not let herself think again the thought that is already putting roots deep into her psyche, she heads home early.

INTERRUPTION

Istanbul

Istanbul is cats, as much as people. And dogs, but more cats. He often wishes he could just be an avatar to the cats, really. Cats don't do politics. Cats don't commit genocide, unless one counts rats, and Istanbul is still raw about the Black Plague so he's fine with those little bastards going down. Cats don't decide to follow this religion one day, that religion another, and some unholy mishmash on a third; they worship themselves, and are fine for it. He's amused that the rest of the country seems to feel similarly; the government won't do much for poor or struggling people, but no one had better dare insult Istanbul's cats.

Istanbul-the-man knows this is his fault. Oh, of course it's not that simple. Whenever a city develops a tic like this, it's more likely the result of a feedback loop. People in Istanbul like cats; Istanbul's avatar becomes obsessed with cats; this feeds the city's liking for cats. He blames himself, however, because it's easier to break a habit in one person than in a whole city. But why should he bother? Nothing wrong with liking cats. And so the cycle continues.

He's walking along the waterfront in Karaköy. This has always been his favorite part of the city, even in recent years as it becomes more tourist trap and less an expression of Istanbul's soul. The tourist nonsense is getting worse because that's how tourist nonsense goes, but he will not give Karaköy up. A thousand years ago, Levantines dominated this part of the city, and though there are few of his people left—well, the people that were his before he became a city—it's still where Istanbul chooses to live. He owns an ancient apartment building in the Old City that has a good view of the Hagia Sophia from the rooftop. And he takes care to walk the waterfront every day, no matter the weather, because this is how he quiets his mind enough to hear all fifteen million of the voices lodged within it. This is how, through plague and famine and war and the rise and fall of empires, he remains Istanbul.

The waterfront is quiet with dawn today, apart from the lovely, haunting calls to prayer hanging on the wind. It's too early for most tourists, but there are a few leftover partiers sprawled in doorways or on benches, sleeping off drunkenness or late-night shisa that made them miss the last Marmaray train. Meanwhile the air is thick with lovely scent. Local businesses have begun to bake bread and grill fish, as they have done every day for millennia. He nods to the local tea seller in his traditional vest and bright, striped pants, who smiles and tilts the massive carafe on his back to pour Istanbul a cup. Istanbul pays more than the tea is worth, to cover any free cups the seller might choose to offer to the poor. They have argued about this in the past, he and the tea seller, because the seller prefers to do his own charity. Even now, the argument isn't settled, but regardless they stand together while Istanbul drinks his tea, enjoying the morning's quiet and chatting about nothing. Then he hands back the cup and nods with pointed graciousness; the tea seller rolls his eyes but smiles in rueful amusement as he walks off. Istanbul has been arguing with tea sellers for more than a thousand years. What is life without such small consistencies? Everything changes, everything stays the same; he is Byzantium, he is Constantinople, he is Istanbul.

Meandering down to the fishmongers as per his usual habit, he smiles as the merchants greet him. Some offer him bags of bycatch—fish too small or net-mangled to sell, rays and seahorses few will want, and so on. He'll take this on his daily walk away from the tourist areas, where the streets are dirtier and the cats are skinnier. That's Istanbul, too. All cities have their showcases of beauty and their blocks of beastliness.

He is aware, as he walks back up a cobblestone road, that the young man who waits on a nearby set of steps is a city. Smaller than Istanbul, but brasher, and with that precocious maturity cities tend to have when they arise in young countries. This one is an infant by Old World standards, but Istanbul supposes that the eldest in any family usually has to grow up the fastest.

He does not slow his steady walk, instead turning onto the street that will lead him away from the tourist areas. "Walk with me," he invites. After a moment, the young man gets up to follow.

He's pleased when the young man doesn't speak first. Young people should show respect for their elders. But because Istanbul is also a city full of brisk-talking professionals, he gets to the point. "You want to tell me about the Enemy becoming more of a threat."

The young man lets out a single, amused breath. "That's already further than I've been able to get with other cities. Yes."

"Which ones have you talked to thus far?"

"Tokyo, Zanzibar, Warsaw—"

Istanbul chuckles. Every one of those cities is crazy—but then, he supposes they would say the same of him. "It's easier," Istanbul explains, "to relate to cities that are born near you, within the same culture. Ankara and I have been close for years, you see." Lovers, too, on and off down the centuries, but such intimate matters are none of this young man's business.

"Unfortunately, we're the first and only American city to arise. Though I guess we do get along with São Paulo."

Istanbul remembers Cahokia and others from the continent now called North America, and sighs. How frightened these newer Americans are by their own history. "Naturally. São Paulo is just as brash and impulsive as you. It takes a few centuries for a city to settle into itself."

"We'd like to have the time to do that. But if we don't do something about our little problem..."

"Yes, I agree, and it's not a little problem. I want to show you something."

"All right."

So they keep walking, in silence this time. Istanbul is amused by the way the young man keeps looking around in wonder. This happens particularly in the older parts of the city that they pass through; the young man can feel their age, naturally, and seems mind-blown by the sheer weight of years embedded in this three-thousand-year-old set of steps, or that leftover bit of aqueduct from the time of Constantine. The awe is rather charming, really. Seeing oneself anew through the eyes of a child usually is.

Eventually they reach Istanbul's city limits proper. There's plenty beyond this, suburbs and exurbs and parks and satellite cities, but for tax and legal purposes the city—and the strongest zone of Istanbul-the-avatar's power—stops here. It's a fairly nondescript area, just a litter-strewn empty lot behind a supermarket. Nothing special to look at, but then he doesn't come here for the sightseeing.

"My favorite cats, this is their territory," he explains. He's given away much of the bycatch along their walk, dropping bits of food into the dozens of dishes permanently set out by building stoops and at the front of alleyways. "They mostly eat garbage from the supermarket, but I bring them fish when I can. Cats should always have fish to eat."

The young man makes a noncommittal sound to show that he's listening. He's very diplomatic, knowing how to appear interested even when he isn't. Istanbul likes him, and wishes some of his own children had turned out so wise. Oh, well.

He points toward the far edge of the lot. "That's the city border. Pay attention, now."

Then Istanbul calls for his cats. Usually a ticking sound works best. Seagulls start circling at once, because they know if they are clever they will surely get some of the bycatch; even cats aren't quick enough to fend them all off. Then the grasses rustle and immediately a dozen or so cats come running out of the underbrush. Istanbul beams in delight and crouches to pet his favorites, rubbing hard little heads and flicking ears whenever they allow. To circumvent the seagulls, he hands a fish to each of the cats directly. Even with this precaution, one cat gets a fish stolen right out of its teeth by a gull. It leaps after the bird and manages to score some flight feathers, but the bird makes its escape. Istanbul gives the poor cat a second, bigger fish, in consolation.

The young man, who is an aspect of New York but not New York itself, watches without comment—but when one of the cats comes up to him with an inquisitive meow, he crouches and holds out his fingers to let the creature sniff, looking fascinated. Ah, a natural cat person! Istanbul offers him the bag, and is pleased when he doesn't hesitate to put his fingers on a slimy undersized eel for the cat to snatch.

Then Istanbul stands. "Watch," he says. He tosses some fish around them, and cats and seagulls swarm like mad. He turns, however, and tosses a particularly big fish into the grasses just past the edge of the lot—the city border. Three cats immediately break away to chase the fish...and stop, tails flicking in agitation, at the border. Gulls swoop, cawing in their eagerness...and then swerve, breaking off their dives, to settle on the blacktop or dumpsters nearby, some clacking beaks or ruffling feathers. This fish is going to remain unclaimed, apparently.

It must be a mark of how bad things have been in New York that the young man suddenly has a knife in his hand. His expression is calm and focused as he edges toward the lot border, ignoring the cats that slink away and the gulls that fly off. Istanbul, who knows what he will see, keeps handing out fish. There's more than enough for everyone, so he tries to make sure the ones who look pregnant get a little extra. Then he comes over to stand by this cold young warrior of a city, sighing at the sight.

Beyond the lot, almost hidden amid the dry grass that's poked its way up through neglected asphalt, are four cats and a gull. They aren't dead; he can see their eyes blinking and flanks moving with steady breath. Otherwise, however, each of these creatures is covered in a mass of fine white tendrils, like fiber-optic wire come to gently waving life. The tendrils cover each animal, rooting them to the ground and distorting their shapes from feline and avian into something more amorphous—and worse, some of them are larger than any cat or bird should be. Growing. Changing. Istanbul can't see that they're agitated or in any pain, which is a relief; their eyes are glazed, sleepy-looking. One of them, a calico whose half-grown kittens he just fed, slow-blinks at him, an affectionate gesture. Istanbul slow-blinks back, despite his own quiet horror at her condition.

"What is the point of this?" asks the New York. He sounds collected, detached, but Istanbul sees that his stance is ready for anything. "In our city, she infected people, but didn't trap them like this. What's happening here is..." He shakes his head in polite confusion. "You've been a complete city for ages. She can't *attack* you with these...creatures, so I don't understand why she would do this."

Interesting, and troubling, that he refers to the Enemy as "she." "This is not a *person* we are dealing with," Istanbul says, which makes the young man frown. "I have heard the details, yes: that she has a name, that she is actually a city herself, that she has only pretended to be a mindless beast all this time. We didn't know that before, so thank you for discovering it. But what we *have* always known about this Enemy is that she is a natural force—and by that I mean she grows and spreads opportunistically. I do not believe she has to *intend* such growth. She is no Atatürk enacting a grand plan, no Aisha. She is more like the bacteria that sits on skin, harmless—until that skin is cut." Istanbul sighs. "I doubt she means to do anything with her...creations. But if my strength ever falters, these abominations are here, ready and waiting."

"That analogy doesn't work," the New York muses aloud. "She didn't come from this universe. She's *alien* bacteria, and she was specifically designed to infect us; she's told us that herself. Designed by whom, though? Who unleashed an invasive predator that specifically targets cities, in our reality?"

Such a smart boy. Istanbul laments that he currently has no daughters to introduce. "That is our true enemy," he says. "Should we be more afraid of the sword, or the hand that wields it?"

The young man narrows his eyes. "I see," he says. Istanbul fears for this New York's enemies, given that look on his face. At least he has the sense to put his knife away. Stabbing, enjoyable as Istanbul has found the act to be during his own warrior phases, will do no good against this adversary.

Istanbul reaches over and pats the New York's shoulder. "I've already called for a Summit," he says, "but I'm only one elder city. If you would hear my advice: don't bother reaching out to the rest. Stick to the younger cities. More likely to listen in any case."

The New York frowns. "If we need to win the elders over—"

"You don't need their agreement, you need their attention. So many young cities have come and gone over the years, you see. It's like in the very old days, when parents had a lot of children because it was understood that so many would die before adulthood. Some doted on all the children, of course, but many parents learned to stay detached until a child had lived long enough to love safely. To us, these days, such detachment seems callous, but it should be understood as a way to cushion the heart against possible pain." Istanbul spreads his hands. "Because of this, you, New York, will not be heeded no matter how diplomatic your approach. You aren't safe to care about until you've been around awhile. But we also like routine, we elder cities. We like quiet. We can ignore one whiny child, but if the whole schoolroom kicks up a ruckus?"

The young man raises his eyebrows, amused. "I *see*." This time Istanbul fears for his fellow elders—but that's fine. All of them are stupid and probably deserve it.

The young man eventually leaves. Not immediately. He lingers first, watching while Istanbul takes out a small thermos of tea—his own home brew, linden flower, good for health—to pour on the trapped animals. He's been doing this every week for years now. He can't keep the patch from being dangerous because it's outside his city limits, but everything that considers itself Istanbul is Istanbul, so he isn't completely powerless. The tea hits the tendrils like acid; they screech and wither and fall away. The gull squawks and flaps off, looking disgruntled at being wet with tea, but the newly freed cats run over to rub up against Istanbul's ankles and shins in what can pass for gratitude. "You don't love me, you just want shrimp," he grumbles at the little calico, but of course he's saved a big one just for her.

Then the New York is gone, and the cats are fed, and all the bad things are dealt with. Istanbul tucks the empty bags into the trash, cleans his hands with some scented sanitizer he carries in a pocket, and then starts the walk home. He hums to himself a little, happily, as he walks. It's always refreshing to meet a young person who has a good head on his shoulders and a clear vision of the way the world needs to go. They aren't always right, but they do make things so very interesting, and frequently better. God willing, those better days will come soon.

CHAPTER SIX

Have Your People Zoom Our People

It's been two weeks since Queens became temporarily un-Queens'd, and Bronca has spent a good bit of that time on cloud nine. It's just the weirdness of bad luck and timing; she didn't plan it at all, but someone interesting made contact via the ten-year-old dating profile on Pink Crawfish that Bronca actually forgot was up. And after several days of cautious back-and-forth chat, a $49 background check, a little bit of stalking on social media to make sure the woman wasn't a TERF or a weirdo, and some very deep soul searching, Bronca has agreed to something that she never thought she would experience again at her age. She's going on a date.

She should probably cancel. Marina, as her potential paramour is named, doesn't know that Bronca's a living embodiment of the city. That counts as a disclosure Bronca should make up front, doesn't it? "Date me and you might end up attacked by monsters from another dimension"? And being a city comes with responsibilities. Bronca should reprioritize, focus on the business of the Bronx, forget all this social-life stuff. She's been pretty happy alone. Her own mom was a single mother who taught Bronca to enjoy her own company and value her own time—a radical way of thinking for any woman, especially back in the Sixties. Bronca liked having a family, back when she and Chris decided to shift from semi-out beards to friends-with-a-baby, but she also likes being able to leave the clean laundry unfolded and sing (badly) at the top of her lungs whenever she wants. If she's feeling a hankering for company again, maybe she's better off getting a dog than a girlfriend.

Except . . . well. If everything really is going to shit, wouldn't it be nice to die in someone's arms rather than alone? Also, never mind the romantic shit, but she hasn't gotten laid in, like, years.

Well. For the moment, Bronca has decided to focus on city stuff. It's been two weeks since Brooklyn declared her mayoral run, and Bronca's honestly a little impressed. She's the last person to throw stones, but it's always been irritating to her that people who would be good mayors for a city like New York never run. Instead, the city has ended up with a cavalcade of selfish and short-sighted businessmen—it's only ever been men—or criminal cronies who use the job to help their friends while screwing everybody else. Which, fine, that's politics everywhere, but it's so relentlessly consistent in New York that the city has suffered for nearly Bronca's whole life, unable to fight for its share at the state budget table, unable to rein in corrupt landlords or the increasingly militarized and mafia-esque NYPD. And now that Bronca is New York, she knows how much the city wants—*needs*—to fight for better. So Bronca decides to pay Brooklyn a visit.

The campaign headquarters are in Bed Stuy, of course. It's just a narrow storefront sandwiched between a laundromat and an old taco restaurant, but Bronca's pleased to see that Brooklyn's already acquired nice, professionally made posters to cover the storefront windows. As Bronca walks up there's a guy installing a marquee sign overhead: BROOKLYN, FOR NEW YORK. Cute. Someone's made her a logo that Bronca instantly hates. The colors are too muted, the whole composition has no balance—but Bronca sighs and reminds herself for the thousandth time that not everyone is an art snob. When she steps inside, the office is neatly set up with tables all around and desktop workstations, and Bronca can see that there are some workspaces in the tent-covered backyard as well. Pleasant-looking young people in casual dress murmur quietly into phones and tap delicately on keyboards.

It's all very professional. Respectable. *Neat.* Bronca's going to kill her.

She marches across the office, ignoring a young woman who gets off her phone and belatedly calls out to ask what Bronca wants, then pushes open the small office door in the back. Brooklyn, who has been sitting with her head in her hands, jerks upright at the interruption. "What the hell?"

Bronca closes the door. "I'm the entire Bronx, how did you not feel me coming?"

Brooklyn just keeps staring. A moment later the young woman who called out to Bronca opens the door, glaring at her before blurting, "Ay yo, Miss Brook, I'm so sorry I didn't catch this person, you want me to call the police?"

That snaps Brooklyn out of it. She composes herself instantly, absently brushing her hair back into place as she sits up straighter. "No, thank you, Haley. She's a friend, it's fine. And we don't call the police here unless there's a life-threatening situation happening, remember."

"Yeah, ma'am, I got you. Okay, then." She gives Bronca a lip-curled once-over, then shuts the door again. Well, at least Brooklyn's hiring people with some real New York in them.

"Can you not," Brooklyn says, finally recovering, "come in here and start a war with my staff? They don't get paid enough to put up with your evil ass."

"Yeah? Pay 'em more, then." Bronca crosses the office to a nice chair, moves a stack of leaflets that's sitting in it onto the radiator, and plops her fat butt down instead. "You know they're going to have to put up with a lot crazier shit than me. And don't you have residuals or royalties or something from back when you were MC Free? Use that to pay your people more."

Brooklyn laughs without humor. "No, 'cause I had an Eighties record contract and a shitty manager. There was a little in my war chest before all this, which I was building up to run again for city council—but that's a drop in the bucket, given what you need to run for mayor in this town. I can't tap my savings, because everything I've got is tied up in fighting the city to get our brownstones back. Can't wait 'til *that* hits the news. And Jojo, sweetheart, tried to surprise me by putting up a GoFundMe after that interview went viral. It pulled in a lot of money, more than I was expecting...none of which I can access. First because it's illegal, and second because three other people—none of whom I know, scammers—started crowdfunding campaigns in my name, too.

So now I'm trying to get the Campaign Finance Board to at least let me take the non-anonymous and non-foreign contributions from Jojo's batch..." She shakes her head. "My poor baby is getting a rough introduction to NYC politics."

Bronca grimaces. "How's her arm?"

"Not bad. She says the cast is itchy." Brooklyn smiles, but the smile doesn't last long. "Doc says she might lose some nerve function permanently. Not to the point of being unable to use it, but it might impair her fine motor skills for things like writing. My father's been in a wheelchair her whole life, so Jojo knows being disabled just means doing things differently. *I'm* pissed, though. Fucking Friendlies hurt my baby."

"We're lucky they didn't kill anybody. Though maybe that would give you a reason to get mad."

Brooklyn looks sharply at her. "What?"

Bronca gets up and leans on the desk. Getting in her face, just a little. "They shot your daughter. But I don't see you out there spitting fire and rolling up the posse. When I opened that office door a minute ago, you looked like you were about to cry. How is this you? Where did your 'bad bitch' go?"

Ah, yes. Brooklyn's brows draw down, and maybe it's Bronca's imagination that suddenly the room feels warmer. "She's right fucking here, same as always. But there's practicalities to consider, goddamn it."

"Like what? So you jumped into a mayoral race with no money and no forethought. And?"

Brooklyn pushes up from her seat, getting right back in Bronca's face. "And I don't have enough staff! I've got plenty of people willing to roll up their sleeves and do street team stuff, but what I *need* are people that can do fundraising and communications, pollsters, strategists! And—"

"So get them."

"With what cash? With what *time*? I have to file a million forms with the Campaign Finance Board and I'm doing everything at the last minute and I'm doing most of it by myself and—"

Bronca decides that if she's going to get slapped for this, then she's going to earn that slap, by God. "Did you fucking forget you're a fucking *city*?"

That startles Brooklyn silent. And yeah, it's about what Bronca figured. She shakes her head but says nothing more, instead finally taking a seat in one of the visitor chairs. Brooklyn is touchy and proud—not much different from Bronca herself, really—and now that Bronca's dropped the hint, she's pretty sure Brooklyn will figure it out in three . . . two . . .

"Oh my God," Brooklyn says. She sits back down, slowly, going on an entire face journey and back while Bronca watches her. "A campaign . . . is a construct."

Bronca suppresses a grin. Prickly bitch will think Bronca's laughing at her, and Bronca needs Brooklyn's head back in the game. "Yeah?"

"Yeah." Brooklyn folds her hands on the desktop, looking prim and put together as always, but Bronca can see how tightly her hands grip each other. "We keep trying to understand how all this city business works, and São Paulo explained about constructs, but I keep thinking small. Music tracks, street haggling, Nathan's hot dogs. Little stuff. But remember when we were kids? That 'I

Love New York' tourist campaign? I still remember the jingle. I remember Koch basically hitching himself to that slogan and all the imagery associated with it. There was even a Broadway play about him. I heard it was terrible, but the point is that he weaponized the city's culture. I don't think he was any kind of great mayor—started out a liberal then turned on the city's poor—but to this day he's one of the people who pops into everyone's head whenever you say 'mayor of New York,' even decades later. Koch got political and public support that every mayor since can only dream of, *because he made himself an icon of New York.*"

"And here you are," Bronca drawls, "already New York, yourself."

"Yeah." Quick as you please, Brooklyn gets up and opens the door of her office. "Folks? I need you to set up for a conference call and then take the afternoon off. I need to do some ...". She pauses, then glances at Bronca, a wry smile on her lips. "Consulting. With some, ah, specialists. See you all tomorrow morning."

Bronca grins and sits back to enjoy the show.

Brooklyn starts a Zoom meeting and texts everyone. To Bronca's great relief, since it means she doesn't have to figure out how to install a new app on her phone—damn things get more complicated every day—Brooklyn has a flat-screen TV on the wall with a camera for virtual meetings. It means Bronca can't join in on the chat, which is mostly Veneza and Padmini making jokes at each other about whether the Avengers have Zoom meetings, too, but that's fine.

"I wondered why you weren't asking us for help," Manny says. He's in his office at Columbia. It's the first time Bronca's seen him in work mode, and he's even more preppy and professorial than usual, with a smart pair of Clark Kent glasses on. "Granted that none of us has experience with a campaign like this, but if the city has chosen you to push back against Panfilo and the Woman in White, then it's very likely we can help you somehow."

"And I need a job," Padmini says. She's in the same room as Neek, wherever that is; same slanting light at different angles behind them, same generic white drywall, though they're on different devices. Probably the Harlem penthouse. "You need data analysis? The fun kind of data analysis, about demographics and patterns and polling? Oh, I haven't been able to do *fun* math for years! Can you pay?"

"Not much," Brooklyn concedes. "The goal is a living wage, of course, but for right now I'm running on fumes. I can pay two dollars an hour over minimum wage. And if I run out of money at any point, you could end up being summarily laid off again."

Padmini laughs. It's the first time Bronca's heard her sound so happy in a long while. "I would have taken minimum. And as long as I can justify it to my advisor—which I should be able to—it's fine for as long as it lasts."

Veneza's on her phone, and her video keeps jolting wildly because she's in the middle of helping Yijing and the other Bronx Art Center staff with an installation. "Uh, I don't know how I can help," she says, out of breath after moving a crate. "I got a job, yo, and Bronca's actually paying me good money for a change. Check it: I got a *retirement fund* now. And real, actual health insurance. Look at me, livin' the not-dying-of-preventable-diseases dream! Anyway, what am I gonna do, answer phones and reposition art for you?"

"You have a whole degree," Bronca reminds her. "In, uh, computer art—"

"Digital design, oh my God, it has alliteration and everything, why can't you ever remember it? *Old B.*" Bronca rolls her eyes. Still, she knows Veneza: the girl is thinking harder about what she can contribute.

"Do you do freelance work?" Brooklyn asks. "I could use a better . . . everything." She glances at a nearby sign and sighs as if she, too, finds the logo awful. "I need graphics, online ads, the works."

"Oh. Huh. Yeah, sure. Never done print design before but I know some folks I can hit up for tips. You don't have people for that already, though?"

"I do, some. But I'd feel better if you worked with them."

"Vale, vale." She's momentarily distracted, while Bronca hears Yijing yelling at someone off-screen. "Oooh, dumb-ass contractor guy decided to talk down to Yijing, and she's verbally *vivisecting* him. I gotta go make some popcorn, so I'm bailing on the rest of the meeting, but cool, glad to be on board." She waves and leaves the Zoom room.

Neek's been silent, and that's bugging the hell out of Bronca. While Brooklyn jots down notes, Bronca leans in. "Your art is amazing," she says to him, "and you know it. I was thinking, if you want, that a series of murals around the city might help spread the word. Any style or design, just stick a campaign logo in the corner somewhere. And *I* can pay for that one." She's been itching to throw some funding at this child ever since she first discovered his quirky, haunting works. He's not Bronx Unknown anymore, and she's pretty sure he could be the next Basquiat, if he'll just let

Bronca spread the good word. Anyone with that much natural talent should be selling works for millions of dollars and being feted by anyone with taste.

But to her surprise, Neek shakes his head. "I might do some murals, but it won't be for this. The city..." He frowns a little, gaze distant. Bronca suddenly gets the distinct impression that he doesn't care about the mayoral race at all. "I keep feeling like *something's wrong*—not just with New York, but with everything. It's like when you're dreaming about...falling, or being watched by something you can't see. Crazymaking shit." He gestures vaguely, in frustration.

Bronca frowns. "If you're opposed to Brooklyn running for mayor—"

"That ain't it." He scowls. "Running feels right. It'll help strengthen the city...but I can't be part of it. I need to listen to the city for a while. Handle up on the metaphysical shit."

They're all surprised, though Bronca's flat-out flabbergasted. She thought...well, she's not sure what she thought. They're six very different people; it follows that not all of them would be 100 percent on board for everything. She just thought this would be one of the exceptions.

In the chat, Padmini quips: *Listen! The city says it wants a snack.* She leans out of sight before coming back with a bowl of something—looks like sliced fresh carambola with salt and chili. Neek chuckles at the joke, for which Bronca's grateful. It clears the awkwardness.

Brooklyn nods as if it makes perfect sense for their primary to be off communing with the multiverse during all this. "All right.

Let me know if there's anything I can do to help. In the meantime..." She turns in her chair to look at Bronca.

Bronca sighs. She knew this was coming as soon as she started getting on Brooklyn's case. "I already got a job, too. But I definitely meet rich philanthropist types as part of that job, and most folks in the art world lean—or pretend to lean—leftish. I'll work the Rolodex and try to get you some big donors. Yes, I still use a Rolodex; shut up."

Brooklyn manages not to laugh. "That'll help a lot. Honestly, that's the biggest thing I need right now: connections. Big names with money or a platform. Endorsements." She sighs a little. "I hate this part of politics, but—"

She pauses, distracted as the chat lights up. It's just one comment—but it's impossibly huge, hundreds of words long and continuing to fill up space as they watch, faster than any person ought to be able to type. Already the name of the commenter is out of sight. And the text of the comment is... Bronca frowns and squints, but it's flowing so quickly that she can barely make out the words. *Comes the eater of sweetness upon the plain whereby there are nought but prey and fellow singers within the light where it is cool to work in endless fascination for the vagaries of imagination*— Gibberish, yet more than mere keysmashes. There are hints of literary references amid the mess, apocalyptic imagery that Bronca can almost place. Dadaist gibberish, then, but why? And who—

Abruptly, a new window opens in the Zoom gallery. "Is that Veneza again?" Brooklyn asks. But no: the window has a big *R* centered in lieu of a personalized icon. There's a name attached to the window, too, but the letters are so tiny that Bronca can't read them. Padmini gasps, however, and Bronca doesn't miss the ripple of unease/anger/shock that flows across the others' faces. *They* can read the name. Manny's face goes cold, Neek's eyes blaze hot. Yeah, okay. Bronca doesn't need to see the name.

A moment later, the new person activates their camera. It looks like a glitch on the other end; where there should be a face, they can see only a heavily pixelated, pale blur, which straightens a little and—Bronca thinks—flashes them a broad smile. "Well, well, and here you are!" says a voice that is aggravatingly cheerful and chillingly familiar. Belatedly it hits Bronca: *She always has the same voice. No matter what face she's wearing or even whether she's pretending to be human or not.* There is a looming epiphany in this, maybe something they can use, something about the Woman in White's true nature being less physical than tonal, resonant, a waveform— But Bronca's getting distracted. They are being Zoombombed by the Woman in White.

"Oh, not today, Satan—" Brooklyn pulls over the laptop she's been using to run the meeting—and yelps, reflexively shoving it away, when bright sparks and lightning arcs erupt from the thing. Her shove knocks the laptop off the table edge, where it clatters to the floor and immediately begins to warp and bubble as if someone's taken a blowtorch to it. "Shit! Somebody else shut the Zoom down."

"I can't," Manny says, scowling as he repeatedly taps something on his end. "I'm not the meeting organizer. But it won't let me leave, either."

"Just close the window, everyone, holy shit," Padmini blurts. She clicks at something, too, and frowns. "Why won't it work?"

"How rude!" says the Woman in White. "Honestly, I don't know why I even bother with you people. You're rude, and you *still* don't understand how all of this works. You're complete now! My guidelines can't operate anywhere within your city's borders. I can't even attack you through this connection; any New York IP address burns us awfully. Not that I *want* to lay claim to any of you." Her voice turns contemptuous. "None of you would last for even a moment on the clean streets of R'lyeh. But I'm just here to talk. Will you listen?"

Neek's eyes narrow, but he says, "The fuck you want, Squigglebitch?"

"I want—" She pauses, and maybe it's Bronca's imagination, but the big chunky squares that comprise her appearance seem to brighten. "*Squigglebitch*, really? Oh, your species is so endlessly creative. That creativity will destroy all existence if it isn't stopped, of course, but I do wish there was some way to keep you around. The things you all come up with! My. Squigglebitch." She shakes her blurry head, chuckling. "Anyhow, I wanted to warn you. Now that we've passed the phase in which I could've killed you quickly and painlessly, I feel that it's only right to give you another chance at a merciful death. The alternative is . . . less merciful, you see, and I'm not cruel."

Brooklyn curses and gets up to fetch a fire extinguisher, because the still-spitting laptop is starting to fill the office with smoke and ozone. Bronca also jumps up to move anything flammable away from the thing—but as she does so, she's thinking frantically, because she doesn't believe for one moment that Squigglebitch just wants to talk. They need a construct ready. Problem is, Bronca's never been the sort to use, hmm, *subtle* constructs. Oh, she can ride the motion of public transportation now, as Manny inadvertently taught all of them to do a while back, and she's been experimenting with using art as well, as the Woman in White inadvertently taught her. But when it comes to offensive configurations of New York's belligerent quintessence, Bronca's generally stuck to what works: her spiritual steel-toed boots, borne of the Bronx's decades of urban decay and her own lifelong battles against injustice. She's used them to literally kick interdimensional doors shut before, but how does one kick an internet connection? She can't think of a way, so she sprays the laptop while Brooklyn opens a window so they won't suffocate.

Meanwhile, the Woman in White has leaned her pixelated chin on one pixelated hand. (She's in some sort of white-walled room, it looks like, and the wall behind her is crystal clear. So is her clothing, which seems to be a plain white T-shirt. Bronca's never heard of a background filter that pixelates just exposed flesh, but . . . maybe it's not a background filter.)

"So," the Woman says, "you're a complex multidimensional agglomeration of entities, I'm a complex multidimensional agglomeration of entities. You've made it clear we can't be friends, but I'm hoping I can at least talk sense into you. My superiors are deeply angry about your refusal to lie down and die, which is why they've decided to deal with you themselves, up close and personal. You *don't* want that, trust me. So let's try doing this your way, to the degree that I can. What can I offer you to reconsider your position?"

Neek just starts laughing. Padmini looks incredulous and says,

"You are actually insane. You want us dead! There's no room for *negotiation* on that!"

"What if I told you that your deaths will prevent the destruction of the entire multiverse?"

Silence falls, broken only by the dying pops of Brooklyn's ruined laptop. The Woman in White beams as they all stare. "So you do care about sapient entities other than yourselves! Now, here's the thing: You understand now that when a city is born, it collapses all of the alternate versions of itself into a single truth, yes? A near-infinite number of other New Yorks, each of them containing nine million people or people-adjacent life forms, each situated within universes that collectively contain uncountable numbers of living things? Those all died a few months ago because *someone* decided his life was more important than theirs." On the flat-screen TV, she tilts her head up and to the right, to where Neek's window is. How she knows the relative placement of windows on Brooklyn's screen, Bronca cannot fathom.

Neek snorts, his upper lip curling. "Now you wanna be all talky. Back then all I knew was monsters, trying to fuck me up. *Yeah* I decided to live."

"But would you have made that decision if you'd known how many would die for your choice?" The pixelated face leans closer to the camera. "Countless versions of people you care about. Countless versions of *yourself*, all dead because of your selfishness—"

"That's a false moral dilemma," Padmini says, with a scowl. "I've been beating myself up about this for months since you brought it up, and then I realized it's bullshit. He didn't know. And even if he had, *one of those other versions of New York was about to make the same choice.* That's the nature of this, isn't it? If we'd chosen no, there was another universe out there with other versions of us, who would've chosen yes. Someone was *always* going to become New York, and the other New Yorks were always going to die. It's horrible, but that's how it works."

"Wrong," the Woman says. Some of the pixels gleam whiter; she's smiling. "My creators have existed since the beginning of everything—certainly since long before the branching-off of realities that gave rise to your little toxic city. Don't you think we would know how to manipulate the endless quanta of possibility by now? To a degree, granted; try as we might, we haven't yet managed to prevent universes like yours from coming into existence. But if you wanted, and *cooperated*, we could manage a little reset, so to speak. A do-over. The only significant difference would be that New York, and all the other living cities which currently infest this reality, would not come to life. You would get to remain ordinary human beings, living your ordinary human lives, and the other universes would survive, too. I can give you that."

She says this last line with such earnest emphasis that Bronca, in the middle of suspiciously poking the laptop with a toe, frowns at the screen. It's almost as if the Woman in White is pleading with them. But why? She is the representative of another universe so inimical that even saying her name aloud hurts the mind and mouth. She can't mean anything good by this...and yet it almost sounds as if she does.

It *has* weighed on Bronca's conscience that others have died that she and the New York she knows might live. It's the way of the world, and possibly infinite other worlds: nothing lives that does not depend at least to some degree on the death of another being. But if there's another way...

Manny catches something Bronca hasn't, however, in her existential distraction. "You said *most* of us would get to remain ordinary human beings," he says. "Which one of us dies to make that happen?"

"Oh, shit," Padmini says, her eyes widening. Of course there's a trap. Brooklyn curses and grabs her phone, muttering about downloading the Zoom app so they don't have to listen to any more of this shit.

"No one dies!" The Woman holds up square-block hands. "Come on, now, I may be a colonial hive mind built to emulate your form of life while providing a conduit for the encroachment of virulent exotic matter upon your reality, but I understand that much about you people. So, no one would have to die at all! We would just have to separate you from *the concept* of New York as a distinct and unique entity. One of you would still need to take on that embodiment." Again she somehow focuses on Neek, whose expression has gone poker-blank. "And then that one, only, would need to come and live within my borders. But I—"

"That won't be happening," Manny says, in such a glacial tone that Neek—in the middle of opening his mouth to say something similar, Bronca guesses—looks both amused and a little taken aback.

The pixels look a little taken aback, too. "I wouldn't hurt him. I've done this before, many times; I know how to be...humane about it. I could paint a version of his own reality for him to dwell within, a pocket universe if you will, wherein he could live out the rest of his life. I could even make shades of all of you, shades of all New Yorkers, to fill it. He would never again know fear or strife! And his presence within my borders would allow me to reset this entire reality, un-awakening the other cities and revamping your species in such a way that you'd never gather into cities at all. The resulting universe would be different, certainly—but it could live. Humanity could live. Will you accept this compromise?"

They all stare at her. "Fuck that," Bronca blurts, apparently before any of the others can muster the words. Brooklyn looks puzzled by her objection, and Bronca speaks as much to her as to the screen. "That's...no. No. Do you have any idea— No!"

The Woman in White fixes her with a glare. Bronca's not sure how she knows this when it's impossible to tell where her eyes are, but she can feel it. "The Bronx, contrary as usual. And what would be the problem precisely with *surviving*?"

"What you're talking about—apart from God knows what you would actually do to Neek if we were stupid enough to let you have him—is just another kind of death." Bronca can feel herself beginning to shake as she fully processes what the Woman in White is proposing. It's monstrous. "All human beings, across every culture, gather in numbers and tell stories and come up with new ways of doing things. Creativity and social living are the only real constants that every single human species has had, from *Australopithecus* to us. The only way to get rid of cities is to get rid of that part of our nature! Without that..." She shakes her head. "You'd have to change us into something other than human. No longer a social species. No longer intelligent. We'd be just mindless animals!"

"Yes? So?" The Woman tilts her head. It's not ignorance, Bronca suddenly realizes. The Woman in White understands exactly what she's asking of them, and somehow she thinks it's a good bargain. "Like I said, you'd be alive."

"But intellectually, *spiritually* dead! You'd 'save' us by making us . . . lemmings or something!"

The Woman sighs. She sounds genuinely weary. "I don't even know why I try. It's always the same response, every time." And yet she does try, taking a deep breath. "Ninety-nine percent of species on your planet and throughout the multiverse lack human-style creativity, or whatever it is that makes you spin off new universes with every stray breath. The Ur-verse lacks it entirely. And like the other 99 percent, we do just fine! You are the problem. *You* are the 1 percent."

"So tell us how *not* to do that," Manny says. His voice is neutral, and his expression reveals nothing, but he's seen that Brooklyn is trying to download the Zoom app. He's keeping the Woman distracted while that happens. "Obviously your people figured it out. Why can't we?"

"We tried to make that happen," the Woman says, shaking her head and looking genuinely sorrowful. "Many times, across many instances of this problem. We tried isolating those branches of the multiverse that began to develop cities, but then other branches started doing it, too. We took some of you in as children, raised you ourselves in hopes that you would learn our ways and take them back to your own kind, but not many survived. The few who did were . . . damaged by the experience. No good to us at all. Then we spent a few millennia manipulating your histories and myths in hopes of channeling your imaginations in safer directions, but that only caused you to start imagining us as monsters. You decided we were 'the Enemy.'" She sighs and spreads her blurred hands. "It's all just...you. What you are. Your species is the quantum equivalent of cancer—cancer that thinks and talks and fights back, and feels insulted when you call it what it is. Still deadly, though." The pixels shrug. "We're getting off topic. Will you cooperate with me, and lose only a little of yourselves, for the sake of the greater good? Please."

"Fuck you," Bronca snaps.

"Oh, *so* fuck you," Padmini agrees.

"No," says Neek.

The Woman seems to draw back. "Now, see? You're angry. And here I thought we could converse rationally."

They're all angry. Bronca can almost feel the hard pulse of blood in five other carotid arteries and hear its rush in five other sets of ears as she leans her hands on the table. Well, Bronca can't drop-kick a Zoom window out of existence, but she can sure as hell speak her mind if she's forced to listen to this kind of nonsense.

"The more I hear from you, the less alien you become," she says to the pixels. "I keep worrying I'm, I don't know, anthropomorphizing you. Seeing you through my own filters...but I can't unsee it. You're a colonizer. All the way from another fucking dimension and still just like the worst people from right here." She shakes her head. "There's probably a way we can coexist. If we worked together on it, we could come up with some compromise that's acceptable to both our peoples. You don't want compromise, tho, do you? That's how equals work out problems, but

you don't think of us as equals. Everything you've described—
segregating us, manipulating us, stealing our fucking children,
remaking us—is what people do when they are absolutely con-
vinced of their own superiority. *That's* what makes us unable to
coexist—your fucking *arrogance*."

The pixels change again. Before, they were pale flesh–colored;
suddenly they go completely colorless, and there is no longer a
humanoid shape sketched out by the flickering blocks. They can't
see her T-shirt anymore, either. The whole screen becomes just a
moving, featureless mass of white broken occasionally by slightly
off-white pixels.

And then the pixels begin to clear.

"We have seen endless ends of existence," the Woman in White
says. Her voice has changed—same voice, but tinny, stuttering in
odd places, like a corrupted audio recording. And there are multiple voices speaking now, all hers but each slightly different from
the others in pitch or pacing or where the stutters are placed, each
echoing in different ways off vast, unseen walls. The effect creates an uncanny valley of voice, proving with every reverberation
that the Woman in White has only been playing at humanity.
And amid these voices, Bronca starts to hear additional sounds—a
chitter here, a cracked growl there, low pops, an eerie minor hum.
And the screen keeps growing brighter. It's already so bright that
it hurts Bronca's eyes.

But why is she looking? *Look away*, Bronca tells herself, sluggish
instincts stirring in warning at last. She's managed to at least pull
her gaze away from the central blob, but this hasn't helped. Now
she can see into the corners of the place that the Woman in White

calls home, and at last she realizes it *has* been obscured in some way, making it look like an ordinary room when it is anything but. Her gorge rises as something about that background triggers vertigo. She can still think: *Stop looking. She wants us to look!* But she cannot muster the strength to speak these words aloud. She cannot make her own eyes move away from the screen.

The Woman in White continues. "By the time they built me, my creators had survived horrors you cannot imagine. They held the line as the last and only universe standing—not just once but again, and again, and again. And you're *insulted* by our request that you be a little less selfish? You want to be treated as equals when you've only just discovered the most basic truths of existence? How dare you!"

The screen has gotten too bright to look at comfortably. Bronca puts her hands in front of the screen, and between her fingers she can see her fellow avatars squinting or trying to cover their faces, too, but it's abruptly clear that none of them can look away. Around her fingers, she sees that the pixels have finally resolved. Whatever the Woman in White truly is, all Bronca has to do is lower her hands and she will see. She *wants* to lower her hands, suddenly. Her arms have grown so tired, even though she's only had them up for a few seconds. Wouldn't it be easier to lower them? It's just a screen. How bad could incomprehensible alien awfulness be in 4K UHD?

Should've had a construct ready, she thinks bitterly, as she feels her will beginning to crumble. She's been trawling on YouTube for "Bronx facts and unique customs" for the past few weeks, trying to find ammunition. It galls because she thought she knew her own borough, but turns out there are all sorts of weird tidbits about the Bronx that she's somehow missed over the years. Nothing useful, however. She's an artist, but visual art doesn't lend itself to instant action to the same degree as Brooklyn's words—

Wait. Words.

She's no Brooklyn, but there's another wordsmith whose skills might be useful in this moment. Not a born and bred New Yorker, but he spent a lot of time in the Bronx. Enough time? Only one way to find out.

"'O-once upon a midnight dreary,'" Bronca manages, barely able to hear herself over the Woman's ranting. It's not midnight. Ugh, she's never been into poetry because she's too damn literal, but she's got to find a way to make this work. "'While I pondered, weak and weary, over many a quaint and curious volume of forgotten lore...'" She's definitely weak and weary, and if she fucks this up she's going to die, solely because she's forgotten more of Edgar Allan Poe than she can remember.

Yet she is relieved to feel a tingle in her skin and a stir along her spine, as the city begins to respond to her desperate call. Energy gathers, raw and hot, and with it comes a blunt, immense sort of nudge. The Bronx is always weary. *Fine, fine*, she imagines her borough saying, with a kind of disgruntled sigh. *Where d'ya want it, where d'ya want it, come on, getting paid by the hour here*. Yeah, there's her asshole of a borough. She's missed it.

Buoyed by that power, she manages to shut her eyes at last. Then she visualizes the Zoom call as the terminus of a series of landlines—literal wires connecting the screen in this room, and the devices of her fellow avatars, to some kind of spectral switchboard. She knows that's not how wireless stuff works, but constructs don't have to be exact, and she's on the clock here.

"'Quoth the Raven: *"Nevermore,"*'" she says, punctuating this poetic brush-off with a mental image: a giant pair of scissors, stamped on one blade with THE BRONX in an old-timey font, chopping through all of the wires at once.

The lights go out.

It's everything, not just the TV. The overhead lights shut off. The air-conditioning unit cuts out. Brooklyn's phone is in her hand, downloading Zoom, and abruptly it buzzes, making her gaze jerk down to it. "Oh, thank God, I can look away—" Then she frowns and slaps the side of the phone as if that will somehow help. "My phone just died. Bronca? What the hell did you do?"

Whoops. Apparently Bronca has accidentally shut off *every* electrical signal, everywhere. Lucky she didn't shut down everybody's brains and heartbeats, too, but maybe it helps that she was specifically imagining manufactured things rather than natural. Also helps that she used the Bronx's power to do it—big attitude, but also lots of casual blue-collar hypercompetence. The borough knew what she meant.

Abruptly there is a loud snap from somewhere a few blocks away, maybe a transformer, and the lights come back on. The big screen lights up, and immediately Bronca flinches—but it's just the TV's startup screen, asking which HDMI connection should be made active.

"My phone is coming back on," Brooklyn says, gazing at her in such awe that Bronca takes a mental photo of it, to savor later. "At least you didn't break it. Did you actually use *poetry* to get rid of her?"

"Edgar Allan Poe lived all over the Northeast," Bronca says. "Maryland's pretty much claimed him because he died there, but he spent years in New York, specifically the Bronx—did some of his best writing here, in fact. Including 'The Raven.'" Deep breath and refocus. "Anyway. We're alive."

Brooklyn sighs and puts her hands on her hips, looking around. The room is a mess—the destroyed laptop on the floor, fire extinguisher residue everywhere, overturned tables and chairs from Bronca's efforts to keep a fire from starting. They stand amid the detritus of a supernatural battle, and it hits Bronca that the mayoral race was always going to be this at its core: the living soul of New York versus the invader city of R'lyeh. Just by democratic proxy.

"All boiled down and crystal clear," Brooklyn murmurs. Obviously thinking along Bronca's lines. And Bronca is pleased to see her take a deep breath, square her shoulders, then nod to herself. "And yeah. Now I'm good and mad. Between this and what they did to my Jojo, I'm ready to throw all kinds of hands."

Bronca claps her on the shoulder. "That's my girl. Let's get this shit cleaned up, and get back to work."

CHAPTER SEVEN

Manny Manhattan and the Terrible, Horrible, No-Good, Fuck-You Day

A month passes.

They've got time. Mayoral campaigns are slow-moving explosions, gathering force and energy until some critical mass is reached and the whole thing fusionbursts into victory—or fizzles into dust. Things are certainly busy, as Brooklyn builds momentum by doing events around the city; her schedule is packed with church visits, corner barbecues, block parties, and the like. People are getting excited about the campaign, and it's nice to see her poster headshot in the windows of bodegas, grinning from between bars of ancient soap. Neek texts them a photo he took from some derelict building or another: some other graffiti artist has been practicing drawing Brooklyn's new, Veneza-improved logo, having left at least three half-done versions on a broken wall. (Bronca critiques the artist's color matching, then says she'll visit the site later and leave a few cans of spray paint in the correct colors. Just as a suggestion.) But no other parts of the city lose "city-ness" during this month, and Neek suffers no more of those bizarre collapses, for which alone Manny is grateful. Not everything is good; Padmini starts muttering about the numbers being off. She can't narrow down the problem, though—which numbers? off in what way?—and they have other problems to concern them, so gradually the looming metaphysical threat starts to feel...less looming. They can focus on other things for a while. Breathe a little.

Padmini moves fully into the Harlem apartment, and after some initial awkwardness—it's not every day that an unromantically involved friend proposes a Green Card marriage—Manny realizes she really has hit upon the best solution to the problem of her status. The six of them are all bound together for life in one way already; why not another? Any of them will do for Padmini's purposes—except Bronca, who declares that she's been married-as-a-business-arrangement before and swore she'd never do it again once same-sex marriage became legal. Veneza shyly volunteers on the condition that she be allowed periodic "dick drops," a term that Manny resolutely does not attempt to visualize. But as Padmini rightly notes, Manny's the one with the spare cash to hire a lawyer and pay all the filing fees, so ultimately he agrees. There's a chance they won't need to go through with it. If Brooklyn wins, she means to hire Padmini permanently to work in her administration. She tells Padmini they might even be able to file for an H-1B on her behalf, on the grounds that few other data analysts would accept a crappy city salary. If that plan falls through, however, marriage is the backup.

Meanwhile, Manny quits his teaching job. He's still in the doctoral program, but he applies to have his new position with Brooklyn's campaign counted as research, and the department accepts the proposal. Then, as soon as Padmini hires a polling firm to assess Brooklyn's appeal to various parts of the city—she's got name recognition, but not enough of it, and outside of her own borough she's not polling well—Manny starts putting together a strategic plan for raising her profile in the other boroughs. That has the benefit of raising her profile nationally as well, which means more donations; always a good thing.

In between his work for the campaign, Manny continues his attempts to sway the younger living cities and basically incite a Summit. He doesn't talk to the others about it. It's not that he thinks they'll disapprove—though if they do, it's easier to ask forgiveness than seek permission. It's more that he thinks they'll want to participate, and in his judgment only Brooklyn, who's too busy, is capable of maintaining the necessary degree of diplomacy. Bronca will make threats the first time some haughty other city catches an attitude. Veneza and Neek will give attitude right back. Padmini sometimes gets overcome by shyness in social situations, Manny has noticed, but her temper is even more violent than Bronca's when it finally blows, as São Paulo once found to his detriment. So it's on Manny, and he's okay with that. He's supposed to be the one that does the city's behind-the-scenes work.

In the meantime, Manny becomes Brooklyn's campaign manager. Padmini does data analysis and advises the neighborhood organizers on where and how to target their street teams' efforts—a field director's job in other words, though at her request

Brooklyn officially hires her with the title "Manager of Quantitative Research." That makes her university more willing to approve the work, and she thinks it will give her a better chance if—when—they file for the H-1B. Then Padmini puts the word out to her school's graduate student association, as does Manny with his former undergraduate students, and quickly the campaign offices are deluged with new volunteers. Bronca, to her deep irritation, gets slapped with "Fundraising Manager" despite only haphazardly volunteering—probably because she immediately brings in a dozenish large donors who contribute the maximum and spread the word further. Veneza gets "Communications Director," to her shock, whereupon she quickly proves herself by getting ads up on all the big sites, sending a press release to the local media, and bringing in an exceptionally witty friend to be their new social media specialist.

Brooklyn puts Neek on the payroll, too, as a consultant. Just minimum wage because she's strapped, but she explains it as a financial acknowledgment of the work that Neek does to help New York. He laughs at the idea, but Manny suspects he's secretly pleased by the title, or at least the irony. He makes a big deal about needing nothing, their primary. Oh, he's more than happy to take advantage of everyone's kindness—he *is* New York—but he doesn't let himself get attached to any of it. On the one hand, it is a reassurance; if Manny's relationship with Neek ever turns toxic, he knows Neek will simply leave, possibly never to be seen again by any of them. On the other hand, they *have* no relationship as such, and no ties that would hold Neek even if they did. Manny has no idea what to do with that.

Manhattanites don't sit around waiting for the world to change on its own. So one morning, at random, Manny decides to make Neek breakfast in bed. Not to suggest anything, even though he has lain awake on more than one night, hyperaware of Neek's nearness in the next room and... wishing. He's not even sure what he's wishing for, but he knows he wants more than he's getting. Breakfast is kind of a corny gesture, sure, but he has to do something—and all his instincts warn against any sort of traditional romantic approach. No coffee dates, despite Bronca's suggestion of such. No dates at all. There's nothing traditional about either of them, or the situation. It's pointless to pretend otherwise.

And one of the things he's realized, after a few months of intensive observation (carefully disguised so as not to *seem* creepy, even if it probably qualifies as such), is that Neek needs... someone. Anyone, really. Neek has no family that matters, per his occasional offhand comments: just a dead father, a mother who disowned him for being gay, a stepfather he would as soon shoot, and some younger half-siblings with whom he has no contact. No close extended relatives, or Manny feels certain Neek would not have been left to the untender care of the streets. Manny's dug into his background—only a little, and no more than one would reasonably do with any prospective partner, and if he keeps telling himself this is normal it might eventually feel true—and found foster homes, a hospital stay for broken ribs, a stint in a halfway house for queer youth, and an arrest record for panhandling and prostitution. No jail time on that last bit, thankfully; the Manhattan DA has had a decline-to-prosecute policy on sex work for years. Mandatory counseling and done. But from all of this, Manny infers that Neek has no real allies—no one to rely on for couch surfing, a mailing address, bail, or even backup in a fight. Manny, and the other avatars of New York, probably constitute the closest thing he's had to *friends* in years.

And friends take care of friends, right? Right.

So Manny knocks on Neek's door with his elbow, and when Neek says something vaguely affirmative from within, Manny finagles his way through the door with the heavily laden tray. He has no idea what Neek likes, so there's pancakes, eggs, fruit, sausage, the works. Neek, sprawled out on the bare mattress he found somewhere and reading a library book, inhales and sits up as Manny crouches to set the tray down beside the bed. "The fuck?" he asks, but it's more wondering and amused than hostile. "It ain't my birthday."

"Just because," Manny says. He fusses a little over the tray. There's a small vase on it into which he's put one of the flowers Veneza is growing on the balcony. The vase has nearly fallen over, caught only by the glass of orange juice. He has no idea what the flower is, except that it's not a rose. Daisy, maybe. That makes this just-friends breakfast in bed rather than hopeful-suitor breakfast in bed, right? He fixes the vase and unfolds one bent petal, but his touch is too heavy; the stem breaks. Wonderful. "I've discovered that I cook when I need to think. It's a handy personality trait that I wish I'd figured out sooner."

"Motherfucker, you obviously think a *lot*."

"Yeah, well. I made enough for everybody." Important to get that in.

Neek shifts to sit cross-legged in front of the tray, watching him with amusement. "You bringing everybody else a tray, too?"

Manny feels his cheeks grow warm, but...it's pointless to pretend. "No. That part's just for you." The flower is just going to be crooked. Sighing, Manny gives up and stands, backing over to the pile of books on one side of the room so as not to loom. He's careful not to knock over any of the books. Neek won't allow Manny to buy him furniture. His room doesn't feel bare since he's completely covered the surface of one wall with abstract imagery, done in varying paints and a style that Manny can't place. He gets the impression of a river? Flowing through a crowd and between rows of tight-packed buildings? The buildings are familiar. Maybe the mural is a reference to Second Avenue, which used to be one of the rivers of the island back in its Mannahatta days. The mural is striking, less beautiful than thought-provoking; Manny suspects Bronca would salivate if she knew it existed. Apart from this, Neek has clean clothes stacked in one corner near a granny cart he's found somewhere and repaired with duct tape, and a surprisingly nice flat-screen TV that he apparently found on the street. The TV is positioned precariously on a discarded Amazon box rather than on the wall—clearly Neek has other uses for his walls—and Manny thinks that tiny device connected to it is a Roku. Is that the only thing he's spent his new income on? The books are Neek's real indulgence, because they occupy nearly the whole wall on one side of the room. There's a fifty-book max on checkouts from the New York Public Library system, and clearly Neek is pushing the limit. There are street finds stacked here, too: coverless return copies probably scrounged from the trash, discards put out for strangers to take, sidewalk-sale and used-store purchases. New York is a city awash in free books. Manny scans the titles and finds fiction, history, a whole stack of popular science texts on quantum mechanics, some poetry, more.

Neek chuckles again—and does not start eating, to Manny's great unease. Neek shifts a little, rubs the back of his head, shifts again, sighs. "Ay yo man, c'mon, let's just fuck."

It hits like a slap, to the degree that Manny winces. "You don't owe me that. Or anything. This—" He gestures at the breakfast. "It's just... friend stuff."

Neek looks skeptical. "Yeah? Where I come from, friends *fuck*."

"Sometimes, yeah, sure, but..." Manny sighs. There's nowhere to sit in Neek's room except the bed. He crouches instead, since otherwise it feels like he's standing over Neek. He doesn't want that. He doesn't want Neek feeling like Manny's lecturing or judging or otherwise assuming a position of superiority. But. "Is that what you want from me?"

He manages, just, not to say *Is that* **all** *you want from me?* But Neek blinks and sits up a little, his expression turning thoughtful. "If I said yeah, what, you strip and get in the bed?"

Pointless to pretend. "If you want."

Neek breathes a laugh. "What about you? What *you* want?"

"You."

He doesn't mean for it to sound weird. Manny knows that if he isn't careful, he can be... intense. He realizes he's screwed it up when Neek's expression turns pitying.

"You don't know me," Neek says. It's gentle, but firm. "You don't even know yourself, *Manhattan*. I don't know why the city's making you like this—"

"Does it matter?" Manny spreads his hands. "If this is coming from the city or from me? I am the city. So are you. Why does anybody fall in love with the people they do?"

"I don't believe in love. People talk that shit all the time, but it ain't real. Fucking is real." He sits back and takes a deep breath, and Manny feels the hit coming even though he doesn't know from what direction or how to brace for it. Neek says, still so gently, "*You* ain't real, Manny. I take up with you now and maybe in a week you remember some shit that blows it all up. Maybe you wifed up. Kids and shit. What then? Like, what kind of fucked-up individual would I be to do anything *but* hit it and quit it with somebody who don't even know . . . anything?"

I know I'm yours, Manny thinks through the ache—but that's meaningless. Because . . . Neek is right. Oh, not about love being an impossibility, but about Manny being little more than a construct of feelings and traits stripped of their context, repurposed for the city's use. Not a complete person with a past or an identity of his own. A tool would indeed think itself made for the hand of its user, wouldn't it? But Neek wants—deserves—a lover, not an object.

Amid his silence, Neek sighs and reaches for the tray. He drinks some of the orange juice. Then he touches the broken flower and smiles a little, like there's something charming about this pathetic thing. Something sweet about Manny's clumsiness and carelessness and utter, useless failure.

Manny gets up and leaves the room and is out of the apartment before Neek's bedroom door can swing shut again.

He heads to Brooklyn's campaign headquarters for work.

Where else is he going to go? He's got no friends, either, outside of the other New Yorks and Bel. God, what an ass he's been, to fret over Neek's deficits. And maybe it's because he's in a welter of self-hatred, but as he approaches the campaign office, he doesn't notice the multiple black SUVs with tinted windows, most of them double-parked, that line the block. Unconscionable. He is New York's protector, or he's supposed to be, and a protector should be the first to notice when things aren't what they should be. But maybe he isn't even a good protector, because he doesn't notice, until he walks into the office and finds it silent.

He snaps back to full alertness then. Padmini stands in front of her corner station, fists clenched and raw hate in her expression. Manny recognizes the head of the Queens street team, a guy from the sign shop with a box of placards in his hands, and a young volunteer sitting near the office phone. All of them are tense, staring. Brooklyn, wearing a politician's empty smile like a bulwark, has moved to the front of the tables, positioning herself between the office's guests and her staff.

And the guests? Three white men of varied middle age and heavy builds. Two wear poorly fitted suits. The third man's suit is tailored, and his hairline is decidedly custom-made, graying in a gelled gradient. Cop or mob boss? Cop, Manny decides in a split instant, though there's so little difference between the two groups in New York that he has to rely more on intuition than any real evidence. What decides him is the man's American-flag lapel pin. Mafia—even ones from long-Americanized ethnic groups—don't need nationalism as one of their weapons.

The man in the tailored suit turns as Manny enters, raking him with a glance and then smiling. "Ah, Mr. Campaign Manager," he says. Long Island accent; Manny's getting better at detecting those Tri-state area subtleties. "*You're* a really interesting guy. Got all sorts of people working for you, Ms. Thomason, don't you?" He glances at Padmini as well. "Grabbing whoever you can get, huh?"

"New York City welcomes all kinds, Mr. Milam," Brooklyn says, smoothly and still with that polite fuck-you smile. "I'll take your offer of endorsement under consideration, thanks, but as I mentioned earlier, you've come at a busy time. I'm happy to meet with you by appointment, when I can."

"Course you are." He pivots a little, as if to leave, but Manny can tell he's just trying to keep Manny in his peripheral vision. Then Milam drawls, "And, yeah, all kinds. I understand you've even got a homeless, uh, sex worker? That's the new term, isn't it?" He glances at one of his men, who grins back. Manny stiffens. "I gotta commend your coalition building. I guess there's a homeless lobby now?"

"Why not?" Brooklyn raises her immaculately shaped eyebrows. "There are something like thirty-five thousand homeless adults in this city, Mr. Milam—a small town's worth of people all in themselves. And political races in New York don't usually run on large margins, as I'm sure you know."

"How are they going to vote without an address?" He and his men laugh before Brooklyn can remind him that there's actually a way to do that. They don't care. "Well, you go ahead with that. Just, ah, let your homeless friend know that we'll be keeping an eye out for him. For his safety."

With a wink, Milam turns for the door, which Manny happens

to be standing in front of. When Manny doesn't move, Milam pauses for a moment, cocking an eyebrow. "Are we going to have a problem, sir?"

"Not at all," Manny says smoothly. He's taller, and he knows this alone will annoy Milam. Some men operate on simpler, more animalistic rules than the ones of civility. "You must be Peter Milam, head of the Police Protection Association. I just wanted to express my sympathy regarding your son. Desk duty, after so many misconduct complaints that he got no discipline for? That last incident must've been pretty bad, then. Or maybe having the PPA boss as a father can only pull strings so far, even in these try- ing times."

One of Brooklyn's younger staffers utters a quick hiss and "Ooooh, *gotem*," before another staffer shuts her up. Milam, to his credit, keeps smiling, although Manny can practically feel the hate radiating from his skin.

"World's changing," he says to Manny, with a shrug. "Sure it is. I told my son that, but he's hardheaded, you know? So we'll be throwing the NYPD rank-and-file's support behind someone who's trying to steer that change in a direction we like." He leans in. "And, uh, I guess we'll be keeping an eye on you, too. Now, can I go?"

Manny steps aside with a graceful incline of his head. Milam eyes him for a moment longer, and then he and his companions leave. Manny moves to the door again, observing through the glass while they get into one of the black SUVs. Only when the whole caravan is out of sight does he turn back to Brooklyn.

She's fuming, but of course that doesn't show in any human

way. She's got a handle on things metaphysically, too; Manny catches only a quick flicker of snarling downtown Brooklyn gargoyles before she takes a deep breath, and the vision fades. She heads into her office and he follows, Padmini moving to join them and closing the office door.

"Thank you for getting him out of my face," Brooklyn says to Manny, moving behind her desk and sitting down, with carefully contained smoothness. "I was never going to accept that son of a bitch's endorsement even if he'd offered it, but I can't just *say* that."

"I don't see why not," Padmini says, scowling. "Nasty, smarmy man. But how did you know about his son, Manny? Does he live in Manhattan?"

"Research," Manny says, taking one of the plush chairs across from Brooklyn. He steeples his fingers, because that's the only way he can think to avoid showing just how incandescently angry he is. They have threatened his Neek. They have *dared* to threaten New York. "I think the son works in Queens, actually. But I started looking into key players with the PPA because they're an obstacle any mayor has to overcome."

Brooklyn smiles bitterly. "I'm a Democrat, a Black woman, and one of my campaign pledges is to rein in police brutality and overtime abuse. I'm surprised Milam even bothered to come visit. Probably just wanted to give me a chance to bribe him."

Manny takes a deep breath and makes himself say, "That's . . . a way to handle it."

He's expecting both of them to glare, but it still bothers him when they do. He always acknowledges the elephant in the room because it *is* an option that would help the campaign, whether they like it or not, and everything he does is in service to New York. Doesn't mean he's actually endorsing bribery. Don't they understand at least this about him, by now?

(No. They don't know him, because he's not real.)

"I know I didn't just hear you say—" Padmini begins, hotly.

Brooklyn holds up a quelling hand, although her jaw is visibly tight. "He's right. The NYPD is either an uncontrolled-but-at-least-not-hostile nuisance for any mayor who pays them off with perks and propaganda, or an occupying army for a mayor who doesn't. I'm not going to be doing anything they like, politically speaking, so bribery is pretty much my only recourse for a chance at the 'good' option." She sighs. "But right now, I've barely got enough funding to field a campaign. No spare cash to grease palms."

Every instinct within Manny warns that this is an untenable situation. Other constituencies within the city might be won over with promises of mutual benefit, but the NYPD must be forced into submission like the rabid beast that it is. Only power or money can do that.

Padmini looks from Brooklyn to Manny with growing incredulity. "You can't give them what they want. They'll be able to blackmail you the instant you offer them anything. And then they'll just terrorize more people and steal more public money! My God—" She laughs a little, wearily and humorlessly. "I just realized. When ICE came to threaten my family, they pretended to be the NYPD. Even ICE doesn't have the kind of power they do!"

Manny shifts his fingers from steepled to folded, and watches his own knuckles slowly turn white. *Warn your homeless friend that we'll be watching him.* They don't know that Neek is housed now;

on Manny's advice, he uses a PO Box for any paperwork that will leave a public record. But if not for that . . .

Manny gets up and walks out. Behind him, Padmini blurts a startled, "Manny?" He cannot bring himself to respond. (That's not his name.) He leaves the campaign office and starts walking briskly up the street. Nostrand again; after the caravan attack, Brooklyn means to promote the avenue as an economic power-house of the city. That's what New York does when threatened, yes? It doubles down. It knuckles up. It steps up to any challenger and gives back as good as it gets. And it always wins, in the end, because it is New York.

But Manny is . . .

Too angry. *Shaking* with it. Veering off Nostrand, he heads down a random cross street, his pace quickening. This street is much quieter, residential, and the number of derelict storefronts and abandoned construction sites reflects the darkest side of gen-trification: sometimes the run down/push out/build up cycle stalls midway. Then, after police and city policies and unscrupu-lous developers have successfully ruined a thriving-but-poor area, no one new comes in. The displaced residents have no way to return. The developers divide the spoils and tax breaks, and the few remaining residents are left to struggle on in a neighborhood as blighted and ugly as any corpse-strewn battlefield.

It's the middle of the day and there's no one in view. There's a wooden fence here, half broken and covered in expired construc-tion notices. On a sudden impulse Manny vaults it. Inside the fence is a half-dug foundation hole, collapsed and full of water on one side. Someone's been illegally dumping trash over the fence, to judge by the pile of disintegrating trash bags in one corner of the site, and there's even a stripped-down car lying half in the hole. Yes. This is what he needs.

Manny does not curse. At first, as he got to know himself in the aftermath of becoming New York, he thought this was simply his nature—but it doesn't make sense that the living embodiment of the most obnoxious part of New York would be so clean-spoken. So, as with his experiments in macrostepping, he's tried on some New Yorkish language just to see what happens. Now he knows.

He focuses on the car. *"Fuck you,"* he snarls through his teeth.

The car explodes.

There's not much of it to explode. It's already missing an engine, all of its doors and tires, and an axle. What's left, however, flies apart as violently as if someone set off a bomb within it. The ground shakes; a couple of Tyvek-covered brick stacks nearby get reduced to rubble; the remaining side of the foundation hole collapses. The ground splits, leaving a crack running across the whole construction site that's a foot wide and six feet deep at its nadir. Manny's got enough control of the power that he keeps any shrapnel from leaving the fenced area, and of course none of it hits him. The city protects its own. But he can hear people in the nearby brownstones crying out in surprise, and every car alarm in a three-block radius immediately starts to *wheeooo* or *dweet-dweet-dweet* or *baaaaaag* in protest.

Manny exhales in relief. Much better. Now he can think.

He hops the fence again and resumes walking down the block at a steady, calm pace. People are already opening their doors and peering down the street in alarm, but for once they don't notice him. Maybe that's the city's doing, or maybe they're just expecting someone who looks like whatever they think car bombers look like. When he's halfway down the block and the alarms have begun to quiet, Manny takes out his phone, not looking as he thumbs through its pass-pattern. Most of his recent text conversations are with the other avatars or Bel. A few are with his fellow students, professors, or other acquaintances from the university. When he stops at the corner of Bedford, however, he looks down, and there just happens to be one name at the top of the screen:

"MOM"

He taps this. The most recent text is from a month ago. *I assume there's a reason for your silence,* it says. *Contact me when you're able.*

His mind is quiet, his thoughts clear. His thumb moves to start a new message.

Hi. I'd like to speak with you. In person.

He waits. He . . . remembers. She's usually very prompt.

A moment later, the app pings a new message, and it appears.

Of course. Tomorrow morning, 9 am, restaurant. Following this, a location link. Washington, DC—not home, but neutral territory.

Manny, who suddenly isn't sure he still is or wants to be Manhattan, sends a quick *OK* and tucks the phone into his pocket. Then he hails a green cab that happens to be passing by. Unfamiliar driver. No magic to it, this time. Maybe the city knows what he's up to, and it won't impede him, but it's not going to help. He can't really blame it for that, can he? New York knows what it deserves. So does he.

The apartment first, for an overnight bag. Then: Penn Station. Back to where it all began.

INTERRUPTION

Elsewhere

Underemployment sucks.

Technically, in Padmini's case, it isn't underemployment. Her work with Brooklyn's campaign is limited to twenty-four hours per week because Brooklyn is scrupulous about the rules for a full-time student. Padmini's a *good* full-time student, on track to finish as some variant of cum laude, so she's probably putting in thirty or thirty-five hours per week on school alone.

The thing is, she's used to working a lot more. Full nights of sleep were nice at first, but at this point the novelty has worn off—especially since she doesn't even need to sleep. Instead she finds herself lying awake for hours, processing a deep disquiet within herself that seems to be growing.

And after a few nights of this, Padmini . . . goes wandering.

She's always loved travel, see. Flying halfway around the world to start a new life at the age of sixteen took all the fear out of the process, so she's pretty sure she would be an adventurous traveler—if circumstances allowed. Being on a student visa means every border crossing is a chance for some Customs official to arbitrarily deny her reentry, whether for an imagined error in her paperwork or just because they don't like the way she looks. Fortunately, the US is huge enough that travel across its disparate regions should be just as exciting as visiting another country . . . but unless she's going to another big city, she'll need a car. Which she'd have to learn to drive, first.

As a result, Padmini's had a couple dozen travel plans on hold for years, waiting for the perfect confluence of free time, money, and legal leeway. Now here she is, a living city, possessed of the magical ability to teleport across time, space, and reality. Gosh. Whatever should she do?

She starts small, only tweaking variables of the relevant equations a little, at first. It rapidly becomes clear that the equations she uses for local travel—more precise than hitching metaphysical rides on public transportation, though none of the others seem to be able to do it this way—are insufficient when it comes to more distant macrosteps. This makes perfect sense given that the field of physics hasn't yet figured out that whole "thought changes reality" business, but it's still frustrating. There seems to be a kind of gravitational lensing effect that takes place anytime she goes too far from New York: the farther she steps, the more energy it takes, and the more spacetime distorts. This makes her "landing" point unpredictable. She manages to make it to Chennai at one point, but doing so wears her out, and after she's finished creepily peeking in on her parents and brother—can't say hi or they'd freak out—and stepping back home, she falls asleep for ten hours.

(Some of that is the crying. Her parents look so old! The

FaceTime filters have been hiding that from her. Her brother, five years younger, is a man grown. Padmini's seen his adult face, but it's a different thing altogether to see him so tall and lanky and strong, laughing as he helps their parents move furniture. She remembers a tiny grinning jokester covered in mud and missing a tooth.)

(She does not go back to Chennai again.)

Through trial and error, Padmini begins to develop her own sense of the laws that govern existence. Staying in New York eliminates the unpredictability altogether; she always hits her target as long as it's within the geographic confines of the city, even when she steps into variants of the city that are utterly alien—and most of those are. All the similar, recognizable versions of New York got bundled into the city's rebirth and effectively erased from existence. What's left are the contradictory New Yorks, like those that stand empty because a super-plague or a neutron bomb took out the population. She freaks out a little upon return from those, until Bronca reassures her that city avatars can't transmit diseases or radiation. After a final very bad scare—a version of New York devoid of *air* because the entire city has somehow been chunked off from the planet and blasted into space, and yes it was only for three seconds but it was still awful—Padmini decides that maybe random macrostepping isn't the best way to get the travel experience she craves.

Instead, she tries meditation, clearing her thoughts except for those that will guide her travels. Doing this is still dangerous. Wanting to go "someplace quiet" is what landed her on Asteroid New York. But the meditation seems to help, especially once she adds a little yoga to it, since she's not walking as much as she used to and needs the exercise. In the middle of Downward Dog she can concentrate on her own breathing and calm mood, and then tell the multiverse that *she wants to be somewhere that makes her feel like this*. Positioning datapoints flow through her mind—a kind of multiversal GPS. It works, and when she straightens from Child's Pose she is . . . elsewhere.

The first time she does this, Padmini finds herself sitting on a tiny island in the middle of a vast, remarkably calm ocean—a classic desert island. That ends up being surprisingly boring, and she steps back home feeling disappointed at the wasted time. Better is the time when she appears in some kind of pavilion, on top of a steep mountain. The pavilion is nothing special, just corrugated steel held up by undecorated timbers, but the view—of nothing but forest and mountains for miles around—is stunning.

She has no idea where these places are, truth be told. None of them are inimical, but they also don't feel familiar, and to judge by the coordinates they definitely aren't in realities anywhere near her own. They're just quiet Elsewheres, context-free and comforting. After the past few years of fear and overwork and bone-deep stress, this turns out to be exactly the kind of travel Padmini needs.

Her all-time favorite of the Elsewheres is the most mysterious of them. Initially she suspects it's another empty version of New York. The place is very obviously a massive city, and while its architecture is like nothing she's ever seen, that doesn't necessarily mean she's wrong. Maybe this is a version of New York that got built by a Mesoamerican culture? Something about the decorative motifs on all the stonework makes her think this, although it also looks Greco-Roman with a side of Dravidian, and there are pigeon towers that make her think of North African cities.

Gradually, however, it becomes clear that this isn't any flavor of New York. Walking too far in any direction brings her to water, so it's an island, but a roughly round-shaped one rather than the long splinter that is Manhattan. Also, there's something really *wrong* about the place. First, it's empty. No people, no clothing or dis- cards of people, no sign that the place was ever inhabited, apart from the fact that it exists. It's always the same time of day when she arrives, a pleasantly bright midday, and it stays that way even when she lingers for hours. No evening. No night. Also, the plants in the parks don't grow or bloom. The grass is a little high when she first starts visiting the mystery city, but it doesn't get higher or go to seed as the weeks pass. In one of the city's numerous small parks, Padmini notices a particular freesia bud that looks poised to bloom, and she starts watching it because it's huge and will prob- ably be gorgeous when it finally opens . . . but it does not open. She can see mountains rising from the ocean on one side of the island, a few miles off and reachable if she was an Olympic marathon swimmer—but on the other side, *there's no horizon*. That is, she can see the ocean stretching into the distance, and she can see the blue, cloudless sky, but she cannot see where they meet. It's just a steady gradient of color, unbroken by any line.

It makes sense when one considers the imagination-sensitive nature of the multiverse. Maybe this artful, unreal city is from a book that Padmini's never read, or a video game—imagined in enough detail to come into being, but not enough to be complete.

It should unnerve her ... but any unease Padmini feels gradually gets wiped out by how *comfortable* the place is. And even imaginary cities need tourists. Don't they?

So the nameless city becomes a regular stop among Padmini's inter-universal travels. She walks its colonnaded avenues and its obelisk-dotted shoreline, thinking of nothing, more at peace than she's ever been. There are pathway mazes in parts of the city, polished petrified wood set into the plainer stone, and she giggles and cheats when they turn out to be stunningly complex. There are strange partially enclosed courtyards amid some clusters of residential-looking buildings, whose purpose she can't fathom for a while—until she trips while crossing one and notices the acoustics of her stumble. She tries drumming on her thighs then, and discovers that getting a good rhythm going makes the buildings amplify it and resonate with syncopated echoes. The courtyard is a *drum circle*, incorporated into neighborhood design rather than pushed into a park or empty lot the way it would be in New York, and treated not as a nuisance but as part of the city's beauty. Some of the larger drum circles are arranged in such a way that the sounds from one get picked up by any others nearby, forming a network that sends their echoes throughout the whole city. With many feet moving in rhythm, or several musicians, the effect would be incredible. A whole city built for music and dance.

She could live here, Padmini thinks now and again, with the same conviction that she felt on her first day in New York, all those years ago. If this were a real city, with people in it ... well. She likes being Queens. But maybe she would like being this place just as much.

Then one afternoon while she's walking up a hill, a man in a neat business suit steps out from behind one of the buildings.

Padmini screams. Loudly. There's one of the large drum circles nearby, so syncopated echoes of her scream dart away down nearby streets, resounding throughout the city. The man—oh, it's Paulo—winces. "If you please," he says.

Padmini winces, too, but only because the echoes are especially shrill; otherwise she feels like the scream was justified. "What the hell are you *doing* here?"

"Looking for you," Paulo says. "The other cities have noticed your travels, and they asked me to track you down."

"They don't give a damn whether the Woman in White eats us alive, but they have a problem with me poking around some empty city?"

"*This* empty city, yes." Paulo inclines his head, whether in agreement with Padmini's outrage or just as some kind of weird genteel gesture. She's never liked him, though she's prepared to acknowledge this as irrational on her part. Paulo is the one who first introduced them to the joys—and horrors—of being a living city, and Padmini can't help hating the messenger. Paulo's sigh lets her know he doesn't really want to be here talking to her, either. "Since I'm New York's designated mentor, they sent me to deal with you."

Padmini narrows her eyes and puts her hands on her hips. "*Deal* with me? What, as in make me leave? If this place is off-limits—"

"No, no, it's nothing like that." Paulo looks around, gazing down the hill toward the harbor, and Padmini is amused to see him visibly relax. There's just something inherently soothing about this place. "It's only that this was a living city, once. Some of the elders knew it back in its day, and that makes them... protective."

A former living city, with its own avatar and everything? For it to be empty now... Padmini's skin prickles with goose bumps. "Did the Enemy kill it during a birthing-battle?"

"No. This one survived its birth, and even did quite a bit of damage to the Enemy, just as New York did. But then the Enemy retaliated in a way that was not understood for many years. If they had simply *talked* about it and perhaps realized sooner..." He sighs with substantial bitterness, and Padmini remembers that Paulo has had more firsthand experience with the other cities' change-resistance than anyone of New York. "Well. What happened is clearer now that we understand the Enemy's nature. Hong has a theory that *she* launched simultaneous campaigns across multiple realities to change how people thought about this city. Over decades and centuries, by altering written texts and tales and songs, she caused the city to move from its natural place on the multiversal tree. It was gradual, at first. No one noticed until it was too late, and by then people had just... forgotten that the city existed. Many forgot even its name." He sighs. "Honestly, I don't know that talking would have helped much. Hong is sensitive to information warfare these days, for understandable reasons. But in those days, such tactics were uncommon."

Padmini inhales, her thoughts racing. "So the opinions of outsiders *can* harm a city." Like what's happening to New York because of Panfilo's mayoral campaign. And there's something in what he just said that has started to tickle the back of Padmini's mind, a distracting irritant rapidly growing toward epiphany. There's a part of this that she needs to understand. Something *important*. She tries to simultaneously focus on it and Paulo as he continues.

"What happened to this city couldn't work today," Paulo says. "It was lost in antiquity, before global communication or photographic imagery—when legends depended on storytellers and musicians, and the occasional chroniclers who bothered to write those tales down. Now? No one could forget New York."

Paulo probably means to sound reassuring when he says this, but it doesn't work—not because he fails at reassurance, but because Padmini's not sure he's right. For one thing, photos and written accounts aren't as reality-affirming as they should be anymore, in this age of disinformation. For another, it's clear now that R'lyeh and her creators, the Ur, are more savvy at multiversal manipulation than anyone in Padmini's reality could ever hope to be. The Enemy doesn't have to erase New York, only make the world forget what New York *is*. New York cannot remain New York if it loses its art, its diversity, its welcome of outsiders, its daring. That means—

While Padmini trembles on the brink of revelation, Paulo sighs into the silence. "In any case," he says, "you should continue to visit this city as often as you like. More, if you can bring yourself to do so."

Wait. "Uh. I thought they sent you to kick me out."

"Yes, they did."

Padmini has grown up speaking English among other languages, but English is a Frankenstein language, and sometimes the ways even other Anglophones use it can be really confusing. "Sssso you're supposed to kick me out, but you just encouraged me to *increase* my visits, because...?"

Paulo smiles, and for the first time Padmini registers the similarities between him and Manny. They're both incredibly stylish and handsome men on the surface, but with a Machiavellian core that's harder to see...until they smile like this. Then she's just glad they're—probably—on her side.

"You wanted the Summit to meet, yes?" That smile grows. "The next step, if the elders decide I'm too incompetent to rein in you upstart New Yorks, would be to convene a full quorum of the Summit in order to determine disciplinary measures."

Padmini inhales, delighted as she understands. "Oh, you're *mean*."

"Thank you. Then, bom dia." With an ironic temple-tap salute, he vanishes.

In the renewed silence, Padmini looks around the empty city that she's grown to love. She gets why, now: it's because there's still a spark of personality here, left over from its better days— or maybe that's just the indestructible core of any city, which lingers after its death. Maybe she likes it here because this is a city she would've gotten along with well, if its avatar had not been lost. The ghost of best friends never met. She wonders if it hurt, when—

Wait.

Wait.

Paulo said *she caused the city to move from its place on the tree.*

Padmini steps back into that bizarre place where she can behold the entirety of the multiverse. The tree churns before her, a fractal shape with a billion branches, each tipped with a quintillion universes, all of them growing and glowing as they spit forth endless new existences. Magic broccoli. And here and there among the boiling clusters of worlds, there are singular points of brighter light: cities, dangling like fruit amid the endless branches. She lets instinct guide her to the blazing mote that is New York, but rather than returning to it, she stops just outside it and lets the other part of her perception unspool—the part that is the Math Queen. There are no equations for the math of the multiverse, other than the tentative ones she has begun to develop from looking at patterns in the raw coordinates, but...

The coordinates are different.

Maybe she's just remembered them wrong? No; numbers aside, the star that is New York usually floats near a distinctive three-pronged fork in the branchings. The tree's crown changes constantly, but the branches tend not to— And when she spots the familiar fork, it's almost out of sight above her, obscured by a cluster of worlds where for some reason Guy Fieri became the US president in 2016. New York now floats near a crooked lower branch, close to a knot of worlds on the brink of World War Three.

Padmini reflexively macrosteps back, landing in her room so hard that she stumbles, but that's partly because she's already trying to reach her desk. With shaking hands, she grabs a sheet of graphing paper; when she wants to be sure about a thing, she likes the comfort of handwritten calculations. There are some variables that she knows she should include, like the impact of people's beliefs and whether the different levels of the tree exist under different conditions from the ones she's familiar with, but until somebody—well, she—figures out how to encode all this madness in some quantifiable way, all she can do is start mapping the city's coordinates relative to their origin point...

There's a curve to the graph.

The city is moving, and the movement is accelerating with time. The city is *falling*, toward the tree's trunk and the unbearable brightness of its roots.

All the peace that Padmini felt in the dead city is gone. Quickly she fumbles for her phone to text the others. She can't manage it—sweaty fingers skate over the virtual keys at first—so finally she has to just toggle voice recognition and speak the words aloud.

"Hey. Guys? Uh, we're all going to die. Thought you should know."

CHAPTER EIGHT

The Sixth Boroughs

In spite of everything, Veneza's not expecting to find so much of New York in Hoboken.

Like, she *should* expect it. She's Jersey City, another suburb located so geographically and culturally close to New York as to make the lines of state jurisdiction metaphysically meaningless. Hoboken is even closer, right across the Hudson from the west side of Manhattan, only a mile or so as the crow flies—but Veneza's still pretty sure Jersey City has more New York in its most rat-infested bush than Hoboken's entire "downtown," laughable as that word is in context. There's just something about Hoboken that clings to its quintessential Jersey-ness more firmly than Jersey City does. For every artist, hustle-obsessed small-business person, and even tourist New York has, Hoboken's got a dude-bro. Or maybe a techbro commuting to work at Google, or a Wall Street finance bro who chooses rental price over the prestige of living in Manhattan. Hoboken isn't all "bro culture," of course; plenty of Hobokeners are non-bros of whatever stripe, from artists and middle-class families priced out of New York to blue-collar workers and retirees. Personally, Veneza feels like the difference between JC and Hoboken is perspective. Jersey City is slightly farther south, with a view of lower Manhattan that is tempered by the grim industrial edges of Brooklyn and Queens just beyond. Hoboken gets to ogle multimillion-dollar condos and experimental-architecture parks and flashes of Times Square. Jersey Cityites might dream of New York success, but they also see its costs. Hobokeners see the same fantastical version of New York as the tourists, but for them it seems in easy reach.

(Okay. Maybe she's being *a little* unfair. But hey, she's Jersey City. It's like her job to hate on Hoboken.)

Veneza's in Hoboken on business, trying to find a better monitor for her at-home setup given that she's going to be doing more design work for Brooklyn's campaign. Hoboken's got good tech shops, and she prefers supporting small local businesses over ordering online or going to the big-box stores. Anyway. It's weird, sensing the city without being in the city. Kind of like sitting five feet away from a swamp cooler on a hot day: you feel something approximating a breeze and maybe it's even cool, but mostly you just end up frustrated and sticky. Being within the living boroughs of New York is more like having really good central air.

But right now, here in Hoboken? She's getting swamp cooler with occasional drafts of solid New York chill.

And she's felt such stirrings before—in Jersey City, during the days before she became an avatar. Back then, she thought nothing of it. Shroom flashbacks. Who knew the occasional yearning for Knicks tickets and Manhattanhenge was a warning of impending apotheosis? Here it is again, though: a subway performer yelling "Showtime!" at the edge of hearing, a waft of the cloyingly sweet scent of a Nuts4Nuts cart, a soupçon of Papaya King on the tongue. When Veneza crosses an avenue that leads toward the harbor, she glances up at the New York skyline and has a fleeting vision of the Twin Towers' fall. Hoboken had a front-row seat for that, didn't it? Some experiences, even indirect, are significant enough to change a city. In Hoboken, it seems to have been the trigger for a gradual buildup of New York–adjacent energy, which is now reaching critical mass.

Wild. But Veneza resists the urge to start looking around for the person or persons who will become their fellow avatar. For one thing, she's got stuff to do. For another, she knows not to linger here outside the city, where she is more vulnerable. She's carrying a set of cracked plastic "brass" knuckles that she found at Goodwill, and a Statue of Liberty souvenir keychain, both of which should be useful as constructs. Jersey City is big in the found-object art scene, and Liberty Island is actually part of JC even though NYC holds official jurisdiction over it for tourism purposes. For a third thing, Padmini has just explained to all of them that New York is currently falling through the multiverse at an accelerating rate toward an unknown but probably really shitty fate. What if Veneza greeting this new proto-avatar somehow speeds up Hoboken's maturation, causing it to pop a consciousness just in time to go blooey?

So she keeps her head down and her thoughts focused on graphics cards. The whole time that she rides the PATH back to Manhattan, however, she ponders What It All Means.

At first she thinks nobody's home when she gets back to the penthouse, which makes sense; it's the middle of a weekday. Manny and Padmini are at Brooklyn's campaign office, and Bel is up at Columbia. Then Veneza spots Neek out on the balcony, so she heads outside, too. "Nu-nunu-nunu-nuuuuuuu yaaaaaaawk!"

"JC in the house," he replies, straightening to exchange a casual dap-and-hug with her before they both lean on the stone railing. It's a nice autumn day in the city, warm but with a dry breeze that hints at the coming cold. The air has that perfect crystal clarity that lets you see for miles, which Veneza has never seen at any other time of year. She spends a silent while taking in the autumn color of the trees and the traffic sounds and the tiny distant human dramas unfolding on every corner and in every window. Any New Yorker can feel like a god whether they're an avatar or not, Veneza figures. They just need a rooftop and time.

"Ay, yo, let me run something past you." When Neek grunts, she tells him about Hoboken. "So, what do you think?"

Neek has rested his chin on his folded arms to listen. "'Bout what?"

"Am I talking to myself? What if Hoboken goes live, and suddenly there's seven of us? Jesus, what if it keeps going? Yonkers? Newark? _Long Island_, God help us all, I don't think I could fucking take that."

He shrugs. "If something's meant to be New York, it's gonna be New York whether we want it or not. I wasn't even conscious when you jumped up. Me thinking about it one way or another don't make no difference."

Veneza shakes her head, thrown by his nonchalance. "Yeah,

but if New York starts changing while we're in the middle of fighting off Panfilo and *her*..." She gestures awkwardly.

"New York *is* change. Hundred years ago this city was so different from now, you probably wouldn't recognize it. A third smaller, full of farms and shit. *Zeppelins* and shit. Avatar probably would've been a European immigrant, maybe a ex-slave, maybe a flapper..." He chuckles, then shrugs. "I been trying to figure out why New York didn't wake up sooner, and that's my guess: because this city changes too fucking fast. Every time it tried to wake up before, it changed and then had to go back to sleep. Right now is like the first time New York's had basically the same culture for more than three decades in a row. And even then, when the six of us finally got our shit together, we lost Staten." He shakes his head. "Still pissed about that."

"What, really?"

"Yeah, why not? Staten Island's always been New York. Even if it thinks it wants to be Jersey—" He breathes out a little humorless laugh. "Shit, Jersey don't want them motherfuckers. People outside New York always tell us to leave the city, move somewhere cheaper, cleaner. New Yorkers actually show up in their little towns, tho, and do anything but spend money and stay out of sight? They be the first ones loading up the shotguns and chasin' us back where we came from."

Veneza chews on this, and ponders the avatar of the newly independent Staten Island. Veneza wasn't conscious when they met, seeing as she'd been taken hostage by a monstrous snack cake from Dimension X. Bronca described her as a little older than Veneza but somehow radiating immaturity and fear underneath her entitled rage. Even without meeting her, Veneza's familiar with the type—young Beckies in training to become mature Karens. Playground tattletales crying to the teacher when Veneza wouldn't let them manhandle her kinky mixed-girl hair. A roommate in college who would spray half a can of air freshener every time Veneza came home. When Veneza finally complained, the girl started shrieking that Veneza was attacking her, intimidating her, a threat. She moved out the next day, and Veneza had to pay extra for a single for the rest of the semester.

Neek wants somebody like *that* back? No, it's not that personal. Neek just gets that Staten Island's twitchy xenophobia is New York, too. Like it or not.

"Early polling says SI is going for Panfilo," she says. "I mean, they usually go Republican, but he has 'support Staten Island secession' as an actual platform item."

"Eh, they always say they want out. Good they found somebody who gives a shit."

Veneza draws back a little. "Uh, it sounds like you're cool with that. With Panfilo winning."

"If it's gon' happen, it's gon' happen. Me thinking one way or another . . ." Another shrug.

Veneza turns a full stare on him. His attitude is incomprehensible to her—but maybe it's why Neek has chosen not to assist them with the project of making Brooklyn mayor. Is this fatalism? Depression? Or is she reading negativity into what is actually neutrality? Maybe it's just what he says: New York is change. Maybe the city made him its first and foremost avatar, the one who could stand on his own for however brief a time, because of his ability to accept this truth.

But the city picked Veneza, too, and *she* doesn't plan to just sit around and let deluded bigots ruin her city. With a low frustrated sound, she leaves Neek and heads inside.

There's an idea in her head. She doesn't let herself think about it much, because that's how her best ideas work. Better just to let the creativity flow; trying to steer the energy in specific directions only clots everything up. Sitting down in front of her desktop, Veneza starts working, even though she hasn't had a chance to install the new graphics card yet. What she's thinking about is simple. She buys a few stock images, sifts through photos she's shot with her own camera that don't show faces, plays around with references and fonts and a central theme. By the time she's done, it's dark outside and her back hurts—but as she sits back and stretches, she feels amazing. She's done real, meaningful work, for the city and for herself. God*damn* she's good.

And although she figures she should probably show this to Bronca for critique, or to Brooklyn so she can get campaign funds for strategic ad buys...Veneza clicks "send" anyway, from her personal accounts on Insta and Twitter and everywhere else. Some things, even if they're about the campaign, aren't *just* about the campaign.

Afterward, she makes herself some dinner. Homemade fried potatoes and Italian hot dogs—a North Jersey staple, complete with pizza bread that she picked up after getting the graphics card. She hits the hay and sleeps like a baby and in the morning stumbles through her usual waking-up routine, which involves massive amounts of coffee and a plea for everyone in the vicinity to use short, simple phrases until her brain wakes up fully.

Then Bel, who is generally amused by Veneza's morning

incoherence, manages to get through to her that he's worried because Manny didn't come home the night before. Which is... huh. Manny's hot as fuck, Veneza would totally hit that if she was into contract killers or whatever, but he's not much given to breakfast in other beds—especially given that he's going long for Neek. It's definitely worry-worthy... as is the fact that, for some reason, Veneza can't "feel" him when she tries to reach out with her freaky magic city senses. He's not dead, because there's not a smoking crater where Manhattan used to be, and he's not temporarily de-avatared like what happened to Padmini that one time. Veneza's not having any trouble remembering that the island of Manhattan exists. Manny, however, is gone.

Neek's at the breakfast bar that morning, munching through kiddie cereal the way he always does. But when Veneza and Padmini ask what they should do about the missing Manny, Neek... says nothing, gets up, and goes into his room, closing the door firmly behind him. Okay. Wow. There are layers of meaning in his reaction, same as in Manny's disappearance, but damn if Veneza can peel off even the topmost of them.

Welp. Nothing to do except wait and see if Manny turns up again.

Veneza's got a different mission for the day. She's off on Thursdays; the Bronx Art Center upped her pay and gave her benefits when they made her full time, but she still asked for a four-day ten-hour schedule because artists don't do no nine-to-five. (Well, they do, until they get a sweet job that lets them have flextime.) And on this bright sunny Thursday, flush with creative purpose and anxiety about her city, Veneza has decided to do what Neek and none of the others seem willing to try.

She DMed Aislyn, the avatar of Staten Island, see, the night before.

It wasn't hard to track her contact info down. They were never formally introduced during that frightening night a few months back, but somehow all the New York avatars know Aislyn's name—probably the same way they knew how to find each other, back before any of them understood city magic. Aislyn's Instagram account has only twenty posts and three followers. Most of the photos have zero likes. The photos are mostly places on the island that she obviously loves: an empty beach, a field of pampas grass, a row of stately side-by-side duplex homes on a pretty tree-lined street. Only one of the shots contains Aislyn herself, and that's with some other folks at what looks like a library branch. The others are all mugging for the camera, and Aislyn stands shyly to one side of this, barely managing a smile. With a digital artist's eye, Veneza can tell that this lone image of Aislyn has been subjected to several popular filters, to make her body look slimmer and her hair brighter. Ole girl doesn't much like the way she looks, huh.

Irony: There are at least a half dozen photos of New York. Mostly Manhattan, but one of Brooklyn and another of, well, well, Jersey City's harbor. When Veneza saw that, she had to reach out.

So now she takes the 1 train downtown to catch the 11:30 Staten Island Ferry. The ride over is boring. She leans on the railing and stares at churning water and listens while tourists ooh and ahh over the (Jersey City) Statue of Liberty. Eventually she sits down beside a young Black guy in a UPS uniform who's using the ride to catch some z's. He slumps toward her at one point, and she decides she'll let him use her shoulder if he gets that far, but instead he just sort of puddles down, snoring into his chest. He's an actual Staten Islander, she guesses from his nonchalance. No tendrils, and it doesn't look like he's been . . . compromised . . . by whatever R'lyeh is doing to the island. He's just a working dude who needs more sleep.

On the St. George side, UPS Guy wakes up and shuffles off, hopefully to home and bed. Veneza gets off the ferry but doesn't move far from the onboarding doors. Neek said the ferry stations were safe territory, but Veneza figures it can't hurt to be extra careful. Also, she thinks it's best to keep everything slow and non-aggressive, re Aislyn. Let her check out Veneza from afar, if she wants. Let the little traitor feel like she's in control.

When they let people back on the ferry, she's got her pick of seats. There's only a trickle of people getting on from this side, rather than the bigger groups that Veneza saw in Manhattan. Middle of a weekday; mostly tourists either way. Veneza's gotten tired of searching people's faces and has started daydreaming, when someone sits down on the wooden bench across from her.

It's Aislyn—and she looks terrible. Sweaty, shaking, pale as a movie vampire, hands twitching on the worn leather purse in her lap. She looks like she's going to pass out.

"Uh," Veneza says. Aislyn's gaze jerks to her. "You okay?"

"Fine," Aislyn replies, too quickly and sharply. Silence falls, while Veneza tries to tell herself not to take offense. Then Aislyn's shoulders drop a little. "I've just. Never been on the ferry. Before."

"Nev—" Veneza bites the words off and blanks the incredulity from her face. Easy now. Got to speak slowly and without judgment, like to a child, or a nervous racist that you have to work with. "Ohhhhkay. Uh, welcome to the ferry. Congrats on your first time."

Skittish Racist Voice works; Aislyn starts to look slightly less ready to jump off the boat. "Thank you." She breathes a not-very-amused laugh that sounds deeply tired to Veneza's ear. "Wish I could tell my mom about this. But she . . . can't hear me anymore."

Whoa, there was nothing about a death in the family on her Instagram. "Oh, shit. Sorry for your loss."

Aislyn stares at Veneza for a moment. Then she lowers her gaze again. ". . . Thank you."

Silence falls. Veneza decides to let it spool out as she contemplates the Staten Island coastline. This part of the island is as built-up as any busy neighborhood in the other boroughs. The rest of the island isn't like this, though, she remembers from long-ago drives through it with her mom, usually on the way to Philly to meet her dad. She remembers being shocked by forests, vast green fields, farms. In *New York*.

"I'm, um, glad to see you're all right," Aislyn says suddenly.

Veneza frowns in confusion, then realizes what Aislyn's referring to. "Oh. Yeah, I'm good. A few nightmares, probably a li'l PTSD, had to ditch my favorite sweater because it stank like alien ass, but y'know, still alive. Could be worse."

She realizes it's too frank when Aislyn looks deeply uncomfortable. Veneza manages not to roll her eyes, just. She's not sure what she wants from this woman—and maybe it's not even her that wants it. Maybe she's acting out New York's desire to have back what was part of it for so long.

A horn blows to signal the ferry's departure, and Aislyn flinches so violently that Veneza can't help twitching in response. Then the ship starts to move, and Aislyn doesn't look at the water, or the opposite shore, or the Statue of Liberty, or anything. She just fixes her gaze on her handbag. Ohhhhkay.

"Why did you come meet me?" Veneza asks, genuinely perplexed. "If you're, like, scared of boats or whatever."

"I like boats fine. When they don't go where this one's going."

"Wait, then . . . you're scared of *the city*?" Veneza has to chuckle. Aislyn throws her a sharp frown, and her hands tighten on the purse. Doesn't like having her irrational fear treated as irrational, huh? Or else she thinks Veneza's going to steal her purse. Veneza is rapidly getting tired of tap-dancing around this woman's fragility.

"Bad things happen in the city," Aislyn says, her jaw tightening. "All the time. You can't say they don't. It's not like I'm scared of nothing."

"And? You think your borough's special? But thank God they're not living in the city, right, where people might hear the screaming through the walls. Can't have that."

"It's not like that."

"It's not?"

"No! We *are* different from the rest of New York. People try to be better here!"

Veneza stares at her, incredulous. "Do you actually believe nobody tries to be better in the other boroughs?— Oh, hell, don't start crying."

To her dubious credit, Aislyn doesn't go full-on White Woman Tears breakdown. She just sniffs a little, rummages in her purse, then dabs her eyes with a tissue held in one shaking hand. "I'm sorry. I just... You're making Staten Island sound awful, like..."

"Like it's a part of New York?" Veneza smiles coldly. Okay, gloves-off time. "Man, you remind me of my dad."

Aislyn looks a little taken aback. "I... what?"

"He's white, too—he pretends he isn't because he's Portuguese American, but last I checked Portugal was in Europe. He lives in the suburbs outside Philly. Most boring place you ever saw. Racist as fuck, too. But on the surface, this place looks like something out of a 1950s sitcom: nice mowed lawns with no crabgrass, everybody driving a new car, kids in soccer and gymnastics, good schools. Guess what, tho? Turns out it's the opioid capital of the mid-Atlantic region. Fentanyl, heroin, the works. There's shootings, robberies, and people OD'ing all over the place. But Dad just... doesn't see it. Doesn't read the crime stats, won't listen when I tell him it's actually safer in New York. It doesn't fit what he *thinks* the world is like." She leans forward; Aislyn draws back a little. "You love Staten Island? Cool. No reason why you shouldn't. But don't act like you're better than the rest of us when you aren't." Now she's done with diplomacy. "And don't pretend you had a good reason to turn on us."

Aislyn makes an incredulous sound. "You came to my house. You *attacked* me."

"*I* was an unconscious hostage, hello. And didn't nobody attack you. They came to talk to you—to ask you to help save millions of people! You attacked *them*. On behalf of your BFF, the giant tentacle monster who kills universes for kicks."

Aislyn sits back and lets out a harsh, angry breath before looking away. "I guess this was a mistake."

Veneza laughs. "Yeah. Maybe so." She sits back as well, shaking her head. Some of her frustration is at herself; she knows how to talk to people like this without losing her cool, but for some reason it's incredibly hard in this case. Partly that's their city natures. New York as a whole doesn't think much of Staten Island, so that's probably influencing Veneza's lack of patience. But bringing up her father has put Veneza deeper into a shitty mood. He is a man who has a perpetual boner for Black women, but who also loves to drop nigger-with-the-hard-r and wear Blue Lives Matter shirts whenever Veneza visits. He, a man living in a literal fantasyland of safe, enforced whiteness, thinks Veneza is "too sensitive" and needs to "toughen up." And Veneza keeps visiting, because he's her father and she feels like she should probably have some kind of relationship with him...but more and more lately she's been questioning that choice. For a relationship to be functional, both parties need to put in effort. Aislyn's starting to look like a bust on that front, same as her father.

But just as Veneza's about to take out her phone and studiously ignore Aislyn for the rest of the ride, Aislyn blurts, "She's changing everything."

There's only one *she* who matters. "What do you mean?"

Aislyn takes a deep breath. Then she lifts a surprisingly steely gaze to meet Veneza's own. "I thought at first that she understood me," she says. "I just wanted to keep my island safe. I guess I was afraid that becoming part of—you—would mean the opposite of that. But now she's *changing* everything. My family and friends, they aren't... It shouldn't be..." While Veneza stares, trying to process this sudden confession, Aislyn's expression contorts into pure fury. "I don't even think she likes Wu-Tang!"

That's. Wow. Veneza blinks. Bites her bottom lip. It doesn't help. She starts grinning. "Oh, well, *especially* fuck her, then."

Aislyn also seems to belatedly realize the absurdity of what she just said. She chuckles as well, weakly but genuinely, and her shoulders slump. "...Yeah. Fuck."

That's when the subtext of Aislyn's little rant finally hits. "Wait a minute. Oh my God. You came here to *ask for help.*"

Aislyn's smile vanishes instantly. "No, I didn't."

Veneza rolls her eyes. "Yeah. Ya did. You just said she was changing things too much for you. She's gonna blow up Staten Island, same as everything else, and you finally figured that out. But what, can't you just boot her off the island the way you booted us—" Oh, shit. "You *can't*, can you? Not by yourself."

Aislyn stares at her for a pent moment, bottom lip trembling, and for a moment Veneza thinks this is it. Squigglebitch loses an ally, New York gains another borough, the multiverse stabilizes and everything is saved, hallelujah.

Then a white tentacle the size of a subway train curls up out of the water next to the boat.

It blocks the sun, a pallid scaled monstrosity that's less like a cephalopod tentacle than a lumpen, eyeless snake. The ferry rocks, violently, and people exclaim—but as Veneza and Aislyn both run to the railing, it's clear that no one else on the passenger deck even sees this thing. Veneza can hear shouting from an upper deck; the ship's crew must be able to see it because they need to, if they're going to do anything about it. City magic works on a need-to-know basis. Everyone else just squeals or even laughs as a spray of water wafts across the ferry decks, showering them all with fresh, grade-A New York Harbor.

"Oh shit," Aislyn says, her eyes huge. It's the first thing she's said that Veneza agrees with.

"How the fuck is this thing even—" Veneza has to yell to be heard over the sound of the water. Passengers who don't see the tentacle look at her oddly.

"We must still be in Staten Island waters," Aislyn yells back, and Veneza's heart plummets as she realizes the depth of her mistake. The ferry and stations might be safe from the influence of R'lyeh, but no other part of Staten Island is . . . and there's plenty of crumbled Staten all over the harbor floor. Plus, as Paulo told them a long time ago, water acts as a conduit for the Enemy.

The tentacle, its tip fissioning into something like a giant fleshy crab claw, begins to turn—yep, toward the ferry. To grab it, maybe, and haul Aislyn back to the Woman in White? To snap the ferry in two and drown them all? Veneza fumbles for the plastic keychain, even though her mind is numb with terror and she can't think of a single Statue of Liberty–based construct to use.

But abruptly the questing tip of the tentacle hits something. Not the ferry; it stops maybe ten feet above the ferry's wheelhouse, almost as if it's hit glass or an invisible shield. The fleshy pincers widen to try again—oh yikes, nope, it's got a small toothy *mouth* in there at the center, like a lamprey—and there is a hiss as they fumble over this blockage, trying to find a way in. Veneza sees a curl of smoke from one of the appendages before it twitches away.

She laughs as she understands. "Can't do it, can you, Squiggle-bitch?" she shouts at the thing. "The ferry's part of New York!"

The tentacle withdraws abruptly as if to regroup, although it continues looming over the ferry, easily keeping up with its forward motion. Its proximity has made the ferry ride rougher, however, by churning up the nearby water to a rapids-level froth. Then the thing undulates suddenly, and the ferry rocks again, so hard that if Veneza wasn't holding tight to the railing, she would topple. A few passengers do fall, and there are screams as others find themselves pitching up against the railing on the other side of the deck. Too late Veneza realizes her error: it doesn't matter if the damn thing can't touch the ferry. It can capsize it without ever laying a squiggly finger on them.

She looks wildly at Aislyn. It's too hard to yell over the screams, the boat's distress signal, and the roaring water, but she raises her eyebrows in as pointed and meaningful a way as she can. *You gonna do anything about your friend?* But Aislyn just stares back at her, shaking her head in mute denial. Can't do anything? Won't do anything? Too terrified to think? Well, shit.

The tentacle writhes abruptly, sending another wave at the boat, and this one actually overtops the lower deck. Veneza barely manages to grab the railing in time. It does knock Aislyn free, and Veneza curses as she has to grab for the other woman's wrist. For a long, horrifying moment, the ferry continues to tilt. Veneza ends up nearly hanging from the railing, groaning at the drag of Aislyn's weight and looking down in horror at what seems like an endless expanse of water looming on the other side of the boat. People there are *under* water; Veneza can see a cluster of them hanging on to the railing while a few already float free, freaking out. Then the ferry rights itself, to Veneza's relief. The captain comes on the PA system. "Anybody injured or in the water?" There are shaken screams and cries from the passengers, but mostly shouts in the negative. A few people applaud.

Too soon for that, Veneza thinks grimly. *This fight's not done.*

She gets her feet under her and tries to catch her breath. Aislyn's no use, so it's up to Veneza. If she doesn't do something before the tentacle tries again, they're going to find out exactly how well the ferry handles being ass over teakettle in the middle of New York Harbor.

The harbor. Veneza gasps and looks wildly around, less thinking than desperately reaching for a lifeline—and there, beautifully close but uselessly far, is *her* harbor: Jersey City's waterfront of industrial piers and yachting marinas, which has been the driver of its economy for decades. There's a dingy-looking blue barge sitting along the shoreline, just off a pier. Veneza's soul shapes a summons, but meanwhile she needs weapons closer to hand. The brass knuckles are useless unless she lets the tentacle get close enough to punch, which...no. Statue of Liberty's too far; she can maybe make it do a march à la *Ghostbusters II*, but it'll take too long to get here. What's New York, and nearby, and construct-izeable? Even something small, anything—

Oooh. Wait. Okay, it's weird, but...Fuck it, she'll make it work.

"You like water, Squiggy?" she yells. At her challenge, the pincers twitch down to press against the barrier right in front of Veneza and Aislyn, which is terrifying—but Veneza grins back at the tiny, toothed maw at the center of those tentacles. "Well, you picked the wrong harbor to fuck with!"

Something churns in the water near the ferry. The tentacle jerks back from probing the barrier, tilting its wiggly "head" down at itself in what seems to Veneza like alarm. A moment later, a lumpen gray mass boils up from below and breaks the harbor surface with a salty-fresh spray. It's growing rapidly, forming a mound like a newborn volcano pushing its way up from the ocean floor, except this volcano is made of . . .

"Are those . . . o-oysters?" From her place at the railing, with one arm hooked around it for security, Aislyn looks at her in confusion. But Veneza can't stop laughing enough to explain. It's perfect. She can't believe she pulled it off.

An instant later, the ferry pitches wildly again as the tentacle flails. This time the Woman's creature isn't trying to capsize the boat, however. It's flailing in what looks like pain as it tries to get away from the rolling, clattering wave of oysters climbing its way up the tentacle's length. Normal shellfish don't swarm like bees, Veneza knows, but city magic can do anything if an avatar just tells it how.

The ferry settles again, and another spray of water wafts over the deck—but the captain has gotten the thing moving again, sensibly realizing the water up ahead seems less troubled than whatever keeps tipping the ferry here. They're pulling away, and the tentacle-snake thing isn't following because it's got bigger problems. There are thousands of oysters on it now, obscuring its root completely and dotting its head like a pox. And Veneza can see that around and between each oyster, the tentacle's white skin has gone a mottled, sickly purple. Are they poisoning it? Eating it? Both? Doesn't matter, as long as the thing fucking dies.

"Oysters," Veneza finally answers, talking half at Aislyn and half to the tentacle, grinning at the tentacle's struggles. "There's a whole Industrial Revolution's worth of shit still in this harbor, some so toxic that it nearly killed off the estuary ecosystem. It did kill off the oysters, decades ago, but people started reintroducing them a few years back to help suck up all the gross crap. And guess what *you* qualify as, Squiggy my squig?"

The tentacle writhes in a way that seems half spasmodic and half desperate, then extends its lamprey mouth toward the sky— toward R'lyeh, in whose pale shadow they travel. Uh oh. Veneza's grin dies as something stirs at the ghostly city's edge. Abruptly two pale cables begin wending down toward them. One is clearly aiming for the tentacle, though to do what Veneza cannot guess. Plug it in and give it a power boost? The other wavers, then wafts toward the ferry—not in pursuit, however, as it stops a few meters short and just hovers there. There's something plaintive about that one. Something almost...beseeching.

"It's after me," Aislyn says, her tone stricken. "She...she wants me back."

"Nah," Veneza says, as her borough gives her a little nudge about something she almost forgot. Baring her teeth in a grin again, Veneza makes a sweeping gesture with her free hand that ends in a fist. "She ain't getting you. I got this motherfucker."

And then, foghorns blaring, the blue barge smacks into the oyster-poisoned tentacle.

The tentacle instantly vanishes under the barge's bow. The barge is bigger than the ferry by a lot, and its wake ought to disturb the ferry even more than the tentacle did—but somehow (the ferry is the city's, the harbor is the city's, Veneza is the city's, and she will not let the city harm itself) the waters have actually calmed. More people scream on the ferry decks anyway, because after all the trouble the trip has already had, Surprise Barge is too much for some folks' nerves. The PA comes on and the captain's voice yells, "Holy shit, did you see that? Barge *Black Tom*, we do *not* need assistance anymore, repeat we do not need assistance, thanks but holy shit, oh, holy fuck. I quit, man, after today I fucking quit." Veneza wishes the captain happy job- and therapist-hunting.

The ferry keeps going, pulling away from the churning water, the barge that has miraculously moved without a tugboat at the nautical equivalent of warp speed, and the now-limp cables of R'lyeh, which Veneza thinks the barge must have basically cold-cocked. As Veneza watches, the cables begin to retract into the city above. Both have noticeable kinks in their formerly smooth length. The tentacle does not resurface in their wake.

Crew members start moving down the deck, checking in on injured people and looking for damage. Veneza's phone buzzes with messages, probably the other New Yorks sensing the flex of the city's power, but when she pulls her phone out, the screen won't light up. Considering she's completely soaked with harbor water, it's amazing the thing can even vibrate. Well, she was due for an upgrade anyway. She closes her eyes for a moment and tries to kind of psychically send her fellow avatars a smiley-face emote, so they'll know she's okay. Can't tell if it works. Then a man stumbles by, disoriented and with his face covered in blood, and both Veneza and Aislyn hurry to help him. Another passenger joins them. "Off-duty EMS," he says, helping them sit the man down.

That takes up the rest of the ride. The ferry pulls in and people practically stampede trying to get off it. The captain comes back on the intercom to say that the ship is going out of service while they check for damage. Another ferry is already on its way across the harbor, however—one that strangely did not encounter the patch of rough water—and that one will arrive in ten minutes to take passengers Staten Island–ward.

After the bloody-faced guy gets carted off on a stretcher, Veneza takes a deep breath and turns to her fellow avatar. Aislyn seems so lost, this self-exile from her own city, standing awkwardly in the middle of a busy ferry station and looking toward its Manhattan-side windows with big eyes. Is that fear or longing? Veneza finds herself not really caring either way.

"You realize," she says, as Aislyn jumps at the sound of her voice, "she would've killed you, too? Capsizing doesn't leave a lot of room for precision maneuvers."

Aislyn knows. Veneza can see it in her face. But she looks away, jaw tightening. "I don't think she meant to. She needs me."

"Does she? She got your borough already, baby. Maybe you are, uh, loose ends now." Aislyn's brow furrows, just a little. Listening. So Veneza presses her case. "Look. You're here, now, in 'the city.' I'm about to go meet the others, they gotta hear about this. You want to come with? Just to talk."

Aislyn looks up, and for a long and terrible moment, Veneza sees pure despair in her face. "My family's back there," she says, very softly. "My home. Everything I care about is already in her hands, and I can't leave them . . . unprotected. I won't." She hesitates, then lowers her gaze. "And . . . *she's* a person, too, you know? She has problems, too. Everybody needs a friend. Everybody."

Well, shit.

So Veneza leaves. What else can she do? Aislyn chose to make her entire borough hostage to an alien monster that wants to destroy the universe. An alien monster that she calls *friend*.

Aislyn watches Veneza until the escalator carries them out of sight of each other.

That night, Veneza checks on the posts she made the night before. The engagement stats make her mouth drop open. She's officially gone viral! Variations on her logo design have popped up, too— Oakland, Houston, Portland, and she laughs to see one for Philly. There's even one from Edinburgh? What is that, Ireland or France or something? Veneza will look it up later. Anyway, she's got twenty thousand more followers than she did the day before and has received an account upgrade on Instagram. In her inbox there are three interview requests from media sites, an invitation to join Substack, monetization instructions for Twitch and YouTube, and she's now got a blue check on Twitter that she didn't ask for. The fuck.

Still. Veneza sends the logo to an online shop, attaches T-shirt and merchandise sale links to her posts, then orders a shirt for herself. After a day like she's had, it's nice to savor the smaller victories.

Then she starts texting the others, to let them know that Brooklyn just gained a lot more name recognition in New York and everywhere else. Support (and donations) are pouring in, and they've finally gotten an international lovefest going that's powerful enough to counter Panfilo's hatemongering. "SIXTH BOROUGHS FOR NYC" is go.

CHAPTER NINE

Mind the Crap

It's been a few months since Bel moved to New York. He's still trying to decide whether it's the city that's driving him mad, or the City.

That's how he thinks of it, capital-C City, as in the living entity that is New York. Manny's explained as much of the business as he could, because Bel demanded that before he made the decision to move into the penthouse. Problem is, even after the explanation, it still makes precious little sense. Not the part about cities having souls; fuck's sake, any Londoner knows *that*. What's hard to swallow is the enemy city from space or wherever, who has the power to possess nosy white women and raise lawns of evil magic grass. Sure, Bel was there while Manny threw cash at the white lawn, and he heard it squeal and saw it burn like a vampire showered with holy water, but to this day he hardly believes his eyes. The memory feels hazy and half-real, even though it was only weeks—months?—ago. He actually suspects he would have forgotten about that day in Inwood Hill Park by now, if he hadn't come to live here in Casa Citypeople. The city protects its own, Manny has said—by letting them see all the weirdness if they need to, and sparing them the horror if not. If people knew about avatars and how many lives depended on their well-being, why, governments might snatch them off to some black ops site to keep them drugged up and wrapped in tissue paper. Bel's not sure that would work. He's seen how restless Neek is, *needing* to wander the city constantly; if that need is part of what makes him New York, then it would probably be impossible to confine him.

And now Bel shares this penthouse with the living embodiments of Manhattan, Queens, Jersey City which is somehow New York now, and New York itself. Brooklyn and the Bronx drop by on occasion. (Never Staten Island, though. He overhears the others talking and gathers it's a sore subject.)

Another crazymaking part is that living with them is all so . . . mundane. Neek leaves the toilet seat up, like a heathen. Sometimes when Bel's near him, the whole world sort of . . . tilts? As if this rude, thin, weedy-looking boy somehow weighs five million tonnes, pulling everything toward him and threatening to make the whole building topple like a late-stage Jenga tower. Well, fine, but can the living embodiment of the City put the fucking cap back on the fucking toothpaste now and again? Honestly.

There's also Veneza, who's almost never home and lives on her computer when she is. She frequently dances through the apartment in socks while singing along to whatever on her headphones—and God help her, such a sweetheart, but she *cannot* sing. And there's Padmini, who apparently can't boil water but brings home the most astonishing meals from her relatives. Bel is half in love with the unseen Aishwarya just for the delicate flavoring of her tamarind rice. Padmini watches the scariest movies late at night. Bel has joined her for a few, and they've sat together cringing and gasping over a massive bowl of curry-dusted popcorn. Impossible to think of her as Queens, that wild and sprawling part of New York where no one gives Bel's brown skin or non-American accent a second thought, and where he can actually find Vietnamese restaurants approaching his mother's cooking in quality. But maybe that's why Bel gets on with her so well.

Despite the relentless normalcy of his life among these strange people, Bel keeps glimpsing weirdness. He's starting to realize the others have been careful to shield him from the worst of it, which is kind of them. Sometimes, though, he walks to campus and notices cracks across the sky, as if the whole thing is a massive iPhone screen. They always fade, but still. And sometimes he rides the subway and catches fleeting glimpses of the tunnel walls vanishing, opening out into a limitless expanse of churning nothingness where the only thing to be seen is a massive, impossible, endlessly churning fractal structure that reminds him a little of a tree. Except the tree is made of exploding suns? Then *snap* and it's back to dirty white tile and CANAL STREET, and some ass deciding to eat an entire roasted duck in the corner seat while tossing greasy bones onto the floor and ignoring everyone's disgusted glares.

She shouldn't bother you anymore, Manny has told him, referring to the force that threatened them on that hazy long-ago day. Bel was amused to learn that hostile extradimensional forces can have gender. *You were collateral damage that day, just in the wrong place at the wrong time, and I didn't know how to defend myself at that point.*

I do now, so I've taken steps to make sure you'll be safe even when I'm not around. But clearly not even Manny's protection, formidable as that might be, can keep all of the fuckery at bay.

Well. When in Rome, et cetera.

Bel heads out one afternoon to explore the city. A first-year PhD student's schedule tends to be light on free time, but he's chosen to hold off on teaching or research for now in order to allow himself adjustment time. Life in the States, and particularly in New York, requires that. He's been using his Tuesdays, which are completely free, to get to know his new home in a semi-systematic way— exploring boroughs and neighborhoods he's never seen before, trying new foods, occasionally playing tourist. Today's journey has brought him to the West Village, which of course meant an obligatory pilgrimage to the Stonewall Inn. Then Bel meanders over to Chelsea, where there's so much lovely eye candy on display that he basically spends the whole afternoon wishful thinking. It's probably just all the unresolved sexual tension between Manny and Neek rubbing off.

For lunch, Bel detours to "Little Britain," which isn't much to speak of. Fifty percent of it is a tiny, quaint little restaurant called Tea & Sympathy, where he is delighted to find Welsh rarebit, along with a sticky toffee pudding that's just about the best he's ever had. He has a delightful conversation with the proprietor about how gentrification did Little Britain in, same as nearly every other quirky ethnic enclave in Manhattan. He apparently earns some goodwill from her, too, and as a result sets out for the rest of his meander with a doggie bag containing two free puddings with custard, "to make you feel at home."

Eventually Bel's feet start to hurt, so he settles in a tiny park to rest. He's trying to decide whether to just take a cab home versus enduring the rush hour subway, when he becomes suddenly aware that he is being watched.

There are six or seven young fellows over by another bench. None of them look like the usual Greenwich Village set. Too shabbily dressed, too bunched up and furtive in their behavior, as if they're nervous here in New York's gayest neighborhood. Also a fairly nondescript and motley group, white apart from one East Asian fellow and another who looks to be some flavor of Middle Eastern. The one who pings the loudest on Bel's trouble radar stands straighter than the rest, and he's dressed in a weird old-fashioned dapper style—muttonchop beard and mustachio, black-rimmed rectangle glasses, suspenders over a button-down. Poor deluded fool probably thinks that mess looks good on him. But the others are all hanging on his words; he's the leader. And he's watching Bel, which means that when Bel frowns, this fellow notices . . . and comes over.

"Pardon me," he says with a smile, while Bel moves his thumb from the rideshare app on his phone to the camera app instead. He makes sure to smile back with distant politeness, however. Americans always seem to expect the performance of friendliness, even when they aren't being friendly. "You wouldn't happen to know a guy who goes by the name of Manhattan, would you? Like the borough."

Bel's skin prickles. "No," he says, getting to his feet and picking up his bag. "'Fraid not. Good luck finding him, though. A Manhattan in Manhattan, ha."

The young man chuckles. His shirtsleeves are rolled up, and Bel notes a number of tattoos on his forearms. Nothing objectionable, and yet. "Oh, we'll find him soon. But are you sure you don't know him? Aren't you Bel Nguyen, his roommate?"

Bel narrows his eyes and taps the "record" button, though he keeps the phone out of the man's line of sight. "What's this about? You looking to borrow money?"

The young man chuckles again. And although it sounds like a good-humored laugh, just two old friends shooting the breeze about a mutual acquaintance, of course it's a lie. The other young men are watching from their bench, and their expressions are all variations on their leader's fake friendliness, ranging from equally "polite" smiles to open, sadistic glee.

Bel can handle himself in a fight. When he came out as trans, his mother made him take vovinam classes—but he doesn't practice as often as he should, and there are a lot of these fuckers. Too many.

"Weeeeell," the young man says, smile widening as he notes Bel's tension. "Don't worry. We just want to talk! Here, my name's Conall." He holds out his hand to shake. Bel leaves it hanging, never taking his eyes off the man's face, and Conall puts on an exaggerated pout before dropping his hand. "I don't want you to feel like this is a threat, but Mr., uh, Manhattan happens to have, let's see, *exchanged words* with a friend of mine. A cop. So we've been on the watch, if you want to call it that, for Manhattan's acquaintances. There's one in particular that we'd love to talk to—skinny, very, uh, Black fellow? We were told he was homeless, but we haven't been able to find him in any of his usual haunts. If you can help us track him down, we'll discuss our business with him. Instead of you. What do you say?"

It's a sickening bargain, and Bel can instantly see the warning in it. If they've tracked Bel down in the middle of New York on a random day, then they'll probably be able to do it again. Unless Bel gives up Neek.

"Well, fuck off, then, yeah?" Bel says. He doesn't intend the code switch. He's well-off now thanks to an inheritance from his father, but for most of his life he lived with his mother in far less comfortable circumstances, and when he's feeling a certain way, the South London just jumps out. Speed's going to be his best asset here, so the gap in the fence behind him might work best. These fellows are all the gym rat sort, big on looking intimidating but probably lacking in actual strength and endurance. It's with these calculations that Bel girds his bravado. "Think I'm stupid? I seen a dozen like you back home, you get me? All the open doors in the world and you still can't make shit of yourself, so you go looking to blame. So *here*—"

He swings the bag. Alas for his puddings, but worth it to see Conall flinch, raising his arms to block the blow in case the bag is heavy. It's not, but the containers burst on impact, the bag tears, and still-warm yellowy custard splatters everywhere.

Bel's moving before Conall's splutter of disgust turns into fury. If Bel can get around a corner, break their line of sight, and duck into a business to hide 'til they pass, he's got a chance. Behind him, he hears Conall's companions jump up to give chase, and among their various imprecations he hears, "Get that fucking cunt!" Which pushes away his fear in a wash of anger, because he knows that on this side of the pond, "cunt" is a gendered thing. Fucking *assholes*.

But Bel's plan goes wrong almost immediately. He's been thinking that his best bet is to head toward Chelsea; more largish shops there, like the Apple Store, and that one's likely to have a security guard. But the gym rats have anticipated his strategy, and the instant he hits the sidewalk outside of the park, he sees two more 'roid-fed hooligans closing in from West 13th Street. Other way, then; other way sounds good. He pivots and runs, with the lot of them—eight men in total—on his heels.

The thing about lower Manhattan is that its street plan makes as much sense as that of London... which is to say, none, to a non-native. Before Bel knows it, he's passing the hat shop he visited not long before—which means he's been heading deeper into the Village, where the city blocks are short and it will be harder to lose his pursuers. Worse, the shops here are tiny; nowhere to hide even if he enters one. But he doesn't exactly have time now to stop and open up Google Maps—

Left, whispers a voice in his ear.

More weirdness, *now*? A woman's voice, but there's no one there, of course. Bel's put a little distance between himself and Conall's crew, since they are indeed slower than lorries, but when he glances back, he sees only two—Conall and another—in direct pursuit. They've split up to try and bracket him in. If he goes left, and they've sent some of their number in that direction... But straight is a trap. Bel's been lapsing on his own cardio, what with being a sleep-deprived graduate student, and he's starting to run out of steam. They'll catch up if he doesn't find a hiding place fast. Left it is, then.

Initially he thinks he's made a mistake. There's an even bigger group of people on the corner—more mixed in apparent genders, body types, and attire, but too many to evade if they're hostile. Something about them, though, pings a note of not-quite-recognition. Their presentation is different, protective camouflage suited to New Yorkish tastes and not Londonish, but . . . And they're looking back at him, with expressions less hostile than assessing.

"Help me," Bel manages. He's got a stitch in his side by this point. "Please—"

That's all it takes. Assessing expressions turn fucking murderous, and the instant Bel passes this new group, they square up and block the sidewalk. One of the bunch, a heavyset, bearded leather-wearer who looks to chuck trees for fun, grabs Bel's arm and pulls him to one side, safely behind the biggest three or four. "You all right?"

"No," Bel pants, trying to orient on Conall, trying to get enough breath to warn his new friends, trying to figure out if he should keep running. "Threatened me—"

"You're gonna be all right." A strong hand squeezes Bel's bicep. "We got you. I'm Christine. She/they, I before E except after C. You?"

Bel stammers out his name. But he's focused on Conall, who's stopped running and is smiling again as he pulls a short metal rod out of his pocket. Conall's old-fashioned taste runs to weapons, too, then; that's a blackjack. "You want to get out of our way?" he says, with that fucking smirk on his face again. Three other of his friends have arrived and moved to join their leader in the confrontation. Bel's group outnumbers them, but weapons level a lot of playing field. "Trust me, you don't want any of this."

"Proud Men?" asks one of Bel's defenders. This one's a thin and weedy-looking probably-white probably-guy, but he's taller than Conall, and somehow Bel can tell just how much Conall hates this.

"You got that fuckin' right," says one of Conall's followers, who looks to be barely pubescent.

"You're in the Village, baby," points out a young blond. She's got her hand in a pocket, and Bel can see the outline of something cylindrical—Mace?—against her jeans. "What you're trying to do wouldn't fly in a lot of this city. But here? You want to try this *here*?"

"Stupid," says a Black femme, somehow putting extra "oo" into the word. "But I guess you gotta be to join these dumb-asses. Hey, you know they not allowed to jerk off?"

Half of Bel's new friends burst out laughing, while the other half look astonished. "The fuck—"

"*No* fuck, that's the point!" More laughter.

"Supposed to make 'em more manly or something."

"It ain't working! They need more hair on their palms!" Everybody's positively screeching now. Lovely comedy show right here on a Village corner.

"I don't have time for this," Conall snaps—but his face has gone blotchy with anger. Too proud to tolerate ridicule, apparently. "If you know who we are, then you know cops love us and hate you fucking freaks. You'll get your asses kicked *and* end up in jail, and we got members in there, too—"

"Your bitch ass would die in Rikers," says Tall and Weedy. "And didn't some of you end up in prison after that bullshit you pulled a while back, beating up people on the Upper East Side? Cops didn't let you slide then. You guys must not be that good at sucking cop dick."

"I ain't no homo—" one of them begins, loud enough for his voice to echo. People on the street oooh and tsk, and one woman yells, *Get out of here, fucking Nazi!* Conall glares at his man, and the guy falls resentfully silent.

"Smile first," says the blond woman, jabbing a thumb upward— at a camera perched conspicuously atop a lightpole. "And you know it's probably fifty or sixty people got cameras on all of us right now. Cops lie, but those don't. We can make you famous."

Several of the Proud Men look around; one curses. Bel follows his gaze and sees that there are indeed several people visible who are holding up phones in their direction. Another of the Proud Men, the babyface, loses his patience and rushes Tall and Weedy, but Conall and the others quickly grab him and pull him back. "Not here," Conall says, glancing around again and scowling. But he focuses on Bel. "We're gonna see you again, friend."

Then they back off, pulling along their more belligerent or reluctant members, and quickly vanish around a corner.

By this point, Bel has caught his breath, though he's at risk of losing it again as the Village group surrounds him, slapping his back, jogging his arm, laughing and celebrating their victory. Bel's not so sure about it being a victory, himself; his heart's doing flip-flops in his chest, and Conall's parting threat has lodged in his mind in the worst way. But he grins, shaky in the aftermath of adrenaline, and nods when the others ask if he's all right. Slowly, as they begin the fine post-confrontation tradition of talking shit about their routed foes, Bel starts to actually *be* all right.

After that, there are introductions, and exclamations of welcome as everyone realizes Bel is new in town. Bel has been wondering how to kick-start what little social life he'll be able to handle around his PhD, but within five minutes he's got simultaneous invites to two mutual aid meetings, a fringe-festival standup show, a play one of the group members wrote ("It's kind of off-off-off-Broadway"), and a private gym for gender nonconforming people.

Afterward, the blond girl takes Bel aside. "You got cab money?"

"Y-yes," Bel says, blushing at his own stammer. Mostly that's leftover adrenaline, but a little of it . . . well. She's really pretty. "Thank you for asking."

She gives him a frank, assessing look. "You look like your nerves are shot. Never mind the cab; I got a car, I'll take you. Where do you want me to drop you off? I was heading up toward the Bronx anyway, so anywhere in Manhattan is fine."

"Inw— Damn, we moved, sorry, Harlem now. If that's not too far out of your way?"

"Got it, and it's not. I'm Madison, by the way. Nice to meet you, Bel." She waves for him to follow, then pauses, frowning a little. "Hey. You don't happen to know a guy . . . Never mind."

"Pardon?"

She's pursed her lips and is frowning. "I don't know. Something about all this just feels . . . I wasn't planning to come out today, see. Tavie wanted me to see this new shoe place, Fluevogs on sale, and I almost said no 'cause I didn't have any money. But then something was like, *You should go.* And the last few times that's happened, shit got weird."

"Lady," Bel says, chuckling in spite of himself, "shit has been *so* weird since I came to this city. I actually feel better to hear it's the same for locals."

"Oh, def." She laughs, and then she pauses, giving Bel a thoroughly blush-inducing lookover. "You're cute. Especially when you smile."

Is she . . . ? Bel clears his throat and grins shyly and tells himself firmly not to turn into a stammering infant. "Thanks. You're fucking gorgeous, if I may say."

"Well, this is going to be a fun ride, then," Madison says, with a knowing grin.

So that's how Bel ends up getting a free ride to Harlem in a restored classic Checker cab—she works for a wedding-props company. "Not supposed to use it for personal stuff, but that'll be our little secret, huh?" And maybe there's some unique property of the cab that Bel can't quite parse, but for the whole length of the ride, he forgets the fear of those moments in the park. There's just something about the cab that makes him feel safe. Because of this, he's comfortable, relaxed, and even eloquent as he cautiously flirts with Madison, and is stunned to find his flirtations reciprocated. American girls, the New York variety anyway, don't fuck about.

When she stops outside of his building, Bel belatedly frets that they might've been followed, but Madison waves this off. " 'Follow that car' only works in the movies," she says. "I drive too damn fast for a bunch of meatheads to keep up without me noticing."

This isn't the reassurance that it should be. Bel knows they're targeting Manny, which means they likely have his address already. It's something the others need to know about, though Bel's not sure it'll make much of a difference given that they're always in the sights of extradimensional assassins. Bel's the one with no superpowers to wield in a pinch.

Maybe he should move out of the apartment. He'd rather not; good roommates are hard to find, and cheap rent is the best deal ever. But staying alive is sort of important, too.

At Bel's building, Madison hands him a business card with her number scrawled on the back. He tucks it away carefully because nothing ventured, nothing gained, right? And he must still be grinning like a fool as he steps into the elevator, because the woman who's already in it—white, messy blond hair, never seen her before—meets his smile with a bright one of her own. "You look like you're having a very good day."

Bel starts a bit, because it's been so long that the woman's blissfully normal English triggers a flare of homesickness. And that accent— "You're shitting me. Another Londoner?"

She laughs and presses the button for Bel's floor. "Well, I'm originally from the north, but London liked me, so Londoner it is. I'm from a little bit of everywhere in the city. You, though... Lewisham, right? You sound Lewisham."

Bel knows he should probably be more suspicious given the day he's had, but this woman is very easy to talk to. "Good guess! Yeah, here to study. You?"

"Just a tourist," she says, firmly enough that he chuckles at the hint of relief in her expression. "But you seem all right? New York's taking care of you?"

He has to think about it a little, but— "Yes, all things considered.

Could be worse. Can't be home, of course, but it's a tolerable substitute for a while."

"That's lovely to hear. Really." The elevator slows on their floor, and the doors open. "I'll be off, then. Take care."

"Are you staying with someone on this floor?" Bel asks as he steps out. Should've let her go first, he supposes, but all his ingrained chivalry is still aimed in the wrong direction. Things to work on. When the woman doesn't answer, however, he stops and turns—

—to find the elevator empty.

Bel stares at this for a moment. And then he closes his mouth, and heads home. When in Rome, right? When in Rome.

INTERRUPTION

London

She reappears on her favorite bridge over the Thames: the Wobbly Bridge, also known as the Millennium Bridge. It doesn't wobble anymore, but that doesn't stop people from continuing to make fun of it, affectionately, because that's what Londoners are like.

A moment later there is a flux and a flex, and New York appears beside her. He leans back on the railing, glances around at the few people crossing the span—it's full night here, not many about except folks stumbling home after drinks or late work—and then eyes her. "Kinda rude rolling up in somebody's house without even saying hi."

"Oh, that." London grins, delighted. Amazing that this slight, soft-spoken young fellow is a huge old city—but then others often say the same of her. "I wasn't really there for you, but I suppose it was hypocritical of me. Especially when the other elders are complaining about *your* rudeness! I apologize."

"Satisfied? With whatever you came to see."

"Oh, yes. I wanted a look at whatever you and your boroughs have been dealing with. Your roommate was a convenient bellwether—ha! Bel-weather. Anyhow, nasty floating city you've got there."

"Right? Like a damn boil on my ass."

"Or a malignant tumor, given the way it's drawing such, hmm, problematic people to you." She could sense the Enemy's influence on that Conall fellow, like the oily sheen left on water by a contaminant. No wiggly tendril to guide him within New York's city limits, but then clearly none needed. R'lyeh's citizens choose themselves. "Anyhow, welcome." London gestures expansively at herself. "I'd offer you tea, but . . ."

"I don't like tea, anyway." She restrains a reflexive gasp, but, well, he is American. He falls silent for a while, absorbing the sounds and smells and glittering lights. Then he eyes her for a moment before speaking again. "They tell me you crazy."

"Now, now, we're meant to use better language than that. Try 'mentally ill,' though I'll admit my personal favorite is 'fucked in the head.'" He snickers; she grins. "And I suppose I am, though better than I was. Hard to shake a reputation once you've picked it up."

He grunts in an agreeing sort of way. "So how'd you *eat* them? Your boroughs?"

"Oh, right, that. Well, know how you have five boroughs and counting? Imagine having thirty-two."

New York splutters. "Fuck outta here."

She chuckles. "It wasn't that many, thirty-two only became official in the 1960s. Even at the time I instantiated, though—mmm, seventeenth century or so? I can't remember exactly but it wasn't long after Shakespeare's passing—London had a lot of distinctiveness between its now-boroughs. Still does, I mean, but we're talking about then. So there were a lot of us when we first felt the city's call. Honestly, be glad you've only five, our meetings were the stuff of nightmares."

New York laughs, though there's an uncomfortable edge to it that tells London he understands, from experience. "And?"

"And..." She shrugs, though in reality it wasn't a shrug-worthy experience. "Some of them didn't want to be London. We tried it for a time, fighting our own version of Squigglebitch for weeks on end—no talking, and we didn't meet a humanish version of her anywhere, but it was bloody monster attacks every other minute, absolutely brutal. Composite cities give her a lot of opportunity, you see." London sighs. "Anyhow, it finally became clear that some of us were never going to be fully on board—and without that, none of us would ever be safe from the Enemy. So I said I would do it. I would be the one, and only, London. The others agreed, and so it was."

"But, like...?" New York pantomimes using a fork and knife.

London can't help laughing. "Oh my God, I'm not Sweeney Todd! I only ate their essence—the thing, or things, that made them an aspect of London. I took all of that into myself, the city latched wholly on to me and me alone, and the others went back to their ordinary lives as ordinary people. Then I vanquished the Enemy and did a little dance, and that was the end of it. Well, apart from me losing my mind for the next couple of centuries, because *this* city of all cities should never be just one person. But one does what one must."

New York frowns, probably because he's trying to figure out

what it would be like to suddenly take on the personalities and skills of so many other people. She hopes he never finds out.

"That's real fucked up," he says. "They just left you to take on all that?"

She sighs. He's right, of course, but she's had a few centuries for forgiveness. "We were strangers to each other, most of whom had families and lives beyond being the city. Life was harder back then, remember. Plagues and war every other minute, and the Great Fire... That happened when I went to mentor another city. Algiers, or maybe Bucharest? Whichever, she almost killed me. Granted, I *was* very Joan of Arc–core at the time, dressing oddly, having visions, speaking in tongues, probably very alarming, but setting me on fire was just rude, don't you think?"

He stares. She thinks he's impressed and preens a little, brushing a lock of hair back over her shoulder.

"I don't know what I would do if the others didn't want to be New York," he says, chewing on his bottom lip as he contemplates it. "I *could* do it, but..."

"Of course you could do it. Cities pick primary avatars who can handle the job alone, if they must. But it's *hard* to be a whole city, especially cities as disparate as yours and mine, so sometimes our cities try to be kind to us. Spread the burden, give us a support network, that sort of thing." She sighs, remembering in spite of herself. Most of the other Londons had wanted to remain avatars, but it had been an all-or-nothing thing. She misses them still. "Never occurred to me to jettison one part and replace it, though. Not sure that would've worked here; London is *particular* about what counts as London."

New York chuckles and says in a terrible imitation of her, " 'One does what one must.' " Then he straightens and stretches. Not much to him in this form, but naturally there is a flicker and for an instant London sees the truth of him, neatly gridded blocks and decrepit subways and fancy rooftop wine bars that make her crave the comfort of a nice cozy pub—but he's got pubs, too. Not many, but those few with the right spirit, sparkling like jewels amid the depths of him. Well, then! They can be friends. Then he's just a skinny Black youth again, lowering his arms and trying to work his way up to leaving with grace. Apparently he gives up on the grace part after a second or two. "Well. I'm out."

"All right, then! By the way, I'm going to tell the others to call a Summit. It's unconscionable that they've let this situation continue unchecked. And if any of the elders give you any more trouble about it, you just let me know, and I'll kill them and steal their stuff."

"—The fuck?"

"Well, I *was* the seat of the British Empire." She reaches over and pats his cheek, fondly, and he blinks. "Now, now, I'm joking, dear. I don't do that anymore."

With that, London heads off. The street market is probably still going, so she'll see if she can grab a kebab there. Then she's going to do an old-fashioned pub crawl, because it's been too long. Talking to baby cities always puts her in a nostalgic mood.

Behind her, New York stares for a moment longer, shakes his head, then vanishes back home.

CHAPTER TEN

You Can't Make It Here,
You Can't Make It Anywhere

Manny remembers his name on the train to DC.

His before-name, that is. Not that he didn't know it already, but now comes the rest: his past, his old personality, his likes and dislikes, the name of his childhood dog. He isn't surprised by this. It happens as soon as the train starts moving, however—before it leaves New York. The train initially has to pass through a tunnel under the Hudson to begin its journey. When it comes out of the tunnel, it will be in New Jersey, but at least the first few minutes of the ride are within New York's city limits. This settles a suspicion that's been forming for a while in Manny's mind: It isn't his presence in or dedication to New York that has kept him "Manhattan" all these weeks. He is Manhattan because he has chosen to be. And now...

"Anybody sitting here?"

Manny, who's been staring through the window at the black walls of the tunnel, sits back. A man stands there who is immediately familiar—but then, this does not quite surprise him, either. He's beginning to see the symmetry of all this, and the ways in which the city moves both overtly and subtly to work its will. This is less than subtle, but he's willing to give the city credit for last-minute improvisation.

"Douglas Acevedo," Manny says, smiling. "Hello, again."

The man, a portly middle-aged Latino, blinks in surprise. "Wait. Hang on . . ." He squints at Manny, then brightens. "Oh, you're that dude who fainted in Penn Station! Hey!" He reaches out and Manny stands to meet him, and it is easy, natural, to exchange a dap. Easy, natural, to remember this part of himself, which was always good at acting like a friend. Right up until he needed to turn—

No. He has remembered who he was, but he's still Manny, too. For now.

So it is Manny who gestures at the empty seat across from him. Douglas sits down on the facing set of seats, plonking down a heavy toolbag beside him.

"Not supposed to block seats," Douglas says with a grunt at the bag's weight, "but I'll move it if somebody asks. So how you doin', man? Not so out of it today, huh?"

Manny chuckles. Then he fishes in his own bag, pulls out a banana, and holds it up pointedly.

"Hey!" Douglas spreads his arms in delight. "Nice to know somebody listens to me, yeah? Where you headed this time?"

"DC. Family business."

"It's always something, huh? Family, man." Douglas sighs and looks out the window as they emerge from the tunnel. This part of Jersey is both a paradise of wetlands and a hell of decaying industry. They both stare for a moment at a marsh thick with cattails, surrounding some kind of abandoned factory. There's a . . . heron? Manny thinks it's a heron, picking its way around an old rusted car half-submerged in the water. He's a city boy. Doesn't know from birds.

"Off to see family myself," Douglas says. He's watching the bird, too. "Just down to Newark. My son had a girlfriend. They didn't get married because my wife was an asshole about them being together. She's Catholic, called the girl a slut even though our son did it outside marriage, too, you know? I'm Catholic, but I just go to mass to shut her up." He grins. "Now, though, the girl got a kid to raise, all by herself. Her family don't got money to help, plus they was assholes, too. She's doing okay, actually—good job, childcare, an apartment, but I still go help out where I can. I fix her car, do handyman stuff around their place, play with the little man. I figure it's what my son would want, yeah?"

It's pleasant, the singsong cadence of Douglas's voice. Some people are just instantly compatible, natural friends. "That's nice of you."

"She wouldn't say so. She don't like me." He laughs when Manny raises his eyebrows. "Ah, she's just grieving, mad at everybody. But that's my grandson she's raising. I'm gonna look out for them even if she cusses me out every other day. And anyway . . ." He sobers a little. "I get how she feels. So when she gets mad, I just remember it's 'cause she loved my boy, too. That makes it easy."

There is a message here. "Family looks out for family, no matter what."

"Well, yeah. But gotta remember family ain't always the one you get born with. *Real* family's the people who are there when you need 'em."

Ah. Manny contemplates this. Contemplates Neek, who has kept New York's other avatars at arm's length, in part because his blood family rejected him. "Once bitten, twice shy."

Douglas laughs. "Yeah, and man, this girl got bites all over! More like: three times bitten, turn around and start biting the shit out of other people." He shrugs, as Manny inhales in sudden understanding. "But she's getting better. Gave me a present for my birthday last time. And her little boy knows his abuelito is always there for him, which is all that matters."

"Huh. Yeah."

"Hey, uh . . ." Douglas tilts his head, watching Manny now. "Not like we got to be besties last time, but you seem a little different today. You okay?"

Manny smiles, and knows it looks sad. "Depends on what 'okay' means."

"Well, that's what you gotta figure out for yourself, man. I just tell people to eat bananas, 'til they do." He grins, and Manny laughs in spite of his mood.

But very well. Manny takes a deep breath and leans forward to prop his elbows on his knees. "My family is . . . like your wife, I guess. Big on tradition, not so big on people stepping out of line."

"Shit, yeah, *just* like my wife."

Manny smiles, though he isn't feeling it anymore. "Well, I stepped all the way out of line when I decided to leave them and come to New York. They were more okay with it than I expected, actually; they let me go. But now I need their help."

"Ouch. Might need a whole *hand* of bananas for that."

Manny chuckles again, though the banana jokes are getting old. "Probably. And some banana bread to top it all off."

"Put some tostones on the side, make it a whole meal." Douglas sobers. "You didn't expect 'em to let you go, right? Maybe they'll do other things you don't expect."

"Maybe." He doubts it, though. "My mother told me this when I was little: After slavery, the family tried doing things on the up-and-up, working hard and saving and all that, but it just... didn't work. They'd join up with other ex-slaves and build a town for themselves, but local white people would come burn it down. They'd defend themselves, but then lose more family members to lynching, or a chain gang, or having to flee north away from the lynchings and chain gangs. They even bought land at one point, a big parcel in Georgia that the whole extended family could've lived on, but then a local bigwig white farmer found a quasi-legal way to steal it." He sighs and spreads his hands. "Same story as most Black families in this country, I guess. And most families, in the same position, just kept at it... or broke apart. Let themselves get beaten down until they gave up. Mine, though, tried a different way. Came up with new ways of doing business—policy wheels, juke joints, speakeasies. Moneymakers that were harder to steal. They bribed the cops and public officials, made deals with Italian and Chinese families so there'd be no fighting... and *that* worked. Over the years we've learned to handle anybody who crosses us, ourselves, since that's the only justice we can trust. We're doing very well these days. Diversified, incorporated, gone legit—on the surface. But everything's still the same at its core. You get me?"

Douglas nods, slowly, and Manny is relieved to see neither discomfort nor admiration in his gaze. Just acceptance. "Yeah, man. Puerto Rico's America, too."

"Right. So. I know my family won't hurt me, but . . . they're hard people. Much-bitten and quick to bite back, like your son's girl—and these days we have very sharp teeth." Manny folds his hands. Lots of scars all over them, and now he remembers how he got each one. Sharp teeth must be honed carefully. "And there's something else happening that's a . . . complicating factor. So this is going to be kind of touch-and-go."

Douglas looks a little sad. "They're your family, man. Family's hard sometimes, sure, but it's worth it. Isn't it?"

When Douglas says *family*, what comes into Manny's mind are Brooklyn and Bronca and Padmini and Veneza. And Neek. Do they know, yet, that Manny's left the city? Have they guessed why, or where he's going? Will they worry? If so, what exactly will they be worried about?

When he doesn't answer, Douglas sighs. But the train is slowing as it approaches a stop, so Douglas gets up and hefts his bag. "Well. Gotta go."

Manny pulls himself out of his own navel. "Already? Oh, you did say Newark." It's just past Jersey City, not even twenty minutes away from New York by train.

"Yeah. You still got my card? Call me, man. Shit doesn't happen by chance in this city. It means something that we met again." When Manny blinks at this, wondering how he knows, Douglas smiles and moves past him—pausing for a moment to put a warm hand on Manny's shoulder. Then he's gone.

The rest of the ride is uneventful. Manny spends it all just . . . thinking. Feeling the spot where Douglas's hand rested, which feels warm for much longer than it should.

At Union Station in DC, Manny catches a cab. The hotel is in one of DC's lovelier neighborhoods, with cute rowhouses and neatly manicured lawns all around. Quiet. He checks in to a suite with a good view, orders room service, and spends the rest of the night staring at the lights and movement of DC while trying not to wish it was a different cityscape altogether.

In the morning he heads downstairs at seven forty-five. He's wearing a dark gray business suit today—one of his tailored ones, which he doesn't usually wear in New York. Jewel-toned twill shirt, no tie. Before leaving the area around Union Station the day before, he stopped at his favorite barber shop—he's been to DC enough to have a favorite—and had them give his hairline a precision edging. A trim makes the neat beard he's let himself grow over the past day or two frame his jawline nicely. There aren't many people in the lobby to stare as he walks through the hotel, but of the few, they all do. He meets their gazes if they linger too long—not to intimidate, but just acknowledging their admiration as his due.

Wants all his power about him, he supposes, as he strolls into the hotel's restaurant.

The restaurant is empty, except for one woman. The hotel, being so far from the Capitol area or DC's downtown, tends to mostly do business from convention overflow, graduations, and diplomats or lobbyists looking to stay low profile. They've both used this hotel before for that reason. The woman, seated at a small table near the window, is as picturesque as Manny in her own way. When she stands, she's over six feet tall; none of that is heels. He knows she's hit her sixties, but she doesn't look a day over forty-five. Pale skin for a Black woman, manicured brows and Fenty contouring, tailored dark brown Armani suit. She is a woman who has never been beautiful in the way that most men prefer: there is no fragility to her, no smallness, no self-diminishing smiles or attempts to lessen her height or presence. She looks powerful and dangerous. Manny supposes that's why he's had a taste for expectation-defying, powerful, dangerous people all his life.

She's gazing through the restaurant's wall of windows at the garden when Manny comes in, but as he approaches, she turns her head only slightly to smile at him. "Well, well. On time as usual."

"Mother," he says, as a greeting.

She glides around the table so they can embrace, and it's . . . good. He remembers this. He remembers her perfume, so distinctive— a custom blend with red sandalwood and cassia. A moment from his childhood comes back to him: this scent wafting past his nose as she strokes his hair. *Don't forget*, she had said, gently but firmly. *Family first and always. We rise together, or fall apart.*

They part then, and Manny sits down opposite while she orders each of them a cappuccino. He nods reflexively to the uniformed girl who comes over to set down their drinks—and pauses as something tickles his senses. The girl is ordinary. Black with a hint of East African bone structure. Slender, college-aged, tired.

There is a welter of whispers about her—seven hundred thousand or so of them.

When the waitress leaves, Manny's mother sits back in her chair and just smiles at him for a moment. "Yes," she says. Her voice is a rich, cultured contralto. "That will be the new DC, if she survives."

Cities know their own, even before they are cities. Manny wonders if Neek will be ordered to come here and mentor the girl. "Here, too, then."

"Oh, yes. At least half a dozen cities in this hemisphere are poised to make the change soon, in addition to ours. It's not just that *she* is delaying their ascension. I'm developing a theory."

"That American cities have only recently developed sufficient reputations and stability, given their relative youth?"

Her smile is wide and approving. "I suppose you would have a better idea of how all this works now. What shall I call you these days?"

"Manny, please. Thank you for asking." He sips his cappuccino.

"Of course. But I'm a little surprised that you didn't become the city as a whole. Timing, maybe? You arrived shortly after the birthing..."

Manny shakes his head. "It wouldn't have been me, anyhow. There was a better candidate. I'm content with Manhattan."

"Boy, haven't I warned you about settling?"

He smiles. "You're also the one who taught me to stay in my lane."

"To avoid the scrutiny of people who would otherwise be all up in our business. But I don't want to argue." She sighs. "You should eat more. I don't like that you've gotten thinner."

They make small talk for a while. Right to business is for enemies and the untrusted; friends catch up first, and family gets all
the gossip. His younger brother is pursuing a career as a rapper
and having some success with his latest single. He's apparently
taken up with "some girl with a PhD who's half a foot taller and
can't dance to save her life." Manny can't tell if this is a good thing
in his mother's eyes or not. His little sister is learning the family
business, and eager to take up the role that Manny abandoned. "In
a few years," his mother says, reassuringly, when Manny raises
eyebrows. "Right now she lacks judgment. And restraint." Apparently she's cost the family a good amount in bribes to clean up her
messes. Well, she'll learn. He did, too.

Finally his mother sits back and sighs, steepling her fingers and
regarding him frankly. "A mayoral race is expensive," she says.

Manny inclines his head. "Keeping tabs?"

"Why wouldn't I? You're my son. Even if you did abandon the
family in our hour of need—"

Oh, here they go. Manny shakes his head, bemused. "You said
you wanted me happy."

"I do! But I'm still gonna talk about you like a dog, baby, that's
my job, too." She grins, and he sigh-smiles as well. Then she
sobers; back to business. "Ms. Thomason's war chest is too small
and she's going to have trouble soon about those brownstones of
hers, or so I've heard from my news contacts. The *Post* will spin it
as irresponsibility, implied corruption—"

"We're going to get out in front of that," Manny says. He's
already discussed it with Brooklyn and hired a PR company to
carefully engineer think pieces about deed theft and the nation's

history of appropriating wealth from African American families. "We can't accelerate the timeline since Brooklyn's court hearing regarding her condos isn't until next week. It's going to land right before the debate and there's nothing we can do about that. But we can prepare the battleground, at least."

She nods in approval. "And the war chest?"

"It's a respectable seed considering we started late. I think that if we can at least get some key endorsements, the donations will roll in."

"Ah. Then if you're not here to ask for money . . ." She narrows her eyes. "The NYPD."

"The NYPD." He nods agreement. "That's going to be a matter of leverage."

"As in, you need some." She sighs. "You never ask for small favors."

"You know I prefer to take care of things myself, when-ever I can." He sits back as well, crossing his legs and steepling his fingers—before realizing he's imitating her. An old habit he's been trying to break for most of his adult life. He folds his hands instead. She looks amused, missing nothing, and he sighs inwardly. "We're prepared to make a concession or two on fund-ing police pensions, but a key component of Brooklyn's platform is going to be reining them in. The overtime abuse, the military hardware and surveillance . . ."

"Oh, of course. Cops there are almost as bad as the ones back home." She considers for a moment or two. "I've had some names compiled. Brass who can be brought around. The PPA is a lost cause, as you've probably guessed. Milam sees a right-wing platform as his ticket to a cushy lobbyist gig later, so he's going to keep spewing foolishness. We might be able to pull the sharpest of his teeth, though; as you already noted, his son is a weak point. Too greedy and racist for sense, and even Milam knows it. Hang him out to dry and we've got Milam. Even better, I think we might be able to swing endorsements from the Benefit Association and the Black Law Enforcement Officers' Union. They don't like Milam much."

Of course she's guessed his intent. It's everything Manny's come to ask for and then some. So he takes a deep breath. "And the price?"

She smiles. "You don't seem happy, Manny."

He manages, just, to keep his expression neutral. "Working on it."

"You're a silver bullet, baby. You're a sword from a lake. Is he worthy? Does he even need you?"

That shot lands entirely too close to the bullseye. "Yes."

"Does *he* know he needs you?" She flicks a hand in frustration. "I'll grant that child might have hidden depths. He'd have to, if New York chose him, and you wouldn't be willing to play number two to just any street meat—"

"Mother." He keeps it flat. Warning.

She gives him an *Oh, it's like that then?* look. "Tell me you aren't falling for him."

Manny flexes his hands, reminding himself to stay relaxed. She's no more tolerant of rudeness than he is, but there are some things he cannot talk about with her, and this is one of them.

Her expression softens. "Then I am genuinely sad to have to

ask this—but I taught you a long time ago that you only exchange value for equal value. We'll even kick in a modest, privately funded PAC." She smiles, which means it won't be modest at all.

Manny's jaw tightens. His throat hurts. "Don't."

She reaches over to touch his knee, soothingly. That makes it worse, that she seems to genuinely regret the pain her words are about to cause. He gets his empathy—and ruthlessness—from her. "*We* need you, Manny. Your family."

Family ain't always the one you get born with. "This is my life you're talking about."

"And you've just mortgaged it." Her smile is kind but brutal. She knows exactly what she's doing to him. "The Woman in White has been active within our borders, too, weakening key institutions and softening what should be our defenses. The writing is on the wall. Should the world survive the current crisis, we will need to be as strong as possible in the moment that our city comes to life."

Manny's jaw is tight. He forces himself to relax it before she chides him for letting his anger show. "*You* run the family. The primary should be you."

"It might very well be! But somehow I don't think so." She sits forward. "So, put plainly: We'll give you everything you need to get Brooklyn elected and save New York. And in exchange, you'll leave New York. Come home, and take the role you were meant for. Are we agreed?"

Manny thinks of Neek's smile. How he so often covers sorrow with nonchalance. So many people in Neek's life have abandoned him—and now Manny will, too. No wonder he didn't want to let Manny close.

But all is fair in love and multiversal war.

His mother waits a moment. When he doesn't answer, she sighs, then puts her napkin on the table beside the fifty she's left for the waitress. The two cappuccinos come to less than ten dollars even with tax. He keeps his gaze on the bill as his mother rises and moves past him. She pauses to put a hand on his shoulder— the one Douglas didn't touch.

"'Manhattan' does suit you," she says. "At least New York gave you the best part of itself. But I've always thought 'Chicago' fit even better."

He just sits there, numb. She lingers a moment, perhaps hoping he'll say something more, but when he doesn't, she pats his shoulder and leaves him to mourn in silence.

CHAPTER ELEVEN

Doink Doink Boom

The courthouse is strangely antiseptic. Brooklyn always expects them to be filthy. A lot of courthouses are, especially in New York, where budgets for cleaning are first to get cut in a crunch and last to be restored when flush. Her expectation doesn't really have anything to do with sanitation, however. Every court is a horror movie setting at its core, where property matters more than human lives and justice gets measured in billable hours. The whole reason Brooklyn went to law school but then immediately went into politics was because she hated appearing in court. Hated moot court, even, back in school. She's just lost too many friends to places like this to view it with a neutral gaze—children sent back to abusive parents, addicts jailed when they needed treatment, innocent people imprisoned for years by lying prosecutors or cops. She could do more for her borough, she felt then, by directing policy and building support systems to keep people out of courthouses in the first place—which should *stink*, damn it, like any charnel house.

This particular one, the state supreme court building in

downtown Brooklyn, looks deceptively well-maintained on the surface. Polished concrete flooring, brutalist design everywhere, "privacy doors" made of clear glass, plastic plants...but the whole place reeks of cheap cleaning fluids. Back when Brooklyn was a child helping to tend her father's brownstones, Clyde Thomason had spent extra money to buy decent cleaning products, and they'd done a lot with plain old vinegar. "People know how loved a place is by how it smells," he'd said, when she asked why. "If it smells like good food, nice wood, fresh paint, they'll want to live there. If it smells like cheap shit, even if it looks clean, they know it ain't got no soul."

No soul in this courthouse, then. Justice is blind, and cruel. Brooklyn's just going to have to hope it's on her side today, for once.

(She's tried to imagine what life is like in R'lyeh. To the degree that life can even exist in such a place, she ends up imagining something like this. Plastic and composite everywhere, spotless white walls and blocks of unyielding stone, and the inescapable nightmare stench of purple Fabuloso.)

"Relax," says her lawyer. Ms. Allen is an incongruously tiny woman, a full head shorter than Brooklyn's six feet and probably half her weight. Brooklyn hired her on the recommendation of a fellow counselor, who said that Allen was as vicious as all the stereotypes about pit bulls. Privately Brooklyn finds Allen a little... much? The woman seems to have taken the Better New York Foundation's attempt to claim Brooklyn's brownstones as a personal affront. "How fucking dare they," she seethes in their meetings. "It's unacceptable. We're taking this to the top and we're not taking no for an answer and then we're going to *sue* the motherfuckers to make sure this never happens again."

Brooklyn feels the rage, too, of course. That two paid-off properties with no liens can simply be sold out from under their owners is so ridiculous as to be Kafkaesque. The city didn't even tax Better New York for the sale. Just snip snap, some paperwork and a few changed lines in a database, and suddenly Brooklyn's family gets an eviction notice for their own damn home. She's feeling the kind of fury over this that can break people—but she's got to wear her poker face through all of it, lest someone catch a photo of her showing momentary frustration and blast it all over social media with an "angry Black woman" caption. She likes Allen's white-woman speak-to-the-manager energy, but it's hard not to resent her freedom to display her feelings.

Well, anyway. "Hard to relax when my father's lifelong dream is on the chopping block," she says. Which isn't even accurate. The brownstones have already been sold; the chopping happened before Brooklyn even became a living city. She can't blame this on the Woman in White or her minions when they just took advantage of the city's preexisting incompetence. "Just as long as I get them back."

"The good news is that we moved quickly," Allen reassures. "And you're lucky Better New York did everything by the book; that's the biggest reason legal recourse might actually help in your case."

Brooklyn knows why Better New York kept everything on the up-and-up. Shady dealings are part and parcel of New York; running this as a scam would only have strengthened the city. Brooklyn might even have been able to fix things with city-power. Alas, R'lyeh in her pale house dreams bigger: she's given Brooklyn a wholly mundane problem rooted in money and systemic inequality—which makes it a lot harder to solve.

Her phone buzzes with a message from one of her staffers. Apparently Senator Panfilo is planning to give a press conference in half an hour. Brooklyn texts back that she'll be in court and her phone will be off. Then the docket gets called, and it's time for Brooklyn's case.

It troubles her to see the public seats full, even though she expected it. She's a mayoral candidate whose star just went national, thanks to Veneza's brilliant viral marketing. If nothing else, she expected the *Post* to be all over this since it's perfect smear material. A lot of these folks don't look like press, however: they're dressed casually, in some cases so casually that the court officer shouldn't have let them in. Two of the guys are in shorts and baseball caps, for example—clothing that's against courtroom dress code.

But Brooklyn doesn't have time to think about the spectators anymore, as the hearing is called to order.

The first ten minutes or so are standard court procedure. The judge is a middle-aged white man who looks really tired. They've lucked out in getting him; Judge Crawford has a reputation for being friendly to property owners who've been hurt by red tape. He's death on people who disrespect his courtroom, however, which is why Brooklyn has asked her father not to attend today's proceeding. Clyde Thomason has never been good at reining in his anger, and is likely to start shouting in the middle of court.

Of more interest is the lawyer representing the Better New York Foundation. Brooklyn half expects to see the Woman in White herself standing there in a suit and French roll, but instead it's another white guy, who looks barely old enough to have passed the bar. He nods politely to Brooklyn when he notices her scrutiny, and there's no malice in his gaze. No white tendrils on his body, either, though Brooklyn hasn't seen any of those in months. She can't relax, regardless. No relaxing when R'lyeh is involved.

Ms. Allen starts presenting their case. Brooklyn and her father co-own the two brownstones in question, paid them off years ago, and have put substantial equity into both. The city program that was used to transfer the deed from their revocable trust to Better New York was intended to address abandoned or distressed properties; the Thomasons' property did not qualify. The pretext that the program used to claim the deeds was an unpaid water bill—which *was* paid, as Brooklyn has the receipts to prove. Just an error on the city's part, but one that has devastated Brooklyn's family.

"This is part of a pattern," Allen concludes. "Across hundreds of cases, this program has misidentified properties as distressed—properties overwhelmingly belonging to Black and Brown New Yorkers who are working-class, elderly, disabled, or some combination of the above. In many such cases, the properties cannot be returned because they were immediately sold by the new owners, and the original owners lack the resources to pursue the matter in the courts. To prevent something similar from happening in her case, Ms. Thomason has requested this hearing to vacate the default judgment in the foreclosure proceeding, and restore her ownership rights."

It's a good opening. Then it's Better New York's turn. Their lawyer, a Mr. Vance, gets up. He doesn't dispute that the Thomason deeds were transferred due to error. However. "This program was intended to benefit the less fortunate," he explains. "Now that the deed has been transferred, sale of the property will help fund our nonprofit organization. Let me tell you how this money will be used." He starts running down a list of the Better New York Foundation's good deeds, starting with its offer of a $23 million donation to the Bronx Art Center. Brooklyn knows full well Bronca turned that down, but the offer still makes Better New York look good, as do the other "benefits" they've offered the city: demolition of out-of-code older buildings (displacing hundreds of poor families), replacing "drug-infested" playgrounds with shiny community centers (taking away a safe free outdoor space for kids and requiring a membership fee that many locals cannot afford), and replacing dirty old bodegas with upscale grocery stores (destroying community support systems and inflating food costs). The sale of Brooklyn's brownstones would contribute to all that. Wonderful.

She leans over to whisper to Ms. Allen. "Are these people trying what I think they're trying?"

Allen's got her own poker face on now, but she isn't taking her eyes off the judge, which means she's worried. "Yep. 'Sucks that we took these folks' home, but we'll do nice things with the stolen goods!'"

It's a tactic that Brooklyn knew was possible, but didn't think could fly: an appeal to the "public good." The city's transfer program is similar to eminent domain—and if Better New York can make the case that the benefit to society outweighs Brooklyn's individual property rights, there's a chance the judge will respond favorably. She watches the judge herself and is worried to see a thoughtful frown on the man's face.

Vance is winding down his argument when one of the shorts-and-cap-wearing men in public seating, the Black one, holds up his phone and starts playing a video. It's loud; the phone's volume is all the way up, and the voice coming out of it—Panfilo—is pitched to carry across a crowd. "Hey," says another person in the public seating, who scowls up at the man. "What are you doing? Sit down." Shorts-and-Cap ignores this. Brooklyn can't make out what he's saying because the judge immediately scowls and calls for order, and the court officer heads toward the man with an irritated scowl.

Before the court officer can take the phone or ask the man to leave, however, another person in public seating stands and lifts her phone. This one's a white woman in her sixties or so, mouth pursed in determination, although her phone's an older model and the volume doesn't add much to the noise. Then White-Shorts-and-Cap does the same thing, however—except worse, because he's holding a portable Bluetooth speaker in his free hand, with enough oomph that it instantly becomes the loudest thing in the room. Now the courtroom is drowning in Panfilo's voice, even as Judge Crawford bangs his gavel and threatens to have all of them held in contempt of court.

Then Panfilo says, "We're gonna Make New York Great Again!"

"Make New York Great Again!" shout six people in the public seats, two standing up belatedly.

"Oh, no, fucking *Friendlies*," says somebody else, but if he says anything else, Brooklyn can't hear it.

Panfilo repeats his call: "Make New York Great Again!"

The Friendlies in the courtroom react as if they're in church, some punching fists in the air in lieu of praise hands: "Make New York Great Again!"

Brooklyn stands as well, though Ms. Allen grabs her arm and pulls her down. Of all the people in this room, Brooklyn is the one who can least afford to lose her shit. She's not angry, though, and she didn't stand because she meant to confront the Friendlies. She stood in pure reactive confusion—because she can feel the city, all of it but especially this borough, *her* borough, suddenly beginning to tremble with every syllable of Panfilo's chant. Panfilo and his followers do the chant a third time, like a mantra, like cultists, their faces ecstatic.

And then the lights go out.

Blackouts, despite the city's reputation, are actually infrequent in New York City. Most often they hit in the summertime, whenever too many people turn on their window units to survive occasional-but-brutal heat waves, but nothing like that should be happening on a chilly fall day. Brooklyn immediately realizes why the power died, however, because this is also the moment when Brooklyn—not the woman, not the municipality, but the metaphysical living entity—dies.

Dies isn't even the word for it. Brooklyn's heard Padmini's account of what happened in Queens, and that's the word she used, but to Brooklyn it seems that the borough does the opposite of dying; it becomes somehow *unborn*. It feels again like it did in the days before the city's awakening—pent energy, stirrings of awareness, whispers and portents and moments in which Brooklyn, at the time, had found herself daydreaming of lives not her own and sites she'd never visited, experiencing unknown traumas and triumphs. Suddenly snapping back to that, after months of the city being vibrant and aware, feels sort of like suddenly being made pregnant again with her daughter, fifteen years after Jojo was born. It's not terrible in and of itself, but it's wrong as hell.

Will it come back to life? That happened in Padmini's case, but Brooklyn curses herself inwardly for not listening more to Padmini on what caused the change, or exactly what she did to speed up its reversal. Brooklyn didn't ask, because on some level, she was intrigued by the idea. She *has* wished, occasionally, to be free of the burden of cityhood; her family has enough to worry about, and she's busy. But this? Is awful. No, she wants her living Brooklyn back, ASAP.

Problem: in that moment of power outage, which lasts only a few seconds but shuts down the chanting Panfilo fans as their phones and speakers go silent...Brooklyn hears the opposing counsel, Mr. Vance, yelp and utter a weird choking sound.

The lights come up. Everyone murmurs in surprise, except the Panfilo fans, who are muttering in frustration. The judge looks relieved, as much by the end of the chanting as by the return of the lights. Brooklyn focuses on Vance—and stiffens in horror.

Padmini described this, too: a cable from on high. It's coming in through the nearby window, piercing the glass without breakage because it is insubstantial on this plane of existence—but its tip is attached, firmly, to the back of Mr. Vance's head.

It's somehow more horrific that no one else can see the thing, a long muscular *something* like a worm made of strung-together boils, wending across the floor and flexing with organic repulsiveness. The business end is flowerlike, with fleshy "petals" spread against the back of Vance's head and flexing now and again amid his short hair, but sticking in place as if suctioned. Vance stands stock-still, his expression slack and eyes glazed, and even though he's working for the people who stole Brooklyn's home, she wants to help him. No one deserves this.

But she is no longer a wielder of the city's power. There's nothing she can do but stare in queasy impotence.

"Take the phones and that speaker," the judge orders the court officer, nodding toward the Friendlies. "That or arrest them, I don't care which. I won't have this disruption again."

One of the guys in shorts protests immediately. "You can't do that, I know my constitutional rights—" The officer snatches the phone from his hand while he's whining, and he gasps and actually tries to grab for it. The officer wins this contest and then puts a warning hand on his belt, where a prominent set of zip ties can be seen.

"You don't have a constitutional right to disrupt my courtroom," Crawford snaps. Then, pointedly turning his attention away from the man, he focuses on Vance. "Counsel, you may finish your statement. Quickly, please, before we have any more interruptions."

"Right!" Vance says, brightening into a smile—and Brooklyn's skin goes cold and prickly. She knows that plastic, manic smile. "Well, you know all the basics. The property's ours. We took it because we could, and because you people genuinely don't seem to care if some of your most loyal and productive citizens get run out of town. If not for the injunction we would've sold it already, and invested the money in something else that would help destroy New York." Then he—though this isn't Vance anymore—seems to remember that he's supposed to have an argument. "Charitably! City destruction can often be charitable, I've found. It's like mercy-killing millions of people at a time. We will do incredible good for the infinite lives of the multiverse when we wipe this particular branch of it out of existence. Now, are we done here?"

Crawford stares at the Vance/Woman in utter confusion. "Counselor, are you feeling all right?"

"Slightly breakable, but otherwise delicious, thank you for asking, Your Honor." The Vance/Woman turns then, and grins at Brooklyn. Vance has a long, narrow face; this makes the grin even more disturbing because it's wide enough to show all his teeth. "Same as you, my dear. I see you no longer have that pesky city-power keeping you safe from me! Well, that's just tragic, isn't it? We should do something about that."

Suddenly, the Friendlies in the room stop arguing with the court officer and go still. Then, as one, their heads turn to orient on Brooklyn, and they all smile. Beyond them, Brooklyn sees the white cable change: now there's a big swelling developing along its length. She's reminded suddenly of *The Little Prince*, a lovely children's book that she found inexplicably disturbing as a child, because children are often frightened by odd things. There's a point in the story that depicts an elephant inside a snake, ostensibly in the process of being digested . . . and now what looks like a baby elephant is moving through the Woman's cable, squeezing itself inexorably toward Vance's head. What is it? What will happen when it gets to him? Brooklyn really does not want to find out.

She grabs for her phone, with a vague and panicky thought of using her "Ladies' Night" playlist. But her phone is still in the lengthy process of rebooting after shutdown—because that wasn't an ordinary blackout of course—and worse, the phone is magically "cold" to the touch. Music works as a weapon for her because she filters and directs the city's power through it; without that power, it's just noise. For the first time in Brooklyn's life, music cannot help her.

Now it's chaos in the courtroom. Several people in the

public gallery—apparently Brooklyn does have a few supporters present—are yelling at the standing, eerily still Panfilo supporters. A couple of the journalists have taken out phones or audio equipment and started recording; great. Allen has stood up and objected: "Opposing counsel is *threatening* my client, Your Honor—" while Crawford rubs his face as if trying to wake up. The court officer tries to grab the nearest Shorts-and-Cap's arm and turn him around, but the guy doesn't budge even when the officer yanks with all his body weight. He *should* move, since the officer looks to outweigh him by a good fifty pounds . . . but the laws of physics in effect right now are not 100 percent local. Not anymore.

The moving mass within the tentacle is nearly to Vance's head.

Brooklyn grabs Ms. Allen's arm. "We need to get out of here. This isn't safe." It's a stage whisper and the judge might hear it, or maybe not given that people in the room are shouting and some of the phones are blinging as they come back on. Why Crawford hasn't declared a recess already, Brooklyn cannot fathom.

But then the judge surprises the hell out of Brooklyn.

"Enough of this," he says suddenly. He sits up, and he's *furious*, raising his voice to be heard over the din. "No. You people want to disrupt my courtroom over politics? You think if you yell enough then people might let you have your way, you bunch of spoiled toddlers? *Hell*, no." He grabs his gavel and bangs it. "Court finds for the plaintiff. All deed transfer fees will be covered by Better New York—"

Scattered cheers break out in the room from those who know enough courtroom lingo to realize Brooklyn has won. But in the same instant, the moving mass reaches the back of Vance's head.

He groans, eyes rolling back, and opens—*and opens*—his mouth. In horror Brooklyn sees that his jaw has detached, unhinging like a snake's as the sides of his mouth stretch and begin to tear; God, she hopes he can't feel pain right now. But much worse than poor Mr. Vance's physical distortion is the fact that now Brooklyn can see something occluding the back of his mouth, welling up from within his throat. It's not vomit or anything liquid, and it's definitely not an elephant... but it does seem to be made of some mottled, grayish-white substance. It pushes up as far as the backs of Vance's teeth and then begins swelling outward, malevolent dough rising on fast-forward—

Crawford points the gavel at Vance as if the horrible gargling noise he's making is actually some sort of protest. "I don't want to hear it, counselor. If you have a problem with how I handled this case, file an appeal, or blame Senator Panfilo for pissing me off. But you think you can pull this in *my* courtroom? 'Not today, not no way, 'cause I'm tellin' you now that I ain't come to play.'" And he bangs the gavel.

Brooklyn-the-woman has a fleeting instant to wonder at the odd familiarity of the judge's last words... before Brooklyn-the-borough starbursts back into life. The blast of *cityness* rolls forth from the gavel like the shock wave of a nuclear explosion. It hits the court officer and suddenly he's strong enough to wrestle the resistant Shorts-and-Cap to the ground. It hits Vance with the force of a sledgehammer, knocking the developing mass of God-knows-what back into his mouth and out of him through the tentacle. He slumps, catching himself on his table as the tendril attached to his head squeals and snaps loose. It flails wildly before beginning to withdraw through the window. However, the strange lump inside the tentacle makes it sluggish, and it can't escape before the wave of Brooklyn-ness overtakes it. To Brooklyn's deep satisfaction, the power sears at it like an invisible flamethrower, blasting the tendril and its cargo apart before disintegrating both. Less than a second and there's nothing but white ash, then even that is gone. Through the window Brooklyn catches a fleeting glimpse of a sharply truncated tendril flailing in the sky before it withdraws toward its point of origin.

Allen puts a hand on her arm. "You okay?" she asks, peering oddly at Brooklyn. "I know this is probably an emotional moment and all, but I didn't think you'd be daydreaming at this point."

Beyond her, the court officer has one Shorts-and-Cap guy in zips and is handing him off to another officer who has come to the room to assist. White-Shorts-and-Cap is loudly asking why his friend got arrested; the first officer glares and clearly contemplates arresting him, too. A few of Panfilo's supporters attempt to revive the chant in a half-hearted way, but their phones aren't able to play the speech for some reason, and without a hook to hang their chant on, they start to look embarrassed and falter into silence. It's still chaos, but winding down.

Then Brooklyn finally registers what Allen has said. "Oh my God. Did we just win?"

Allen bursts out laughing, and it's the best sound Brooklyn's heard in a good while.

That's it, then. The Friendlies have converged on the court officers, yelling that they want to speak to the manager of the courthouse. At this rate they're all going to get themselves hauled off.

Poor Mr. Vance has slumped into his chair; his mouth is back to normal, but he looks exhausted and rubs at one jaw joint as if it aches. Brooklyn swings past him on her way out, pausing to peer into his face—but it's just him again. "You okay?" she asks, just to be sure.

He blinks in surprise, then nods blearily. "Thanks. But you shouldn't be talking to me, Ms. Thomason—"

"I know, I know. You just looked like you were about to faint. Take care." She takes a step back, just to make it clear that she respects the boundaries of protocol. Crawford has come off his bench in preparation to leave, though he pauses as Brooklyn passes. Brooklyn nods to him, more relieved than he can possibly know; if not for his outburst of New Yorkish temper and irreverence, she's not sure what would have happened.

But then, belatedly, she remembers that line he quoted at the end of his finding. *Not today, not no way . . .* God. That's one of *her* lines, from one of MC Free's late-career hits, "Hell to the Naw." She's forgotten her own damn music; she really must be getting old.

"Have a nice afternoon, Ms. Thomason," Crawford says, to her surprise since he's not supposed to speak to her, either. And then he glances at Mr. Vance to make sure he's not listening before flashing her a wink. "I'm a huge fan."

CHAPTER TWELVE

Bagels, Meet Baguettes

By her second date with Marina, Bronca starts to think *This is the one.*

That's because everything that can possibly go wrong with the date does—and in all her previous relationship experience, Bronca's only had luck this bad when she's found someone worth her time. First, she gets the time wrong. They're supposed to meet at the Angelika Film Center on Houston, to watch some arthouse movie whose name Bronca has forgotten. It's got lesbians in it and they don't die at the end; this is still a novel-enough experience for her that it's all she really needs to have a good time. She forgets that the film starts at nine instead of eight, however, though she remembers the plan to show up an hour ahead of time so they can just chat and maybe get some quick eats. As a result, Bronca ends up sitting by herself in the theater's lobby, *two* hours early. That's way more time than she likes to spend, unoccupied, in her own company.

But as she stares out the theater window and tries (but fails) to not think about the latest nonsense from the board of directors, and the follow-up phone calls she needs to make for Brooklyn's campaign, and the photos of her new grandson that her son just texted, oh yeah and the imminent death of the universe, she spies another woman approaching through the mirror reflection. It's not Marina, who's on her way after Bronca sheepishly confessed her error regarding the time. This woman is short but savagely thin, with a small-boned frame and loose, wavy dark hair framing a tan-skinned face. She's dressed to the nines in a brown suede skirt, cropped blouse, and striped socks of all things, topped by a shiny orange satin duster. Somehow it looks amazing. Fashion model, maybe? She's way too dressed up for a movie, but then here on the edge of tony SoHo, "too dressed up" isn't a thing. The most notable feature of this woman, however, is the fact that she looks deeply disgruntled to be in this place, with its stale-popcorn smell and worn carpeting, even though the Angelika is one of the nicer theaters in the city. It's beneath her to be here, Bronca reads in this woman's face. Everything in New York is beneath her.

As she sits on the couch across from Bronca, and Bronca's metaphysical weight shifts as another large gravity well takes up close proximity, there's a moment when her perception flickers and she finds herself sitting across from *crowded tenements and ancient ossuaries, cigarette smoke laced with herbes de Provence layered mille-feuille-deep over the acrid smoke of protest fires—*

Bronca blinks as the woman crosses her legs. The striped knee-highs would look silly on anyone else, but she's wearing the hell out of them. Of course she is. "Paris," Bronca says.

The woman rolls her eyes. *"Hello,"* she says, pointedly and in rapid, barely accented English. "Delighted to meet you. Yes, of course I am Paris, who else did you think would be sent to explain things to you, clearly this is my sad fate. You are New York."

Bronca spends a moment trying to decide whether to go off on this woman. She decides to opt for courtesy, if frostily. "I'm *a borough* of New York, yes, specifically the Bronx. If you want to meet our primary—"

"I don't care what you call your arrondissements here. I'm talking to you because you're the one I could find most easily. I'm also told you're the only one who actually acquired the lexicon we assembled in order to educate you younger ones, and I don't feel like explaining myself. You'll do."

Yeah, no. "I suppose I'll have to do," she says, speaking with emphatic slowness to offset this woman's machine-gun speech, "because if you step to any other part of this city with that attitude, you're likely to get punched in the nose. Me, I'm only *thinking* about it. I'm a grandma now. Gotta be a role model."

Paris looks taken aback, but then she takes a deep breath. "I apologize," she says, after a moment. "Everyone here seems rude to me. It's hard not to respond in kind."

The apology actually helps. Bronca supposes she can relate; New Yorkers don't handle it well when outsiders disrespect their greeting customs, either, even though those customs amount to "Get to the point and don't waste our time with small talk." "Yeah, well, when in Rome. But fine; hello, pleased to meet you, Paris. What can I do for you?"

Paris relaxes, though she uncrosses and recrosses her legs in a way that Bronca reads as nervous. Maybe it's not. Maybe the living embodiment of one of the oldest European cities has restless legs syndrome, or maybe this is how she embodies the energy of the Tour de France or a UEFA championship. Whatever. "We've set a date for the next Summit," Paris says, flicking at an imaginary spot on her skirt. "It will be on Friday, noon your time, on the island of—"

Bronca's already shaking her head. "Friday? It's *Tuesday*. You know how much airline tickets are going to cost at the last minute? And one of us has to arrange childcare—"

"You're the ones who requested the meeting be set up as quickly as possible," Paris says, looking annoyed.

"Yes, 'cause *the whole world is going to die* and we figured the rest of you might be *concerned* about that—"

"Consider the difficulty of arranging meetings at all for several people in their fourth or fifth *millennium*. Normally we don't allow new cities to address the Summit before they're a hundred years old because they don't yet understand how much of a burden it places on the rest of us. For God's sake, Luoyang only became willing to travel by train in the 1950s. Won't macrostep outside his city at all! Such a nightmare."

There's a lot to unpack in this, so much that Bronca struggles to hold on to her anger. "You've put us off for weeks at this point, so I don't see what difference it'll make to give us more than three days' notice. I saw your star falling through the branches of the tree same as ours, but Padmini—Queens—says we should have a few weeks before things get acute. And if your elders can't make it to the meeting, then we're willing to go to them—"

Paris lets out a long, irritated sigh, though it doesn't sound personal this time. "You fail to comprehend that a good number of us are *in denial*," she says, her tone going sour. "I used to think only Americans could be so selfishly self-destructive during an emergency, but I suppose it is a human failing."

"*Denial?*" Bronca can't believe what she's hearing. "Do they not see what's happening? Have they been to the tree lately? Do they think that falling sensation is just a nice breeze?"

"I don't know what they tell themselves. But what they tell *me* is that they blame New York for causing the problem, and they want you punished for it."

Bronca sucks in a breath. "The *fuck—*"

Paris holds up a hand. "Please! I am just the messenger." She recrosses her legs, gracefully looking down Houston Street through the window. "In any case, I assume you or some representative of New York will attend?"

Bronca's still trying to wrap her head around... what, multiversal apocalypse truthers? "Uh, yeah. Shit. We might all attend, but let me talk to the others, and Paulo."

"How democratic. Though I suppose you have no choice, given there are so many of you."

"What, the other compound cities do things differently?"

"Each city does things in its own way. While you of New York aren't the only multiple birth by far, it hasn't happened in recent centuries. Some had begun to believe it was a thing of the past. Instead, as we sense the stirrings of life from several other cities in this hemisphere, we can tell that quite a few of those will be multiple births as well. That's also what has upset the change-resisters, you realize: so *much* change, all at once. And do not forget that some of us are still in mourning. Colonialism was a mass casualty event for us, and not that long ago by elder standards." Paris sighs, then sits forward. "But never mind that. Regarding the Summit, I simply want you to understand what you face. The recent discovery that the Enemy has played us for thousands of years, your city's persistent instability, this multiversal descent that we cannot seem to stop... The complainers want to be done with it all. And they cannot stop the Enemy, but they can attack you. Infuriating as it must be, is it not understandable?"

"Sure," Bronca says, trying very hard not to think about her own frustrations with the rapid change of technology, protest movements, and just about every other aspect of life. Veneza calls her a Luddite sometimes, and Bronca takes a private pride in the designation... but it hits her now that she's going to have to let go of that. Otherwise—assuming they all survive the next few weeks—she might end up a thousand years old and still pissed off about the demise of landlines. "But them attacking us, and the rest of you humoring their nonsense, isn't going to save anybody. Only solving the problem will do that."

Paris tilts her head in a way that Bronca reads as belligerent, though she reminds herself that body language varies across cultures. "Do you have a course of action to recommend?"

"Yeah, I think we need to get rid of—" Bronca refrains from saying the name, instead jerking her head southward to indicate R'lyeh. "We got her out of most of the city when we awakened our primary, but before that, she latched on to one of our number. If we can break that linkage, somehow..."

"Yes. And how did one of the New Yorks somehow fail to bond

with the rest of you, and become vulnerable in this manner? This is what the others will say, I'm just preparing you."

Bronca feels a muscle start to tighten in her jaw. "Partly that's the nature of New York; that borough's relationship with the rest of the city has always been...um, contentious. But mostly it happened because we had no idea what the hell was going on, at first. Don't blame the cities who came to help us, São Paulo and Hong Kong, either; they didn't know any more than the rest of you did. So it's time we all woke up and started trying to adapt to the brave new world we're stuck in."

Paris sits back in her chair, rubbing a temple. "I agree with you. But your...confrontational nature...won't play well with the angry ones."

"Tough titty, said the kitty." Bronca shakes her head. "You said it yourself: New York is rude. We'll give you the shirt off our backs and our last subway card swipe if you're lost, but step to us with wild accusations about things that aren't our fault and any one of us will go off on you. Except maybe Manhattan; he's mostly too nice to yell. He'll just—very nicely—cut your throat."

To Bronca's surprise, Paris snorts in amusement. "I respect honest murderousness. But if the danger is caused by *her* attachment to your former piece of New York..." She pauses, delicately and dramatically. "There are only half a million people on this Staten Island."

Bronca shakes her head, suppressing a bitter laugh. She knows that some of the others—Manhattan, almost surely—have considered killing the avatar of Staten Island as a solution to their problem. She cannot help feeling that this is a peculiarly settlerish way of resolving the issue, however. Half a million people are still people. The most expedient solution isn't always the best one. She's so proud of Veneza for trying to talk to Aislyn again, even if the attempt failed.

But she'd better head Paris's little assassination plan off at the pass for a different reason. "We don't even know if that would work," Bronca says. "One of us tried to meet with the avatar of Staten Island recently, to convince her to come back to us. R—*She* attacked them, even though the assault could've easily killed Staten Island, too. Would she have done so if killing the avatar threatened her foothold? Maybe she's just stuck to this world now, like Velcro, regardless of our active assistance."

"Then...?"

"The one thing we haven't tried is an all-out attack." Bronca stretches out her legs. Getting tense amid all this talk of war. She looks at her feet and imagines them in boots rather than the nice, date-worthy Converse she's got on instead. "We hit her with everything we had when we found our primary and joined our power with his—but because of Staten Island, that wasn't enough to drive her away. If we could get help from other cities, however, maybe apply *enough* force..." They don't know if that'll work, either. But she spreads her hands. "Better than more useless bitching."

Paris nods. "Yes, agreed. Well. Come and make that argument to the others, and we'll see what sort of help we can get you." She gets to her feet, brushing imaginary wrinkles out of her skirt. "And tell your Manhattan not to visit any more cities before the Summit. Some of the angry ones..." She grimaces. "The rhetoric has gotten out of hand, and the situation is delicate. Be as careful as possible."

Bronca rolls her eyes. "Lady, we're New York. But fine, I'll pass that along, too." She's sick of this. She's tired of having to spend so much time stopping stupid, selfish people from destroying themselves and everyone around them. She rubs her eyes, then sighs out, "So where is this meeting?"

"An island near the mouth of the Mediterranean. There is an amphitheater at the heart of the ruins; it's been our traditional gathering place for a few centuries now. We'll send an . . . invitation." The pause lets Bronca know that this is city magic again, not a fancy printed card to expect in the mail. Maybe the island's so small that macrostepping is the only easy way to get there or something.

But wait. "Do you mean the Azores?"

Paris smiles, almost to herself. "Ah, we give the new cities all the knowledge they need, but it still takes time to shed the old ways of thinking, doesn't it? You know the island I mean; we were careful to put that in the lexicon of knowledge. It isn't accessible from this world, however. It never existed, here."

Oh, shit. "You're talking about *Atlantis*," Bronca blurts. She's told the other New Yorks the story of how a city can fail so spectacularly as to be erased from reality, relegated to nothing but legend. "I thought it was *dead*, not someplace we could actually go."

"It is dead, yes. But when a city dies, there is always something left behind." Paris offers a thin smile that is surprising in its bitterness. Did she know the avatar of Atlantis? Maybe it isn't even that. Maybe it's just that Paris is old enough to have seen many cities die, and one tragedy melds into another, after a time. Bronca can relate.

So out of respect for the grief she can see—and the fact that there's always more, out of sight—Bronca takes a deep breath and allows a moment's silence before she speaks again. "All right. We'll be there. Thanks for the heads-up."

Paris blinks in surprise, as if she hadn't expected Bronca to have the manners for thanks. Bronca decides to overlook this, under the circumstances. Then Paris stands and goes to the big window, her gaze drifting south. After a moment her eyes widen. "My God."

R'lyeh. "Yep," Bronca says. It's a breathtaking sight, in its way: the gleaming city in the clouds. That city looks like a fairy tale, not like the hammer poised to smash everything that it is.

Paris shakes her head. "I must remember that this, all the madness that is so sudden and bizarre to us, is all you have known in your short time as one of our kind," she murmurs to herself. "A child-city, born in war; how cruel. I'll do what I can to make things easier for you."

With that, she nods to Bronca and heads toward the bathroom. Bronca thinks fleetingly about warning the woman; the Angelika's bathrooms are terrible. But Paris passes behind a column and does not reappear on its other side, so just as well.

And here's Marina, a stocky middle-aged Latina with the sweetest smile Bronca's ever seen, driving away all the awfulness just by walking across the lobby.

"Hello, Early Bird," she says, sitting down in Paris's old seat. "You look like you just saw a ghost."

Bronca chuckles—and then, on impulse, she goes over to Marina's chair, bending to kiss her forehead. It's too awkward an angle, and things are still too new between them, or she would've gone for the lips. But to her surprise, as she starts to straighten, Marina shoots a hand up and catches her by the front of her shirt. Then she hauls Bronca down, tilts her own face up, and...oh. *Well*, then.

"No ghosts," Bronca says, grinning, once Marina has taken her fill. "The future, maybe."

"Fuck the future," Marina says. "Everything's going to shit anyway. Let's just make the next five minutes amazing."

Bronca stares down at her and thinks, *Marry me.*

Slow your roll, Romeo-ette, laughs the little Veneza that lives in her brain. And fine, Bronca will check herself, but still. There's always a moment when you know, isn't there? No matter how bad things are, there's a chance for them to get better. Just gotta keep working at it.

So Bronca sits down and, in spite of looming apocalyptic transdimensional destruction, enjoys the rest of her date.

CHAPTER THIRTEEN

The Pizza of Existential Despair

Aislyn sits in her bedroom, seething, while her mother talks to her about loyalty.

The words don't matter. Aislyn's been tuning her out for the past twenty minutes. She's not actually angry with her mom, either—because it's not Kendra Houlihan that's talking, right now. Right there on the back of Kendra's neck, peeking over her shoulder, is one of the delicate, not-quite-real fronds that the Woman in White calls "guidelines." Such an innocuous name! After wearing one for three months and finally breaking free of its influence, Aislyn's started using a different word for them: *leashes*.

What's troubling is that she doesn't even think the Woman meant to be deceptive about the guidelines. Strictly speaking, the term is entirely correct. Leashes guide, don't they? The fact that they also *control* is incidental.

Well, I'm not a dog, she thinks. But if she has to listen to one more word being forced out of her mother's mouth, she's going to start barking.

"I'm going out," she says, getting up in the middle of a sentence.

"But if you just think about— What? Oh." Kendra blinks. Then she brightens, and for a moment it's almost as if she's back to her usual self. Almost the mother that Aislyn loves, and misses badly. But this is a trap. "Back to the ferry today? You actually made it on, last time . . ."

"No," Aislyn replies, to her mother and to the entity that she once thought of as a friend. "I'm not going to try to leave again. I just need some space to *think*, okay? Can I have that at least?"

Her mother sobers. "Human thought is always a problem," she says. "So quick to meander away from the simplicities of problem-solving, so *creative*. But fine. Will you at least be home for dinner?"

"No," Aislyn says, on impulse. She grabs her jacket and keys. "Don't wait up for me." Her mother says nothing else as Aislyn heads out.

For a while, Aislyn simply drives around her island. It's one of the things she's done to clear her head ever since she got a car, and in retrospect she thinks it's one of the things that made her a good avatar for the borough, because she definitely knows every inch of it by now. She's stopped at all the usual scenic locations— O'Donovan Pond and the Fountain of the Dolphins, Great Kills Park—and found or made a few cool spots of her own over the years. There's this one area down by Sharrott's Shoreline where she can sit on the beach for hours, staring out at the water and the industrial mess that is New Jersey. When the wind is wrong, it carries the stench of countless unidentifiable chemicals. When it's right, however, there's a thick, briny marine scent on the air that she absolutely loves, because she's smelled nothing like it anywhere else. It is unique to her borough, the scent-essence of Staten Island itself, and it has never failed to soothe her...before today.

Today, Aislyn sits in her spot on the beach and feels nothing but dread. Some of this is because of the falling. She is always aware of it now, and when she closes her eyes at night to sleep she can barely manage it, because in that other place she is a mote of light surrounded by growing brightness, suffused with the awareness of onrushing doom. Right now, however, her unease is because the beach doesn't smell the same this time. The briny smell lingers, but there's a strange, somehow fungal undernote to it that she's never noticed before. As if something, somewhere amid whatever creates this scent, has started to decay. It makes Aislyn pay more attention to the strange, fleshy white columns dotting the landscape around her—pylons, the Woman has called them— which connect the island with the ghost city floating above it. No part of Staten is free of them, and they actually seem to be increasing in number with each week. And although the Woman once compared them to cable adapters, translating the signals of one world into something comprehensible by another, Aislyn has started to suspect there's also a double meaning in that description. The pylons feel more like roots—which she guesses are cables of a sort, too? Just biological instead of mechanical. She's done enough gardening to know that some plants give back some of what they take, like clover or beans, which fix nitrogen. Most plants just take, however, sucking out water and nutrients, and if nobody adds compost or fertilizer, then eventually you end up with a lot of useless dry crumbly stuff in which nothing can grow. So what exactly are these pylons taking out of her island? She doesn't know, but she has her suspicions, based on what she's seen missing from her fellow islanders. Vitality. Individuality. Reality, even. Things quintessential to making Staten Island the weird and wonderful place Aislyn's loved all her life.

You realize she tried to kill you, too?

Yeah. Aislyn doesn't like that, either. Not one bit.

The sun starts to set and it's getting October cool, so after a while Aislyn heads back to her car. She's not hungry, but sometimes comfort is its own food, so she heads to Denino's, a restaurant that holds a special place in her heart. It's classic Staten Island cuisine, with menu items like the white-sauce clam pie she orders, but she likes going there for a bonus reason: because her father doesn't like Italian food. ("Too greasy, like the people who make it.") Eating pizza has always been one of the ways in which Aislyn defied her father and laid a little more claim to herself.

As she sits down this time, however, she feels no comfort, only sadness. Where is the pleasure in defying a man who no longer cares? Can the smiling, blank-eyed thing that is Matthew Houlihan even get angry anymore? She's not sure. What shocks her is that she's actually starting to miss the walking spike-covered powder keg that was her father, in spite of everything. There's probably some kind of psychological weirdness to that, Stockholm Syndrome or masochism or something else she's heard about from Maury Povich reruns, but what it all really boils down to is that at least Matthew Houlihan loved her, in his terrible way. She's not sure the new version is capable of that, either.

But then Aislyn bites into her clam pie, and discovers that however bad things have been lately, they can still get worse.

It tastes *awful*. Like, so awful that she immediately spits it out. Is the cheese bad? The clams? It even smells wrong—also fungal, which makes no sense because there shouldn't be a mushroom within a mile of this pizza.

While Aislyn stares at the bitten-into slice and wonders if maybe she's caught some weird disease that ruins her sense of taste, the waitress stops nearby. "How is everything, ma'am?"

When Aislyn looks up, she blinks. Denino's is a family-run place; after years of coming here, she knows most of the staff. She's never seen this woman before. "Uh, it doesn't taste good. Maybe something's wrong with it, or... I don't know."

"Oh." The waitress looks pleasantly puzzled. "That's unfortunate."

Aislyn, who has been braced for pushback—another Staten Island tradition, arguing with customers—finds herself a little taken aback. "Uh, yeah, unfortunate. Look, I can't eat this. Can I maybe get the shrimp pie instead?"

"Oh, I'm sorry." The waitress's expression turns tragic. "We've removed that from the menu. Actually we're about to remove the clam pie, too. Sorry."

Aislyn's mouth falls open. "But... Those are the only two things I eat here!"

"Oh, all right, then, no problem." The waitress reaches down to take the plate. As she does so, Aislyn notices that her guideline is on her forearm; it flicks around as she collects the plate, and then orients sharply on Aislyn's face. Aislyn tries not to look at it or think about it, which is easy because she's incredulous at the waitress's response.

"*Hey*," she says, sharply because the woman has already turned away with her plate. When the waitress turns back, pleasantly puzzled now, everything is pleasant on Staten Island these days and that's so *wrong*, Aislyn blurts, "Aren't you going to offer me a refund or something? I'm hungry, and that pizza is bad, and you don't sell the only other thing I might have wanted. Can I get at least an apology, or, or . . . an explanation?" She stops short of demanding to speak to the manager, because she doesn't want to be *that* kind of white woman, not right now. But it's on the tip of her tongue.

"Oh, I'm sorry," the waitress says, with a bright smile. "We changed our recipes a few weeks ago. Most people like the new ones fine. Guess you're not one of them!"

Aislyn really can't wrap her mind around this. "It's *bad*. Like, really gross."

The waitress just stares. Aislyn counts her own breaths: one . . . two . . . a third. Ten seconds of being stared at. Finally she realizes the waitress isn't responding because she doesn't know how. She lacks the initiative even to say *Well, what do you want me to do about it?* That would at least give Aislyn something to work with—a little New Yorkish attitude to react against, a nonresponse that would at least allow her to continue the conversation. But there's just this . . . nothing. Everything is pleasant on the new Staten Island, but arguments aren't pleasant, and there isn't even enough Staten Islander left in this woman to tell Aislyn off.

Suddenly Aislyn can't take it anymore. She focuses on the guideline peering at her from the woman's arm. "Get over here. Right now. I want to talk to you."

The little white frond, which she once thought of as pretty, draws back a little, as if surprised by her bluntness. A moment later the waitress's hair flickers from dark brown to tawny white, and her clothes get an instant bleach job. "Oh dear, you really don't sound happy," says the Woman in White. She moves to sit in the open chair across from Aislyn, setting the pizza plate down and folding her hands. "And here I thought I could cheer you up by giving you a nice mother-daughter talk and not bothering you at the beach. I was going to give you the pizza for free, too."

Aislyn shakes her head. "Why would you think that *making my mother talk to me* would help? Especially about loyalty? That's the last thing she would ever—" In their last real talk, before all of this madness, Kendra all but told Aislyn to leave Staten Island. At the time, Aislyn had been horrified. Since then, she has become a city and fought off hostile invaders and ridden the ferry all the way to the city and back—even if the ride did get interrupted by a harbor monster. And she cannot even properly share this triumph with her mother.

"You made my mom *wrong*," Aislyn says finally. "You made her—" She gropes for the wording. It's clear that the Kendra who spoke to Aislyn that morning was not as much the Woman in White as this waitress is right now. There hadn't been another mind in there, just a . . . flattening, somehow, of Kendra herself, from a complicated, quirky woman into the most generic Mother imaginable. Personality gentrification. "—like you," Aislyn concludes. "You're making *everybody* here like you."

The Woman looks honestly confused. "Yes? That was the idea all along, which I thought you understood. Should I have spent more time explaining things?"

"You couldn't have explained this." Aislyn gestures at the plate, meaning to encompass the food's foulness and the waitress's detachment and everything in between. "Nothing can explain this!"

The Woman raises her snowy eyebrows. "Of course I can. New management, cost cutting, replacing the olive oil with faux truffle oil, using premade crust bought in bulk—"

Aislyn flinches. Blasphemy. "It's ruined!"

"Is it? The new management taste-tested the recipes with a focus group." Her gaze unfocuses a little. "Let's see. The group seemed to like it. They said it was just as good as stuff from California Pizza Kitchen?" She frowns, thoughtful. "But there are so many kitchens in California that make pizza; how did the group pick just one?"

Aislyn shakes her head. *This isn't California.* I mean, nothing wrong with California pizza, I guess, but they like it their way and we like it our way!"

"Well, yes. That's precisely the problem." When Aislyn falters silent, the Woman sighs. "Why are there a thousand different ways to make pizza? That's not hyperbole, I've counted, and it's actually one thousand four hundred and twenty-two. Those are just the recipes. Add in different cooking techniques and equipment, normal variances in ingredients across source—mozzarella from buffalo, mozzarella from cows who only eat grass, low-moisture pre-shreds with sawdust filler—and the actual number of ways to make this one dish becomes exponential. So, yes, in order to make Staten Island less *New York* and more *me*, I need to make its pizza consistent with that of several well-regarded national chain restaurants." The Woman tilts her head, a *why do I have to explain something so basic* look on her face. "I can't stop your species from doing what it does, but while I'm preparing this universe for annihilation, I can't very well let you keep spinning off yet more multiversal branchings, now, can I? What if the next world you spawn creates something even worse than cities? My superiors would never forgive me."

"But..." For a moment Aislyn can't word. Then she manages, "I thought you liked Staten Island for what it was?"

"I do! It's so weird, even by my standards! And everyone here is so delightfully contrary."

"Not anymore! You're making them..." She shakes her head. "*Nice!* It's...it's just..."

The Woman in White considers for a moment as Aislyn flails into frustration, and then she apparently decides to explain further. "New York—and this borough when it was included in New York—is legendary for its rudeness. The legend isn't as true as it should be; lots of people here are perfectly nice. But to contain a city's threat—to *un-New-York* New York—I have to destroy its legend. Do you understand? That is *my* nature. I don't do it out of malice, but because it's what I was built to do, in order to save countless other universes. I thought you agreed with that idea?"

"I—" Aislyn falters. Did she? She understood from the beginning that the Woman's goals were in conflict with...well, everything...but still, back when this all started, she just liked having a real friend. She liked standing with the Woman against the rest of New York. It made her feel strong, supported, and supportive in turn. Brave, instead of the coward that she has been for so long. But maybe she should have paid more attention, asked more questions.

The Woman watches her through the waitress's eyes. She seems genuinely troubled by Aislyn's unhappiness—and doesn't that mean something? She *cares* about Aislyn. Even though at the end of the day, Aislyn's having a breakdown over pizza.

Except it's *not* just about pizza. She's upset about her mother's soft, too-pleasant smile, and her father's frictionless friendliness. She hates that she suddenly has "friends" she neither knows nor trusts, and even that the racists are just ordinary hateful people instead of fitting into Staten's unique brand of pro-Wu-Tang anti-Blackness. She hates that the shoreline scent has gone rotten, and that the island's unique, iconic, weird-but-delicious food is being remade into something…normal.

She has always known that Panfilo's slogan is a lie. Fun, at first. A way to claim control of the uncontrollable, like all her little rebellions—but just as disowning her family is something Aislyn would never do, the kind of change that Making New York Great Again actually demands is a bridge way too far. What the slogan really means is *Make New York What It Never Has Been* except in the fevered imaginations of people who would destroy what they can't (or won't) understand. At the same time, she believes the Woman when she says this is the only way to save the multiverse. Friendships are supposed to be about trust, after all. More importantly, Aislyn's parents raised her to be self-sacrificing, and for the most part she has accepted this imposed duty. She didn't need to go away to college. She doesn't need dreams of her own, ambitions of her own, friends or lovers of her own; a person can be happy without those things, damn it. And until lately, she's been grateful that so much of what she does need to be happy is located here in this singular, once-perfect place. But this isn't her Staten Island, anymore.

The Woman in White sighs and puts a hand on Aislyn's. "I can make you happy again," she says, very gently. "It's your nature to chafe against the changes I must impose. You were once New York, after all, even if you didn't want to be. I won't lie: It doesn't bother me that you shed my guideline, because I've *missed* the complete you, my Lyn. My first friend! All your strangeness and contrariness and anger . . . these are the very things that make you Staten Island. They are what make you *dangerous*. But it has been hard, having so little of you around." She looks momentarily surprised by this, and the frown that's already on her brow furrows further. "I should not feel reluctance about this. I should not *ask*. But I've come to realize that what is best for you . . . isn't necessarily what's best for our friendship. So out of respect for our friendship, I offer you the choice. Shall I make you happy again?"

The Woman smiles, and it hurts, because Aislyn can see the sincerity and loneliness in that smile. And Aislyn understands loneliness, doesn't she? She's *lived* it. If the slow destruction of herself and everything she's ever cared about is indeed the only way to solve the unending problem that is New York City, then what the Woman is offering is a way to be content with that. A way to be at peace, until death.

It's wrong, though. Maybe it's not wrong to be selfless and choose the greater good, but it definitely feels wrong to . . . to drug herself into oblivion while it happens. If Aislyn has chosen this path, then she feels like she should face the consequences head-on, with eyes open. She owes that to her island, and her family, and herself. It's the Staten Island way.

To Aislyn's surprise, the Woman only sighs a little as she pulls her hand back. She looks so sad, though, and because of this Aislyn impulsively reaches out to grab her hand in turn. Aislyn half expects to feel the sting of implantation again, but there is nothing. The Woman really is leaving the choice to her.

"Is this okay for you?" Aislyn asks, troubled. The Woman has her own Matthew Houlihan to answer to.

The Woman shrugs a little, but there is something deep and meaningful in her gaze. "I was made to interact with planes of existence like yours. It means I have certain known flaws."

It's an evasion, and not. But Aislyn gets it.

Then the Woman takes a deep breath. "Well. Matters are coming to a head, anyway. There's going to be an actual *confrontation*, apparently—a nice proper mano-a-mano, good-versus-evil moment! I'm rather excited." She beams, and Aislyn cannot help smiling with her. "I've always wanted one of those! I'll give a 'the reason you suck' speech, and they'll monologue about how evil I am. I'll reply with some bitchy one-liners. Then we'll fight. I'll make it properly climactic, all the best special—well, actual—effects. Then goodness and righteousness will win out over badness and selfishness! Then I gather I'm supposed to kiss someone, but everyone in this universe will be dead so I suppose I'll have to handle that part myself." She folds her arms, thoughtful. "I should come up with a way to roll credits."

"You are so damn strange," Aislyn says, but it's affectionate.

The Woman beams. "Thank you! Now, may I please return to my important work of plotting your inevitable doom, and let this poor woman get back to her job?" Aislyn nods, and the Woman gets to her feet. A moment later, she's the waitress again, brown-haired and blue-shirted and wearing again her pleasant customer-service smile.

Aislyn takes a deep breath, then reaches over to take the plate back. "I think I'll give it another try," she says. "Sorry to be a bother."

"Oh, no bother at all, ma'am." The waitress smiles and heads off.

It still tastes awful. The cheese is bland, the crust gummy, and the fake truffle oil's funk pretty much overwhelms any better aromas that the slice might have. But it isn't so terrible, is it? To be less unique, more common. All cities change, after all. Change isn't always a bad thing.

So Aislyn chokes the slice down and orders a Coke to wash the taste from her mouth, because sometimes that's the kind of sacrifice you have to make, for a friend.

CHAPTER FOURTEEN

Brooklyn's Get Me Bodied Shop

Debate night.

Specifically, it's the first mayoral debate that will have both Brooklyn and Senator Panfilo on the same stage. The mayoral race has an unusual timeline this year, with the city rearranging several key dates due to the Bridgefall disaster; most notably, the primary has been moved to the day after the debate, barely a month before the general election. Despite this extra time, for reasons that the press is calling "a perfect storm of political problems," all the other Democratic candidates have dropped out or been so thoroughly excoriated for various scandals as to be polling in the low single digits. One of Brooklyn's fellow candidates apparently ignored rampant sexual harassment and a racial pay disparity among his campaign staffers; another turns out to have bribed various city officials and is likely to be indicted; a third was just revealed to be on the payroll of a right-wing think tank (but nobody liked her anyway). A recent profile in the *New Yorker* declared that "It's a bad year to be a Democratic mayoral candidate in New York, unless your name is Brooklyn Thomason," which frankly is excellent press. The article is largely complimentary and the full-page photo that accompanies it looks great—even though the article writer attempts a bit of scaremongering by suggesting that Brooklyn might be *too* perfect of a candidate and that there may be more to the matter of her disputed brownstones. Surely she has a few skeletons in her closet? But as long as they're only speculating about skeletons and not making some up from scratch, Brooklyn will take it.

(She does have skeletons, brand-new ones. Suddenly there's a mystery PAC spending millions on behalf of her campaign, and she hasn't been able to identify the backers. They haven't contacted Brooklyn or asked for anything . . . but Manny, in his quietly unnerving way, simply suggested that she not look that particular unrestricted-gift horse in the mouth. She's got her suspicions, as a result, but she'll deal with the fallout if and when it happens.)

Meanwhile on the Republican side, Panfilo is very clearly the front-runner, though his main challengers have been more serious—some right-wing talk show host, and a tech CEO who seems to think that all New York needs is a hefty dose of libertarianism and ten thousand extra cops, never mind the contradiction. The state party has chosen to support Panfilo, but the truth is that with both Brooklyn and Panfilo effectively backed by opposing supernatural interest groups, the other candidates had no real chance to begin with. American politics aren't truly democratic; if it isn't whole demographics being excluded from the franchise, it's corporations and wealthy donors endlessly meddling with the whole system. Extradimensional meddling fits right into that tradition, but Brooklyn can still mourn the loss of fairness and ethics, even as she uses every means at her disposal to win. She'll work on reform once she's in office.

After a series of hashtag storms and a request from local TV networks, both parties and the Campaign Finance Board have agreed to start the inter-party debates early. They've invited the top three candidates from each party to face off onstage. Ought to make for great ratings, since this setup will just cause the trailing candidates to trip all over each other saying hopefully memorable things. Running for the next election, basically.

This means that Brooklyn's strategy for the first debate is to shut up and let everyone else hang themselves. She's prepped for anything Panfilo can throw at her, of course, with some choice-but-not-too-sassy put-downs on standby for any policy issue. Still, a mayoral debate ain't got nothin' on a rap battle for excitement, and she actually kind of hopes he'll try her. As the night progresses, Panfilo largely refrains from coming at her—probably following the same strategy as her. The talk radio host has shown up ready to be outrageous, which interjects a little welcome tension and amusement into what would otherwise be a boring affair. The guy's relentless enough that Panfilo finally has to flatten him by reminding the audience that the host was born and raised in Boston. This delights everyone in the TV studio and even gets the debate moderator snickering. Some hatreds are universal in New York.

Panfilo smiles at Brooklyn whenever there's a lull in the back-and-forth. Just smiles, never says anything. It's a mind game and she doesn't fall for it, favoring him with a perfect bless-your-heart smile of tooth-rotting sweetness right back. Panfilo is damaged in this effort by association: his attempts to be creepy fall well short of the Woman in White's natural gift for same. Also, he's been getting some bad press about his partnership with a fellow by the name of Conall McGuiness—founder of a charming little bunch of wannabe Brownshirts called the Proud Men. Some of them are even on his security detail, per the reports. *McGuiness's* smiles, when the articles include photos, are creepy as shit. Brooklyn's met his type before, because there are plenty in both the music business and politics: pure narcissists, happy to use and abuse anyone stupid enough to let them. Panfilo's a fool to get in bed with a monster like that, because McGuiness will shank him as soon as Panfilo is no longer useful. But that's Panfilo's problem, not hers.

Apart from this little bit of passive aggression, however, it's a mostly boring night for Brooklyn. After the audience has started to file out and the cameras have shut off (though first rule of both politics and rap is *always assume the mic is hot*), Brooklyn chats with her team and the TV station staff a little, then waits to see which of the other candidates try to talk to her. Her people do an excellent job of running interference when the other two Dems and the lesser Republicans drift close. The Democrats can't help her and the Republicans are probably hoping for a nice photo op of themselves cursing her out. However, she's given instructions that Panfilo be allowed to approach, because she can't be seen avoiding him—and because she's genuinely curious to see if he will. When she realizes he's working his way toward her, she finds herself... pleased? Man, it really has been too long since she played that rap game. She must miss having worthy opponents.

"Good to see you again, Senator," Brooklyn says when he arrives. It's important that she seem polite and gracious, even though she despises this man. She even manages a genuinely friendly smile as she extends her hand to shake. "We met a few years back when you came to address the city council about that New York / New Jersey joint tunnel venture."

"I remember," he says. "If I recall, you opposed it." And he does not take her hand to shake. Well, there's that photo op. Brooklyn keeps her hand in place, pointedly. The right-wing papers will report favorably on his disrespect, but if she hangs a lampshade on it and shows that she hasn't been upset by his posturing, then the gracelessness and incivility in his gesture might galvanize some of the independents. If she's *really* lucky, Fox News will make up some lie about the incident; that'll get the fact-checkers ranting about it all over Twitter, and many more eyeballs on the video. Brooklyn smiles in Panfilo's face and thinks, *Maybe I'll take your senate seat next.*

Meanwhile, she says, "Only because you wanted New York to pay the bulk of the bill. Thank you for the reminder on that incident, though! I'll be sure to mention it at the next debate."

"You do that." He glances down at her still-extended hand and shakes his head, amused. It's a contest of appearances, winner gets the most donations—and they both know that the longer it goes on, the worse it'll look for him. "Good night, Ms. Thomason. We'll talk more later...if you can." With that veiled threat, he heads off.

Brooklyn glances around, pleased to spot Manny off in the shadows behind the cameras. He waggles his smartphone and nods approval. Excellent; if video of the not-altercation doesn't go viral on its own, they'll give it to Veneza and let her work her magic, city and otherwise.

Panfilo and his people leave. Brooklyn lingers a while longer, but it's getting late and she's always tried to get home early enough to see Jojo to bed every night. The girl's arm is healing well, but she's been anxious about the whole campaign—understandably, given her experiences thus far. Brooklyn's already found Jojo a good therapist, but some things just take time.

Now that the campaign has money, Manny makes sure Brooklyn has a car and driver at all times, hired from a firm that specializes in employing ex–Secret Service members as guard detail for VIPs. (Brooklyn tried to look the firm up to research it herself, but they don't have a website. No one talks about them on social media. As for where Manny heard about it . . . He's been different since his return from that unexplained out-of-town trip. Colder, and more intimidating. Brooklyn's sure she'll get used to not asking him questions she doesn't want to know the answers to, any day now.) For major campaign events they've also been able to rent a small fleet of nice vehicles for her staff. Brooklyn isn't fond of the message this sends; how's she supposed to frame herself as a champion of the subway set from a car? But security considerations have won out. Brooklyn has opted for hybrid SUVs, at least, to show environmental consciousness.

Once inside her own SUV—alone; at this point in the campaign her staff has figured out that she needs recharge time after a public event—Brooklyn feels herself start to come down off the adrenaline. Their little caravan pulls away from the curb and separates to deliver the others home. She's annoyed to realize it's later than she thought—nearly midnight, and past Jojo's bedtime. Brooklyn knows that the girl sneaks e-books under the covers for a good hour after she's supposed to turn in, however, so there's still a chance Brooklyn will make it in time.

Her driver, an older white gentleman whose actual name she can never remember because he looks like a clean-cut Captain Kangaroo—apparently he actually *was* some kind of captain before his retirement—nods to her in the rearview. "Waze is saying there's a wreck on the FDR, ma'am," he says. "Queensboro Bridge looks open, but the tunnel might be faster. You have a preference?"

"Faster," Brooklyn says. The Midtown Tunnel has a toll, and she tries not to charge the campaign for nonessentials, but the toll is less than ten dollars, and damn it, her daughter is essential. "Definitely faster, thanks."

He smiles and heads that way. Brooklyn pulls out her cell and starts a text to Jojo saying that she's on her way home, and simultaneously telling the girl to at least turn down the brightness on her screen if she's going to read under the covers. Between the moving car, the bumpy potholed streets, and her giant Gen-Xer butterfingers (she misses physical keyboards on phones so much), it ends up taking her a while to type out the message coherently.

And because Brooklyn is concentrating on minimizing typos, she momentarily forgets that she's been avoiding tunnels in the city for the past few months—ever since the day a giant tentacle took out the Williamsburg Bridge. For reasons that they might not ever understand, water makes it easier for the Enemy to break through the city's barriers. It's an awkward problem in a city that sprawls across a series of small islands. The bridge-breaking tentacle is long gone, driven out of the city along with all the other bits of R'lyeh when Brooklyn and the others woke up Neek. Still, she's been picking bridges over tunnels because if something comes at her from the water, on a bridge she'll at least see it coming and maybe be able to do something about it. Tunnels provide fewer options.

She's about to hit "send" when Captain Not-Kangaroo speaks again, with an edged note to his voice that immediately gets her attention. "Ma'am." He's looking at the rearview again, but not at her. "Please make sure you're belted in. We're being followed."

"What?" She turns in her seat and looks before sense can kick in. Never good to let a tail know they've been spotted. But the instant she sees the absolutely huge white vehicle that has slid into the tunnel a few cars behind them, her skin prickles with unease. Hummers are a somewhat unusual sight in New York. The kinds of people who like them as status symbols often don't like the city's narrow, messy street configurations, which can be hard for bulky vehicles to manage. Even now, this one is hugging the lane paint-lines, occasionally brushing against the plastic guard sticks meant to warn drivers when they're drifting into oncoming traffic. Damn thing can barely fit in the lane. It has a *brush guard*, of all things. Not the decorative look-how-fashionably-tough-I-am chrome kind, either, but one made of heavy-looking black metal wrapped around the entire front end of the car, from bumper to hood. And as a final bit of irony, she's pretty sure that's the new EV model. Fully electric, unlike Brooklyn's hybrid.

(She does not like that vehicle color choice. Not one bit.)

"It's been following us since Second Avenue," says Captain Not-Kangaroo. "Connecticut plates and I've memorized the number, but plates could be stolen. I saw the exhaust when it turned, and that's a working ram intake on the lid. Those aren't standard manufacture for EVs yet; means it's had some custom engine work."

"Tell me that's just somebody showing off their detailing budget," Brooklyn says. But the tickle of warning at the back of her mind—the city's tension compounding her own, both growing sharply from unease into *Danger, Will Robinson*–level alarm—tells her otherwise.

Then the Hummer pulls abruptly into the oncoming traffic lane and speeds up, a lot, as if to show off its fancy custom engine. One of the tunnel cameras flashes to register the moving violation, but clearly the driver doesn't care about license points. There's a significant gap in the oncoming traffic and the Hummer navigates it expertly, darting back into its lane with hardly a waver. Now there's only one car between it and Brooklyn's vehicle.

Yeah, no. Brooklyn starts thinking of constructs—but she can't think of anything, so she looks for a backup option. "Hey, you wouldn't happen to have a hip-hop station on satellite you can switch to, would you?"

Captain Not-Kangaroo's expression flickers with disgust just before he blanks his face. Well, nobody's perfect. "No satellite at all, ma'am. I can put the radio on when we're out of the tunnel, if you really need to hear something right now. Meanwhile I can notify the police that we've got a situation."

She's not fond of that, given past experience. Cops are just as likely to kill her as whoever's in the Hummer. But the white Hummer suddenly swerves outward again, attempting to pass the car in front of it. It has to move back into lane when the oncoming car turns out to be faster than the driver estimated, but it's clearly trying to get closer to Brooklyn's vehicle. And Brooklyn got a good look that time. There are several people in the car, but the Hummer's driver is Conall McGuiness, grinning maniacally behind the outsized wheel. Shit.

"Call them," she says, after an endless second. "Don't tell them I'm in the car, but do mention that we've got a high-speed chase about to hit the streets of Queens. Maybe they'll at least try to help with that." The captain nods and gives the voice command for 911.

Would city magic be useful here? She banished the vehicles of the Friendly caravan in Bed Stuy that day. Those vehicles haven't reappeared anywhere, and rumor has it the caravanners are struggling to file insurance claims as a result—but Brooklyn only managed that feat with the help of Neek and the others. Helped also that she was on her home ground at the time. Without these boosts, when she tries to "grasp" the Hummer now, the thing is slippery to her metaphysical touch, impossible to lock down. That's not how this stuff works anyway; she's not a Green Lantern or anything. City magic is liminal. It likes the hidden stories, the perceptual-conceptual shifts, the space between metaphor and reality. The more Brooklyn tries to treat it like a video game power blast, the greater the chance the power might go wrong. And what would a misfire of city magic do? She's not willing to find out.

Then again, what will it do to the city if her car gets rammed through a tunnel wall? Okay, the risk means she has to—

The Hummer swerves and suddenly it is behind them, accelerating sharply. Her own vehicle feels like it's flying; belatedly Brooklyn realizes Captain Not has been speeding up this whole time, trying to get them out of the tunnel before their assailant gets into range. Regardless, the Hummer's gaining because it's got a monster engine and is being driven with monstrous intent.

"*Ma'am,*" Captain Not says, sharply enough to make her jump. "Please keep your head down. This vehicle isn't armored."

"Fuck, right," Brooklyn murmurs, obediently flattening herself across the back seat.

There is a jolt from behind. The Hummer has rammed them, although Captain Not is doing an amazing job of cross-controlling the steering wheel to keep them stable. But Brooklyn can hear the thing gunning for another strike, and yeah, that does sound like an engine pimped out for murder—

Wait. Ooooh. Really? Yeah. Should work.

"I need you to drive us somewhere else," Brooklyn yells, over the sound of her own SUV's revs. They're out of the tunnel now, thank God, and have accelerated even more as Captain Not tries to lose their pursuer. "Not to my home."

Captain Not's voice is still professional, but tense and distracted; he's focused on keeping them alive. "I understand your concern about not leading danger toward your family, ma'am, but where?"

Best way to protect her family is to stop these fuckers, one way or another. And she's got something for their asses— "Can you get to Williamsburg?"

"*Williamsburg?*" She knows what he's thinking, and she doesn't blame him. These days, Williamsburg is trust fund baby central, its main thoroughfares crowded with boutiques offering sample sizes and tax write-offs, and small eateries trying to start the next trend like "kimchi gnocchi pizza." But up until fifteen years ago or so, Williamsburg was primarily a neighborhood of poor people: Puerto Rican families eking out a working-class living, artists homesteading in illegal lofts, Orthodox Jewish families just scraping by. Doing better than a lot of neighborhoods, but everything was relative back then. Brooklyn can remember visiting friends there in her childhood and having to step carefully around crack vials and stripped cars.

Things are better these days, in part because of initiatives that Brooklyn and her fellow city council members pushed to help a lot of those poor families put down roots instead of getting swept away by the tidal wave of gentrification. But there's a secret about this neighborhood of Brooklyn that she and the other long-term locals have always known: the crime didn't go anywhere. Well-off white people in the neighborhood means less police surveillance, so the various organized groups still meet in never-open storefronts right next door to the boutiques—or else they open fancy shops of their own, selling expensive imported meats and cheeses alongside other, more lucrative goods. A different neighborhood makeup means new opportunities as well. The drug dealers do bike deliveries now, taking orders via apps they coded themselves. But as for the cars on blocks—

"Williamsburg," she confirms, directing him to a specific street. He looks skeptical, but twitches the wheel to obey.

They get rammed twice more. Brooklyn can't see much of

what's happening, but she can hear people on the street yelling angrily as they streak past, or screaming when they realize they're witnessing a car chase. Captain Not-Kangaroo is driving with a precision like Brooklyn's never seen, but then of course Manny would hire the best, taste in music aside. Still, there's a dull, soft thud against the side of the trunk at some point—a sound that Brooklyn has dreaded hearing. She gasps despite herself, covering her mouth with both hands. "Sidewalk fruit stand," the captain says, to her deep relief. "Did a number on some mangoes."

"Oh thank God."

"We're almost to that intersection, by the way. I hope you have a plan. No cops have shown up."

She does have a plan, as she pushes herself up just enough to see. They're passing by an incongruously dilapidated block, only three streets over from the tony new condo buildings of the Williamsburg waterfront. Taking a deep breath, Brooklyn shuts her eyes and pings her city. Ah, yes, right there, ready—and the instant she summons her memories of the old Williamsburg, the city knows what to do. It laughs, even, in an echoing stadium-crowd ripple through the back of her mind. Brooklyn-the-borough, like Brooklyn-the-woman, just loves itself some good petty.

"Turn there!" Brooklyn says, leaning between the seats to point at a nondescript corrugated door that is now rolling open, halfway down the block. The building that this door belongs to is a lumpy brick of a thing that looks abandoned, with small trees growing on its roof and faded graffiti on its crumbling sides. There's an ancient sign, and the only letters she can make out on it are B 's B DY S OP. There's nothing around it except an overgrown meadow and the remains of a brickyard where some even older building got demolished long ago. Prime real estate in the city's most gentrified neighborhood, left completely undeveloped? Yeah, even if Brooklyn wasn't New York, she would know there was something shady about it.

Because she *is* New York, however, there's a bright, slightly green-toned light coming from within the old body shop.

"Into that building?" Captain Not asks. He sounds highly skeptical. "Is that place even still—"

"Yes. I've got . . . friends there. It's a drive-through!"

He actually turns his head enough to look at her, though only for an instant. Whatever he reads on her face, however, is apparently enough to decide him. Shaking his head, he turns the wheel sharply, leaving rubber on the road, and takes them into the now fully open doorway.

They're still going fast enough that what's inside blurs past indistinctly, though part of that is also because the space within the building is so brightly lit. Light is usually the mark of the Enemy—but the peculiar greenish quality to this light marks it as something else. This is light that Brooklyn has seen her whole life, so ubiquitous that she only realized she associates it with New York when she started traveling and noticed that other cities have their own color schemes. San Francisco, from an airplane window, is cool white light in a mountainous cup. Paris is amber sprawl. New York green is the light of old subway stations, and the Coney Island rides at night, and poorly maintained streetlamps. It is the light of the lost Williamsburg Bridge, first and worst casualty of R'lyeh's hostile occupation, along with the hundreds who died when it fell. Brooklyn starts grinning as they fly through the building. This shitty green light means that everything is going to be just fine.

(There are shadows moving amid the light, unclear but unmistakably there. Lanky and predatory figures sit perched on old engine blocks, or hop down ladders with power tools in hand. Most, she knows somehow, are just echoes. The ghosts of chop shops past. But at least one of them is a real person, she feels certain. As Paulo once told them, those who need to know and are attuned enough to the city—those who are themselves true citizens of New York—are granted a measure of its power. This figure stands hipshot under a car on lifts, and for an instant she sees him clearly. He's an older Latino, skinny and balding and mean-faced, though he grins and winks at Brooklyn as they blast past. *We gotchu, mami.* Flirt. She blows a kiss back.)

Then the Hummer comes growling after them, so huge that its girth seems to push at the walls of the place. Behind the wheel Brooklyn can see Conall shouting in thwarted fury, and when he sees her looking, he points in the universal gesture of *I'm coming for you, bitch.*

But by this point, Captain Not-Kangaroo has threaded the needle. Their SUV yeets out of the far end of the shop fast enough to scrape the tailpipe as they bounce over the driveway curb. An instant later, the corrugated door behind them slams shut—in front of the white Hummer.

As their car turns away, Brooklyn sees light from the other end of the shop vanish as the door slams shut on that side, too. *We gotchu.* There is no crash of the Hummer against the door, no gunfire or sounds of violence—but the light inside the shop, visible through flyspecked ancient block glass windows and the building's skylight, suddenly flares to eye-watering oxidized-copper brightness. Just for an instant there is a deep, earthquake rumble from within the building, loud enough to hear over the SUV's screeching tires, hard enough to rattle the corrugated door. Then the light goes out. Total blackness inside.

Brooklyn, staring over the back seat as they pull away, curses in wonder, and even the unflappable Captain Not murmurs, "What the heck...?" Two seconds later, the building lights flicker back on, as dim and murky as they were before. The doors do not open again. Nothing comes out. Brooklyn thinks she hears a faint, echoing belch, but that's probably just her imagination.

She sits back. "We're fine now."

"Uh," says Captain Not. "I've seen chop shops at work, ma'am. They're fast, but not *that* fast."

"This one had a little extra labor on hand. Folks who could help with a big job, rush rush."

"Help from your...friends."

"Yep." Brooklyn starts to grin. In the rearview his eyes linger on her for a moment, confused and wary, but then he finally shakes his head and focuses on the road again. She supposes he's spent enough of his career in what-the-heck situations that this is just one more. She can't resist fucking with him a little, though. "Just one big friend, really—but that one's got lots of connections. Two point five million deep."

"Uh-huh." She can hear him deciding that he doesn't need to know. "Ma'am, if the police responded, they haven't caught up.

I'm going to let them know we lost our assailant. They might want us to come in."

Brooklyn sighs. "Fine, though we'll be lucky to not end up charged with reckless endangerment or something, given how little the NYPD likes me. But drop me off at home first, please. I'll go make a statement or whatever they want after I've seen my little girl."

"Can do, ma'am."

The Hummer is gone. The driver and passengers in the Hummer...well. New York can be dangerous. People go missing all the time. She tries to feel bad about Conall McGuiness's fate and can't bring herself to. They tried to kill her first—but they clearly forgot that Brooklyn goes hard.

Which reminds her.

Brooklyn's been trying to rely on only her own resources up to this point. She doesn't like that Manny's brought his shadow backers into the situation, but she must reluctantly acknowledge that he was right to do so; can't be a successful mayor of this city without powerful friends. The Big Apple dreams big, flexes big, and needs big allies, especially if it's going to fight another whole-ass universe.

Also. Brooklyn has been slowly coming to realize that she's been going about one part of this wrong.

She's been trying to run from her old self. MC Free was a performance. The world has so much hate for Black girls, and by sneering at a camera and pouring her rage into lyrics, she could at least make it pay attention to her for a time. She could *demand* the respect that the world gives to everyone else by default. But when that part of her life was over, she shed her MC Free skin and tried not to look back. That was childhood, she told herself, and it was time to put away childish things.

But she is both the woman and the child who became the woman, just as she is both a human being and a city, and just as any Black woman must both be hypercompetent and keep it real. Some of that isn't fair. No one should have to be so many things. But since Brooklyn *is* . . .

She opens her phone's address book, quickly scrolling past all her political contacts: other council members, her intrepid aides, reporters and donors and preachers and business leaders and union bosses and mutual aid organizers. Brooklyn had a pager way back in the day, and she's just been transferring numbers from one device to another since then, resulting in a cluttered mess of a contacts list in which millionaires rub shoulders with ex-boyfriends from thirty years ago. Most of the old numbers she hasn't called in years; they're probably defunct. But there's one number that she knows is still good, because she and its owner exchange texts every now and again, just to check in on each other. That's not friendship, not really. They're colleagues at best. It's just that back when they were both young, ladies in the business had to look out for each other, and things along those lines haven't really changed for either of them since.

So Brooklyn hits the dial button. And when the call is answered, she smiles. "Hey, Bey," she says. "Sorry to hit you up out of the blue, but—yeah, you got it. I need a favor."

CHAPTER FIFTEEN

Run Up, Cities Get Done Up

One day 'til the Summit.

Padmini spends the day in a flurry of activity. She visits Aishwarya and the rest of her family for breakfast, just because. Then she heads off to work at Brooklyn's campaign headquarters, in this new job that she's actually starting to love. Not enough theoretical stuff for her tastes, but she's getting plenty of that elsewhere—and Elsewhere—since she's been using her observations of the multiverse to try and come up with theories about how it works. (She's looking forward to the Summit because maybe there are math- and physics-heads among the other cities! Maybe they could write a white paper together! And get laughed out of academia, but anyway.) For the campaign, she's been doing lots of juicy applied predictive analytics. Survey design and interpretation, too, which is messier and less fun, but she still watches with glee while the numbers change whenever Brooklyn acts on her recommendations. It's just so nice to finally use her skills to help make the world a better place, instead of only making shareholders richer. She hopes Brooklyn wins, not just because New York might die otherwise, and not just because it keeps Padmini in the country, but because she wants to keep doing this good work.

When she gets home that evening, she's still in this introspective, warmfuzzy mood—which is why she stops when she glances at the balcony and sees Neek. He spends most of his time there when he's at home. And because she can see the math of existence (she loves saying that in her head; Math Queen *of the fucking universe*), she's started to realize that he's doing more than just moodily gazing out at the cityscape. It's hard to put words to what he's doing, really, but the closest she can come to it is *tuning*. Right at this moment he's gently influencing some of the younger newcomers to the city—only those who are sufficiently New York in spirit, naturally—to go volunteer with the Mermaid Parade or J'Ouvert or their local block association, all of which could use the youthful energy. He's sending hyperawareness toward all the corner barbecues selling plates, helados carts, and churro ladies, helping them see NYPD coming before the cops can see and harass them. He makes that one dog walker with twenty leashes in hand turn down a different sidewalk, where he'll interfere less with foot traffic.

All of the avatars do a version of this for their respective boroughs; Padmini doesn't even drive and yet she's always fixing traffic. Neek's doing more than traffic, and he's doing it more subtly than Padmini ever managed. All the energies of the city smooth out at the merest touch of his attention, including things that it would never have occurred to her to mess with, like the tides at Far Rockaway or wind speed atop the Empire State Building.

He's not even *actively* doing it all, as far as she can tell; the city changes—improves—simply because he's observing it.

How does that work? Padmini can't guess. How did he know to try it? Because he is New York. And maybe because, as Padmini is rapidly coming to suspect, Neek is some kind of polymath genius, self-educated and unacknowledged because Americans don't actually seem to like when people who aren't well-off white men turn out to be smart.

As Padmini settles beside him, she feels his attention shift toward her own borough. Curious, she follows along. On one block in Forest Hills, Neek has made the brakes on a tow truck grind loudly, causing the driver to get out and peer at the under-carriage in concern. This means that a person who's parked in front of a driveway two blocks up won't get towed until five min-utes later—which means the doctor parked in that driveway is still there, stuck and annoyed and yelling at the tow driver over his phone, when an old homeless man groans and doubles over ten feet away. Neek doesn't push the doctor to do anything he doesn't want to do, Padmini notices. Like the Woman in White, the avatar of New York just encourages people to be who they already are—and because the doctor is ethical despite being an asshole, he hurries to help. The homeless guy thus ends up getting treated by one of the best cardiologists in the city. And as Padmini watches all of this unfold, she sees the math of the city change again. The change is insignificant on its own, infinitesimal. *Many* such changes, however…Ah. And as *x* approaches *infinity*—

No. There's an effect, but something's off about it. The effect should be stronger. Why isn't it?

"I don't know, either," Neek says. Somehow he's following along with her reasoning. They can see each other's thoughts when they're in "city mode" together; apparently her watching him work qualifies. He sighs in frustration as she blinks. "No matter what combinations I try, something always mutes the colors."

Oh! What is math to her is art to him—but there's not as much daylight between art and math as most people seem to think. Padmini leans on the railing as well. "Something?"

"If I knew, I'd say. It just feel like . . . somebody else holding on to the brush. Not trying to take it or paint what they want, just dragging on it. Can't do as much as I want because I can't shake the motherfucker off." He sighs in frustration, rubbing at the back of his neck. "Probably just tired."

"So what are you trying to do?" Padmini asks. "Make New York actually be a good place to live, or something?"

Neek chuckles. "Just making things easier for the folks who get the most shit," he says. "Back before, when it was me getting the shit, there would be days when I wished for . . . I don't know. A little luck. Just one or two more people around to care, or even just *notice* what I was going through." He shrugs. "Paulo said cities make their own luck. Figured I could . . . spread it around. Fuck, everybody else keeps trying to make New York what they want. Why can't I?"

"Because you *are* New York."

"Exactly." He looks at her. She is struck, suddenly, by the realization that he looks *bad*. There are lines around his mouth that shouldn't be there given how young he is, and he looks as if his head hurts. As if it's been hurting for a long time. "Maybe I wanna change on my own terms, instead of whatever a bunch of mother-fuckers in Alabama or Utah want."

New York's Campaign Finance Board has a matching-funds program meant to help less-resourced candidates run for office, but the program demands a level of transparency that makes it hard to hide funding sources and amounts. Brooklyn's in it, so it's public record that the bulk of her donors are New Yorkers mak-ing small donations. Panfilo refused to join the program. Between internet sleuths and some investigative reports, however, the truth has come out: He's being funded primarily by Mormons, Evangelicals, and a slew of dark-money PACs—just a few of them, donating staggering amounts. Padmini's seen some of the mailers the PACs are sending out and it's lurid stuff, meant to get engage-ment from people who ordinarily wouldn't give a damn about New York. *America's greatest city has been a captive of liberals and special interests for too long!* and *Ever wanted to do Christmas in New York? Not while it's full of perverts and Commies!* The result is that Panfilo, for all his claims of being a favorite son who just wants to restore his hometown to greatness, is doing so primarily on behalf of rural Midwesterners and Southerners, corporations, bil-lionaires ... and the Ur-verse.

That's beside the point. "It's hurting you," Padmini says, with a frown. "Panfilo's campaign."

"Been hurting." He shrugs. "I'm fine. S'why I'm doing this, though." He waves at the city.

"Trying to make yourself stronger ..." The small changes that Neek has been encouraging don't have the acute power of a shady extradimensional nonprofit corporation or a political candidate imposing non-New Yorkers' will on the city. They do create a pervasive opposing pressure, however, as each small New Yorkism saves lives and reinforces the city's best aspects. Inoculations, sort of, so that eventually no single future populist will be able to wreak the degree of harm that Panfilo has managed in a short time.

"Then we should do this, too," Padmini says, brightening. She can handle tuning a lot more than traffic, and this sounds much more interesting. "You've been tired lately. It shouldn't be just your burden. Let me try—"

"City's mine."

She frowns, narrowing her eyes and putting other numbers together—like two and two. "And *ours*. What, is working yourself to death a New York thing, too?" He throws her a skeptical look, and Padmini belatedly realizes she just called herself out. "Don't answer that. But..." She shakes her head in frustration. "Where the hell is Manny? He's supposed to be taking care of you!"

Neek lets out a long sigh. "Iono. Can't feel him anymore. Not since he left town and came back."

"What?" It's been days since then. Padmini asked Manny where he went herself, and he simply said *Needed to take care of something* without actually answering the question. There's been distance between him and Neek since then, but Padmini's romance-dar isn't good; she's always mistaking sexual tension for actual conflict, and vice versa. If Neek has actually lost his sense of Manhattan as an avatar, however, then something is very wrong.

She lets herself slip out of the normal world a little, searching for Manny. There's Manhattan-the-borough, alive and teeming with people and money and tourists and a thousand iconic buildings and sites, but...Manhattan-the-avatar is nowhere that she looks. As if he's not in the city. That's not right, is it? Has Manhattan become unborn, the way Queens did on the day she left Evilcorp? No, that part of the city still feels alive and thrums with power. Yet there's no personality to it right now. None of Manny's conscious kindness and habitual cruelty. None of his quiet, wistful yearning for something more.

Padmini stares at Neek. Neek shrugs. "Okay, what," she says.

Neek sighs. "I think Manny is deciding...to stop being New York."

"He can't. We're stuck like this now, ever since we woke you up and became New York together. Aren't we?"

"The fuck you think I know? All this shit mad crazy."

"But..." All of them know Manny is in love with Neek. And Neek tries to ignore him, pretends not to care, but everyone's noticed that Manny's the only person he lets come into his room. Padmini sometimes tries to bully Neek into resting or eating or otherwise letting himself be cared for, and he mostly just laughs at or ignores her attempts—but for Manny, he does it. For Manny, he smiles way more than he does for the rest of them.

But if Manny is thinking about leaving, then— "My God," she says. "You're going to let him go."

"Kinda fucked-up if I don't, ain't it? If that's what he really wants?"

Her mouth drops open. "What he wants is to be with you!"

"Yo, weren't you trying to marry him?"

"As a business arrangement! I'm just going to be the completely platonic piece on the side, except when Immigration comes around. But he loves *you*."

"He don't know me. That's just city shit talking."

"Well, yes, hard to get to know somebody who won't talk. But getting to know each other is the whole point of getting into a relationship, isn't it?"

Neek is too low-affect to show bashfulness, but they are New York, and right now New York is radiating unease and starting to fidget. "I don't do relationships."

Padmini shakes her head in confusion. "So just have sex and read library books together. What's wrong with that?"

"Because *that's a relationship*."

"What, you aren't even doing friends, then?"

Neek makes a little sound of frustration. "You know what I mean. He's gonna want exclusivity, and...Iono, *cuddling* and shit." Neek shakes his head in disgust. "I used to run that game, let strangers and old dudes play like we were in love, always kissin' on me and shit. But for real, that ain't for me."

Padmini groans and puts her head down on the railing. "I can't. My God. I've never understood Americans' revulsion for arranged marriages when romance clearly makes everyone stupid. You want him, he wants you, the fate of the city rests on both of you working this out, but no, why would you do *that*?" She straightens and throws up her hands. "My God, I think he's the only one of us who actually wanted to become New York!"

Neek turns to glare. "I forgot Queens is the part of the city that gets on my goddamn nerves the most."

She glares back. "You're damn right. Queens doesn't quit. *Especially when we know we're right.*"

He pinches the bridge of his nose. "Look. I— I been fucked over so many times I can't even count, so I know this much: It's worse when you get used. When somebody fucks with your head, makes you think you want something that you really don't. The city made him the way he is. What the hell am I if I take advantage of that?"

Okay, that's a legitimate concern. But— "What the hell are you if you push him away when he doesn't want to go? He bloody *loves* being New York. Every day he looks at this city, at *you*, like it's the best thing that ever happened to him. And you're telling him it's not. That what he feels isn't really what he feels. You're gaslighting him because *you're* scared to let him get close!"

That, finally, seems to get through to Neek. He falters silent, frowning...and then, to Padmini's absolute horror, Manny steps into the open balcony doorway.

Neek flinches, then glares at Padmini. Padmini does feel bad; she knows her voice carries even when she isn't yelling, so Manny probably heard the whole thing. He doesn't look angry, though. Just...sad. Sadder than Padmini's ever seen.

She knows an opportunity when she sees one. "Well, um, now I'm going to go to my room and let you two talk—"

"No need," Manny says softly. "I've been looking for a way to say this, and I guess this means it's time." He takes a deep breath and focuses on Neek. "I'm...not New York. You were right; I never truly have been. I wanted to be. Thought I could *make* myself be." He falls silent for a moment, lowering his gaze and seeming at a loss for how to continue, as Neek stares and Padmini tries to process what she's hearing. "After the Summit, assuming they help us figure out how to stabilize the multiverse and push the Woman in White out for good, many other cities in this hemisphere are due to awaken. Some have been on the brink for years; New York's not the first, just the only one to complete the process so far. *My* city has been on that brink for years. So once New York is safe . . . I'm going back there. To finally become what I was always meant to be."

Neek has gone very still, his expression trying for poker face and mostly just landing on *shocked but pretending to be cool about it*. Padmini splutters for a moment. Her mind latches on to one argument, maybe pedantic but it's all she can think of. "But you can't. The city is complete now. The time to leave was before we woke him up—"

"That's true for the rest of you." Manny's manner is resigned, despite his palpable sorrow. "You were all real New Yorkers—but I knew that I was meant to be a different city. My whole family was called to it, years ago. We're going to be another composite city, with me as the primary."

Padmini shakes her head stubbornly. "That's not how it happens! None of us knew about any of this nonsense before it smacked us in the face!"

But Neek says, very softly, "I did." When Padmini frowns at him, he seems to pull himself together a little. "Felt it coming on for weeks, months, even before Paulo showed up. If I'd had the rest of you to talk about it with . . . We probably would've started figuring shit out on our own. Might not have needed Paulo's help at all."

Manny nods, once. "There's information out there to be found about city ascension, if you know to look for it. If you need to know. So my family, we've done everything we can to prepare for when the day comes. We're planners like that; it's part of our city's nature. But when I decided to come here for school..." He looks away. "I told myself it was one last chance to enjoy normal human freedom before I took on the responsibility of cityhood, but on some level...I think I wanted a say in my own fate. A choice. But it's time I stopped being selfish."

Oh, fuck. Padmini looks at Neek, who has gone quiet, looking lost. No help there. She tries on her own. "Manny, you're so New York I can't imagine you being another city. This is crazy. If you leave, what happens?"

"Someone else becomes Manhattan." He shrugs. So calm about leaving when they have fought together, suffered together, sung the city together. So sad—but not sad enough to change his mind. "There are plenty who suit the city as well as I do, and I have my suspicions. Check out a guy called Doug Acevedo, or a woman by the name of Madison, once I'm gone. New York just chose me because I was already a suitable vessel, and because I wanted it. Or I thought I did."

Padmini's never heard anything so awful in her life. "You did, Manny. We can feel it. Even now, you want to stay."

His expression is cool and professional. "It's been arranged. But I'm allowed to stay until after the city's stabilized."

That sounds like—Padmini gasps. "Your family. Oh, no. All that money for Brooklyn's campaign." Neek looks sharply at her. "They're *making* you come back?"

Manny smiles thinly. "They're helping me do what's best for New York."

Yes, then it's the worst thing Padmini's ever heard. She flounders for something else to say, anything that might encourage him to change his mind again and fight that mysterious powerful family of his. Choose his fate, like he said he wanted. But she's never been eloquent like that, and silence falls instead.

"Which city?" Neek asks, at last. His voice is soft. The poker face is impenetrable this time.

Manny gazes at him for a long moment before answering. There's a whole other conversation happening here, in tones and silences. "Chicago."

"Fuck." Neek laughs. It sounds forced. "Nah, bruh. New York claimed you 'cause Chicago always talks that big noise about New York. You know we petty."

Manny smiles. It's just as forced. "Maybe so. Sorry."

"For what? Ain't like you *Boston*." Neek looks away. Playing it off again. He's always playing it off, like he's too tough and cold to be hurt—but Manny is the true monster of the two of them, and his emotional displays always belie the image that Neek keeps trying to claim. What's in Manny's expression right now isn't apathy or cruelty, just resolve and that terrible, ocean-deep sorrow. He's doing this, giving up everything he wants, for them. If Neek asked him to stay . . . But Neek falls silent.

Padmini steps away from the railing, toward him. "Manny—"

He slides his hands into his pockets. "We should get some rest before tomorrow. Going to be a big day."

"Manny, *damn it*—"

He walks away. She hears him go into his room and close the door.

Padmini rounds on Neek, spreading her hands in mute incredulity. Instead of responding to her—or going after Manny like he should—Neek turns back to the balcony railing and props his chin on his forearms. Conversation over.

For fuck's sake.

Padmini heads inside, muttering to herself in three languages, and grabs her phone. She doesn't know what, if anything, the others and she can do about this, but they need to know that they've got one more *huge* problem, on top of everything else.

The Summit is in Atlantis. And Atlantis turns out to be . . . the pretty, dead city where Padmini's been spending so much of her off-time.

She should've asked Paulo for its name, she supposes. It never occurred to her to ask, in part because he floored her so much with his little plan to force the Summit to happen—but really, the reason she never asked the city's name is because the name doesn't matter. It's dead. What remains of it, its quiet beauty and its mosaic mazes and its dancing courts, is just the last fragmentary memory of the people who built it, and the avatar that embodied its soul. Visiting it has been like . . . doing puja. Padmini has always been only nominally Hindu at best—less so with every year that she sees the ugly rise of Hindu nationalism back home. Politics aside, though, she still *believes*, because the universe—all the universes—are too complex and beautiful for her not to see divinity in the whole arrangement. In coming to Atlantis, she has made an offering of herself, she supposes; instead of fruit and incense, one last tourist to ooh and ahh at its sights. But the names of the dead are always lost to time, eventually.

"Whoa, check it." Veneza stands with Padmini at the top of a long, broad avenue that leads downhill to the sea. From here, they can see all the way to the strange, not-quite-there horizon, and Veneza seems fascinated—and disturbed—by the visual paradox. "Is it just me, or is there nothing left to this place except this city, and a rim of water around it, and maybe enough sky to see and... nothing else? Flat Earth, for real."

Padmini, crouched beside her and trailing fingers along the edge of a little lily pond, nods. It's the same conclusion she came to about this place a while back, and it never really bothered her... but it does hit different to know that this used to be a living city. Before Paulo told her that, Padmini just chalked up its strangeness to being a different and possibly imaginary universe, with different physical characteristics. Nope; the strangeness is because they're walking through crematory ashes.

Wow, that got dark. Padmini sighs and stands up.

They're standing at the arched entrance to a walled amphitheater where the Summit will take place. Padmini's never been to this part of the city. There are a few other city avatars lingering outside, chatting with each other in clusters and throwing hooded looks toward Padmini and the other New Yorks. From the archway of the amphitheater, she can hear many more voices murmuring. A small crowd's worth.

It's what they've spent all this time trying to achieve, at last. Now they can get help and maybe fix everything. So why, Padmini finds herself wondering, does all of it feel so... foreboding?

Manny, who's been cordial but hasn't answered any of the others' questions since his surprise revelation the day before, has already gone in. Neek and Brooklyn, too. Bronca stops and calls to them from just within the archway. "Hurry along, children." Veneza reflexively flips her off, but they both get up to follow.

It's not like the Greek or Roman amphitheaters Padmini's seen in books, or more modern ones like the Delacorte Theater back in New York, where Shakespeare in the Park happens during the summertimes. Those are ovals or semicircles. Atlantis's amphitheater is teardrop-shaped, with a flattened, stagelike area positioned at its narrowest point. Despite hearing the size of the crowd from outside, it's still something of a shock to see just how many city avatars there are gathered here—maybe a hundred altogether. That figures, given that there are thousands of cities in the world, but relatively few that are large or well-known enough to transcend. The avatars themselves run the gamut of appearances, with most leaning toward flamboyance. There's a handsome, bearded elderly man who nods politely to her for some reason. (Istanbul, her city supplies.) And a tan-skinned woman sitting next to another who's so identical that they must be twins, except that the other has albinistic pink-white skin and tawny hair; somehow she knows they are Budapest. To Padmini's immediate left is a thin middle-aged Black man dressed to the absolute nines, and who sucks his teeth loudly when the New York avatars come in; Kinshasa. Then there's a familiar face: Hong Kong, who merely nods in greeting, though the last time they saw him was in the middle of a Staten Island battle to the death. When Padmini passes near, a plump Indian aunty beams and waves at Padmini in delight; her sari is royal blue with gold stars all over it. Mumbai, wearing the colors of her city's football club. (Padmini waves back awkwardly.)

There's a spot big enough for all of the New York crew about midway down the length of the amphitheater, where Neek and the others have already parked. Padmini sits by Veneza and tries to decide how nervous to be. There's a small lectern with some incongruously mundane metal folding chairs positioned nearby on the amphitheater's stage. No one's standing at the lectern, but several avatars are clustered there talking with each other, including a woman who fits Bronca's description of Paris. These folks glance at the New York avatars as they settle in, some with decidedly unfriendly looks. The most powerful of the legendary elders, Padmini guesses.

"Why the fuck do I feel like I'm back in my high school lunchroom," Bronca mutters.

She's said it under her breath, but a woman just behind them chuckles. "Oh, you are someplace far worse!" As if to emphasize this, half the row starts laughing with her. Bronca exchanges a look with the other New York avatars. Yeah, Padmini doesn't think it's funny, either.

"At least you had school, and lunch," says a white woman sitting on Padmini's other side. The infamous London, Padmini's city-senses tell her. London leans forward to wave at Neek for a moment; Neek looks surprised but lifts his chin in a return greeting. Then the woman sits back, sighs dreamily, and resumes her musing. "When I was that age, I just starved all day. And *everyone* was mean, not just people who had lunch."

"Uh," Padmini says. To her relief, she then sees Paulo's lanky form, stepping around other chatting avatars to approach them. To London, Padmini quickly says, "Oh, um, pardon me, there's a—" Wait, Paulo's not their friend. Padmini thinks Neek likes him and has maybe slept with him, and she doesn't really know how that works given that Paulo and Hong have some kind of thing going, but Padmini herself tried to beat the shit out of him once and she should probably apologize for that at some point. "—person I know."

"Oh, I've unnerved you and you don't want to talk to me anymore," London says, though she doesn't look particularly put out about it. She flashes a friendly but not-quite-here smile. "Sorry. Don't mind me, then!"

"Ah, right." Padmini focuses on Paulo with more attention than the meeting quite merits.

"Apparently I'm to speak on your behalf," he says. Straight to business without so much as a hello; Padmini wonders if that's a São Paulo thing or just a Paulo thing. He glances past them, and Hong gets up to come over with a sigh. "That's the tradition, here—but since I'm also 'too young' and have never attended a Summit myself, I have no idea how it works. Maybe they'll have Hong speak for us both."

"No," Manny says. "We'll speak for ourselves. Anything else is unacceptable." He's sitting with them, but at the other end of the bench from Neek. They're still presenting a united front, and he's still one of them. But for anyone who's previously seen Manny hovering near Neek, quietly ready to stand between him and the entirety of a hostile multiverse, it's an awful warning, and

Padmini hates it. Even Paulo does a little double take as he registers their positions, because it is screamingly obvious that something is wrong. But then Hong reaches them.

"It will have to be acceptable," Hong says. "They're bending the rules enough as it is to let any of you in here. Piss them off enough and—"

"And what, they gon' throw us out?" Neek has sprawled across his own seat, elbows propped on the seat behind him (to the visible annoyance of the Berlins, who sit nearby). He snorts out a bitter laugh. "Enforcing the rules supposed to make these motherfuckers feel real good about themselves while R'lyeh eats 'em alive?"

Silence falls in their immediate vicinity—shock, Padmini gathers, from hearing the R-word spoken aloud. (It does sort of ring in Padmini's ears, like the aftermath of a slap.) The lull in conversation is noticeable enough that its silence spreads, people who didn't overhear stopping their conversations and looking around to see what's going on, until the whole room is staring at Neek.

Neek gives them all a contemptuous glare worthy of any rapper or real estate developer. "Look at this shit," he says to the rest of the New Yorks. He's normally soft-spoken, but the amphitheater picks up his voice easily; he's pitching it deliberately. "All of us falling through the multiverse and y'all wanna stand around playing Who's In The Club."

"We're in danger because of *you*," snaps a man on the third tier. "No other city has had the problems you have. Of course fucking *Americans* would screw everything up—"

"We're not in danger at all, you fool." That's a tall older male avatar on the top row. He waves a hand with put-on gentility.

"The Enemy is nothing more than the monster it always was. New York just made up this business about it having a face. The danger lies in giving these whores for attention—"

"The danger," says a bronze wall of a woman, with short hair in a squared-off buzz cut, "is that too many of you have gotten used to 'tradition' and are too fucking slow to react when the situation changes. If you think—"

She's interrupted by a loud clacking sound. There's a thin, hard-faced young man standing at the lectern now, with a large rounded stone in one hand. He's just banged this on the lectern's surface. "Children," he says, a little testily. He looks about Manny's age and has similar coloring, though with a redder undertone, straight hair, and sharply angled cheekbones. There's a small earring—shaped like an alligator's head?—in one of his ears. The earring makes Padmini like the man a little. It's so cute. Faiyum, she knows somehow. She's never heard of that city and isn't sure where it is, but apparently he's the person in charge. Does that make him an elder? He looks so young.

Faiyum sighs and eyes Neek. "Clearly you've already decided to begin. But if you respect nothing else, avatars of New York, at least have some respect for order so this doesn't turn into a free-for-all, will you?"

"Yes, yes, please, let's have an orderly discussion of the end of the godsdamned universe," quips a person sitting not far behind the lectern. They're wearing a man's suit and the most amazing silver-and-black cut crease Padmini's ever seen, which makes their subsequent eye-roll very dramatic. Tripoli; another elder city. "Sit down, Fai. You're not the person we need to hear from right now."

"How dare you—" blurts another man seated near the lectern, but Fai holds up a hand and favors Tripoli with a sour smile.

"I'm not a tyrant," he says. "Who, precisely, would you like to hear from at this time? Our newest members, the conurbation of New York? Very well. New York, or whoever chooses to speak for you, please answer the question on everyone's minds: How *do* you plan to save us all?"

It's a completely unfair question. Padmini instantly decides she hates this man, cute gator earring or no. Several people in the room laugh, with a malicious edge that really does sound like high schoolers playing Mean Girls. It's like Paulo and Hong tried to warn them: Even though everyone in this room knows the danger they face, some would rather take pleasure in watching New York fail than do what's necessary to save it, and themselves.

But New York didn't show up without a plan.

Neek glances at Padmini, and she stands up to address Faiyum. She's nervous, of course, but talking to a room full of fractious cities isn't nearly as nerve-racking as making a presentation to her thesis advisor, or for that matter her co-workers. And at least this, like her work for Brooklyn's campaign, is also good work.

She takes a deep breath. When she speaks, the amphitheater picks up her voice as beautifully as any microphone. If only her news wasn't so ugly. "At the rate we are falling through the multiverse, I believe we will pass the point of no return in less than a month."

The laughter trails off, though there are still a few persistent chuckles. Faiyum, his expression caught somewhere between boredom and disdain, narrows his kohled eyes. "Very dramatic. 'Point of no return'?"

"The point past which bad things will happen. I'm not a physicist, but I've run the numbers a hundred ways, and we're approaching a threshold beyond which matter, energy, and everything that comprises our universe will be utterly crushed."

Specifically, what she's talking about is called a kugelblitz—a kind of black hole formed not from the collapse of matter, but from an overwhelming intensity of heat or radiation . . . or light. Like the light that awaits them at the base of the tree. She's given this explanation to the others already, but they suggested she hold that part back; best not to confuse everyone with theoretical physics terminology when what she needs to do is simply make them understand that they need to act now. "Plus or minus a week. Something keeps throwing off my calculations, so I'm including a margin of error that—"

"Bullshit," someone near the back of the amphitheater shouts. "Not everything is some American blockbuster movie with a countdown! This is bullshit, New York is bullshit, *you're* bullshit, all of this is—"

Manny stands as well. "Denial won't save you," he says. He doesn't raise his voice, yet the edge to his tone silences the shouting man. Everyone in the room stares at him, which irks Padmini just a little. It's his nature to draw attention, as the flashiest part of New York, but he's stealing her spotlight. "I'm sure it's comforting to pull the covers over your head and hope the monster goes away, but whether you believe in it or not, it'll eat you just the same."

The man who shouted just stares at him in mingled affront and revulsion. Manny inclines his head to Padmini, passing the spotlight back. Awkwardly she resumes.

"It seems clear that this is not a natural process," she continues. "I don't know how the Ur initiated it—maybe through the Woman in White's foothold in our city, maybe something else—but knowing what they did to *this* city"—she gestures around them at Atlantis; several members of the audience gasp at this alone—"I think we can assume the results will not be good. To be honest, we might not make it to the event hor—point of no return. If we fall far enough that the unique conditions which support our reality aren't replicated within that place, all our cities will end up just as empty as this one. Dead in every way that matters."

Murmurs break out around the room. Someone cries out and is quickly shushed. Padmini hears one guy nearby say, "You understand that?" And another replies, "Yeah, I understand we're fucked." Well, they're not wrong.

"As for what we do about it," she concludes, turning pointedly to Faiyum, "we need to do the metaphysical equivalent of igniting booster engines. Generate a force sufficient to counter whatever the Ur is doing. Even if we can't stop our fall, we might at least buy time to think of something else."

Faiyum, who has been staring at her in consternation, recovers himself and pinches the bridge of his nose. "Well. I did a stint as a magician, once upon a time, invoking the spirits and arcanity in order to impress my pharaoh—and *that* was less impenetrable than what you just said. Please explain, child, how we are to generate this . . . counter-force. Use whatever language you feel most comfortable speaking."

Oh. He's *that* old. How much to explain, though? Half of it is math, and half is . . . psychology? The collective unconscious, at least. Psychic energy, prana and chakras, quantum theory; on some level it's all feeding into her understanding of how the world, *all* worlds, really work. A unified field theory of cities as nuclei of hyperreality... aaaaaand she'll play with that idea once they've saved the universe.

"City magic," she finally says, turning to face the room. "Let's just call it that. But we're going to have to upgrade our language at some point, because part of the problem we're having is that there are rules to this, a science that we don't understand on anything but the most basic and instinctive level. We've only just learned to add, and the Enemy is doing differential equations."

"The *Enemy*," says Tokyo, who sits with other Japanese avatars, "has operated the same way for more than ten thousand years of human history. 'She' had no face and no name. What we did— those traditions you scorn—allowed us to survive."

"Yes," Padmini begins, "and that's commendable, but it has no bearing on—"

"The traditional ways no longer work," says Paulo, standing to speak. Padmini sighs, resigned to interruption. "Younger cities have faced dangers at birth that none of the rest of you had to—systemic attacks, sociopolitical poisonings, ideological assassinations. You've all noticed that the rate of city births has slowed, and even stalled altogether in the Americas; I believe this is why. There's no shame in acknowledging that we've been outplayed by this Ur-verse. The only shame will lie in failing to act, now that we know."

"This is nonsense," says a tall blond man—Amsterdam?—over the murmurs that have risen in the room. He stands up, scoops up his jacket, then begins descending the steps of the amphitheater to leave. "Nonsense! All of this trouble started with New York. Did you know one of them is actually trying to become *mayor* of her city? Power-hungry, self-absorbed Americans! Let the Enemy *have* New York. Then the rest of us can get on with our lives." When Faiyum starts to speak, the man rounds on him. "No! I don't want to hear this, Fai. We don't even know if—"

Padmini blinks and suddenly Manny is blocking the man's path to the exit. When did he— "'Let the Enemy have New York'?" he asks. His voice is soft, but clipped and clear. Oh, shit.

Amsterdam takes a step back, his eyes widening, as Padmini throws a look at Neek, who actually looks alarmed for the first time since she's met him. He sits up. "Yo. Pretty boy." Manny's back is to them, but his head turns, just a little, in response. Neek, Padmini sees, is watching Manny's hands—and is one of them canted a little, as if he's about to let something drop out of his sleeve? Okay, no, New York can't be going around just stabbing other cities. Neek grimaces. "Man, he's just talking shit. Don't start acting like pretty *crazy* boy up in here."

"These people would let us all die if it would save them." Manny turns, and it's deeply unnerving to see him assess not just Amsterdam, but the whole room, with the same eerie butcher's calm. He's not even trying to hide it as he continues, "We've held our own this far. Maybe we don't need them."

"We do," Padmini says, scowling and going up to his back. He glances at her and there is a flicker of sleek glass skyscrapers, saber-sharp—to which she responds by spamming him with a thousand Queens-specific sensations: the smell of fresh-cut grass and barbecue grills, children swimming in backyard pools, *parking your car in a driveway*. These things counter the overbuilt quintessence of Manhattan as surely as a towel can end a knife fight, and he flinches as she moves around him to get in his face. "You want to do this now? Really? You're leaving us and still acting like it's your job to protect him?"

That hits him like a slap, and the otherworldly threat display vanishes like a snuffed candle. He throws a taut, desperate look at Neek that tells Padmini everything she needs to know about his supposed resolve to leave, and then he looks away. "...Sorry," he mutters. She keeps glaring, and after a moment, he sits down.

"Well, that was sordid," Faiyum deadpans. He eyes Neek and Manny, shakes his head in annoyance, then focuses on Amsterdam. "Am, *please* sit down. I know the city of New York used to be yours, but do try not to provoke our newest members into a fight that will kill thousands in both your cities. Yes?" The blond man still looks affronted, but with a final sour look at Manny he returns to his seat. Faiyum inclines his head to Padmini, while twirling a finger to indicate that she should move it along.

Yes. Padmini takes a deep breath, all nervousness gone after that little episode. She supposes she should be grateful to Manny for that. "I believe that if all of the cities of our world manifest their full power and join us, we will collectively be able to tear loose R'lyeh's foothold on New York. Additionally, such a joining fits into a powerful archetype, at least within our world. The brave team of adventurers facing off against a monstrous enemy..." The underdogs fighting a nigh-hopeless battle against a bigger, better-prepared foe. She refrains from mentioning this. "This is an archetype that exists in the stories of nearly every culture of our world—a shared construct, basically, which any of us can utilize. And if we succeed, I believe our collective will can then compel the tree to return us to our original position. The Woman gone, everything right with the multiverse again, a happy ending for all."

She also refrains from mentioning that in most cultures of the world, those stories end in tragedy. They need the unrealistic American version of the archetype this time, for their universe's sake.

"Still nonsense," says Amsterdam, who apparently doesn't want anyone to think he backed down even if he did. "All of this is about New York getting other cities to do what they can't manage on their own."

"Yeah, that's *right*," Neek snaps, standing and turning to glare at him. "We can't do it on our own because you motherfuckers had like a thousand years to handle this shit yourselves *and you didn't*. Sitting around calling yourselves 'the Summit' like that means something. Letting new cities die and blaming 'em for it! So either sit your bitch asses down, or shut the fuck up and *help*. Do or die, show and prove. Can't be no in-between." There are a surprising number of murmurs of assent throughout the amphitheater, at this—the majority of the room, Padmini notes. She's letting the histrionics of the denialists fool her; there's only a few of them. They're just loud. But then everything goes very, very wrong.

"Yes, *exactly*," says the Woman in White, stepping out of thin air.

This time she's shaped like a stoop-shouldered white woman in her sixties or so, who wears an ugly holiday sweater and jeggings. Her hair is frizzy gray-white, in a schoolmarm bun. "Do or die," she continues, as people gasp and Manny leaps to his feet again and Bronca yelps out a very loud *Fuck!* "Always liked that phrase. So very fitting, for so many situations."

Many things happen, very fast.

Padmini raises her hands, fingers splayed in cat's-cradle position, and imagines three-dimensional vector equations forming a shimmering, translucent barrier around the Woman to seal her in. She's been working on a theory, see, that instead of constructs they need to try something more fundamental—

"Oooh, honey, no. You want to go non-Euclidean with me," the Woman says with a bless-your-heart grin—and Padmini's barrier shatters in the next instant. Veneza scrambles to her feet, fumbles a vape from her pocket, inhales, then blows forth a great plume of thick, foul smoke. It blasts forth instead of just billowing, dragon's breath made of 100 percent pure New Jersey air pollution. Before the blast can strike, something makes the air around the Woman grow hazy, as if a cloud has moved between her and the smoke. Padmini can't see it clearly, but she has a sudden impression of many small whipcord tentacles curling out of nowhere, moving so fast that they essentially fan the pollution away. Manny bares his teeth and doesn't bother with city magic at all, instead throwing a fucking knife at the Woman's face. She *catches it* between two fingers and looks at it scornfully. "Really?" Then she throws it right back. Manny dips his shoulder and actually manages to dodge it, though it's a near thing. The knife thunks into the bench where he was sitting, its blade sunk three inches deep into the stone.

It's not just the New York avatars who react. Padmini sees Hong Kong grabbing for something in his jacket pocket and Paris pulling a handful of . . . rectangular butter cookies? from her purse. But before anyone else can attack, the Woman smiles, holds up a fist, and then spreads her fingers. "Boom," she says.

An unseen concussion of force hits them all like a bomb, knocking down anyone who's standing and flattening the rest.

As Padmini struggles back upright, trying to think through panic to figure out some other means of attack, she sees that quietly, behind the Woman, another figure has stepped out of nothingness: Aislyn, avatar of Staten Island. Her unhappy eyes meet Padmini's by chance, and then she looks away.

"Now, then," says the Woman in White. She beams in genuine delight, stretching out her arms in parody of a group hug. "Here are all of you, in one convenient place. It takes a great deal of effort to shove universes into a kugelblitz. Much simpler if I just kill you all here and now; less dramatic, and fewer archetypes to trip over. No waiting!"

Then she raises her arms, and the whole amphitheater begins to shake.

CHAPTER SIXTEEN

We Are New York?

*G*ot to push her out of here, Manny realizes.

A piece of the amphitheater's entryway ceiling crumbles nearby, though fortunately not very nearby. The fallen rubble does effectively seal off the way out of the amphitheater, but it's not like there's anywhere to run within a dead universe. A few of the gathered avatars immediately vanish, macrostepping back to their home cities—but then Manny sees another shut his eyes in concentration, then gasp as nothing happens. "Rude," says the Woman in White. "I brought all my best grotesque murder techniques. The least you can do is stay long enough to *appreciate* them—" Sharp saw-teeth suddenly jut up from the floor around the man. His eyes widen, and he lunges away just before the white bear-trap jaws snap closed around him.

The avatars who ran might be cowards, but Manny honestly can't blame them; the situation is bad and racing toward worse. He doesn't know why their constructs are so ineffective against her. Maybe because none of them are on their home ground?

Whatever the reason, if they don't either return to New York or drive her out of Atlantis quickly, they're all dead.

"How—" Faiyum, behind the now-toppled podium, drags himself upright. "How the hell—"

London hurries over to help him up. "Perhaps now's not the best time to question the reality before you, old friend." Abruptly she yanks him out of the way, right before the Woman in White flings an arm in their direction. The arm becomes an enormous, doughy appendage that in no way resembles human flesh, and a great lump of it splats against the wall right about where Faiyum was standing a moment before. The Woman tsks and sends thinner tendrils out from this mass, grasping after Faiyum's ankles. Before she can catch him, however, London bares her teeth, shoves Faiyum behind her, and then she—

the rush of the Tube, people packing the car, excuse me can you let me out, EXCUSE ME, shut up we're all trying to get home here

—sends a great blast of pure, formless *London-ness* at the Woman in White. It's not the totality of the city by any stretch, just a flicker of commuting rudeness, but for some reason this hits the Woman harder than anything they've sent at her thus far. The small tentacles snap back, and then the larger lumpen mass twitches and catches fire, shriveling and sizzling. The Woman winces, snatching it back and turning it into an arm again, which smokes. "Hmm," she says, examining the arm.

"You okay?" Aislyn steps forward, frowning.

"Oh, fine," the Woman replies, with a bright smile for her. "This is basically a broken nail. But my nails are made of a high-tensile-strength element your species hasn't discovered yet, so usually they're unbreakable."

Why was London's attack effective, when Padmini's and Veneza's were not? Manny tries to figure it out as he helps Neek up from where he's been bowled over by the Woman's attack.

The Woman refocuses on London with a pout. "I thought you crawled into your own sewers to die a few hundred years ago. Or go mad, at least."

"Quite," London replies, with a chilly smile. "Madness isn't as bad as everyone makes it out to be—and I wasn't going to die from a little identity confusion, come on."

"She's really—" Faiyum's shaking his head at the sight of the Woman. "My gods. I didn't believe it. She *can* talk."

"Talk, sing, break-dance," the Woman says, flexing her regenerated fingers and then favoring Faiyum with a sour look. "Kill all of you, too, if you'll just stop *wiggling*."

"Why isn't anything working?" says an Asian woman on the third row. Seoul, holding a groggy man up while a massive tiger crouches in front of them on guard. "I tried a weather construct, the winter wind, and it didn't work at all."

"*Constructs* are the problem," London calls to them. She raises her fists in some kind of old-fashioned boxer's stance. "Those can only carry a small portion of a city's essence; concepts work better. Use a bigger gun!"

"Got it," says Neek.

All of a sudden, Manny is suffused with a rage so intense that it makes his skin feel hot. Blink and he is staggering beneath fists in Howard Beach, raising his own fists in Crown Heights' riotous rage, inhaling Harlemite affront at both predatory police and predatory neighbors. Every dram of resentment that New Yorkers have ever felt toward other New Yorkers, every moment in which the city's legendary tolerance snap-flashed into violence, burns in his brain. *Get out of our neighborhood*, he hears in ten thousand voices that churn in his belly, then boil up from his throat until he opens his mouth to shout it, too—

Then it's gone. Manny staggers, then blinks at Neek, who has squared up beside him with elbows jutting and hands loose, legs braced and knees slightly bent. It's a specifically New Yorkish threat display, the bus rider's Back-The-Fuck-Off before a fight that will require extra agility because it's on a moving vehicle. That wave of neighborhood territoriality was part of this, too—New York as fuck even without Staten Island, and a warning that Neek is prepared to fight with his whole self.

"Yeah," Neek says, jerking his shoulders forward. "You forget me, Squigglebitch?" His gaze flicks toward Aislyn. He's never met her, Manny knows, and yet Aislyn flinches as if this glance has struck her a blow. She looks away. Neek snorts in contempt and focuses on the Woman in White again. "You forgot that last beatdown? It's six of me now. Want a reminder?"

"Careful," the Woman says, waggling a finger at him. "This dead universe is as fragile as an emptied-out eggshell. The other cities chose it for their gatherings because that fragility is an incentive to avoid violence—but they gave no thought to its defensibility." She nods toward Faiyum, who stares in dawning horror. "They always believed they were safe here. That only *cities* could enter." She laughs. "Well. I suppose that part's true."

Faiyum sets his jaw and draws himself up. "Then we should

greet you as a fellow of our number, R'lyeh," he says—wincing as he says the name. "If you have some grievance with us—"

"Your existence," the Woman says, with a weary sigh. "That's the grievance. Stop existing and we'll get along fine." Faiyum opens his mouth to reply but can only manage a few shocked noises. The Woman dismisses him and looks around at the whole Summit. "And there's no real point in discussing the matter further. All of you are just so very *crushable* here. A whole room full of Bubble Wrap. I can't resist!"

Suddenly the room is full of lumpen white horrors. Some are familiar: multicolored wavering Munch-painting silhouettes; spiderlike X-shapes of creeping flatness; an immense nosing thing like a great hairy worm, which fills the open space before the podium. Then there are the new nightmares: gibbering monkey-like things, featureless but covered in human teeth; a cluster of floating translucent spheres each containing a tiny skeleton; a small and innocuous cylinder about the size of a soda can—the sight of which fills Manny with inexplicable dread. Even Aislyn seems alarmed as she stumbles back from some of these creatures, though none of them make any move to attack her. Manny hears Veneza shriek when a lumpen black thing appears and utters a low, reverberating *da-dump*. Bronca grabs Veneza's jacket, hauling her away from it and turning in the same movement to throw a perfect side kick at the thing. Glowing, pristine Timbs have materialized on her feet. The wave of force that hits the Ding Ho makes it gulp and disintegrate into a swirling cylinder of gory colors before vanishing. At least constructs work on R'lyeh's minions, if not the Woman herself.

But there are more minions popping into the amphitheater by the second. As the assembled cities scream or haphazardly fight back, Manny thinks, *We've lost this battle.* They're too disorganized, caught by surprise and surrounded. It's not a matter of courage anymore; they're all going to die if they don't retreat. If they *can* retreat.

Then . . . amid all the chaos, Manny spies a figure descending the amphitheater steps.

Manny's in the middle of trying to jiggle out his credit card, which has jammed in a fold of his wallet. He stops fumbling, however, as his mind registers this . . . person. A city? Only cities can enter Atlantis—but for some reason, Manny can't see this one, even when he squints. That is, he can tell there's a person walking down the steps, but every detail of this person's appearance is obscured. It's as if a pall of shadow, fog, and blackout rain surrounds them and them alone.

The figure raises a hand, and all of the Woman in White's gibbering, quivering hordes . . . vanish.

(Aislyn remains, Manny notes.)

The Woman gasps, then whirls to stare at this shadowed figure. Her gaze narrows into vicious fury. *"You."*

The figure only nods. They look around the room. Even though Manny cannot make out the face or eyes, he is abruptly aware of the weight of this entity's gaze upon him, and a sense of warning. Why?

Doesn't matter why. He grabs Neek's arm.

Neek throws a startled look down at his hand. "What—"

The world explodes. Everything around them—the amphitheater, the light, the universe—is blasted by a nuclear fireball of *rejection*. Before Manny can even begin to understand what is happening, the pocket universe that is the last sad remnant of Atlantis cracks open around them. The amphitheater, the blue sky above it, the ancient marble beneath his feet, all of it crumbles, separates, scatters. Beyond it is

—oh, God. Not the hot, bright, churning universeburst of the tree, but *a negative phantasm of same*. Drying, twisted branches wend around them, grayscale against shadowed black. The clusters that should be boiling at the tips of each, where new universes are born, are still and cold in this place, lumped together like black knot fungus. As Manny stares, the closest of these knots crumbles away into dust.

All of which is academic. Manny is in human form, not an abstract concept, and there is no *air* here—

Blink. They are in Central Park.

On the Mall, specifically: a broad paved pathway framed by two rows of graceful elms. There are dozens of people around, strolling along and enjoying the gentle fall of amber leaves, while Manny and the others stand shaken and gasping in the middle of the path. There's plenty of room, so no one pays any attention to them. Manny sees one elderly gentleman on a walker pause and squint sharply at them, then shake his head and move on.

Manny sweeps the scene and verifies that everyone's there. Padmini's sitting on the leaf-strewn ground, groaning in relief; Bronca's standing but bent over, with her hands propped on her knees. Veneza, not helping, is leaning on Bronca's back; Brooklyn's trying to get the girl to ease off. Neek . . . is in Manny's arms, standing but resting against him, and blinking around in disorientation.

"You all right?" Manny asks. It was instinct to grab Neek as they were blasted out of Atlantis, but he cannot regret doing it.

"Yeah, shit. The fuck was—ay, *yo.*" Neek pushes away from Manny, fists clenching, furious.

This is because where six should stand, there are now seven. Staten Island's Aislyn stares at the park and all of them with equal horror.

"Oh, hell no," says Brooklyn. Bronca's shoulders take on a belligerent set as well. (A child runs by, licking a Push-Up from an ice cream truck. "'Push 'em up, push 'em out, smack it up and all about,'" he chants. Some jingle.)

"Wait," Manny begins.

"Whoa, whoa, shit, hold up—" Veneza says, running to stand between Aislyn and them. She raises her hands. "Hey? Old B One and Old B Two? *Mature ladies who should be role models?* Before you both start breaking off your steel toes or really nice heels in anybody's ass, somebody want to tell me what the actual fuck just happened?"

"A-Atlantis," Padmini says. Her voice is still shaky and she looks ready to faint, though she has gotten to her feet. She also looks distraught, however—so much that Neek goes over to put a hand on her back in concern. "It pushed all of us out. No matter how powerful the Woman in White was, she wasn't going to beat a city on its own home ground. But she didn't lie, either. Atlantis *broke itself*, doing it. We got dumped into . . . wherever that place was. Then our city pulled us home."

Neek lets out a whistle. "Damn, Atlantis. Respect."

(A passing young woman throws Neek a puzzled look, then resumes talking on her phone.)

Padmini smiles shakily. "It touched me as everything came apart. It *thanked* me. 'How nice to be loved again,' it said." She shakes her head, on the brink of tears. "All that time . . ." She covers her mouth. Veneza comes over to give her a hug.

Manny focuses on Aislyn, who stands apart from them, holding herself as if she's freezing even though it's only jacket weather. She seems less afraid of Bronca and Brooklyn than she is of Central Park itself. A leaf flutters past, and she flinches violently away. (Two young Asian men roll their eyes at her and walk on.)

Brooklyn shakes her head. "What the hell was that other place, though? Like the tree, but . . ." She grimaces. "Oh. Dead. Answering my own question."

"Now we know where the dead worlds go," Bronca says, very softly. Her gaze has gone distant, and haunted. "But did the rest of you see . . . ? Beyond the tree."

"There were *a lot of* fucking trees there," Veneza says. She looks deeply shaken. Manny understands; he saw it, too, in that endless second of suffocation. "I could see into the distance. That's not just one tree's worth of dead worlds. That's a whole forest of them."

"A tree is a multiverse." Padmini looks ready to faint. "That means *the entire multiverse* has died before. Again and again and again."

"Squigglebitch been busy," Neek says. "But we ain't got time for this."

Manny follows his gaze up to the sky. At first he thinks there's nothing to see. But—he narrows his eyes. There are swirls of deeper color against the sunset-streaked sky, beginning to shift across the clouds. Fast-moving, low-hanging aurora borealis, which should not ever be visible in New York. But it's clear that no one can see the new colors except Manny and his fellow avatars.

"I don't think we gotta get dragged all the way to this white hole or whatever the fuck," Neek says, as all of them fall silent and stare. "She heard us talking—probably been spying on the Summit all along."

"Of *course*," Padmini says, her voice still hollow with shock. (A college student stops, follows their gazes upward, frowns at the sky in confusion, then shrugs and moves on.) "But her attacking now means we must be right, she *can't* keep dragging us down if all the cities get together and kick her off the island."

"She trying to take us out before we come for her," Neek says.

"I didn't think she could still just attack us," Veneza says. She's shifting from foot to foot, breathing hard with anxiety. Manny doesn't blame her; pretty or not, there's nothing good about that sky. "What was all that shit about us being complete, then?"

"Maybe that's why she's been moving us," Bronca says slowly, swallowing as she stares at the sky. "The Ur is the first universe, she said—the seed that grew the tree. It would be down the trunk, in the place of light. The farther we fall, the more power that must give her."

Veneza glares at her. "You don't know?"

"No, I don't fucking know, why the fuck do you think I know everything?" (Two teenage girls overhear this and burst out laughing until they have to hold each other up.)

"She likes this tactic," Manny says. "Pretend to be bound by a set of rules so her enemies will get complacent. We relaxed. Gave her plenty of time to arrange this whole setup. Now we find out what rules she *actually* follows..." He hesitates, not wanting to state the horrible obvious.

"If any," says Brooklyn, who has no patience for obfuscation.

Well. Yes. If any.

"Anybody got the magical ability to send a group text to the Summit?" Veneza asks. She's got her phone up, taking photos of the sky. She catches Bronca's look and spreads her hands. "What? It's pretty, or it will be if my phone can pick up interdimensional aurora borealis. But if she's coming for us now, backup would be nice."

"Nope," says Neek. "On our own same as always."

Manny turns and advances on Aislyn, fast enough that Bronca starts and Veneza puts her hands up again and Brooklyn blurts, "You're the one that told us to hold up, Chi-town."

At this moniker, there is a ripple of—not exactly pain. It's more visceral, more *psychological* than that. A sudden jolt of *Who am I?* blurriness that he belatedly realizes is exactly the same confusion he experienced on a train to New York several months before. He shuts his eyes against the dizziness and thinks hard at himself, *I am New York. I am **Manhattan**. I will be New York until I, only I, decide otherwise.*

(A sudden sharp gust, Chicagoesque, stirs up leaves along the Mall. People yelp, grab for hats and press down skirts.)

The dizziness fades. Manny opens his eyes to see Brooklyn frowning at him, perhaps belatedly realizing that his home-city status is no joking matter.

"Please don't call me that again," he says.

"Yyyyeah, nah," Brooklyn replies, unnerved for the first time since they've met. "Sorry."

"You know you, uh, got kinda *see-through* there, Mannahatta." Bronca's staring. But he is grateful for her nickname, which reaffirms who he is and allows him to focus on what matters again.

"You need to make a decision," he says to Aislyn. He knows he sounds cold. He knows that he is looming over her, in part because he's nearly a foot taller—but he also remembers those awful days when Neek was barely alive, sleeping on trash in a forgotten subway station, because *they weren't there for him*. They could have found him sooner, taken care of him and each other better, if not for this woman. Manny might even be able to stay Manhattan, stay with New York, if not for this woman—

But New York doesn't want me.

He closes his eyes. Fights off the grief. Takes a deep breath. Starts again. "You betrayed us before. Now you have a better idea of what happens if that fu—" He reminds himself that however satisfying it might be to blast Staten Island into a crater, it won't actually solve any of their problems. "If your *friend* wins. So are you with us, or—"

"Nah," says Neek. He moves up beside Manny, touching Manny's arm in absent apology for the interruption. Manny just manages not to flinch. Neek is touch-averse, usually. And apparently there's still a part of Manny that *hopes*, in defiance of his decision to leave New York. And *aches*, and—("Baby I neeeeeeed you!" sings a woman jogging past.)

Neek either doesn't notice all of Manny's existential flailing or doesn't care. "That ain't the question," he says to Aislyn. "Real question is, you New York or not? We know you don't give a shit about nothing but Staten, but if you ain't with us, then I guess you hate Staten, too."

Aislyn backs up a little. Manny wonders if she'll run. "What, you, you think I hate *myself*?"

(Two people in business casual walk past, chatting. "Did you see that Pete Davidson song about Staten Island on *SNL*?" "No, what about it?" "I can't explain it. Just go watch. Funny as shit.")

"Yeah, you hate yourself," Neek says. Aislyn gapes at him, and Neek laughs, once and viciously. "Squigglebitch eating you alive. Half a million people getting mind-raped every damn day, 'cause of you." He shakes his head, while Aislyn goes pale. She does not protest, however. "So yeah, you hate yourself. I mean, how you gonna love something if you hurt it like that?"

"That's . . . I didn't mean . . ." Aislyn doesn't finish the sentence. She just shuts up, trembling, and stares at the cobblestones.

Abruptly there is a rumble in the sky—not thunder. More of a mechanical rattle, or the thuds of something heavy striking something rigid. There is a scraping screech as well, nails the size of girders scraping across a city-sized chalkboard. When Manny looks south toward the floating wonder that is R'lyeh, he notices a churn in the clouds there.

"Time's getting short," he says.

"God, what *is* that sound?" Veneza asks, shuddering. She puts her hands over her ears.

Padmini looks queasy. "I hope that was rhetorical, I don't want to imagine an answer."

To Manny's surprise, Aislyn blurts, "It's not her fault. Look, her creators treat her like shit, because she's like us. But she's *nice*."

"She tried to kill us, you included. She tried to kill my whole family." Brooklyn bursts out laughing, bitterly. "You people really will overlook anything so long as the monsters are polite."

"You people?" Aislyn glares at her. "*White* people?"

Brooklyn laughs again, and for a brittle instant the ground shudders, as Manhattan feels the distant thudding reverberation of a thousand boom cars cranking up the bass. "Child," she says, "I don't care if you're white, black, polka dot, or purple, as the racists say. If you say *she's nice* one more time, about that creature, whose *flunkies* broke my baby girl's arm and tried to steal my father's house—"

"Yo, fuck all this talking," Neek says. Aislyn tenses, and he shakes his head at her in disgust. "Fuck you, too, 'cha Benedict Karen ass. Hope your family forgives you in the afterlife, 'cause the rest of us never will. Bye."

He turns his back on Staten Island's stricken expression and raises his hands. Manny, who is nearest, takes his hand and tries not to think *One last time*. Padmini grabs Neek's other hand, but asks, "Do we have to hold hands?"

"What, too touchy-feely for you?"

"No, I just feel like we're about to start singing 'Kumbaya' or something, it's very strange."

Brooklyn takes Padmini's hand, and Bronca grabs Veneza's. "'Kumbaya' isn't a New York song," Brooklyn says. "If we're gonna break into song it's gotta be 'New York, New York.' Except which version?" She frowns, thoughtful. "Sinatra? Eh, we hear that one everywhere, boring."

"I can't believe *you're* not suggesting Grandmaster Flash or Funkmaster Flex," Bronca says. "You get hit on the head while we were falling out of dead-tree-space?"

"I think Jay-Z's version outsold both of those," Brooklyn says, her brow furrowed in thought.

"Leonard Bernstein, the one about it being a hell of a town?" suggests Veneza. "That's actually my favorite. Though I gotta give some props to the Beastie Boys. They actually mentioned Jersey City! Just Ellis Island, but still."

"I like that one, too," says Brooklyn, amused. Veneza takes her hand and Bronca takes Manny's. "Bobby Short did a good cover—"

"We ain't singing no motherfucking song," Neek declares, his accent adding a "w" to the last word. "Have some goddamn dignity."

Manny, who is partial to the Sinatra song, decides it wouldn't be politic to suggest anything when he's planning to leave. This thought sends a renewed surge of powerful sadness through him, however—and perhaps this is why he looks over at Aislyn again. She hasn't left, despite them ignoring her. She's looking furtively at them, and there is a longing in her gaze. It is this, the longing, that decides him.

Manny lets go of Bronca's hand, ignoring her grunt of surprise. He extends his hand instead to Aislyn, letting the gesture and the moment speak for him. Last chance.

She stares at the hand, then his face, then back at the hand. The expression on her face is ugly—a combination of jealousy and misery and frustrated pride. But.

She comes to him.

She takes his hand. Hers is clammy, and trembling.

And while all of them stare at her, and the cringing discomfort of the moment stretches into expectation, Aislyn slumps in defeat. "I'm . . ." She stops, takes a deep breath, tries again. "Okay. I, I *am* New York. Damn it."

A tooth-vibrating thrum rings throughout Manny's whole body: synergy. He sees the others inhale or shut their eyes in shared response. In the same instant, that awful scrape-clatter in the distance abruptly stops. Manny finds himself smiling with quiet viciousness. R'lyeh still floats above Staten Island, sucking on its vitality, but Manny suspects the milk just turned sour.

Veneza lets out a loud breath. "Oh, thank fuck," she says, when they look at her. She grins shakily. "Still New York. I mean, magically speaking."

"Were you actually worried about that? After all your 'sixth boroughs' shit?" Bronca says with gentle fondness. "New York takes anyone who wants in, remember."

"Aww, yeah," Neek says, with a sharp-toothed grin. He glances at Manny, to Manny's surprise, and Manny cannot help returning that smile. It's beautiful, this feeling. Neek is beautiful—Well. He's going to savor what he's got for now.

Neek raises his eyebrows a little, and his smile turns softer, more weighted. But he squeezes Manny's hand. "Wanna help me put this motherfucker on a bus home?"

"Yeah," Manny says softly, and with conviction. That much, at least, he can do with a whole heart.

So New York takes off its spiritual earrings, turns its extradimensional rings around, and surges forth into battle.

CHAPTER SEVENTEEN

These Streets Will Make
You Be Brand-New

They are R'lyeh, and they are very ready for all of this to be over.

By *they*, they mean *she*, because over the aeons they have learned to ape the concept of individuality. The key to good acting is to *believe* the performance, at least while one is onstage . . . but since she is always onstage, having been built for the stage, the performance has developed more than a little truth with time. Her creators permit it because having an identity seems to make her more effective. When in Rome (or trying to shank Rome), one does as the Romans.

The problem is that she's developed not just an identity, but a personality. This part isn't R'lyeh's fault, she feels certain. She's an emulation of a city rather than the real thing, certainly, made from Ur-matter rather than leftover starstuff like most entities in this universe—but cities innately have personalities. No one would mistake Boston's passive-aggressive belligerence for Toronto's passive-aggressive friendliness, or Atlanta's overtly aggressive superiority—

Wait. Where was she? Oh, right. Murder.

It's time. For the fleece to come off and the claws to come forth, even if they're attached to the tips of tentacles rather than paws. End of line. That it is probably the millionth time R'lyeh has destroyed a universe is irrelevant; each world-murder is unique and deserves to be savored and contemplated in its turn. She enjoys them all, of course. It's the only art she's permitted to practice, and by this point she has become quite good at it. The wolf cannot help but love a full belly. And yet, in spite of everything, she finds herself regretting the necessity of this particular world's death. This is the first one where she's found a friend, for one. A friend, after countless aeons! She shouldn't be so surprised; it would've happened eventually, seeing as some part of her actually admires the creatures of these tainted, dangerous branches of existence. It isn't their fault that they're such monsters. They're just built that way— and if anyone in this multiverse can understand the inescapability of a monstrous nature, it is R'lyeh, the city where dreams go to die.

So when she senses that Aislyn has betrayed her... she is not sad. Monsters betray. It's just their nature. R'lyeh has been betraying Aislyn all this while, in fact, promising her comfort while stripping it away, proclaiming friendship while harming her family, her island, her universe. Even now, as R'lyeh gathers her resources for the moment of excision, she's mostly surprised that Aislyn's stuck with her this long.

Well. She's sucked up more than enough strength from Staten Island. Not enough to get all the cities of this plane; she'll have to rely on the Ur for that, once the others land at the roots of the tree. But if she gets to personally take out New York, she'll be satisfied.

(Even if she is also sad. Personalities are full of contradictions! How beautiful, and also annoying.)

Then someone knocks on the door to R'lyeh's reality.

R'lyeh's home—her "staging area," as she's metaphored it for Aislyn—is not a complete reality. A whole world centered around her would be precisely the thing the Ur despises. She is permitted pocket realities: simplistic spaces consisting of a single environment designed to meet her needs so perfectly that no decisions beyond her mission, no creative impulses, are ever necessary. She usually keeps the other parts of her self there, whenever they aren't needed onstage. None of those parts are missing. So who has come to speak to her, here in her bright house?

There's a tiny hole floating amid the nothingness, so R'lyeh assembles herself into a form compatible with speech and goes over to it. Through this tiny, completely circular portal, she can see Aislyn peering through with one eye. Wise of her, that; without depth perception, she probably won't be able to fully take in the paradoxical dimensions of the staging realm, or at least not to a degree that will harm her mind. In spite of everything, R'lyeh does not want her friend hurt—not until R'lyeh can do it, and personally ensure that it is quick and painless.

"Are you there?" Aislyn asks. Her eye rolls, peering around. Beyond this, R'lyeh hears someone else say, "You sure—" Aislyn frowns at someone to her right. "Yes, I talk to her through mirrors in my car all the time."

That works because Aislyn's car is an object of transportation; its role is to move between one place and the next. What Aislyn is using right now is a compact mirror. However, its purpose is to transform, and since R'lyeh has no singular shape and also seeks to turn living New York into dead New York, it's close enough for interdimensional government work.

"Aislyn," R'lyeh says. She cannot help smiling. Hideous as her friend's human face is, even in the depths of betrayal, it is a good face to look upon. "I've missed you, my bipedal friend! But somehow I get the impression this isn't just another of our friendly chats."

"No," Aislyn says, with genuine sadness. She hesitates and looks frustrated—because, R'lyeh intuits, the others are nearby and she has no privacy to speak her mind. R'lyeh does her a favor, then, and reads her mind without words. It's not telepathy or anything. She just really knows this lone human-city after being connected to her for months, and... did she just call R'lyeh to say goodbye? After telling the others she meant to negotiate. Well, R'lyeh can say vaguely negotiatey things if Aislyn wants, but they both know that's pointless.

"It's fine," R'lyeh says when Aislyn flounders for something to say. The gentleness of R'lyeh's voice is surprising even to her own ears, to the degree that her ears chide her about it. She ignores them. "Really."

Aislyn's expression grows pained. "I'm sorry. I just—"

Foolish vertebrate. "You probably shouldn't be," R'lyeh says. "I was always planning to kill you, after all. If you've chosen to die fighting rather than just letting me remove your strong nuclear forces, I can't do anything but respect you for it. And frankly, I expected it—because you are, in spite of everything, New York."

Aislyn sighs. "Yeah. Guess I am."

Silently R'lyeh sends an alert through the layers of her consciousness. The legion of nightmares that moonlight as her citizenry gathers its weapons. "I won't hold back, of course. Anything less would be disrespectful. But should the opportunity arise for me to be merciful, I will offer that to your fellow New Yorks as well. An ex-friend pain discount of sorts."

Someone on Aislyn's side mutters, "This motherfucker..." But those parts of New York do not matter to R'lyeh. Aislyn smiles a little. She, of all the entities in this branch of reality, knows how hard it sometimes can be to stay true to oneself.

Then Aislyn lifts her chin. "See you soon, then," she says, and closes the compact.

Yes. Very soon.

It takes a great deal of energy for R'lyeh to snap herself into true existence within the world that living New York inhabits. She's been *almost* there all along, parked in a more liminal adjacent reality that facilitates feeding, her "ghostly" visibility an implicit threat for months. Because of all that feeding, she has just enough strength to overcome the city's rejection of her presence, for a few hours at least. More than enough time.

Shunting an entire city into New York's airspace is immediately devastating, as all the local laws of physics hasten to accommodate her presence. There are cries of alarm from Staten Islanders, who suddenly find their sunlight blotted out by the twitching, hungry infrastructure of R'lyeh's underside. The blast of wind from displaced air hits the whole city with a titanic thunderclap, loud enough to blow out eardrums and flatten people all over the island, Jersey City, and lower Manhattan. The resulting minor tsunami isn't that high because the harbor is an estuary—a river that flows in two directions, so typical of New York—and the tidal flow is outward at the moment. Still, New York is not built for such fluctuations. The Gowanus Canal overflows, flooding streets and basements with toxic water. A transformer in lower Manhattan dies in a blaze of electric glory, right before all the lights go out below Thirtieth Street.

Through the thin air of this dimension, R'lyeh can hear panic erupting on all of its communication channels: shouting over the radio, screams from helicopter and plane pilots trying to swerve around a sudden obstacle, terror on Twitter. Images burst forth all over Instagram: the looming white bulk of R'lyeh floating impossibly overhead, just like a dozen photos previously dismissed as deepfakes. Hilariously, a number of humans immediately decide that the appearance of a floating white city is a sign of approval from their god, or an invitation from aliens, or something. A couple of helicopters, having managed to right themselves after the initial concussion of her manifestation, alter their flight paths to intercept instead of avoid. One's even angling to land somewhere on R'lyeh's upper surface. Ah, tourists! R'lyeh quickly shapes something resembling a helipad on the northeast side. She could use a snack.

Then she begins drifting toward Manhattan. She's not really floating anymore, since fighting gravity would be a wasteful drain on her strength. Instead, she has manifested hundreds of thin tendrils and plunged them into the harbor, "walking" along its bottom. No phantom unreality, this; for the first time, the Ur-matter of her substance comes into contact with the solid matter of New York's harbor waters and even a few boats that have ventured too near. (The people on the boats scream as rootlets invade their flesh, sucking away blood and bone as well as willpower, aaaaand... there! New minions, hot off the presses. She'll fix their limbs later.)

Bedrock along the harbor floor cracks as she works her tendrils deeper, starting one taproot toward the core of the planet and spreading leaping, rippling roots toward Manhattan, Brooklyn, and Jersey City because they're nearest. She needs fuel, plus it might be helpful to set off some high-intensity earthquakes.

But naturally, New York will not take attempted murder lying down.

Its first retaliation is a feint. A phalanx of approaching helicopters turns out to be not tourists or police, but reporters. A few are still intrepid despite the depredations of hedge funds and billionaire ideologues and both-sides-obsessed pundits, and the memory of the lost *Village Voice* is still powerful enough to imbue them with a good bit of city-energy, which surrounds them like a sheath. Before R'lyeh can smack them out of the sky, they veer off, windows flashing from photographers' cameras—but the sheath of city-energy riding in their wake keeps coming. It smacks into R'lyeh's newly formed helipad, which is still busy trying to consume the fools who landed on her. The helipad screams as it is torn apart, and the tourist helicopter quickly takes off, snapping loose the few tendrils that are still wrapped around its landing skids. She makes a last grab for the chopper's tail, but misses, and then they are away.

How frustrating! It does not hurt her much, of course; that strike was the equivalent of a bee sting. She strikes back at both helicopters by manifesting actual bees—Ur-bees, to the degree that they qualify as bees at all given that each is spherical, three feet in diameter, and covered in detachable, sapient stingers. A cloud of these bumbles after the helicopters, knocking one out of the air simply by blundering into its main rotor; the bee gets shredded, but so does the rotor, and the people inside scream as the helicopter goes down somewhere near Battery Park. There; now nobody gets a snack.

Despite this small victory, R'lyeh stays ready, because she remembers: New York can fight harder than this.

And sure enough, the moment she sets a cilium on the soil of Manhattan, something erupts from Midtown. At first it is inchoate, formless energy; a shout of rage from seven throats, transforming from sound into rippling air and then into streamers of light. Quickly this energy coheres: Girder-fingers spread into claws, high-rise arms glimmer with MoMA-armor made of abstract color studies, swirling in pixelated swarms. A torso of train switchyards locks into a protective cage around a verdant park-heart. The head of this beast, now standing tall enough to brush the wispy autumn clouds, is apelike—but of course! R'lyeh laughs to see that Manny has brought his battle persona of King Kong to the fore again, this time directing the strategy of all the others. The beast's lower half is elsewhere, ethereal, transcending the realms again so as to minimize damage and loss of life. The upper half, however, has formed very real fists of tough, ancient Manhattan schist. And . . . is that a pahkàskinkwehikàn in its hand? A Lenape war club! Well, well, look at that, Bronca's decided to go *really* old-school.

They really believe they can defeat R'lyeh with brute force. R'lyeh, the city built to kill cities! How precious.

In anticipatory delight, she manifests her own battle configuration. The circular disk of her now spreads out like a *Monstera* leaf, streets splitting and walls folding back. From the splits emerge extra heads on long, armored necks. Each has its own eyes, mismatched and in clusters, some with slitted pupils and some with horselike bars and a few with wavy cuttlefish eye-smiles. Beyond this, R'lyeh has allowed them limited individuality: one has a chainsaw tongue, another a vacuum nose, while another is covered in mouths all singing an atonal, screeching battle hymn. They are more than they seem, these appendages; not just physical threats, but conceptual weapons. The mouthed head is formed from concentrated Staten Islander hatred of paying city taxes, for example. With it, R'lyeh means to rip out New York's civil service—all the bridge painters and street-sweeper drivers and even the people who work at the DMV, who are as vital to a city's life as any living thing's intestines. The chainsaw tentacle is powered by NIMBYism, meant to chop up chunks of affordable housing and public transportation expansions. And there's more, more, so much more. R'lyeh has spent these past few months learning all her prey's weaknesses, and—with the help of its most reluctant borough—designing a weapon to target each and every one.

New York swings, bedrock hips bracing for leverage, the war club's ball singing through the air. R'lyeh laughs in bloodthirsty glee and raises a corrosive tendril to meet it. She'll tear that arm open and then pump a million Ding Hos into its veins, bleeding its infrastructure dry and—even better—traumatizing its Jersey City component.

But before this tendril can connect, the war club strikes at the tendril's root with a blast of *We still set trends that the world follows, we drive whole economies toward or back from the brink, maybe we aren't called the greatest city in the world because we have the biggest skyscrapers but because here the American Dream has a hope of someday becoming truth—*

A conceptual attack, riding along with the brute force, and it *hurts* when it hits. Damn it! R'lyeh has made the mistake of thinking Manny's running the combat show, but this familiar ferocity is the primary avatar's, he whose truest name is New York. Little bastard's just naturally good at weaponizing complex emotional memes and hyperreality.

This means that the blow of the club leaves R'lyeh's tendril numb and nerveless, flopping off to one side and spilling dying Ding Hos everywhere. Maybe that will work to R'lyeh's advantage? The citizens of New York are screaming and running through the streets, and if she can eat enough of them— But no. Plenty of the Ding Hos are still functional, but as they hop after potential victims, the manhole covers blow off and the subway grates pop up, and R'lyeh's footmonsters are suddenly met by an equally vast flood of—oh, God, rats and pigeons and cockroaches, and *pigeons carrying rats holding cockroaches*! She's never seen anything so nasty, and she's a Lovecraftian horror. The verminous creatures surge out of the sewers and set upon the Ding Hos, which are born of a completely different ecosystem and should not be in any way palatable . . . but they're not trying to eat, she realizes in revulsion. They're just shredding the Ur-matter, and *pissing* all over it, and poisoning the Ding Hos with diseases too exotic even for her alien immune system to manage. Too late, R'lyeh senses Neek's influence upon even the lowest life of this terrible city. The rats chitter with his attitude: *We caused the Black Plague, bitch, who the fuck you think you are?*

R'lyeh snatches her numb, damaged tendril back and shakes off the vermin, recalling her surviving Ding Hos so she won't lose them all. If New York thinks this minor setback is enough to—

Wait, what's this?

The world shivers to the south. R'lyeh turns to behold another half-ghostly giant striding across the landscape. Its structure is just as urban as New York, but its body is broader, with more sprawl. The favelas of its fists curl round ghostly Tupiniquim knives, and there is a strange X-shaped bridge pylon on its chest, like a superhero emblem. Well, well. São Paulo has entered the ring.

And from the east, she can see another city approaching as well—higher-tech and cleaner than New York, and swinging a massive, glowing, golden umbrella. Hong Kong.

And there are more coming, she marks, in growing alarm: Paris, walking with a runway model's forceful confidence and lowering the unicorn horn of the Eiffel Tower to bear on R'lyeh's central business district. London, mad as a hatter, giggles in a dozen voices as she crouches atop the Palisades. Istanbul has shed his kindly-old-man facade, now manifesting simply as a giant barechested wrestler doused in olive oil. In his wake comes a clowder of enormous, ghostly calico cats, weaving around his ankles and lashing spectral tails at the sight of R'lyeh. Barcelona punches the air as it comes, jabbing with fists covered in Gaudí architectural mail. Mumbai pats New York on its Queens shoulder as she stops beside the other cities and strikes a pose, sparkling with pure Bollywood fight-choreography energy.

And Faiyum, small and old compared to the rest but canny with long experience. And Abidjan, another composite city, multiple avatars sparkling within its commune-parts. And Tokyo, still grumbling in annoyance as she brings her skyscraper-long naginata to bear. And Bangkok, and Accra, and—

It's not all of the living cities of the world. Less than a third, actually, have come to New York's aid. The problem is that they're all the ones who gave R'lyeh the most trouble during their birthing-battles—the most belligerent and dangerous of the living cities she's tried to kill over the ages. And at the sight of them, R'lyeh begins to worry that she might be in trouble, for the first time in her aeons-long life.

Before she can brace for these new foes, however, the absolute worst happens. She feels it coming and fights it, even shunting a part of herself into the staging world to shout at her masters: "No! Not now, I can take them, don't—"

But it is too late. Hooks set themselves deep in her substance, so painful that she screams before New York is able to land another blow. Her city-foes draw back in confusion as the Ur's power overwhelms her, forcing her to anchor herself more deeply into this dimension. Then, using her as the hook, it reels in this upstart city, ignoring R'lyeh's shriek of agony in the process.

It works. The falling mote that is New York abruptly becomes an utterly still mote—now trapped in a stark, empty white space.

Human self-concept does not bear gestalt identity well. The people who become cities are better at it, but even they have their limits, and getting snatched into an alien reality is more than enough to push past those. Abruptly the New Yorks are no longer a vast ethereal warrior; they materialize in the white space as small and fleshy individual human beings, looking around in alarm. Except Neek, whose fists are still clenched as he glares at R'lyeh. "The fuck? I know we didn't hit you that hard."

Manny adds, "And what did you do to the other cities?" The others are nowhere to be seen.

R'lyeh, exhausted and reverberating with pain now that the Ur has released her, lies sprawled on the ground before them. Because she has been forced into this space as well, she wears the closest thing to an avatar shape that she has—which she hates, because she's never managed to get its details completely right. The eyes are always too far apart, the cheekbones too angled, the teeth too white, something. It's why she usually just inhabits one of their number instead; in this form, she is ugly to both them and herself.

"Leave me alone," she mutters, sulking.

"Where are we?" asks Jersey City, looking around in alarm. "I can't see anything but white—" The Bronx catches her arm. They all turn to stare at Staten Island, who has dropped to her knees with both arms out and eyes shut tight in concentration, whispering *"Get off my lawn"* to herself over and over. Ah, then that's why they're still alive. R'lyeh feels a perverse pride in her ex-friend.

"We're in the kugelplex," Queens says. She's trembling a little, eyes wide. "Not just being pulled toward it but actually *inside* it. That shouldn't be possible! We should all be, I don't know, spaghetti with burned-out eyes. *Dead*. I don't understand how—"

"The Ur brought us home," New York says. He stands tense, chin down and shoulders up, still braced for a fight. "This *is* the Ur."

"A universe existing in a singularity? That's..." But then Queens' expression turns to calculation, not in the Machiavellian sense but the mathematical. She starts murmuring to herself. "That means...but if the collapses are..." She covers her mouth, thoughts racing so fast that R'lyeh can practically see speed lines.

But they are not alone, here in the empty whiteness.

R'lyeh knows it's coming, but that makes it no less humiliating or uncomfortable when forces that the New Yorks cannot see drag her to her feet. She is made to float a few feet above the "ground," arms outstretched and back arched as if to emphasize that she is only a puppet in this moment. The Ur doesn't outright take over her mouth to force her to speak, but that's because it doesn't communicate in words. The whiteness around them ripples with vibration, deep and powerful as an earth tremor. With a sigh of frustration, R'lyeh obediently translates, adding an echoing basso underlayer to her voice in order to more accurately convey the Ur's presence.

"'You are required to die for the good of the multiverse,'" she says, "'or to be transited to a state of inert existence as a dead universe. Either outcome is acceptable.'"

New York tilts his head. "No."

Nothing happens that the rest of them can perceive, but Staten Island winces and murmurs "Get off my *fucking* lawn," louder than usual. Neek glances at her, then focuses on R'lyeh and shakes his head. "Fuck it. No. We're not gonna die to make you happy. I don't even believe this is about saving the multiverse anymore. We saw all those other dead trees—dead multiverses! You been killing everything, all this time, and *it hasn't fixed shit.*"

That is . . . R'lyeh blinks in surprise. They think *the Ur* is causing the problem? "We've been doing everything we could to prevent the proliferation of universes, you rude creature. If not for us, this multiverse would have collapsed already!"

Stop talking and thinking, her masters tell her, and she sighs. "'We seek to avoid a repetition with this multiverse,'" she blurts again, in the Ur's voice. "'You are required to die.'"

"Bullshit," Queens says. Something's different about her, all of a sudden, a subtle change to her face. R'lyeh's not great at interpreting human faces—so symmetrical and static, ugh—but she takes a wild guess: Queens looks as if she's suddenly figured out the solution to a very complex and frustrating problem. "Killing us doesn't solve anything. *It's just the only solution you'll accept.*"

Brooklyn's eyes narrow as she sees the look on Queens' face, too. "You've thought of something."

"I've thought of everything." Queens suddenly spreads her arms, fists tight, biceps flexing; she lets out a shout of glee that actually sends a faint reverberation throughout the kugelplex, to the mild alarm of R'lyeh's masters. "I am the *queen*, long may she reign! I get it, finally. You fucking—fuckers!" She rounds on R'lyeh and points, only a little flustered by her own failure to come up with a good insult. "The problem isn't proliferation, it's *observation*. You Ur people, or whatever you are, you *live* in Schrödinger's box. *You're causing the collapses!*"

"What?" R'lyeh asks in confusion—before her masters speak through her again. " 'You are required to die.' "

"Shut the fuck *up*, yo, I'm already tired of hearing that," New York mutters. But Queens is still pointing at R'lyeh, and jumping up and down a little, too, in her excitement.

"You're saying the same thing over and over again *because that works for you*. You're used to quantum reality! Say something enough, believe in it enough, and it becomes a thing. That's how you became the seed of all the universes, everywhere. You imagined the first few into existence. And you liked those universes, didn't you? You wanted them, because they were just slightly different riffs on your own—just decisions you made, given life of their own. But they did the same thing you did, generating new universes of their own—making different decisions. And *those* universes were less of what you wanted. Right? Then as the whole thing kept going, the tree exponentially growing and infinitesimally changing with every new iteration, beyond even your ability to comprehend—"

"We comprehend things you cannot even imagine," R'lyeh says, and the Ur doesn't even have to tell her to say this. It's just the truth.

"Except equality." Queens is grinning. "That's what all this boils down to. You're older than any other universe, you have power and knowledge that the rest of us don't, so you think you get to dictate how the multiverse grows! You think of all new universes as your decisions, your creations—and to you, the ones that are wildly different from your own, like ours, are aberrations. Not universes in our own right, but just mistakes you made. And you keep trying to control those mistakes, or erase them. Like you're *embarrassed* or something."

Abruptly Queens starts laughing, harshly and maniacally enough that R'lyeh wonders if her sanity is finally starting to give way, as it should have done the instant she entered the kugelplex. But it's schadenfreude that R'lyeh is hearing, not sanity slippage. "And guess what? I bet that's what eventually created us, a species that instinctively spins off new universes in its sleep. We're the antithesis of everything you are, and you have to do all this, sending your minions and meddling with our histories and harassing us at every turn, because *you can't stop us.* You've killed the entire multiverse to get rid of us, again and again and again, and we just keep coming back!"

R'lyeh frowns, pondering this. It's simplistic, and dangerously so. These beings can barely comprehend the existence of multiple realities, let alone their workings ... and yet. "Cities destroy," she says. Just her voice this time. The Ur is silent within her; are her masters listening? She thinks maybe they are. "Just by being born, cities suck up all the realities around them. I've seen it happen— most recently with your birth." She narrows her eyes at New York.

"And that doesn't make any sense, either," Queens says. Her tone is triumphant. "The cat should be both dead *and* alive. When our New York came to life, all those other New Yorks should have kept existing! But all this time, we've been feeling like someone's watching us." Neek inhales, turning to stare at her himself now. "I thought I was just paranoid, but no, that's you ... people. You keep observing us, and you think we're bad, so in the moment when we are most quantum, lost in our own rebirth, your observation is what takes precedence. You want the cat dead when the box is opened, so our adjacent realities collapse because *you think they should!*"

"Uh," says Jersey City. "Padmini, baby, I know you're all about the math, but it sounds like you got some tainted weed. All I want to know is how do we *stop* these Ur people? Because I'm tired of them fucking with my life."

" 'Dying would stop it,' " R'lyeh blurts—and then she scowls in annoyance and replies to the Ur herself. "But only temporarily. It's true that you haven't been able to come up with a permanent solution."

Silence within her. Her masters don't like it when she talks back. But this whole conversation has floored them, to the degree that they're apparently listening to her, too.

New York sets his feet. "Yeah," he says. "Dying would stop it. And I think y'all aren't prepared to take the shit you been dishing out all this time. That's why you made her, yeah?" He jerks his chin at R'lyeh, who blinks. "She's your little bouncer, kicking everybody out of the existence club whenever you decide we don't belong in the VIP suite. But if we roll up into the suite and start knocking heads, that might help you see the error of your ways."

Staten Island mutters something that isn't "Get off my lawn," then raises her voice. "Hey, look, I don't know if you feel it or not, but this place is trying to *crush* us and I can't hold it back much longer!"

"Ain't nobody relying on you, Staten Island," New York says. It isn't even said angrily, just as a statement of fact. "Let your little xenophobia shield go if you want. It don't matter if the Ur kills us— because this is just gonna happen again." He grins, as R'lyeh feels a distinct resonance of unease from her creators. "I get it, too, now. First you couldn't stop those first few universes from making decisions you didn't approve of. Then you couldn't stop creative universes from being born. Then you couldn't stop cities, the ultimate form of human collective creation, not without killing everything else in the process. But now we're here. First time you got guests up in your kugelplex that you couldn't kill—but it's gon' be others, after this. You been making us cities stronger without even realizing, and eventually? You won't have to drag us here. One day the cities of a thousand universes gon' come for you, right here in your little ball of light, and slit your fucking throats."

Manhattan nods slowly, frowning as he processes. "Unless they collapse the whole multiverse. It's the only defense that still reliably works: kill everything and start over from zero."

"Wait, I thought that was happening because they were observing us?" asks Jersey City, shaking her head. "Is it deliberate or not?"

"Doesn't matter," says the Bronx, speaking slowly as she processes out loud. "If I understand it right, the fact that they're *afraid* when they observe cities is enough to affect the outcome. They hope we'll all die before we become more of a threat, which causes the collapse. Then they start over—probably can't help that, or there wouldn't be so many dead trees. But every time, the process repeats, and the multiverse goes out of control again."

"It's not out of control," Queens says, annoyed. "It's just *wild*. Life runs on chaos math. It's supposed to be varied and hard to predict—and yes, dangerous. But if something attacks you, you deal with that, you don't just smash everything! For fuck's sake! My toddler cousin has more sense." She takes a deep breath, visibly reaching for calm. "There's one way to break this stupid cycle and save yourselves before it bites you on the ass, again. *Mind your business*. Just stop trying to control other worlds, stop even looking at them. You're the problem. Just let go."

"Before we *make* you let go," New York adds.

And though it's mostly just senseless posturing because he doesn't have a clue how to really hurt the Ur, R'lyeh feels a little chill. There's a disturbing truth in the posturing. New York is the culmination of everything the Ur has feared: a multidimensional entity in full control of its creative abilities and perfectly willing to deploy them—aggressively, relentlessly—not only in its own defense, but on the offense. Worse, there are other cities just as fierce, and if Queens' theory is right, there will be more with time. It feels right. Each iteration of the multiverse *has* been growing more dangerous with time. Schrödinger's cat has grown longer claws, sharper teeth, spikes, and acid blood. Already the multiverses resist their rebooting, and at some point in the future, the next multiverse might not be rebootable at all. If this is a war of attrition—and it is, R'lyeh sees suddenly, she's been too deep in the thick of the fighting to pay attention to the overall map, but now that she contemplates it, the pattern is *there*—then the Ur is doomed to eventually lose.

R'lyeh waits. The response takes some time by the Ur's standards, and comes only a moment later by human standards. Perhaps her creators already suspected that they were the cause of the problem—but people are people everywhere, and denial is denial. Sometimes people have to get slapped in the face with a fish before they'll admit being allergic to seafood. (She's been working on her metaphors, and feels that this one is especially good.)

" 'Proposal accepted,' " the Ur says, finally. " 'Your deaths are now optional. Our current influence upon and observations of city instantiation will be minimized where possible and negated entirely going forward.' "

There is a pause, during which all of the New Yorks stare at each other and R'lyeh in confusion and dawning understanding.

Then the Ur adds, reluctantly, " 'Sorry about all the murders. But we still don't like you, so please leave.' "

And just like that, it's over.

CODA

I am New York, and because of me, no more universes will die. Unfortunately, that includes Squigglebitch. See, once the Ur dropped her squiggly ass to the ground and started sending us back where we used to be on the tree, Quisling Island ran over and *hugged* R'lyeh and started yelling that she deserved to live, too. Surprised the fuck out of all of us, R'lyeh included. But then Squiggy kind of blinked and looked even more surprised and said the Ur had just told her to GTFO, too, and that her "generative restrictions will be lifted." Translation: now R'lyeh is a real city, like us, just as free as any other city to live and sprout other iterations of herself. That's the thing I finally figured out, see, from all that shit about physics and math that Padmini was spouting: cities are *seeds*. Each and every one of us that comes to life can sprout a new branch upon the great tree of the multiverse—or maybe even start a new tree altogether. Fuck if I know what that means, but as long as Squigglebitch don't come back to fuck with me and mine, I don't give a shit what she does.

Imagine it, though. There might be a billion new universes out there someday, all spun off from New York. Wild.

I got no beef with Staten Island anymore. She pulled up and

was New York when it mattered, and we ain't all gotta like each other to work together. Veneza seems willing to forgive and forget, but Veneza's nice, and I guess she figures Staten's fuckery is how she got promoted to cityhood. But Staten didn't apologize for sleeping with the Enemy, either, so when we all popped back into Central Park, everybody except Veneza just walked off and left her. I guess Veneza'll help her get home. If Staten wants more than tolerance, well. She's gonna have to show and prove before any of us will trust her.

Better New York vanished overnight. Nobody knows exactly why, but its parent company, Total Multiversal War, LLC, filed for bankruptcy, and that was the end of BNY. A bunch of court cases all got dropped, several politicians in New York and elsewhere suddenly went down in weird scandals, and several other organizations—like the Proud Men—went bankrupt, too. Even NYPD suddenly had a pile of motherfuckers resign or retire, including the Police Protection Association boss, Milam, for reasons that I guess will come out over the next few weeks as city investigations—

—wait, hang on.

Baaaaaaaahahahahahahahahahahahahahahahahahahahahaha-hahaha.

Okay. Had to get that out. Next.

Brooklyn won the primary so easy it was like she didn't even try. Main election is in a week. Panfilo's still campaigning, spewing shit all over Republican radio and Fox News and Telegram, but without Better New York's super PACs he's suddenly short on funding. His poll numbers are shit and getting worse, 'cause people don't like some of the stunts his "Friendlies" been pulling. They tried to protest about Critical Race Theory at a couple of PTA meetings before the parents themselves ran 'em out. Risk a bad score on the AP history test? In *this* city? Shit.

Connor Whasisname is mysteriously MIA. Awww, so sad.

Everybody else is cool. Padmini's happier than I ever saw her, and it ain't all because the Math Queen saved the multiverse. I think she just really likes the new job and having time for a life. Veneza cussed out her father about something and went no-contact after; she says it was overdue. Old B must've finally got some, 'cause she don't cuss us out like she used to. Paulo says he and Hong are on-again, too, after like twenty years off; fuck knows how that works. Even Bel, our regular human roommate, is dating somebody now. Love, or at least some good fuckin', is in the air.

So . . . Manny.

I find him on the balcony one night, a few days after we all get back from Cityfight At The WTF Kugelplex. He's thumbing his phone with this look on his face that lets me know his family's reaching out, wanting to know if he's on his way back. Chicago's birth will happen the instant he sets foot in that city; I can feel it trembling on the brink, ready to supernova into life, even now. Without the Ur messing with everything, half the big cities in the Western Hemisphere will probably go live within the next few months. Nature making up for lost time. But for right now, he is still Manhattan, and miserable with the imminent loss of himself.

Shit. Padmini was right, again. If he stops being mine, that'll be on me, not him.

He glances at me. Face doesn't change, but he puts the phone away, 'cause I'm special like that, I guess. We both lean on the balcony railing and look out at the city for a while. I don't do any tuning, for once. He gets my undivided attention.

"Don't leave," I say. It's soft.

He looks at me for a moment. I scuff my foot and play it off like I'm not tense. "Okay," he says.

That's all it takes.

I chew on my lip and kick at the railing and keep fidgeting, while he takes out his phone again and composes a text. That's all it takes, too. The instant he hits "send," all the jittery not–New York energy that's been pulling at him suddenly snaps away, and he stabilizes. He gets to be who he wants to be—and that is Manhattan now, Manhattan forever.

"This gon' make problems?" I ask. He's pressing the "off" button on his phone. Deal with the fallout later.

"Yes. Significant ones."

"What kind of problems?"

He shrugs. "Ones I'll handle, as best I can. But we should probably touch base with the Summit and ask them to suggest someone else as a mentor for when Chicago comes alive. The situation will be . . . fraught, for a while."

"Fraught like . . . ?" I pantomime shooting a gun.

"Guns can't hurt us. But if we aren't very careful, we might find out how, exactly, one living city goes to war with another."

Shit. None of the others are gonna want to hear that. I don't want to hear it. We just got done with one fucking crisis.

But if I gotta fight again to keep what's mine, then . . . so be it. Square up, Chicago.

Manny's quiet awhile. Then: "You still believe it's just the city that makes me want you?"

Damn it. Old Manny didn't push shit like this. Chicago ain't got no chill. "Yeah," I say. "But we *are* the city, so what it wants and what we want…" I shrug. I hate talking sometimes. "Maybe it just be that way."

I see him smile out of the corner of my eye, which is good 'cause I'm looking at my feet. "I suppose so."

"Yeah, you *suppose*. With your proper ass." Now I'm just talking shit 'cause I'm nervous. I take a deep breath. "Look, uh. I ain't done a relationship in a minute. Not a real one. Maybe not ever."

He looks at me again and this time I can feel it, like pressure against my skin, though his voice is soft as velvet. "We don't have to do anything. That wasn't a condition of me staying."

Yeah, but still. I make myself stop scuffing my damn feet and straighten up. I'm New York, damn it. "Maybe I want to try."

Manny takes a deep breath and lets it out. "Maybe we can take it slow, 'til you're sure."

"Yeah." Then I sniff and stretch and roll my shoulders a little. Restless. "Not doin' no damn *coffee dates*, tho."

Manny chuckles. "I, ah, was actually thinking that since you're most comfortable with it, we could just start with sex."

Hey, now. "For real?"

He glances at my face, then blushes. Cute-ass motherfucker. "Yeah," he says.

"'If I want'?"

"If we *both* want. And yes." He looks me in the eye, lets his gaze be all the things he normally conceals. Like *hungry*. "We do both want. Don't we."

Well, damn. "Yeah." Then I lick my lips and step a little closer. He doesn't move away. Okay, good sign. "Tonight?" Pushing it, maybe.

He takes a deep breath again. Then he turns to me, and steps close, and all of a sudden I'm backed up against the balcony railing. Uh. He smells good. I just stand there while he reaches up and cups my jaw and drags a thumb over my mouth and...um. Shit. Nobody's ever touched me like that. It's just a *thumb*, what the shit. But just to fuck with him, I open up and suck his thumb in, letting his salt skin settle on my tongue. His pretty eyes get big, and I give him a little twirl for good measure. Then he licks *his* lips, which is...fuck. Yeah, okay. He leans in. For the first time, a kiss actually feels like something more than wet and somebody else's breath.

Dumb-ass romantic shit.

So anyway.

We are the city. Fucking city. And...pretty sure we gon' be okay now.

Acknowledgments

Wheeeeeeew. This one was rough.

You know the problem with writing a fantastical paean to a real city? The real world moves faster than fiction. When I started it, I did not intend the Great Cities series to be a metaphor for the COVID-19 pandemic, nor for my country's swan dive into Deep Fascism (we've always been swimming in the fashy shallows). All of this meant I ended up writing about the soul of a city at a time when that soul was, as we used to say in my old counseling career, "in a transitional stage"—i.e., midlife crisis.

The New York I wrote about in the first book of this series no longer exists. I decided not to mention COVID because there was no way to know what the pandemic's status would be by the time the book made its way through the publication schedule. I had to change one of my initial planned plots for this book—a monstrous president waging war on his own hometown—because Trump got there first. The Great Cities trilogy that I'd initially planned became a duology because I realized my creative energy was fading under the onslaught of reality, and I didn't have it in me to write three books in this milieu. I came dangerously close to quitting after book one, in fact—but I absolutely hate leaving stories unfinished (and readers disappointed!) once I've begun a thing, so I finished this out of sheer bloody-minded stubbornness.

To get it done, I needed lots of help, so many, many, *many* thanks to all of the following:

My friends and father, who kept me sane. My beta and expert readers: several fellow New Yorkers who shall remain unnamed by their request and also wandering fictional facepuncher Cassandra Shaw; Danielle Friedman, who offered suggestions on medical stuff in addition to beta-ing; Emily Lundgren, who helped me get legal stuff right in the chapter where Brooklyn goes to court; Mikki Kendall, who told me amazing stories about Chicago's history and culture; Whitney Hu, who offered sage advice re political organizing, immigrant family dynamics, and NYC mayoral campaigns; and Crystal Hudson, another NYC political strategist who explained How to Run for Mayor of New York in byzantine detail. There are other experts who've chosen not to be named, including my advisors on Istanbul and London. I would also like to thank those institutions around the world and in New York which put virtual tours online, as I chose not to travel due to the pandemic and really needed to "see" some things for research purposes. I should probably also thank current NYC mayor Eric Adams for motivating me to finish the book because that way my city at least gets a good mayor in my imagination, but nah fuck him.

And of course big thanks to you for buying my books, reading my books, and talking about my books. I wouldn't have a career if not for word of mouth and people who are willing to take a chance on all the weird things I write. Success has been a huge surprise for me, in both wondrous and unpleasant ways.

(Remember, for those of you who read my intro to *How Long 'til Black Future Month?*, I started this journey just hoping to pay some bills.) But knowing that people *are* reading my work, and thinking about it, and yelling about it, and putting it on class lists, and wait-listing it at the library, and *everything*... gives me the greatest joy. Thank you so much.

And last but not least, many thanks to my personal trainer, Tanya of Power Moves, who pushed hard for me to name this book *New City, Who Dis?* I tried, T. I really tried.

Please take care of yourselves, and each other. As Neek would say, we all we got.

extras

orbitbooks.net

about the author

N. K. Jemisin is the first author in history to win three consecutive Best Novel Hugo Awards, for her Broken Earth trilogy. She is a MacArthur 2020 Genius Grant Fellow. Her work has won the Nebula and Locus Awards, and the first book in her current Great Cities series, *The City We Became*, is a *New York Times* bestseller. Among other critical work, she was formerly the speculative book reviewer at the *New York Times*. In her spare time she's a gamer and gardener, responsible for saving the world from Ozymandias, her dangerously intelligent ginger cat, and his destructive sidekick Magpie. Essays and fiction excerpts are available at nkjemisin.com.

Find out more about N. K. Jemisin and other Orbit authors by registering for the free monthly newsletter at orbitbooks.net.

if you enjoyed

THE WORLD WE MAKE

look out for

THE BALLAD OF
PERILOUS GRAVES

by

Alex Jennings

Nola is a city of wonders. An alternate New Orleans made of music and magic, where spirits dance the night away and Wise Women help keep the order. To those from Away, Nola might seem strange. To failed magician Perilous Graves, it's simply home. Then the rhythm of the city stutters.

Nine songs of power have escaped from the magical piano that maintains the city's beat, and without them, Nola will fail. Unwilling to watch his home be destroyed, Perry will sacrifice everything to save it. But a storm is brewing and even if they capture the songs, Nola's time might be coming to an end.

1

HERE I'M IS!

Perry Graves tried not to think about summer's arrival—the heat devils hovering, breathless, over the blacktop as if waiting for something to happen—or even about the city streets. Tomorrow was the last day of school, and he'd be free to roam the neighborhood soon enough...But it *wouldn't* be soon enough. Perry and his little sister, Brendy, sat cross-legged on the living room floor watching Morgus the Magnificent on the TV. The unkempt, hollow-eyed scientist was trying to convince a gray-haired opera singer to stick his head into a machine that would allow Morgus to amputate the singer's voice with a flip of the switch. From here, Perry could hear his parents and their friends gabbing on the front porch as they sipped sweet tea and played dominoes.

"Why you ain't laughing?" Brendy said.

"Don't talk like that," Perry said. "Daddy hears you, he'll get you good." Then, "I don't always have to laugh just because something's funny."

"Oh, I know, Perry-berry-derry-larry." Brendy stuck her tongue out at him. "You in a *mood* 'cause you ain't seen Peaches in a week. You don't want me talkin' like her because it remind you of the paaaaaain in yo heaaaaaaaaaart!"

Perry scowled. "Shut up."

"I'm sorry," Brendy said. "I'm sorry you luuuuuuuvs Peaches like she yo wiiiiiiiiife!"

"Little bit, you be sorry you don't shut your mouth," Perry threatened. He had no idea what he could do to silence her without getting into trouble.

"Nyeeeeowm! Zzzzzrack!" For a moment, Brendy absently imitated the sound effects from Morgus. "You just want her to say 'Oh! Perilous! I luuuuuvs yew tew! Keeeeeeess me, Perry! Like zey do een—'" Perry was ready to grab his baby sister, clap his hand over her mouth at least, but before he could, a clamor rose up outside. "Looka there!" some grown-up shouted from the porch, his voice marbling through a hubbub of startled adult exclamations.

Whatever was going on out there had nothing to do with Perry, so he ignored it. He was sure that someone had just walked through some graffiti, or that a parade of paintbodies was making its way down Jackson Avenue. He grabbed Brendy's wrist, all set to give her a good tickle, but when the first piano chord sounded on the night air, Perry's body took notice.

Perry let go of his sister, and his legs unfolded him to standing. By the time the second bar began, his knees had begun to flex. He danced in place for a moment before he realized what was happening, then turned and made for the front door. Brendy bounced along right beside him, her single Afro pouf bobbing atop her little round head.

Ooooooooh—ooh-wee!
Ooooooooh—ooh-wee!
Ooo-ooh baby, ooooooh—ooh-wee!

Outside, Perry's parents and their friends had already descended to the street. Perry's grandfather, Daddy Deke, stood at the base of the porch steps, pumping his knees and elbows in time with the music. "Something ain't right!" he shouted. "He don't never show up this far uptown—not even at Mardi Gras!"

Perry bounced on his toes in the blast of the electric fan sitting at the far end of the porch. The night beyond the stream of air was hot and close—like dog breath, but without the smell. As soon as Perry left the breeze, dancing to the edge of the porch steps, little beads of sweat sprang out on his forehead and started running down.

From here, as he wobbled his legs and rolled his shoulders, Perry saw a shadow forming under the streetlight. It was the silhouette of a man sitting at a piano, and the music came from him. The spirit's piano resolved into view. It was a glittery-gold baby grand festooned with stickers and beads, its keys moving on their own. Shortly thereafter, Doctor Professor himself appeared, hunched over, playing hard as he threw his head back in song. He wore a fuzzy purple fur hat, great big sunglasses with star-shaped lenses, and a purple-sequined tuxedo jacket and bow tie. Big clunky rings stood out on his knuckles as his hands blurred across the keyboard, striking notes and chords. Perry smelled licorice, but couldn't tell whether the smell came from Doctor Professor or from somewhere else. The scent was so powerful, it was almost unpleasant.

All Perry's senses seemed sharper now, and he tried to drink in every impression. He danced in place to the piano and the bass, but as he did, guitars and horns played right along, their sound pouring right out of Fess's mouth.

Ooh-wee, baby, ooooooh—wee
What did you done to meeeee . . . !

By now, everyone for blocks around had come out of their houses and onto the blacktop. A line of cars waited patiently at Carondelet Street, their doors open, their drivers dancing on the hoods and on the roofs. It was just what you did when Doctor Professor appeared, whatever time of day or night. They danced along to the music, and those who knew the lyrics even sang along.

You told me I'm yo man
You won't have nobody else
Now I'm sittin' home at night
With nobody but myself—!

Perry gave himself up to the sound and the rhythm of the music. The saxophone solo had begun, and it spun Perry around, carried him down the steps and across the yard. His feet swiveled on the sidewalk, turning in and out as he threw his arms up above his head.

Just as quickly as he'd come, Doctor Professor began to fade from sight. First, the man disappeared except for his hands, then his stool disappeared, and then the piano itself. He had become another disturbance in the air—a weird blot of not-really-anything smudged inside the cone cast by the streetlight, and just before he had gone entirely away, Perry heard another song starting up. The music released him, and the crowd stopped moving.

"Oh, have mercy!" Perry's mother crowed. "That's what I needed, baby!"

"That Doctor Professor sure can play."

"Baby, you know it. Take your bounce, take your zydeco—this a jazz city through and through!"

Wilting in the heat, Perry turned to head back inside and saw Daddy Deke still standing by the porch. The old man wore a black-and-crimson zoot suit, and now that he'd finished his dance, he took off his broad-brimmed hat and held it in his left hand. He looked down his beaky nose at Perry, staring like a bird. "Things like that don't happen for no reason," he said. "Something up."

"Something bad?" Perry asked.

"Couldn't tell ya, baby," he said. "Daddy Deke don't know much about magic or spirits. But I gotta wonder... why *that* streetlight in particular? That one right there in front of Peaches's house?"

Now Perry turned to look back at the space where Doctor Professor had appeared. Daddy Deke was right. It stood exactly in front of Peaches's big white birthday cake of a house.

"I didn't see her dancing," Perry said. "Did you?"

"If she'da been there, we'da known it," Daddy Deke said. "Can't miss that Peaches, now, can you?"

Perry and Brendy's parents resumed their seats on the porch, but Daddy Deke headed past them into the house. Perry and his sister followed. In the foyer, Daddy Deke paused to breathe in the cool of the AC and mop his brow with a handkerchief. "Ain't danced like that in a minute," he said.

The living room TV was still gabbling away. Brendy twirled and glided over to shut it off—and Perry wasn't surprised. After seeing Doctor Professor, the idea of staring at the TV screen seemed terminally boring—but so did porch-sitting.

"What you doing tonight anyhows, Daddy Deke?" Brendy asked.

"Caught a couple bass in the park this morning," the old man said. "Might as well fry some up and eat it."

"You went fishing without us?"

"Y'all had school," Daddy Deke said. "If you comin', come on."

Daddy Deke's house sat around the corner on Brainard Street, a stubby little avenue that ran from St. Andrew to Philip, parallel with St. Charles. The low, ranch-style bungalow with the terracotta roof and stucco walls looked a little out-of-place for the Central City—it was the kind of place Perry would expect to see in Broadmoor, crouching back from the street like ThunderCats Lair.

As Perry and Brendy crossed the lawn, Daddy Deke broke away to head for his car, an old Ford Comet that seemed like a good match for the house in that it was also catlike. But instead of ThunderCats Lair, it reminded Perry of Panthor, Skeletor's evil-but-harmless familiar. Daddy Deke turned to look at his grandchildren over his narrow shoulder. "Gwan, y'all. I just gotta stash something real quick, me."

As always, the door to Daddy Deke's house was unlocked. Perry let himself and Brendy inside and took a deep breath. Daddy Deke's place had a smell he couldn't quite identify, but it was unmistakable. A mix of incense, frying oil, and Daddy Deke's own particular aroma—the one he wore beneath his cologne and his mouthwash, the scent that was only his.

At one time, the house had been a doubled shotgun. Daddy Deke had had the central dividing wall and a couple others knocked down, but the second front door remained. Perry and Brendy took off their shoes and stored them in the cubby underneath the coat rack. By then, Daddy Deke had followed them inside.

"Do the fish need scaling?" Perry asked. Daddy Deke had shown him how to descale, gut, and fillet a fish, but Perry was still refining his grasp on the process. There was something about it he enjoyed; figuring out how to get rid of all those fins, bones, and scales felt a little like alchemy—transmuting an animal into food. It made Perry think of the Bible story where Jesus fed thousands on a couple fish and two loaves.

"Naw," Daddy Deke said. "Did it my own self this time—wanted to get them heads in the freezer. Gonna make a stew later on."

Perry's mouth watered. Daddy Deke's fish-head stew was legendary—no matter what form it took. He could make it French-style, Cajun, or even Thai. On those nights when Daddy Deke made a pot for the family and carried it around the corner, the family would eat in near silence, punctuated with satisfied grunts and hums of approval.

"Why I can't never fix the fishes?" Brendy asked. "I wanna help make dinner!"

"You didn't want to learn," Perry said. "You said it was gross."

A flash of anger lit Brendy's face, but it blinked away as quickly as it had come.

"You promise to be careful with the knife," Daddy Deke said, "and we put you on salad duty, heard?"

"Yesss!" Brendy hissed. "Knife knife knife knife *knife*!"

"Lord," Perry said with a roll of his eyes.

In the kitchen, Daddy Deke turned on the countertop radio and stride piano poured forth to fill the room like water. "You know who that is?" Daddy Deke said.

Perry listened closely. He recognized the song—"Summertime"—but not the expert hands that played it. Hearing it made him feel a sharp pang of loss. He hadn't touched a keyboard in more than a year. He pushed that thought away—thinking about playing was a dark road that led nowhere good. "No," Perry said. "Who is it?"

"That's Willie 'The Lion' Smith," Daddy Deke said, "outta New Jersey. Used to work in a slaughterhouse with his daddy when he was a boy. He said it was horrible, hearing them animals done in, but there was something musical about it, too. That's the thing about music, about a symphony: destruction, war, peace, and beauty all mixed up, ya heard?"

Perry frowned and shut his eyes, listening more closely. He could hear it. At first the tone of the music reminded him of water, and it was still liquid, but now he imagined a bit of darkness and blood mixed in. He saw flowers unfurling to catch rain in a storm. Some of them were destroyed, pulverized by the water or swept away in the high wind.

"That's the thing about music," Daddy Deke said. "It can destroy as much as it creates. It's wild and powerful, dig?"

Perry opened his eyes. "Yes," he said, trying to keep the sadness from his voice. "I understand—a little bit, I think."

"Hey, now," Daddy Deke said.

Perry shook his head. His attention had been off in the ozone somewhere as he, Daddy Deke, and Brendy played rummy. Perry liked rummy okay—he liked the shape of the rules, the feel of the game itself—the cards against his palms, raising and lowering them to the table, keeping track of points—but tonight, he'd been going through the motions. "I'm sorry," he said. "What's going on?"

"What's going on is you won and you don't even care!" Brendy huffed.

"Y'all, I'm sorry," Perry said. "I just—I still feel the music on me. I'm thinking about what it means and what Doctor Professor wants with Peaches."

Brendy rolled her eyes. "'And where she at? What she doing? She thinking bout me?' Blah blah blippity."

Daddy Deke laid down his cards and shook his head. "Don't tease ya brother for caring—and besides, Perry ain't the only one miss Peaches when she gone. Is he?"

Brendy pulled a face where she flexed her neck muscles and drew her mouth into a flat, toadish line. Then she let the expression go and sucked in a huge mouthful of air to pooch out her cheeks. She let that go, too. "Okay, no he ain't," she said. "We all be missing Peaches. I get left alone, too, but I don't make a big deal. Just like when—"

Perry knew his expression must have darkened because Brendy cast aside whatever she'd meant to say next. "En EE ways, Peaches *always* go away for a lil bit after a fight."

This was true. Thirteen days ago, Peaches had fought Maddy Bombz on the roof of One Shell Square after Perry and Peaches figured out how to predict the location of her next display. Each of her fusillades was part of a grander display—similar to the ones above the Missus Hipp on Juneteenth or on New Year's—and since she didn't care about the safety of her "audience," of course she intended to launch her grand finale atop the tallest building in Nola. Perry and Brendy watched from a Poydras Street sidewalk as one of the explosions tossed Peaches down to the street.

She hit hard and lay still for a moment, then sat up, shaking her head angrily. A glance into the parking lot to his right told Perry what she'd do next. Peaches pushed up imaginary sleeves and bounded over to a big green dumpster. She lifted the bulky metal thing over her head easy-as-you-please and jumped. *Hard*. Watching her reminded Perry of the moon landing videos. It was as if gravity simply worked differently for her when she wanted it to.

When she leaped back to the street, the dumpster she carried had been crimped closed like a pie crust. She set it down right there on the pavement.

"Five-oh on the way," she said. "I seen 'em from up above. Let's get to steppin'." And they had. Perry and Brendy had spent the night at Peaches's house, watching TV and eating huckabucks and Sixlets late into the night because there was no school the next day.

Perry and his sister awakened the next morning to find Peaches's pocket of pillows and blankets empty—and nobody had seen her since.

"I know she coming back," Perry said.

"I know you know," Daddy Deke said. "But I'll tell you sumn for free—there ain't nothing wrong with the feelings you having, but them feelings are yours. Ain't nobody else responsible for 'em, dig? You can't carry nothing for nobody else, and cain't nobody carry what's yours for you."

Perry frowned. In the past, Daddy Deke had never failed to offer him comfort when he was feeling low, but this advice seemed important. He turned Daddy Deke's words over in his mind for the rest of the night. *Cain't nobody carry what's yours for you.* What burdens did he carry, and why? Well, there was the dream he'd had...but some dark, quiet presence in the back of Perry's mind told him that it hadn't been a dream, it had been a warning, and he'd be a fool not to heed it.

Music might be the most powerful magic in Nola, but it couldn't help Perry—not really.

———— ≀ ————

Dryades Academy was an old square-built art deco building that looked more like a courthouse than a place of learning. Its façade was a riot of ivy, full of ladybugs the size of baseballs, which marched up and down the outer walls, keeping them clean. Chickens roosted in the trees out front, and one of the substitute teachers, Mr. Ghiazi, had told Brendy that every evening, after hours, when the last students and teachers had gone home, the chickens would come inside and hold their own lessons, learning about corn and how to find the best worms and bugs. Something about the way he said it made Brendy think Mr. Ghiazi was probably joking—or at least that he thought he was.

Inside, the building boasted green marble floors, old-fashioned mosaics, and vintage furniture maintained by an invisible custodial staff. What Brendy loved most about the place, what she couldn't imagine ever parting with, was its smell. Crayons, glitter, oil soap, and cooking. It smelled best on cold winter days, but even on the last day of school, Dryades Academy smelled like home. How her brother could leave it made no sense to her.

This year, Perry and Brendy had attended separate schools. Last summer, Perry abruptly asked to transfer out of Dryades Academy and wound up at a new school over on Esplanade Avenue. Brendy didn't understand the choice, and she knew she should have asked Perry about it, but every time she tried to bring it up, Perry's face took on a lost, hunted look, and she backed down. Still, it made her sad and angry to be without him, and sometimes those feelings formed a little knot of tension in her throat—like she'd tried to swallow a pill and failed.

All year she had avoided thinking about it, but now, as she sat at her desk by the window in Mr. Evans's class, ignoring the movie playing on the classroom livescreen in favor of a Popeye the Sailor Man coloring book, she wondered whether Perry had decided to leave because he wasn't good at music.

Brendy bore down with her Fuzzy Wuzzy brown, filling in the outline of Popeye's left arm as he slung a string of chained-together oil barrels over his head. She'd taught herself a trick earlier this year: She liked to color in her figures hard, in layer after layer—careful, of course, to stay inside the lines—then go back with a plastic lunch knife and scrape away the wax. The process resulted in smoother, richer colors that had won her an award from the Chamber of

Commerce in its Carnival Coloring Competition. The grand prize had been a beautiful purple-and-white bicycle that Daddy Deke taught her to ride without training wheels.

Brendy frowned, listening hard, as she finished coloring Popeye's exposed skin and tried to decide what color Olive Oyl should be this time. The chickens in the tree outside had gone quiet. Brendy had earned the right to sit by the broad classroom window because Mr. Evans thought she did such a good job fighting the temptation to stare outside at the trees and the play yard, and the neighborhood beyond. This was only partly true. Brendy found it easy to keep from staring out the window because she tended to listen out it instead. Most of the time she spent at her desk found her listening to the swish of cars on the street, the noise of other classes bouncing balls and running riot on the play yard blacktop, the squabbles of the chickens and the neighborhood cats— who seemed, lately, to have resolved their differences by banding together against the raccoons and possums.

Hey, girl!

Was that Peaches? Brendy raised an eyebrow.

Hey, girl. Hey!

Brendy frowned and selected another crayon. "Peaches?" she whispered.

Yeah, girl. Come on. We gots to go!

Brendy considered briefly, then raised her hand.

It took a while, but Mr. Evans noticed. "Brendy?"

"Can I go use it?"

Mr. Evans nodded curtly. "Two minutes." But he'd never remember.

Enter the monthly
Orbit sweepstakes at
www.orbitloot.com

With a different prize every month,
from advance copies of books by
your favourite authors to exclusive
merchandise packs,
**we think you'll find something
you love.**